The Dragon master's Quest

The Dragon Master

By
Anne Renee Schellen

Dedication

Dedicated to my daughters, Danielle, Ashleigh and Rebecca. My support, inspiration and encouragement with a dash of critique thrown in. Thank you for being my muses.

Table of Content

Chapter 1: The New Teacher

The students walked in twin lines through the enormous arched doorways and out of the school's courtyard. The initiates, first-year students, led the way, followed by the novices, the apprentices, and finally the fourth and final-year students known as the academics. They followed the winding path through the vale, beneath the arbor where picked-over vines hung like lifeless threads from skeletal trellises. On the other side of the valley, the path climbed again, leading to the top of Ackley's Plateau. There, in the fading glow of daylight, the students whispered among themselves as they waited.

Niko nudged his best friend. "How long do you think we'll have to wait?"

Caius shrugged, his dark eyes scanning the plateau before glancing back toward the school perched atop the opposite mesa. "I don't think anyone said."

Beyond the plateau's edge, Darbin's Woods stretched into the horizon like a vast, ominous curtain. To the north, just beyond the forest and moors, lay Caius's hometown. He couldn't see it, but the thought comforted him in a way.

"I hope not long," Niko muttered. "It'll be dark soon."

"Quiet over there," Master Pell called out. "Your new teacher should be arriving momentarily. Best to make a good first impression. Be alert."

Caius frowned, curious about the odd location. Why had they been led up here, rather than assembling in the Assembly Hall or even the school's courtyard? And why wasn't the new teacher entering through the front gates like every other member of staff?

Fourteen-year-old Caius couldn't help but feel relieved the old Sorcia Master wasn't returning. Master Lorek had taught him during his initiate year and had all the personality of dried parchment. Rumors said the sorcerer was finally retiring due to forgetfulness. Caius hoped that was true. Now a novice in his second year, he was looking forward to his first Combat/Defense class and to wielding a real rapier instead of a branch. That alone made this term promising.

Even more exciting was the arrival of a new Sorcia Master. Ackley's hadn't hired new staff since Master Dak, the Elements teacher, joined fifteen years ago. And Sorcia? It was the most challenging class offered. Speculation had run rampant all day. Most assumed the new instructor would be an experienced elder from another academy. Ackley's, after all, was said to be the finest school in the realm.

"Hey… look!" one of the initiates shouted.

Niko rolled his eyes. "Initiates," he muttered.

Caius, remembering his own first-year awe, said nothing. His parents, his father a paymaster, his mother a cloak maker, had never imagined he'd attend a place like Ackley's. But his father, Liab, had ambition for his only son. Caius remained grateful. He was pulled from his thoughts when Niko smacked his back and pointed upward, eyes wide with excitement.

"A dragon!" someone gasped, though it was clear to everyone.

Sailing above Darbin's Woods, the enormous serpent glided effortlessly, wings stretched wide and tail working like a rudder as it banked toward them.

"Someone's riding it!" another voice cried out. "A dragonmaster!"

Caius turned to Niko, wide-eyed. "Our new teacher is a dragonmaster?!"

Even in the dimming sunlight, Niko's blue eyes sparkled. "I didn't think dragonmasters were even allowed on school grounds!"

"Everyone quiet down!" Master Pell barked, but his eyes stayed fixed on the approaching beast. There was wariness in his tone, and Caius noticed it. He couldn't blame the lore master. None of them had ever been this close to a dragon.

"The Tribunal is aware of the new Sorcia Master's… uh, credentials," Pell added, visibly uncomfortable. "And the Sage Master assures me that everything is under control." The lack of conviction in his voice said otherwise.

"My mother won't like this," one of the older girls muttered.

There were murmurs of agreement, though most students seemed more curious than concerned.

Caius wondered what his parents might think. Dragonmasters had never been a topic in his home.

"My mother'll probably be one of those throwing a fit," Niko said with a laugh.

The dragon began circling the plateau, gliding lower and angling its body toward the flat rock. With a tremendous whoomph, it landed on its rear legs, the ground trembling beneath them. Its shorter front legs touched down more softly. The dragon stretched its wings wide, flapped once with force, and folded them neatly at its sides.

The students collectively stepped back as the creature's long neck curled toward its rider.

From the leather saddle slung across its back, the rider stood, one hand patting the dragon's neck. The dragon snorted, this time more gently. Compared to the beast's towering frame, the rider appeared small, but power radiated from the figure even from a distance.

The rider descended the leather strap ladder with practiced grace. Master Pell stepped forward with visible hesitation.

"Welcome," he said formally, extending a hand. "The Sage Master wished to greet you personally, but he was called away by the Tribunal."

Caius rose on tiptoe, trying to get a better look at the new teacher, but the hood of the silver robe hid their face. It wouldn't have mattered, night was falling quickly.

The dragonmaster scanned the group. Beneath the hood, Niko glimpsed eyes bright amber, sharp and watchful. Something about them made him shiver. They reminded him of the dragon's glowing eyes.

"Master Fane said accommodations have been made for your…" Pell hesitated, glancing at the dragon, "...your mount. Stable hands are waiting…"

"No stable hands," the rider interrupted, raising a gloved hand.

Caius's eyes widened. The voice was unmistakably female.

As if responding to the moment, the dragon snorted again, lifting the hood of the rider with its breath. There was a collective gasp.

"Calla?" Master Pell said, stunned.

The new teacher stood young and upright, wearing her titian hair short and tousled, framing a face lit only by her gleaming golden eyes.

"I see you remember me, Master Pell," she said.

"You're a dragonmaster?" Niko blurted.

Amber eyes landed on him. Caius flinched, expecting Calla to scold his friend. But she laughed.

"I am," she said brightly. "And I've the dragon and the robes to prove it."

A few uncertain chuckles broke the silence. Caius grinned. He liked her already.

"My name is Calla, and I'll be your Sorcia Master," she continued. "This is a spiketail for those unfamiliar with dragon breeds. His name is Valor." She gestured at him with pride. "And we won't need stable hands. I tend to Valor myself."

Master Pell nodded faintly, clearly out of his depth.

"I appreciate the welcome," Calla added, glancing across the plateau at the school. Her smile faded. "Perhaps Master Pell will escort you back. It's getting late. I'll see you all in class tomorrow."

Pell motioned for the students to form lines. They obeyed, but whispers echoed through the night air.

"This is going to be great!" Niko said, glancing over his shoulder at the dragon and its master. "A real dragonmaster!"

Calla remained on the plateau, watching the flickering lanterns bob along the path as the students returned. Valor shifted his weight, his snout nudging her shoulder.

She gave him a sideways glance. "Well… this is certainly going to be interesting," she murmured.

The sight of Ackley's hadn't changed. The same proud walls, the same towering structure it looked nearly identical to the day she'd left seventeen years ago. Her stomach turned. She hadn't wanted to return. But there hadn't been a choice, not really. The Sage Master had made that painfully clear.

Valor snorted and nudged her again, more insistently. She chuckled. "Alright, alright. Time for dinner."

With that, she turned and started toward the stables, her dragon lumbering faithfully at her side.

Ackley's School of Sorcia Arts had once been a fortress. Perched atop the plateau, it was surrounded by a massive stone wall with watchtowers at each corner, their views stretching endlessly in all directions. The courtyard enclosed by the curtainwall housed stables, gardens, and at its center, the Castle of Ackley of the Rune.

Long ago, the castle had been steeped in violence and dark magic. There were those who believed the school should change its name, but its historical significance proved too great. And so, it remained. The stories of duels, executions, and magical battles that once took place within its walls were quietly buried beneath centuries of textbooks and student traditions. Most current pupils had no real idea of Ackley's bloody past. The history was kept vague, reserved for the curriculum of the final academic year. In the same spot where sorcerers once died defending their lives, students now picnicked, sparred, and crammed for exams.

After breakfast the next morning, despite the warm sunshine, the students remained clustered just inside the arched doorways, staring out into the courtyard. No one dared step outside.

Niko and Caius pushed their way to one of the archways, and immediately saw why. In the center of the lawn, the spiketail dragon reared back on his hind legs, tail slamming the ground with a force that tore deep gashes into the earth. Several girls shrieked and backed away. Caius slipped forward into the space they'd left; Niko was right behind him.

Valor roared, stretching his long neck skyward and spreading his massive wings. The stable hands scrambled away, clearly unsure whether to flee or attempt to calm the beast. Judging by the panic on their faces, it was a question they hadn't answered yet.

A gust of wind stirred the air as silver robes swept past them. Calla strode across the courtyard, fury etched into her expression. Her voice rang out sharp and commanding.

"What is going on here?!"

The stable hands looked just as afraid of her as they were of Valor.

"He… got out," one of them stammered.

Calla didn't even glance at them. She moved straight to the dragon, planting herself in front of him. "Valor," she said sternly, "we talked about this."

The spiketail snorted, tossing his head. His tail stilled. The ground no longer trembled beneath them. In moments, the dragon lowered his head and looked into her eyes, his growls fading to a low, contented hum.

From inside, no one could hear her words. But the quiet murmur she spoke seemed to wash over Valor like a spell.

In daylight, Caius could see her clearly. She didn't look anything like the grim, robed dragonmasters depicted in their lore books. Her short red-gold curls were tousled and untamed. Her eyes glowed with that same amber fire, and her face though still young bore a thin scar across her right cheek. It wasn't disfiguring, but it was noticeable. Striking, even.

He wondered briefly why she hadn't had it removed. A trained healer could've made the scar vanish without effort. Maybe she didn't want it gone.

Valor turned obediently toward the enclosure, guided by Calla's presence more than any leash or spell. The stable hands hurried after him, trying not to make eye contact with either beast or master.

Once the dragon was inside and secured, Calla rounded on the stable hands. "No one is to come near that pen," she warned. "Next time I may not intervene. And if Valor decides to make a meal of one of you, it will be your misfortune."

The stable hands nodded quickly, looking grateful just to be alive.

Calla turned, her gaze sweeping across the students who had cautiously stepped into the courtyard. For the first time, they saw the scar that crossed her cheek. It seemed to sharpen her features without marring them. Her eyes held the gleam of quiet command.

"Perhaps you should all be getting to class?" she said lightly.

The students scattered like startled birds. Caius and Niko remained frozen.

"Did you have a question, gentlemen?" she asked, her tone mild but expectant.

Niko hesitated. "Um… we have Sorcia class first… but, well, if you're not there yet… are we late?"

The corner of Calla's mouth twitched, though her eyes remained serious. "No. Of course not." She tilted her head slightly. "Shouldn't you be getting along then?"

Without another word, the boys bolted inside, dashing through the corridors and down into the lower levels of the castle, where the Sorcia and Combat/Defense classrooms were located.

When they reached the Sorcia classroom, their classmates were already seated in a semicircle of desks. Snickers echoed through the room as Caius and Niko rushed to their seats.

Calla stood at the front, arms crossed, lips curled in a half-smile. She was no longer wearing her silver dragonmaster robe. Instead, she wore a simple leather tunic and brown leggings practical, clean, and indistinguishable from student attire, save for the power she wore like armor.

"As I was saying," she resumed, "I'd like to begin by seeing what you've learned up to this point."

Caius and Niko exchanged uneasy glances. Several hands went up. Calla nodded at a girl with dark curls.

"Master Lorek didn't let us do actual spellwork last term," the girl explained. "We mostly studied theory, proper phrasing, posture, incantations. He called it the fundamentals."

Calla gave a thin smile. "Yes… I might've guessed. Well, I prefer a hands-on approach. We'll be doing things differently this year."

Caius raised his hand. "Did Master Lorek really retire?"

Her eyebrows lifted. "Do you have reason to believe otherwise, Caius?"

He blinked. "You know my name?"

She nodded, the corners of her mouth lifting. "As for Master Lorek, I assume his retirement is genuine. Sage Master Fane said he wished to travel. If there were other reasons, I wasn't told."

More hands shot up, and Calla, instead of calling on anyone, climbed atop her desk and sat cross-legged. With casual grace, she answered each question.

"No, this is my first teaching appointment."

"No, you can't ride Valor."

"No, spiketails don't breathe fire."

"Yes, dragons are dangerous. They're dragons."

"Why did Master Fane appoint you?" one bold student asked.

She raised her hands, and an arc of glowing light rose from one palm and vanished into the other in a rainbow of color.

"I am a sorcerer," she said. "Why shouldn't he?"

"Because you're a dragonmaster," the student replied.

Calla's golden eyes settled on the speaker. "And your family has long disapproved of dragonmasters. I suspect Sage Master Fane will soon be hearing from your parents and others."

Gan leaned back in his chair, arms crossed. "No dragonmaster has ever been allowed at Ackley's. The Tribunal forbade it."

Calla tilted her head. "You should pay better attention in lore class, Gan. It's true that dragonmasters have been discouraged from attending or teaching at Ackley's, but it was never formally forbidden. Most simply chose not to. Or at least… that's what the Tribunal believed."

She stood, her voice growing firm. "But things are changing. You may not notice it yet, but the apprentices and scholars do. And by the end of this term, likely so will you."

With a wave of her hand, all the students' books snapped open to the first chapter.

"Read this for tomorrow. We'll discuss it in class."

As the students packed up, Calla strolled casually toward Caius and Niko.

"Seeing as you didn't make it to class before me," she said lightly, "I really should mark you as tardy."

Niko grimaced. "Sorry, Master Calla."

She smiled. "Perhaps I'll let it go if you can tell me what you've learned."

They paused.

"Well," Niko said, scratching his head, "you can travel faster with spells than we can by running."

Caius shook his head. "No. We learned not to count on something just because it seems like a sure thing."

Calla chuckled. "Both are correct. But I think the latter is the more useful lesson. Chapter One for tomorrow. And don't be late."

>

The dining hall at Ackley's was always lively, but tonight the buzz had an extra edge. Rumors about Calla and Valor filled every table. Students whispered theories, repeated overheard gossip, and speculated wildly about the Tribunal's intentions. The High Table sat in uneasy silence as the masters exchanged stiff pleasantries.

At the novices' table, Niko stabbed a hunk of bread and waved it like a baton. "I'm telling you, Valor's wingspan is wider than the courtyard."

"That's impossible," Paka said, rolling his eyes. "He's big, sure, but don't exaggerate."

"I'm not! I measured it visually."

Dara reached over and snatched the bread from Niko's fork. "Visual measuring. Highly scientific," she teased.

Niko lunged for it, but she held it just out of reach. "You weren't even there!" he said, frustrated.

"I didn't need to be. I saw him from my dorm window. Looked more like a giant chicken to me."

"Take that back," Niko said, scandalized.

Caius grinned into his soup, letting the siblings squabbling and the noise around him wash over his thoughts. He'd never seen anything like Calla. She moved with quiet authority, but without arrogance. When she taught, she didn't just lecture she listened. That alone set her apart from every other master at the school.

"I heard the Tribunal didn't approve her," Paka muttered. "That it was just Sage Master Fane who appointed her."

"I heard she was exiled," someone else added.

"I heard she used to be a student here," Dara said, eyes gleaming. "That she left before finishing because of something big."

"Well, I heard she was kicked out," Gan said loudly. "My cousin's in the Tribunal's council. He said there were… incidents. Dangerous ones."

Caius's spoon paused midair. "What kind of incidents?"

Gan shrugged. "The kind where someone ends up dead, probably."

"That's ridiculous," Dara snapped. "She's our teacher now. Fane wouldn't hire a murderer."

"Fane's been getting soft," Gan muttered. "He's not what he used to be."

"Better soft than pompous," Niko fired back.

Gan's face reddened, but he didn't reply. Across the hall, Calla walked past the open archway toward the stables, her silver cloak fluttering in the wind. She didn't eat with the other masters. Caius noticed.

Later that night, curiosity gnawed at him. He pulled on a cloak and slipped quietly from his dormitory. Niko joined him a moment later, equally silent. Neither of them needed to say where they were going.

The stables were dark but not empty. Valor's silhouette loomed even in the shadows. A single lantern flickered near his enclosure. Two voices drifted toward them.

"…they're already complaining," a man said. It was Dak, the Elements Master. His voice was gravelly, familiar.

"I expected that," Calla replied calmly. "Gan's father? Senator Berrin?"

"And his uncle. And the Morrigan estate. And two from House Valence."

Caius and Niko ducked behind a stack of hay bales. Caius's heart pounded.

"They've filed formally." Dak said. "The Tribunal may demand a hearing."

"They want me to leave."

"They want to call out Fane first most likely. Make him rescind the appointment himself."

Calla didn't respond immediately. When she did, her voice was quieter. "They never forgave me for the events here...or in Soronu."

Dak sighed. "Calla, you need to tread carefully."

"I'm not here by choice," she snapped, then softened. "I'm here because I was asked. More like I was ordered. Because there's something at stake."

There was a pause.

"Someone should've warned me," she added. "About how much it still hurts to walk through those halls."

"I wouldn't think they needed to."

A longer silence followed.

"I'm glad you came back," Dak said at last.

"I'm not," Calla replied. "But I'm here."

Valor shifted behind her, tail swaying gently.

"I know you've heard the rumors," she continued. "You want to ask. So ask."

"...was it true?" Dak said quietly. "Back then? The reason they expelled you?"

Calla met his gaze. "You were there. You know I didn't lie. Dragonmasters can't."

He nodded slowly. "Well it wasn't fair."

"It never is."

From their hiding place, Niko shifted, making a faint crunch on the straw.

Calla turned sharply. "Who's there?"

Caius stood before Niko could react. "I'm sorry," he said quickly. "We weren't spying...well, we were but we didn't mean to."

Calla crossed her arms. "Come out, both of you."

Niko sheepishly followed. "We couldn't sleep," he offered.

"You decided to wander through the stables in the dead of night?"

Caius hesitated. "We… wanted to know more about you. The Tribunal stuff, the past…"

Dak frowned. "Boys, you shouldn't be out."

"It's alright," Calla said, cutting him off. "I expected you'd be curious. Just… don't believe everything you hear."

"Gan said..."

"I don't care what Gan said," Calla interrupted. "What matters is what I do here. What I teach you. And how well you learn."

She looked at them, and for a moment, Caius felt as though she saw straight through him.

"I'm not like your other teachers," she added. "I don't believe in sugarcoating the truth. But I do believe in second chances."

"Did you do it?" Niko asked suddenly. "Whatever they accused you of?"

Calla's eyes narrowed, but not in anger. She looked at Valor. "No, not exactly. But that didn't stop them from casting me out."

"Why did you come back?"

"Because sometimes the thing you least want to face is exactly what you're meant to."

The silence that followed was thick with something heavier than fear or awe. Caius nodded slowly.

"Are we in trouble?" Niko asked, fidgeting.

Calla's lips twitched. "Not tonight."

As they turned to leave, Niko looked back. "Is it true you can't lie?"

"Yes."

"How do we know you're not lying about that?"

She raised an eyebrow. "Would you know either way?"

Niko blinked. "That's… actually a good point."

Calla smiled faintly. "Now go. Before someone catches you out of bed."

Caius and Niko hurried off, their thoughts racing. Behind them, Calla watched until they vanished into the night. Valor nudged her gently, his golden eyes mirroring hers. She leaned against his side, one hand resting on his warm scales.

"Seventeen years," she whispered. "And nothing's really changed."

The dragon's tail curled protectively around her, and in the quiet night, Ackley's held its breath.

Chapter 2: The Legend of the Dragonmaster

Caius fidgeted in his seat, drumming his fingers against the polished wooden desk as he eyed the classroom door. Around him, the other students of Sorcia sat in varying states of anxiety, curiosity, and boredom. The desks formed a wide half-circle, and the sunlight from the high windows caught floating specks of dust that danced between them. But all eyes when not subtly glancing toward the doorway occasionally drifted to the vacant teacher's chair.

"She's late," Gan said loudly enough for half the room to hear. He leaned back in his seat, arms crossed, a smirk playing on his lips. "Maybe she got sent back to wherever dragonmasters go when they get fired."

Caius rolled his eyes but said nothing. Niko, seated beside him, didn't bother with subtlety. "She's not getting fired. She probably had to check on Valor. Dragons don't exactly feed themselves."

"Maybe she's already back in exile," Gan pressed. "Maybe this whole thing was a mistake."

"Or maybe," Niko snapped, "she's not on your schedule, Gan."

Before any further retorts could fly, a sudden pop of blue light burst in the center of the room. Students gasped and flinched back as a small creature appeared hovering three feet above the ground. Wings glittering like shards of ice, the sprite flitted about the classroom, laughing with a voice that sounded like bells over chimes.

"Miss me?" she chirped, spinning a tight loop in the air. Moria was no larger than a teacup, with silver-blue hair piled atop her tiny head like a crown of clouds and eyes that sparkled like starlight. She zipped around the classroom with chaotic delight, brushing the tops of heads and sending stray papers fluttering from desks.

"Back! Shoo!" Gan waved his hands as she darted toward him.

She grinned wickedly. "Still afraid of tiny things, Gan?"

"Get out of here, sprite," he muttered, swatting at her like a fly.

Moria zoomed directly in front of him and held her position, wings buzzing like a hummingbirds. "Now, now. That's no way to talk to the trusted courier of Ackley's most mysterious new teacher. I bring messages, secrets, and sometimes baked goods. You never know."

"What do you want?" asked Alora, amused despite herself.

Moria placed a hand on her miniature hip. "To witness history, of course. Our dragonmaster is teaching her second lesson, and I wouldn't miss it for all the apples in the orchard."

"She can't be a real dragonmaster," Gan muttered.

"Oh, but she is," Moria said, her tone abruptly dropping into a whisper. "You've seen the dragon. You've heard the stories. Dragonmasters don't lie. They can't. It's part of the bond. Even you must know that."

"She could just be a good liar with a big pet," Gan grumbled.

The sprite arched an eyebrow. "You think Valor is a pet? Adorable." Then, with a twirl in the air, she added, "But it's not just about dragons. It's about history. About power. About what your world refused to understand."

"Why are you even here?" Niko asked, squinting at her. "Isn't Master Calla the one teaching this class?"

Moria tsked. "And you're supposed to be paying attention. But here we are."

The classroom door opened with a faint creak, and silence fell instantly. Calla entered, her presence quiet but arresting. She wore a simple dark grey tunic, her robes nowhere in sight. Her eyes flicked once to the hovering sprite.

"Moria."

The sprite spun in place, throwing up a salute. "Present, punctual, and full of facts."

"You're not needed at the moment."

"Aren't I always?"

Calla raised an eyebrow. "Go."

With a dramatic sigh, Moria gave the students a last wave. "Don't forget what I said," she whispered, then winked and vanished in a flash of light, her wings leaving a trail of blue sparkles in the air.

Calla crossed the room without another word and sat on the edge of the teacher's desk. "I apologize for the delay," she said. "Valor needed attention, and dragons don't wait patiently."

A ripple of laughter passed through the class. Even Gan cracked a smile.

"Today," she said, scanning the room, "we're going to test what you actually remember from last term. Think of it as an oral review. No grades yet. Just performance."

Groans filled the air, but Calla didn't wait. She pulled a small slip of parchment from her pocket and read the first name.

"Alora."

The girl sat up straighter. "Yes, Master Calla?"

"Name one elemental spell and demonstrate its casting technique. No materials."

Alora nodded, stood, and drew a practiced circle in the air. "Ignitus minorum," she said, and a tiny flame burst to life above her hand.

"Controlled, balanced, good diction," Calla said. "Thank you."

The list continued: a whisper of names followed by spellwork. Students cast minor illusions, produced small weather effects, levitated objects or temporarily silenced their classmates all textbook basics, but done with varying skill and confidence. Gan's spell sputtered briefly, and his annoyance deepened when Calla raised an eyebrow but said nothing.

Then came Caius's name. He stood, heart pounding.

"Your spell?" Calla asked.

He closed his eyes and focused, channeling what he'd practiced endlessly. "Luxor magnitus." A bright orb of light appeared above his palm, slowly rising like a miniature sun and bathing the room in warm gold.

Calla's gaze sharpened slightly. "Very good."

Caius sat down, trying not to grin.

"I'm impressed," Calla said once the review ended. "Some of you need more control, others more confidence. But all of you can perform. That's something." She stood and addressed the group more broadly. "This term won't be like the last. You'll cast every day. Theory has its place, but sorcia is a craft learned by doing, not watching."

As students exchanged glances some excited, some nervous she nodded toward the door.

"You're dismissed."

They rose and began gathering their things. Niko elbowed Caius. "That spell was brilliant."

"You think so?" Caius asked, trying to sound casual.

"She thought so. That's what matters."

As the students exited into the corridor, Caius nudged Niko, and they lingered back, letting the others file past.

"Let's hang back," Caius whispered.

"You think she'll talk to the dragon again?" Niko asked.

"Maybe."

But Calla didn't return to the stables. Instead, she entered a side hallway that branched toward the faculty offices. Her footsteps echoed faintly.

Caius pulled Niko toward the corner, and they ducked behind one of the tall woven tapestries lining the stone walls. From here, they could see the open doorway to a small office empty but with voices filtering in from the next room.

"…You shouldn't be here," came a man's voice sharp, clipped.

"I was invited," Calla answered evenly. "By the sage master himself."

"You know as well as I do that your presence disrupts more than it helps. The Tribunal is already restless."

Caius recognized the voice now, Master Arrio. He taught Combat/Defense, and while he rarely interacted with younger students, his reputation for cruelty and rigid control was well-known.

"Yet here I am," Calla replied coolly.

"You were removed for a reason," Arrio said. "Your kind always pushes too far. There are rules. And when dragonmasters break them, people die."

There was a pause.

"I broke no rules," Calla said quietly. "But I will expose the ones that serve fear, not justice."

Arrio's voice dropped lower, but the bitterness was no less potent. "You humiliated me once. That won't happen again."

"I didn't humiliate you, Arrio," she said. "You did that to yourself."

The door creaked open, and the boys scrambled further behind the tapestry, heartbeats hammering.

Calla emerged first, walking calmly down the hallway. Her face was unreadable, but her hands were clenched into fists.

Arrio followed a moment later, his expression stormy and jaw tight.

"Do you think he's trying to get her fired?" Niko whispered.

"Definitely."

They waited until both adults were gone, then hurried off before they could be discovered.

Later that afternoon, as they walked past the Sorcia classroom again, Caius paused. Through the door's glass window, they could see Calla alone inside. The room was dim except for the glow of something on her desk; a stone, smooth and red like polished blood, pulsing with a faint inner light.

"That's it," Caius breathed. "A peril stone."

They leaned closer, watching as Calla stared at it with an unreadable expression. Her fingers hovered above its surface, but she didn't touch it.

"What does it do?" Niko whispered.

"No idea. I've read about them but no one seems to know their purpose."

Calla turned slightly, and they darted away before she could spot them.

The next period brought them to Lore, where Master Pell was hunched over his desk and scribbling notes with a quill that looked older than most of the students. He didn't even look up when they entered.

"Open to page ninety," he muttered. "Start reading. Quietly."

Alora raised her hand. "Master Pell, can we learn more about dragonmasters?"

Pell froze. His pen stilled mid-stroke.

"No," he said curtly.

"Why not?" Niko asked. "They're in the old scrolls, aren't they?"

"Not anymore," Pell said, voice clipped. "Much of that material has been… redacted."

"Redacted?" Alora asked, frowning. "Why?"

"It's above your grade level," he snapped.

"But we're being taught by a dragonmaster," Caius said. "Shouldn't we know their history?"

Master Pell looked up at them for the first time, and his face was drawn tight with something close to fear.

"There are things that are better left in the past," he said. "Focus on today's reading."

The classroom fell into confused silence.

Later, in Elements class, Master Dak stood before a flickering flame suspended in midair. His long coat was scorched in places, and he smelled faintly of smoke and pine resin. He smiled at the students.

"Let's talk about what your other teachers are afraid to say," he began. "Let's talk about dragonmasters."

Several students exchanged surprised looks.

"There's a reason you're not learning about them in Lore," Dak continued. "Politics. Fear. History rewritten to protect certain reputations."

He waved a hand, and the flame expanded, forming into the shape of a dragon mid-roar.

"Long ago, before the First Treaty, dragons weren't just beasts they were guardians. Symbiotic partners to a rare few humans. These people could connect to dragons through magic, thought, and emotion."

"Dragonmasters," whispered Caius.

Dak nodded. "The first was Rait, a young man damaged by war and left to die in the highlands. The story says he was saved by a dragon fairy, who gave him the blood of a dragon. That magic re-shaped him."

He let the fire-dragon dissolve.

"And with that bond came power but also isolation. Dragonmasters were feared and revered. Eventually, that fear overtook the respect. The Tribunal rewrote their stories, some turning them into villains. As a result, the dragonmasters secluded themselves away from the sorcia and gaol."

"So Calla's … one of them?" Alora asked.

"She is one," Dak said. "And from what I know, a powerful one."

Gan scoffed. "That's all just storybook nonsense."

"Maybe," Dak replied, voice calm. "But then again, you've seen Valor for yourself. Does he look like storybook nonsense?"

No one replied.

Dak crossed his arms. "You'll find that legends tend to resurface especially the ones people try hardest to forget."

After class, the students spilled out into the courtyard, their chatter low and uncertain. The legend of Rait lingered in their thoughts like an echo too loud to ignore.

"Do you think it's true?" Niko asked as he and Caius made their way toward the dormitories. "That Calla had dragon blood given to her or something?"

Caius shrugged. "I don't know. But Valor is not an ordinary dragon, is he? He listens to her. Like he understands everything she thinks."

"Maybe he does," Niko said. "Maybe that's what bonding means. I still can't believe no one talks about dragonmasters. Like people think if they ignore them, they'll vanish."

"They won't," Caius said firmly.

"Gan's not going to shut up anytime soon though."

Caius smirked. "No. But he might learn to be quieter with a mouth full of feathers."

They both laughed, and the tension eased.

Later that evening, while the other students prepared for dinner, Caius stood at the edge of the stables again, watching from behind the post as Valor curled beside the hay bales, one golden eye half-open.

Calla stood nearby, her back to the school, arms folded. The sky above had turned dusky purple, clouds drifting low and heavy. From the shadows of the stable, it was quiet until Calla spoke.

"I know you're there, Caius."

He stepped out slowly. "Sorry. I wasn't spying."

"I believe you."

He hesitated, then asked, "Is it true? What Master Dak told us about Rait, the dragon fairy and the blood?"

Calla didn't look at him. "It's one version of the story."

"Is that what happened to you?"

She glanced at Valor, then shook her head. "No. What happened to me was quite different."

"Why do some people seem to be afraid of you?"

"They're afraid of what they can't control," she said softly. "And dragonmasters have never been easy to control."

Caius didn't speak for a moment. Then, "I don't think that's necessarily a bad thing."

Calla gave him a small smile faint but real. "That you can say that is what scares them most."

As Caius turned to go, Valor shifted slightly, his tail curling protectively around Calla's feet.

"Caius," she said suddenly.

He stopped and looked back.

"Some people will tell you that truth is dangerous. That it stirs things best left quiet."

He nodded slowly. "And do you think that's true?"

She met his eyes. "I think it's more dangerous to pretend the truth is something it isn't."

That night, as darkness settled over Ackley's, the wind howled faintly beyond the tower windows, and the red stone on Calla's desk pulsed once just once with an inner light. Like something waiting.

Watching.

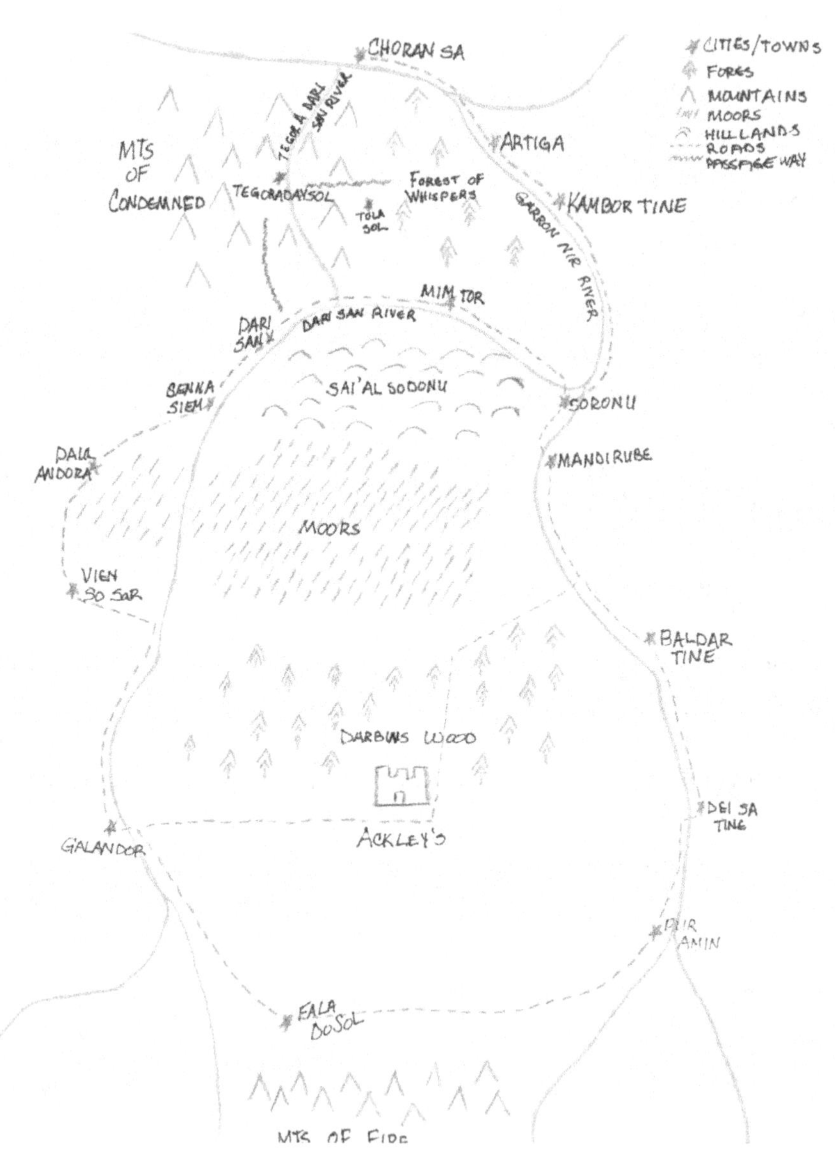

CHORAN SA
CITIES/TOWNS
FORES
MOUNTAINS
MOORS
HILLLANDS
ROADS
PASSAGE WAY
ARTIGA
TEGOR A DARI SAN RIVER
MTS OF CONDEMNED
TEGORADAYSOL
FOREST OF WHISPERS
TOLA SOL
KAMBOR TINE
GARRON NIR RIVER
MIM TOR
DARI SAN
DARI SAN RIVER
SAI'AL SODONU
BENNA SIEM
SORONU
DALA ANDORA
MANDIRUBE
MOORS
VIEN SO SAR
BALDAR TINE
DARBINS WOOD
DEI SA TINE
ACKLEY'S
GALANDOR
PIR AMIN
EALA DOSOL
MTS OF FIRE

Chapter 3: Secrets Revealed

If they wanted to know more about the dragonmasters, something beyond legends and speculation, Niko and Caius would have to get it from a dragonmaster. And they only knew one.

Their sorcia master.

But as personable as Calla seemed, they both agreed she wasn't about to pour out ancient secrets to two novices already deemed too curious for their own good.

After lights out, students were confined to their dormitories. Normally, Caius welcomed the chance to collapse into bed, but recently, sleep eluded him. Nights were long. His thoughts restless.

From the bunk above, Niko groaned and dropped his head over the edge. "Will you stop all that tossing and turning? I've not gotten a decent night's sleep this week."

Caius sat up with a sigh, fingers dragging through his already-mussed hair. "Sorry. I just… can't sleep."

"Obviously," Niko muttered, rolling back onto his pillow.

Caius shoved his feet into slippers and tugged his navy wool robe over his pajamas. "I think I'll get a drink of water."

"And a sleeping serum," Niko mumbled.

"I vote for that," Paka grumbled from the next bunk over.

Caius slipped quietly from the room, pulling the door shut behind him. He understood their irritation. His preoccupation with dragonmasters was becoming an obsession. And he didn't fully understand it himself.

He crossed the hall, drank a full glass of water from the basin, and started back toward the dorm. But voices from the lower corridor caught his attention. Pausing, he moved toward the stairwell and crouched at the top step, peering down into the shadows.

"I think he should know the truth sooner rather than later," Calla was saying. Her voice was tight with restrained emotion. "That decision was made long ago."

The other voice was unmistakable. Sage Master Fane. "It was."

Until now, Fane had been conspicuously absent from day-to-day affairs. In Caius's first year, the Sage Master had often visited classrooms and made long speeches at mealtimes. These days, he only appeared at dinner and spoke rarely.

"As I see it," Calla continued, "this matter's been put in my hands. You sent for me, if you recall. I didn't volunteer."

"I realize that."

"And the summons was hardly subtle."

"I had doubts you'd respond to subtle," Fane replied mildly. "I considered sending a note, but would you have read it?"

Calla gave a short, dry laugh. "No. You're right. I wouldn't have."

Caius leaned forward slightly, curiosity sharpening. Even now, Calla's tone held barely restrained irritation.

"Having a falcon swoop down on me was far more effective," she added.

"He wasn't instructed to swoop," Fane said, a hint of amusement in his voice.

"Well I'm here now but you're tying my hands."

"That's not my intention, Calla."

"You know my first loyalty lies with my own. It has to."

"I understand that."

"To be honest, I don't know that you do, Master Fane," she said, her patience thinning. "You certainly didn't seem to understand it when you failed to mention that Arrio was here. Or Dak."

A long pause.

"Calla," Fane said at last, his voice smooth, "after all this time… are you still so angry?"

"Angrier," she snapped. "It's not in my nature to let bygones be bygones."

"I remember. As to my message I thought it better to keep it brief."

"It was certainly that."

"And Arrio's presence shouldn't affect the matters at hand."

"It shouldn't," Calla agreed tightly. "But it does."

"All of that is in the past, Calla. Let it stay there."

"That's easy to say. Following through is another matter."

"Because you won't let it go," Fane said gently. "Why else would you still wear that scar?"

Caius held his breath.

"I keep it," Calla said, her voice low, "to remind myself that there are dangers in this world far worse than dragons. Prejudice. Arrogance. And to remember never to let my guard down again."

"You were treated unfairly. I won't deny that. But there must've been some expectation on your part of how this might go. You revealed what you were in front of your classmates, and you cast a spell against another student, turning him into a goat."

"I'm familiar with what transpired," she replied sharply. "And I won't allow such things to happen again."

"And is that why you're out roaming the corridors after dark?" Fane asked, his tone light. "Worried about what might happen?"

She sighed. "I couldn't sleep. I just wanted to check on things."

Fane chuckled softly. "Even dragonmasters need rest, Calla. Go on to bed. I'll take care of things."

"I'm expected to trust you," she said bitterly.

"But you do," Fane replied. "Despite your hurt and anger, despite what you believe I allowed to happen, you trust me. You always have."

There was another silence.

"Yes," she admitted. "I know."

"You're not ready to forgive. I can wait."

"It might take time," she said quietly.

"I can wait," he repeated.

Suddenly, Caius realized their voices were growing closer. They were ascending the stairs.

Panicking, he bolted for the dorm, leaving the door ajar as he dove under his covers, robe and slippers still on. He yanked the blanket to his chin and squeezed his eyes shut, heart pounding.

Footsteps entered the room.

He heard Paka snoring faintly. A bed creaked somewhere down the row.

Caius tried to slow his breathing, willing his heart to quiet. The shadow of the Sage Master crossed the threshold. Caius squeezed his eyes shut tighter.

Fane walked slowly down the line of bunks, pausing briefly, then moving on without a word.

Caius was sure he stopped at his bed. Certain Fane knew he was awake.

Then, just as quietly, the Sage Master turned and left.

As silence settled again, Caius lay still, staring into darkness. He was exhausted. His thoughts tangled in the questions that now loomed above all others:

What was the dragonmaster doing at the school and who was the 'him' she referred to?

>

To most students, Moria was just part of the school like the worn staircases, the drafty hallways, or the smell of old parchment in the library. She shelved books, delivered messages, filled in for missing teachers, and most notably knew everything about everyone.

Caius and Niko, after reviewing what Caius had overheard on the stairs, decided it was time to test her knowledge and willingness to talk.

Dragon fairies were said to be among the most powerful of the fairy clans, and while Moria had never claimed to be one herself, she was, as she reminded them often, *cousin* to the dragon fairies. She would know the lore. The problem was getting her to share it. She loved secrets. Guarded them closely. Boasted about what she knew, but rarely said too much.

Fortunately, she had one tragic weakness: she loved gossip.

The boys made a plan. On the evening before their free day, when curfew was later and students lingered in the lounge, they claimed the table nearest the fire. Open books and blank parchment spread before them, they bent their heads close together, speaking in staged whispers. Moria would never ignore a whisper.

"She'll be angry if she thinks we're trying to trick her," Niko muttered.

"Then we'll just have to make sure she doesn't find out," Caius replied.

Niko glanced toward the edge of the room. "Well… she's looking."

They leaned in again, carefully pretending not to notice the glittering blur zipping toward them.

"The novices are hard at work," Moria chirped, hovering over their table. "Or are they?" Her gaze flicked across their blank tablets. "Having trouble?"

Caius shrugged and picked up his quill. "We're fine. Just figuring out what to write for Master Caden's assignment."

Niko hunched over his book, just as rehearsed. "I don't think we know enough to write about. Peril stones are... kind of a secret."

Caius lowered his voice to a stage-whisper. "But no one else picked this topic. We could get top marks."

Moria narrowed her eyes. "Peril stones are *not* a proper topic for a school paper."

Caius frowned, rubbing the spot where she rapped him sharply with her tiny knuckle. "If they're not, why did Master Dak teach us about them in Elements?"

"Master Caden said to be original," Niko added. "And it's not like we plan to make things up."

"I could ask Master Calla to show it to me again," Caius offered casually. "Just to get the details right."

"You've seen a peril stone?" Moria asked, suspicious.

"Sure," Caius said with a shrug.

"In the Sorcia classroom," Niko added, as if it were the most ordinary thing.

Moria blinked. "Strange happenings," she muttered. "Dragonmasters… peril stones…" She trailed off.

"I guess it's all part of the Tribunal bringing dragonmasters back out of seclusion," Niko said confidently.

"Master Dak thinks it's better that way," Caius nodded. "He says people fear what they don't understand."

"Humans are *always* fearful," Moria scoffed. "Middlings are the worst. Claim to believe in nothing but fear everything. Sorcia aren't much better except dragonmasters, of course. Fairy blood makes them wiser."

"Fairy blood?" Caius echoed.

Moria smirked. "That's why dragonmasters know what should be feared and what shouldn't."

"Master Calla isn't afraid of anything," Niko said proudly.

Moria twirled in midair, wings catching the firelight. "We would likely never know. Dragonmasters rarely admit fear. Nor will they deny it."

"They speak in riddles," Caius said. "That way they don't lie but they don't exactly tell the truth either."

"Exactly." The sprite spun again. "Never lie. Never tell. That's the way of the dragonmasters."

"Sounds… exhausting," Niko muttered.

Moria cocked her head. "You forget I can't lie either."

Both boys froze. "Oh," Niko said sheepishly.

Moria grinned. "It's *lying* that's hard. Keeping stories straight, covering your tracks. Fabricators always slip up."

"Some even lie to themselves," Caius added without thinking.

The sprite's smile grew sly. "Yes. Some do." she said, winking at Niko.

Caius nudged Niko under the table before his friend could bristle. "Master Calla doesn't seem like most dragonmasters," he offered quickly.

"No," Moria agreed. "She isn't."

"She's the best teacher Ackley's ever had," Caius said with conviction.

"The best *and* the worst," Moria teased, fluttering behind his chair. "Depends who you ask."

"Well, I say best."

"You're biased." She hovered over the fire, glowing blue in the light. "But yes, many have strong feelings about dragonmasters."

"Master Arrio, for one," Niko muttered. "He has *feelings*."

"Bad blood there," Moria said, giggling. "Quite literally."

"I guess I'd be upset too if someone turned me into a goat," Niko said with a snort.

Moria's peal of laughter echoed through the room. Nearby students winced and covered their ears. The boys joined them.

"So, you *do* know," she said, settling back down.

Caius glanced around. The other students, mostly older, ignored them again.

"He asked for it," Caius said quietly.

"That and more," Moria replied. "It's a terrible thing to give your word and not keep it. Especially to a dragonmaster."

"He didn't know she *was* a dragonmaster, though," Niko pointed out.

"No. Only those who needed to know were told."

"Was that why she was expelled?" Caius asked. "Because of Arrio?"

"Oh no," Moria said. "Students cast spells on each other all the time; some end up as worms or tree frogs. That only gets you demerits. No, Calla wasn't expelled for what she did. She was expelled for what she *was*."

"Master Dak and the Sage Master both she was treated unfairly," Caius said.

Moria nodded. "He spoke for her. Others did too. But most weren't ready to accept what she represented."

"Just because she's a dragonmaster?"

"That's enough for some." The sprite twirled again, slower this time. "But it wasn't *just* that. She was clever. Willful. Sharp-tongued. Too bright for her own good."

"And some of the teachers didn't want her at Ackley's," Caius said quietly.

"No," Moria agreed. "Some truths are difficult to accept. Then and now." She paused, glancing around. "I've said more than I should. You remind me of Calla when she was a novice, full of questions. Be careful. Curiosity can be your undoing."

"Wait!" Caius stood suddenly, knocking his book to the floor. "Calla's here for more than teaching! Isn't she? You know what she's really doing here!"

Moria regarded him with interest. "Of course, I know."

"So…?"

"I can't tell you," she said lightly. "Still, I'll give you this much: you already know more than you should. Be careful not to learn more than you really want to know. Or more than is good for you."

With a mischievous grin, she zipped out of the room and vanished into the corridor.

"Well, we learned a few things," Caius said, retrieving his book and stuffing it into his satchel.

"We did?" Niko followed him out of the room.

"Sure," Caius said. "She wasn't expelled for turning Arrio into a goat. And he broke a promise to her. I forgot to ask about the scar," he added with a sigh. "I meant to."

"Everyone thinks it came from a dragon."

"No. Calla made it sound like it came from something *worse* than a dragon."

Niko frowned. "What's worse than a dragon?"

Caius didn't answer right away. "All I know is the Sage Master brought it up while talking about Master Arrio. So, he must've had something to do with it. And Moria said dragonmasters have fairy blood," Caius added. "Are they even human?"

"Of course, they are," Niko said.

Caius looked troubled. "But if they have dragon's blood… and fairy blood… how do we know?"

"You've seen Master Calla. She doesn't *look* like a dragon or a fairy. And she uses sorcia. Sorcia are definitely human."

"Are they?" Caius asked. "What if dragonmasters are something else? What if they're immortal?"

"Fairies and dragons aren't immortal," Niko said. "They can die. If it can die, it's not immortal."

"But they don't really *die*. Fairies become sprites."

"They have to die *first*," Niko insisted.

"Who has to die?" asked a voice.

They turned to see Paka sitting cross-legged outside their dorm room with a book in hand. "Elak's meditating," he added, gesturing at the closed door. "So… who're you two planning to kill?"

Caius and Niko grinned and dropped beside him.

"We're not killing anyone," Niko said. "We were talking about fairies. And sprites." He leaned close to get a look at what was in Paka's hands.

Paka held up the book. "*Mysteries of the Mountains.* Doria lent it to me. It's full of stories about dragonmasters and Dragon's Lair."

"Dragon's Lair?" Caius blinked. "I thought that was a myth."

"Probably is," Paka said with a shrug. "Who knows? So what's with the interest in dying fairies and sprites?" Paka asked, closing the book with a casual thump.

"Actually," Niko said, "we were talking to Moria about dragonmasters."

"Are they evolvers too?" Caius added.

Paka tilted his head. "No one really knows, do they? There's not a lot known about dragonmasters outside the Tribunal."

"Are they human?" Caius asked again.

Paka looked surprised. "Why wouldn't they be?"

"Because they have dragon's blood," Niko said, like it explained everything.

"And maybe fairy blood," Caius added.

Paka chuckled. "You two have been listening to Moria too long. Sounds like she's filling your heads with wild ideas."

"She said dragonmasters know more than *other* humans," Niko offered.

"Then there's your answer," Paka said, rising to his feet. "She wouldn't have said 'other humans' unless they were human too."

Caius let out a breath. "Good point."

"So, they *can* die."

"According to this book, they certainly can." Paka tapped the cover. "Some died in battle. Others were killed by rogue dragons."

Caius's brow furrowed. "I still wish I'd asked about the scar."

"Master Calla's scar?" Paka laughed. "I thought everyone had heard by now. Master Arrio told us in class a few weeks ago."

"What did he say?" both boys asked at once.

"Just that she got it during a fencing tournament. He was teaching about distraction...said you wait for your opponent's moment of hesitation and strike. That's how she got the scar."

Niko frowned. "That can't be right. Calla said it was worse than a dragon."

Caius stared at the floor. "It was," he said softly. "Arrio gave her that scar. With a rapier. That's what's worse than a dragon."

"What is?" Niko asked.

Caius looked up. "Someone who breaks their word."

Paka shook his head. "You two should worry more about studying and less about dragonmasters and fairies. Testing starts soon."

He rapped on the dormitory door. "Elak, your time is up!"

Caius and Niko gathered their things and were about to follow when a voice from the top of the stairs stopped them.

"Just a moment, boys."

They turned slowly.

Master Dak stood before them, arms folded.

"You two seem to have quite an interest in your Sorcia Master," he observed.

"Well… she *is* interesting," Caius said cautiously.

"I suppose she is," Dak said. "But getting tangled in rumors and speculation can be dangerous."

"It wouldn't *be* speculation if someone told us the truth," Caius said.

Dak eyed him. "You're perceptive, Caius. But most of what's known about dragonmasters really is no more than speculation. That's the nature of the dragonmasters."

"You knew her when you were students," Caius said. "You *must* know something."

"I didn't know she was a dragonmaster back then." he reminded them.

"Did Master Arrio give her the scar?" Niko asked.

"Yes and no," came a voice behind them. All three turned as Calla stepped into view, a glimmer of amusement in her eyes. "I really should be getting paranoid. That's the third time I've walked in on a conversation about myself."

Caius blushed. Niko stared at his boots.

Dak gave her a dry look. "Perhaps if you stopped prowling around the school like a shadow, you would hear fewer people talking about you."

Calla smirked. "What fun would that be?"

"Honestly, Calla," Dak said, exasperated, "are you ever going to grow up?"

"I hope not," she replied, resting her hands on the boys' shoulders. "I think it's time the three of us talked."

Niko made a noise halfway between a cough and a whimper. Caius swallowed hard.

"I think the nook will do," Calla said, guiding them down the corridor. "You're welcome to join us, Dak."

The turret rooms were cozy by day, but eerie at night. Still, Calla entered as if it were the sunniest space in the castle. She sank onto one of the cushioned window seats and gestured for the boys to sit across from her. Dak followed, looking both wary and intrigued.

"Curiosity is a wonderful thing," Calla began, tone deceptively light. "It inspires invention, leads to discoveries. But it can also get you into trouble."

Caius's stomach twisted.

"To be honest," she continued, "you're not very good at spying yet. Arrio didn't notice you behind the tapestry only because he was too angry to see straight."

Caius's mouth fell open. "Y-you knew?"

"I knew," she said with a chuckle. "You were more subtle on the stairs. I didn't realize you were there until just before I left."

"Because you were angry," Caius murmured.

She nodded.

"But why were you angry at the Sage Master?"

Calla sighed. "That's… complicated."

Dak looked at them both. "You've been spying?"

"I don't think it was intentional," Calla said kindly. "Just… timely."

"I don't see the point," Niko said. "No one wants to tell us anything."

"Oh, but you've learned plenty," Calla smiled. "You know I was expelled. That I turned Arrio into a goat. That he gave me this." She touched her scar. "You've figured out more than most."

"Why a goat?" Caius asked.

"We'd studied satyrs that day," she said sheepishly. "It was on my mind."

Dak burst out laughing. "I always thought it was a statement about him being a stubborn little bully."

"That version *is* more poetic," Calla agreed, grinning. "But this?" She traced the scar again. "This wasn't about satire or statements. I was careless."

"You were betrayed," Dak said fiercely.

"I should've known better."

"You were dueling?" Niko asked.

"Fencing," she corrected. "There's a difference."

Caius nodded. "Fencing is a sport. Dueling is combat."

"Exactly," Calla said. "And the first lesson?" her gaze moved questioningly to Dak.

Dak sighed. "Fencing is a sport, and a sport requires rules and honor."

"Correct. Power, money, fame… they mean nothing without honor." Her tone grew firm. "Of all the things you'll possess, nothing is more valuable than your word."

"Arrio broke his," Caius said.

"He did," Calla agreed.

"In fencing, you vow to abide by the Sorcia Abeyance," Dak explained. "No spells. No magic."

"Is that really necessary though? There hasn't been war in the realm for centuries," Niko said.

"And in a real war, no one would offer the Sorcia Abeyance. That is used strictly in sport. Master Pell likely told you the last war was fought right here at Ackley's," Calla replied. "And you'll be learning more about that sooner than you think."

Dak gave her a sharp look. She only smiled.

"So, what happened at the tournament?" Caius asked.

Dak answered. "Arrio was top of our class in fencing. Then he heard rumors of a younger student who could best him, and a girl at that. He took a great deal of teasing so he finally challenged her."

"And I declined," Calla said.

"But Arrio pushed for a school tournament," Dak continued. "And the combat master approved it. Eventually, they had to face off."

"I should've just walked away," Calla said. "But I was proud. I wanted to prove myself."

"Calla had him beat," Dak said. "So Arrio cheated. He cast a de-materializing spell on her rapier."

Caius and Niko stared.

"That's how you got the scar?" Niko whispered.

"I don't think it was intentional. Like a fool, I tried to summon my weapon back with a spell," Calla said. "But it didn't work, of course. I was never sure if Arrio intended to cut me or it it just happened in all the confusion."

"Why couldn't you get your weapon back?" Niko asked.

"Because I'm a dragonmaster," she said softly. "I'd sworn not to use magic. And dragonmasters *can't* break their word."

"Seriously?" Niko said.

"Seriously. The bloodline won't allow it. I might think about doing it, but the vow of the dragonmaster will not permit me to act on those thoughts. Unfortunately, Arrio was not likewise restricted. Even to save my life I could not have broken the Sorcia Abeyance."

"And that's when everyone realized what you were," Caius said.

"Most didn't know what to think."

"Remember, Calla was the first *female* dragonmaster ." Dak pointed out. He gave Calla a searching look. "I sent you messages...but you never replied."

"I thought it was better that way." she said with a shrug. A weary smile crossed her face. "You didn't need to be linked to a dragonmaster. Besides, my father was forced to confess what I was and I was expelled by midday. And by the end of the day…"

"Arrio was a goat." Dak said flatly.

"He was in the front hall, gloating over my expulsion. I overreacted," she admitted.

"That's an understatement."

"Oh, a few hours as a goat didn't hurt him." she said dismissively.

"How did you know you were a dragonmaster?" Caius asked.

"It was the peril stone, wasn't it?" Niko said excitedly. "Master Dak told us the legend."

Calla exchanged a glance with Dak. "Oh he did, did he? It's mostly true, what you've heard. Most dragonmasters get their calling before they learn to walk. I didn't even know I had one until just before I enrolled here. My father kept it hidden. When Tangor came to the house on that day, he helped me summon it."

Dak looked thoughtful. "Tangor's the one you left the school with?"

She nodded. "Master Fane called for him after the tournament was announced." She looked solemn. "Probably had an idea what could happen."

"So, Fane *knew* you were a dragonmaster?"

Calla laughed harshly. "Fane knows everything. He let me attend because he believed in me and didn't agree with the dragon-masters staying in seclusion."

"He defended you?" Caius asked.

"Yes. But there was no real hearing. No one wanted that, certainly not my father and the Tribunal ."

"Your father's in the Tribunal?" Niko gasped.

Calla nodded. "He was at that time...which made things worse."

Dak glanced at the corridor. "Calla, it's late." he decided, rising.

"These boys needed to know," she said. "They are asking a lot of questions and they need to hear the truth." She gave the boys a stern look. "But you *must* come to me with questions in the future. Not Moria. No other teachers. Just me. I'll tell you what I can and the rest...you'll just have to trust me."

Niko nodded without hesitation, but Caius looked apprehensive.

"Master Calla," he asked worriedly. "...are we in trouble?"

"No," she assured him. "And I'd like to keep it that way. You have to promise me, discuss this with no one but me."

With a grunt of disapproval, the elements master dropped back into the window seat but Calla paid no attention to him.

"I need your word."

"I promise," Caius said.

"Me too," Niko echoed.

Calla looked relieved. "Then off to bed with you." she crossed to the doorway, her back to them. "But there's something else you should know." she said quietly. "Things are not always what they seem to be. It doesn't hurt to have a bit of skepticism. If you feel uncertain or uncomfortable about anything...trust your instincts.

"Calla, are you trying to frighten them?" Dak asked, rising again.

Turning towards him, she nodded. "Yes Dak, that's exactly what I'm trying to do. Asking questions of the wrong person now could have serious consequences." Her gaze rested on the boys again. "But Dak is right...it's late and you've had enough for one night."

As they walked back to their dorm, they could hear Calla and Dak beginning to argue again but this time, the boys didn't try to listen.

They had enough to think about.

Chapter 4: The Masters' Duel

Though the semester was only half over, the Academy was already buzzing with excitement for the Festival of Fairy Lights. Once the last week of classes ended, students would return home for the winter break, some by coach, some by spell but all eager for the comfort of hearth and family.

All except one.

"I still can't believe you're not going home," Caius said, tossing a soft-tipped practice sword from hand to hand as they walked toward combat class.

Niko shrugged. "It's not as if there's a big celebration in Cenna Siem. Paka, Dara and I would rather be here...at least there's always a lot to do here during Festival."

Caius looked sideways at his friend. "Well... maybe you could spend the holiday with *us* this year. My mum always makes too much food and she would be thrilled to entertain a guest."

Niko's face lit up. "Seriously?"

"Why not? I'll ask my parents tonight."

"Done," Niko said, grinning. "I'm officially adopted for Festival." he exclaimed as they headed to Combat/defense class.

They entered the questing arena, the vast stone chamber that housed all combat and defense classes. Today, students were abuzz with rumors that fencing would finally be introduced. Caius had only practiced with a rapier once, but he'd liked it. Niko was surprisingly good with the weapon, having trained with Paka at home.

But as the class gathered in a loose circle around the supply carts, Caius's excitement began to fade.

He spotted Master Arrio, arms folded, wearing his usual smirk. His gaze swept over the students with a kind of bored contempt.

"I don't like the look on his face," Caius muttered.

"Looks the same as always,to me." Niko whispered.

The rapiers were polished and gleaming, looking deadlier than they were. The ends of the teaching weapons were blunted, the blades dull. Everyone was disappointed as they examined the weapons and discovered that the rapiers were hardly sharp enough to cut butter, but Caius was secretly relieved. Now more than ever, thinking of Calla's scar.

Arrio raised his voice. "As you can see, the time has come for you to engage in actual fencing, of a sort." Murmurs of approval swept around the room and several hands shot up. "I appreciate the enthusiasm." Master Arrio said, seemingly amused. He gestured to the line in the center of the questing ring. "This is the dissecting line. For today's lesson, you are only going to be defending your side of the line. If you allow your opponent to cross the line, he takes a point."

"Now," Arrio said, planting his blade in the floor, "who would like to demonstrate?"

Several students raised their hands eagerly.

Caius stepped back.

Arrio pointed. "Gan. And… Caius."

Niko glanced at him, wide-eyed. Caius hesitated, then stepped forward slowly. Gan, broad-shouldered and a head taller than Caius, smirked and twirled the weapon in his hand.

"Are you going to have us give the Sorcia Abeyance?" Caius asked cautiously.

Arrio turned toward him, eyes narrowing. "What?"

"The vow," Caius clarified. "Shouldn't we say it aloud?"

A few students murmured in agreement.

Arrio's mouth twitched. "This isn't a true fencing match, it's only a classroom exercise. Is that a problem?"

"No," Caius said quickly. "It's just that… well, it's tradition, right?"

Gan snorted. "Scared you'll get a scar on your pretty face?"

Laughter rippled through the group.

Caius flushed. "Just wondering if we're doing it properly." His stomach twisted. Something wasn't right about this lesson.

"Halt!" The voice rang out like a thunderclap. The class turned, surprised to hear the command called to end a fencing match before it had even begun.

Calla crossed to the edge of the arena, arms folded. "The Sorcia Abeyance should always be used when two sorcerers face one another with weapons. " she said coolly. Her eyes were glowing brilliantly. "Unless, of course, the weapons are drawn in true combat."

Arrio raised his chin. "You weren't invited to this lesson, Calla. And the vow is hardly necessary. These rapiers couldn't do any serious damage and you know it."

"I don't need an invitation when a student is being threatened." Her tone was icy. She stepped into the circle and faced Arrio directly. "You are the combat/defense master. It is your responsibility to teach them the rules of wielding, sport and combat."

Gan opened his mouth but Calla pointed over at him without looking in his direction. "Not a word from you. You're dismissed."

Gan scurried back into the group.

"We can deal with this later," Arrio said, starting to turn.

Calla didn't move. "We can deal with it now."

The air between them crackled.

The tension in the arena was so thick, even Niko stood still.

Arrio squared his shoulders. "You're out of line, Calla. This is *my* class."

"Then take responsibility for it," she replied evenly.

"This is the reason you were sent here? To protect the students. " Arrio sneered, glancing at Caius. "Is that what the dragonmasters have sunk to? Babysitting?"

"My reason for being here is none of your concern."

"I will say it again, you are not welcome in my class. Dragonmasters have no business in a school, I know that from first hand experience!"

A ripple of murmuring spread through the students.

"Enough of this," Arrio said, stepping forward. "You're still here under a trial appointment, aren't you? A mistake in judgment could..."

"Could what?" Calla interrupted. "Earn me another scar?" Her fingertips grazed the scar on her cheek. "As I recall, it wasn't a dragonmaster that broke the Sorcia Abeyance and attacked an unarmed opponent. Do you think it a victory to draw blood from an unarmed opponent?"

"I wasn't the one expelled." he reminded her.

She shrugged indifferently. "But you should have been." Her voice was soft but filled with malice.

Arrio stopped. His hand gripped the hilt of his sword.

"Try it," Calla said softly.

"Don't underestimate me, Calla."

Her expression hardened and her eyes seemed to glow with more intensity. "I will not make that mistake again, rest assured." Stepping back a pace she cast a glance around at the students, staring in shocked silence at the two masters.

Arrio drew his sword in a flash of silver. Unlike the training rapiers, this one was well honed and gleaming wickedly.

The students gasped, withdrawing several steps.

But Calla seemed unconcerned by the rapier only inches from her chest, her eyes on Arrio rather than his weapon. Her right hand rested casually on the hilt of her own sword, an arming sword rather than a rapier. Niko and Caius both doubted that she would have time to draw her weapon before Arrio could act.

"It will take a sorcerer more powerful than you to defeat a dragonmaster, Arrio." She said quietly. "And I no longer pledge the Sorcia Abeyance." She raised one hand and with a simple twist of her fingers, bent Arrio's rapier in half.

The weapon curved like warm wax, the metal hissing with residual heat. Arrio staggered, stunned, staring at his ruined blade.

Calla's finger flexed on the hilt of her sword. "I would suggest you never again draw a weapon against me. I am a dragonmaster...keep that in mind. I do not wield my weapon for sport and I do not take being threatened lightly."

With a bellow of rage, Arrio flung his rapier to the floor. "Get out." he said, his voice low but racked with contempt.

No one spoke as Calla nodded and headed towards the door.

Arrio watched her leave, then bent and retrieved his damaged rapier. "Class dismissed." he muttered, still regarding his blade.

The students filed out in stunned silence, casting glances over their shoulders at Arrio. No one spoke a word until they were well out of the questing arena.

Caius and Niko lingered near the back of the group, their minds buzzing.

"She bent it," Niko whispered.

"I saw."

"She didn't even touch it."

"I *know*."

They stopped just outside the corridor as Calla approached them.

"I assume you two have questions," she said, her voice low.

Caius swallowed. "A few."

"Come," she said. "My quarters."

Calla's quarters were tucked away in the highest turret of the west wing, accessible only through a spiral stair hidden behind a tapestry of the founding sages. Most students didn't even know the tower *had* a fourth floor. Caius and Niko followed her silently, boots thudding on worn stone.

The room, when they entered, was unlike anything else at Ackley's.

Soft green light filtered through hexagonal stained-glass windows. Bookshelves arched like trees against the walls. A small hearth crackled beside a table covered in maps and tiny crystal shards.

She waved a hand, and two armchairs spun to face the boys. They sat. Calla remained standing.

"I imagine you want answers," she said.

"Yes," Caius said at once.

Calla walked toward a low table and picked up a smooth, obsidian disc rimmed in gold. She held it in her palm. "This is a summoning mirror. Dragonmasters use them to track and protect those they are bound to. Not physically, but magically."

"So, it's like a scrying tool?" Niko had never heard of a summoning mirror, but looking at the one in Calla's hand made him uneasy. There was no reflection in the disc, just a foggy swirling that seemed to have no depth...to just go on endlessly.

"Much more," she said. "They help us to communicate over distances. They are attuned to our peril stones and can be used for tracking as well as communicating."

"Peril stone?" Niko echoed. "Like the one you summoned."

"Yes. Every dragonmaster has one. A peril stone is part of our essence. Only...peril stones are like living things."

"Alive?" The boys exchanged glances.

"There are two types of peril stones," she went on. "Spirit stones and patron stones. Spirit stones are rare. But that's a lesson for another time."

"And the stones find the dragonmasters somehow?"

There was a knock at the turret door.

Calla frowned, flicked her fingers, and the door creaked open.

Dak stepped inside, expression unreadable.

"I figured I'd find you here," he said. "You left the arena rather abruptly."

"I had students to reassure."

Dak raised an eyebrow. "You mean to protect?"

Calla didn't smile. "You disapprove?"

"I disapprove of dragging students into any sort of Tribunal or Triad business," he said.

"It isn't always an option."

Dak folded his arms. "You were always impulsive, Calla."

"And you were always reluctant to accept the things you couldn't control."

Niko coughed.

Neither adult acknowledged him.

Dak stepped closer. "You said you were summoned here. Why now? After all these years?"

"There's been a shift in slayer activity," she said. "Four attacks reported in the last three months. One apparently unprovoked."

Dak paled. "Unprovoked?"

"They're not just tracking dragons anymore."

Caius spoke up. "What are slayers?"

Calla turned to him. "They were once referred to as dragonslayers." she explained. "Members of the sorcia that were trained to kill dragons."

"It took someone with a great deal of nerve to study to be a dragonslayer, and most of those that trained didn't make the cut." added Dak.

"That's true." Calla looked grim. "There have always been dragons that simply refused to be...controlled, for lack of a better word, though I would never say Valor is controlled. It's more involved than that. And dragonmasters can do nothing to harm a dragon, even if our lives are in danger. So dragonslayers were trained to handle the rogue dragons." Her voice dropped. "But they aren't dragonslayers any longer. Now they are simply slayers."

"What changed?" Niko wondered.

"We haven't determined that exactly. We only know that they are no longer under the Tribunal and they have killed beings other than dragons." Calla's eyes narrowed. "Which is part of the reason I'm here. This school is vulnerable. The Tribunal seems reluctant to act so the Triad sent me here...to observe."

"Then why not tell me?" Dak asked.

"That wasn't my call to make."

"Well whatever you're here to do...antagonizing Arrio can't be helpful."

"I needed him to know that he is being watched. That I'm no longer the student he could get expelled."

"That was personal and we both know it."

She shrugged. "Perhaps a little. I will not tolerate students being threatened, however, or being improperly taught."

"And that's why you're here?"

"One reason." she replied elusively.

"So it's back to the language of the dragonmaster." Dak said, folding his arms across his chest. "Riddles and half-truths."

If Dak expected Calla to be offended, he was disappointed. She laughed. "Isn't that what you expect?"

His face darkened. "That's not fair."

"It's *true*," she said.

The silence was heavy.

Caius shifted uncomfortably. "Are you two..."

"Complicated," Calla said quickly.

Dak ran a hand through his hair. "And old." He sighed, giving Calla a calculating look. "But I find myself looking for your hidden meanings and motivations. We didn't used to have trouble trusting each other."

Calla's amber eyes flashed briefly, then she shook her head. "That isn't my doing, Dak. I haven't changed who I am."

He was silent for a moment, staring hard at her. "You're saying I have." he finally said.

"I'm saying you took me at my word before you knew I was a dragonmaster. Now, when you know that it's impossible for me to lie, you have doubts. You wondered why I didn't tell you the truth about being a dragonmaster while we were students here...I think you have your answer."

"We were friends, Calla."

She arched an eyebrow in his direction. "Yes...and I noticed you used the past tense there." Calla looked at the boys. "You need to go. It's past curfew."

"But..."

"No arguments," she said. "You've learned enough for one night."

They obeyed, slipping quietly out the door and down the stairwell.

Just before the door shut, they heard Dak's voice:

"You still don't trust me. After all this time?"

Calla's reply was nearly a whisper. "I want to. But it's hard to trust someone who once looked away."

>

The next day, combat class resumed.

Arrio, noticeably subdued, instructed students to repeat the Sorcia Abeyance before every match. No one complained, buy eyes were constantly glancing towards the doorway to see if the sorcia master was watching.

Caius and Niko moved stiffly through drills, both distracted. As the class ended, Dak met them in the corridor.

"I need to speak with you."

They followed him to the arched opening nearby and out of the student traffic flow.

Dak looked at each of them in turn. "You're in over your heads."

"We know." Caius assured him.

"And you don't care?"

"I *do* care," Caius said. "But I trust Master Calla."

Dak's expression softened. "That's what worries me."

Niko nudged Caius. "We should go."

As they turned to leave, Dak called after them. "If things start changing or if you feel something strange come to me."

Caius nodded.

"I wonder what they're expecting?" Niko murmured.

"Nothing good."

Chapter 5: The Festival

The wind had changed.

It carried a crisp bite that hinted at snow, rustled banners atop the Academy towers, and stirred the high pines lining the northern walls. The breeze had teeth now sharp and sudden and when it gusted across the practice fields, even the bravest sorcia tucked their hands into their sleeves.

The school's ancient stone bones didn't warm easily, but the halls were filled with the heat of excitement. It was nearly time for the Festival of Fairy Lights, a celebration that marked the start of winter, the strength of enduring friendship, and the magic that bound the natural world.

Students hung paper lanterns from dorm windows, tied tiny crystal droplets to the banisters, and rehearsed songs in corridors until their masters scolded them for echoing too loud. In the kitchens, syrup kettles steamed and silver molds were pulled from cupboards with great reverence. Even the staircases, usually aloof and practical, shimmered faintly in anticipation.

But Caius felt hollow.

At his desk by the turret window, he unfolded a letter from his mother for the third time. Her handwriting, gentle and looping, carried the warmth of a smile he missed deeply.

My beloved boy,

I hope Ackley's has been kind to you. I do wish you were coming home for the Festival this year. There will be no dragonfruit this season. Mandirube canceled the markets due to unrest in the eastern borders. It's all been very strange. Your father says it's nothing to worry about, but I think it's more than just whispers.

Try to enjoy the Festival at the Academy. I've no doubt it'll be grander than our little street party ever was. Write when you can.

Your loving mother, Saya

Caius folded the letter slowly.

He could still picture their old neighborhood clay chimneys puffing smoke, candles in the windows, his mother's arms wrapped around him while music played from the bakery across the lane.

He hadn't realized until now just how much he'd counted on returning. It wasn't the lights or the treats he missed, it was *them.* His family.

He tucked the letter into a drawer and tried to shrug the weight off his shoulders.

The creak of the door pulled him from his thoughts.

Niko peeked in. "Ready for breakfast? I heard they're serving the honey cakes early."

Caius stood, grabbing his cloak. "You hear everything."

"It's a gift." Niko grinned. "Also, there's a rumor the Mandirube Festival got canceled."

"It's not a rumor," Caius said. "My mum wrote to tell me."

Niko blinked. "Seriously? That's the biggest festival in the eastern provinces."

"I know. It's been going for over two hundred years. They don't cancel it for weather."

"So why *did* they cancel it?"

Caius hesitated. "She said something about unrest. Border skirmishes, maybe. But my father said not to worry."

Niko frowned. "We should ask Calla."

"Nothing ever happens in Mandirube." Caius said quickly. "I doubt she's even heard of the place."

"Well obviously something has happened." Niko pointed out. "We could at least ask."

"No."

"Why not?"

"Because if there's unrest big enough to cancel Festival, it means something's wrong. And if something's wrong…" He trailed off.

"You don't want to know."

Caius nodded.

"That's dumb," Niko said.

"Thanks."

"No, I mean *you're* not dumb. Just the idea of pretending everything's fine."

"I'm not pretending. I'm… trying to focus on happier things."

They descended the turret stairs in silence.

The halls below were glowing with dawn light, windows glinting like gems. But as they turned the corner near the sorcia classroom, Niko suddenly grabbed Caius's arm.

"What's that?"

Caius followed his gaze and stopped cold.

A massive, red handprint had been burned into the stone just outside the classroom door. It was nearly seven feet tall, the fingers unnaturally long and jagged, with claw-like edges. The color pulsed faintly, as though it were still hot.

Other students were gathered around, gaping at the mark in fearful silence.

Then Caius whispered, "I think it's a Dragonslayer's Mark."

Niko took a step back. "You're sure?"

Caius nodded. "It matches the drawing in Master Pell's book. Only… bigger."

A voice behind them spoke coolly. "So, you've read *Pell's Histories*? I'm surprised."

They turned. Moria leaned against the wall, her arms crossed, a half-smile on her lips.

"It's not liked that book is easy to get through," she added. "Most people fall asleep before chapter three."

Caius gestured at the mark. "Why would someone put this here?"

"Maybe a prank?" Moria offered.

Niko shook his head. "A prank that can burn stone?"

"You'd be surprised," Moria said. "There are spells in the restricted section that could simulate that kind of heat."

"That *is* the Dragonslayer's Mark, isn't it?" Caius asked.

A long silence stretched.

Moria's voice dropped. "Yes. It is."

"Then why are you so calm?" Niko demanded.

"Because if I panicked every time something strange happened at Ackley's, I'd never get anything done."

Before they could respond, a shadow fell across the corridor.

Calla had arrived.

She didn't speak immediately. Her eyes moved over the mark, her expression unreadable. Then she stepped closer, held her palm just above the surface.

A faint flicker of energy sparked.

"This is old magic," she murmured. "The kind that doesn't fade."

Niko swallowed. "So, it *is* a warning?"

"Possibly," Calla said. "But perhaps not just a warning. Also, I suspect, a message."

Moria's eyes widened. "You've seen this before?"

Calla nodded once. "The last time I saw a marking like this was my last day in Soronu, in my parents home. Before Tangor took me to Tegoradaysol."

"Tangor?" Caius asked. "Your mentor?"

"Counsel, but yes. It's the same basic idea. There was a time when the mark meant one thing only: that a dragon had been killed."

Silence fell.

"But now," Calla continued, "it seems to mean so much more, and clearly there is a slayer or one of their supporters close by."

"Close?" Niko echoed.

"Closer than we realized," Calla said. "We may have misjudged their numbers." She stepped back from the wall, voice tightening. "This time, it would seem they have marked us."

"Us?" Moria asked.

"Dragonmasters? Perhaps all Sorcia. Maybe even students."

Gan appeared behind them, arms folded. "Or maybe they're trying to protect us."

Everyone turned to him.

"Don't look at me like that," Gan said. "Dragonslayers weren't bad. They took out rogue dragons. Saved cities. What if this is a warning *for* us, not against us?"

Calla studied him. "The old slayers were guided by the Tribunal. The new ones aren't. They answer to no one as far as we know. And the ones who leave the path… don't stop."

"They're vigilantes," Moria said grimly.

"They're worse," Calla corrected.

Caius stared at the mark. "So, what happens now?"

Calla's jaw tightened. "We prepare. We stay inside the wards. And we pay attention."

"But the Festival..." Niko began.

"The Festival will continue," Calla said. "That's probably *why* they chose now to place this. They want us afraid."

"Well… it's working," Niko muttered.

Calla's eyes remained fixed on the mark. "And that," she said, "is exactly why we don't change our plans for the day."

>

By weeks end the campus of Ackley's had transformed.

Crimson and amber pennants fluttered from towers and turrets. The west lawn had been reshaped into a sprawling fairground, with food stalls, juggling platforms, music stages, and makeshift arenas where students attempted everything from riddle battles to feats of strength.

Caius and Niko wandered through the festival, drawn first by the smell of cinnamon, sugar and kettle cakes.

"Three tokens for two?" Caius asked the vendor, eyeing the warm stack of honey-drizzled pastries.

"Three tokens for *three* if you answer my riddle," the vendor said, winking.

"I got this," Niko said. "Let me redeem myself after last week's sprite debacle."

He leaned in as the vendor recited:

"I have hands but no fingers,

I have a face but no eyes.

I measure your hours,

And yet I do not lie."

Niko grinned. "Easy. A clock."

The vendor clapped. "Correct! Three cakes, coming up."

They took the pastries, handed over the coin and found a spot beneath the floating lantern trees, which blinked in pastel shades as if nodding approval.

Caius licked honey from his thumb. "I could live off these."

"You practically do," Niko replied, biting into his.

The two boys sat quietly for a few minutes, watching a group of upper-year sorcia students play a glass harp, their hands moving without touching the strings.

"Hey," Niko said suddenly, "do you think Calla will come to the festival?"

Caius shrugged. "She's probably busy watching for slayers hiding in food stalls."

"She deserves a cake and I'm going to *give* her one," Niko declared. "Right after I find the unicorn."

Caius laughed. "There's no unicorn."

"Then what did that gnome mean when he said he had one 'from the wilds beyond the wall'?"

"He meant he had an animal with a horn glued to its head."

"I'm still going."

They rose and continued through the fair. Jugglers passed flaming spheres back and forth, while students crowded a tent labeled "Enchanted Fortune Fizz."

They passed a stage where a talebearer stood in flowing robes, retelling the Legend of the Moon-Stitched Cloak. Children and younger students sat cross-legged, wide-eyed.

Caius and Niko paused to listen.

"And so the lady crossed the river of ice, her cloak shimmering with stars, and the dragon of the third moon bowed low, saying, 'Even I cannot fly where you walk…'"

The crowd leaned in.

Behind them, a voice muttered, "Ugh. Talebearers. Always so dramatic."

Caius turned to see Lore Master Pell, arms folded in disdain.

"Have you read the verified transcripts of the Moon Cloak records?" he asked the boys. "These stories are full of factual inconsistencies. There was no river of ice or moon dragons."

"It's just a story," Niko said.

"It's *fiction* masquerading as history," Pell huffed. "Foolishness."

As he stormed off, Niko whispered, "He needs a honey cake."

They walked deeper into the fairgrounds until they reached a small, unassuming tent with a crooked sign that read:

"BEHOLD: THE LAST TRUE UNICORN"

A squat gnome stood outside, arms outstretched. "Come, come! Witness the wild magic of the beyond! One token!"

"I told you," Niko said smugly.

"I'm still not convinced," Caius replied.

Before they could enter, Calla appeared beside them.

"You two are looking for your daily dose of disillusionment, I see." she said dryly.

"Missed you too," Niko grinned. "Want a cake?"

She raised an eyebrow. "Only if you acquired it by winning a riddle duel with a kettle witch."

Caius held out the pastry. "Something like that."

Calla accepted it with a small nod.

Just then, the gnome looked up and froze.

His mouth opened. He dropped his performance voice.

"*Genesi Ney,*" he whispered.

Calla stiffened.

The gnome stepped back and lowered his head respectfully. "Welcome to my humble display, dragonmaster."

Caius gave the gnome a startled look, making him cackle. "But...how…?" How could the gnome know Calla was a dragonmaster? He wondered. She wasn't wearing the silver cloak.

"Dragonmaster are a bit of a novelty here, trader." Calla said amiably. "We're generally identified by our cloaks."

The gnomes wrinkled face crinkled even more. "Odd ones you are, dragonmaster. And you the oddest, eh?" He looked up and smiled, though it didn't appear to be a friendly smile in Caius' opinion. It was probably the small but sharply pointed teeth, he determined.

Calla nodded, chuckling. "I'm sure you're right."

"The day is at hand." the gnome continued. "Deius protect us all," he said quietly.

Calla looked at him for a long moment. "Sar sei al." she murmured softly.

The gnome pointed toward the tent. "The unicorn awaits."

Inside, the air was cool and scented with mint.

The creature stood in a silver stall, small, dark gray in color with a short twitchy tail. A spiral horn rose from it's brow, dark in color and dull tipped.

It looked directly at Calla.

"Is that…" Caius began.

"A true unicorn," she confirmed.

"I thought they were bigger...and white."

"That's would be a mystic. Rarely seen by human eyes."

"Why is it looking at you like that?" Niko asked.

Calla didn't answer. Her expression was unreadable.

As they exited, the gnome gave her a slow salute. "Good tidings to you, dragonmaster."

Calla's voice was firm. "And to you."

Back outside, music swelled as fireworks burst in the sky silent, but radiant, like falling stars and Niko looked at Calla. "What was that you said to the gnome?"

"Sar sei al." Calla repeated. "It means luck and peace in the Language of the Old Age." She turned to the boys. "Stay within the walls tonight,"

"Why?" Caius asked.

"Because the world outside them isn't as festive as it used to be. Stay inside Ackley's walls until I tell you to do otherwise."

With that, she turned and disappeared into the crowd.

>

As the sun dipped below the hills, casting long shadows over the Academy, Caius and Niko wandered toward the Watch Wall, where students were gathering to view the terra fairies; tiny, floating creatures that illuminated the sky during the Festival's finale. Entertainers were packing their tents and vendors were scrambling to make last minute sales.

Caius leaned against the stone ledge, full of honey cakes and thoughts he couldn't quite string together.

He closed his eyes for just a moment.

When he opened them, the world had changed.

The crowd had gone still. A single cry echoed from below.

Niko was shaking him. "Caius. Look."

Caius turned to follow his gaze and saw it. The Dragonslayer's mark.

But this time, it wasn't on a wall or a door. It had been burned into the ground, deep and searing, right outside Valor's dragon stall.

Its red glow pulsed like an angry wound.

Students screamed. Staff sprinted toward the barn. Some sorcia formed protective barriers. One of the acrobats dropped a flaming torch, which sputtered at his feet.

Calla was already there.

She pushed through the crowd with terrifying speed, cloak flaring behind her. Dak followed close behind, arguing but she didn't slow.

Caius and Niko rushed down the stone stairs and across the courtyard, finding Calla had reached the stall.

Valor stood inside, nostrils flaring, wings twitching with unease.

Calla touched his snout.

"We have to move him," she said.

Dak placed a hand on her shoulder. "Calla. Think."

"I *am* thinking," she snapped. "This is targeted. If they're here, if they're watching, he's already in danger."

"We don't know it's them."

She turned. "Then *who*? Who else carves slayer sigils in dragonblood magic?"

Dak didn't answer.

Calla stepped into the stall.

The moment she crossed the threshold, Valor let out a low, rumbling cry; a sound Caius had never heard before. It wasn't anger. It was sorrow.

Calla pressed her forehead to his.

"I'm sorry," she whispered. "But you have to go. Tonight. Now."

Valor's wings lowered.

Niko leaned close. "Where would he go?"

"Dragons are said to have sanctuaries," Caius replied, "but they're sealed. You need the old words to open them."

"Old words?"

"From the Language of the Old Age," Caius said. "Like Calla used earlier, though it's rare I've heard."

Calla stepped back, eyes shining.

She raised her hand.

Then, in a voice that echoed with strange cadence, she spoke:

"Val'oraii shenthar veraduum.

Thriin sol'dakai haruun.

Atraak veyen moril.

Go now *fly, and remember."*

The stall doors burst open.

Wind surged outward. Valor reared, wings fully extended, then leapt into the sky with a thunderous beat. The air cracked behind him.

The dragon circled once above the Academy, then vanished beyond the western hills.

Silence fell.

Even the festival lights seemed dimmer now.

Calla turned away, eyes unreadable, and began walking.

No one tried to stop her.

Back in her turret quarters, the fire had gone cold.

Caius and Niko stood just inside the door as Calla tried to use the summoning mirror. Nothing happened. She waved her hand again. Still nothing. "Useless mirror." she snarled.

Dak entered, followed by Sage Master Fane; tall, pale-skinned, with silver rings on every finger and a long cloak that shimmered like polished dusk.

"What are you planning to do now?" Fane asked.

Calla shook her head. "I tried summoning Tangor three times. He doesn't respond." She glanced over at the boys, then back to the Sage Master. "I sent word of the slayers mark and told them things were moving quickly. We would have to leave."

Dak eyed her, his expression sullen. "If that's the case, you should have left with the dragon and gone back to the City of Dragons."

She gave a half-hearted shrug. "I can't go...not just yet. And not to Tegoradaysol anyway...not until I finish other tasks." She stared out the window. "I have to take my charge to collect his peril stone."

"Charge?" Dak echoed in surprise. "There's another dragon-master here?"

"Yes."

"Does he know?"

Calla shook her head. "Like my own parents, his chose not to reveal the truth." her mouth was turned downward and there was anger in her eyes. "I don't know why they believe they can deny the truth."

Dak gave a snort and Calla regarded him coolly. "A dragonmaster is what he is. Born of the blood. Truth cannot be hidden away forever, as my father discovered." She heaved a sigh. "When Tangor arrives we can leave."

Fane looked somber. "Tangor will not be coming. Sadly, he is dead. Madoral too. The camp near Harrowrun was destroyed. Burned. Nothing left but ash." He stepped towards her with an expression of compassion. "It becomes more important than ever for you to be in Tegoradaysol. Camalaron fears for your safety, Genesi Ney."

Niko's head jerked around in astonishment. That name again. What did it mean?

There was a long pause.

Calla stared down at the summoning mirror and without warning, she picked up the disk, raised it high and smashed it against the stone floor.

The glass shattered into black shards.

"And what does Camalaron want of me now?" she asked harshly.

Fane didn't flinch. "The Triad wants what they have always wanted," he said. "All of the last generation united in Tegoradaysol. They want *you* to assume Tangor and Madoral's charges."

Slowly, she shook her head. "He cannot ask this." she murmured. "I'm not ready for that, Deius knows...asking me to be counsel to one was already asking too much." She regarded the Sage Master. "Without Tangor...he cannot ask this." she shook her head again, her frown deepening. "This is too much."

"You don't have the luxury of waiting."

Dak stepped forward. "This isn't fair."

"No," Calla said. "It isn't."

"But it's necessary," Fane added. "And you're the dragonmaster on hand at the moment. Tangor's responsibility passes into your hands. You know that, Calla."

Backing away, Calla looked down at her hands, then back to Caius and Niko, still staring in shocked disbelief. She gave a final shake of her head. "My hands are not ready for this." she whispered. Before anyone could move, she was out the door in a blur.

Fane looked at the boys now, gaze intense. "Come. Both of you. And Dak, find and bring the other one, Gan, is it? We'll be in the North Tower."

Niko frowned. "Why?"

Fane didn't blink. "Because your part in this story has now begun."

Chapter 6: The Dragonmaster's Charge

The North Tower loomed at the far end of the fortress, centered on the rear watch wall. From its summit, so the stories went, one could see beyond Darbin's Wood and even across the distant moors. But no student had ever proved it. The stairway leading upward was sealed behind a rusted iron gate, its padlocks enchanted with a barring spell that deterred even the most daring apprentices.

Paka claimed the tower was haunted. Caius and Niko had always laughed that off, until now.

Standing before the open gate, the cold stone yawning into darkness, the boys were not so certain. It wasn't just the tower that made them uneasy; it was the calm, unreadable presence of the Sage Master beside them. Or maybe it was the thought of who waited above.

Caius tugged his cloak tighter. "How did Master Calla get in?"

"The barring spell deters most," Fane replied. "But dragonmasters aren't 'most.' The enchantment yields to their presence." He raised his hand. "Iridesci," he murmured, and a glowing orb of silver-blue light floated up from his palm, bobbing gently ahead to illuminate the narrow stairway.

Niko glanced at the shadows, his voice small. "Sage Master… is the tower haunted?"

Fane gave a thoughtful hum. "It's said to be. I've never ventured inside myself. But your Sorcia Master knew this place well. Even as a student."

"I thought it was forbidden," Caius said, his brows knitting.

Fane chuckled softly as they began their slow climb. "It was. But Calla… has always had a dragonmaster's heart. Willful. Curious. Rebellious."

There was something almost fond in his voice, and Niko glanced sideways at Caius, who only shrugged, focusing on the cracked steps ahead. The air was dry, heavy, and colder than it should have been.

As the orb guided them upward, the sense of foreboding dulled, replaced by quiet awe. Maybe the haunting rumors were exaggerated. Still, Caius found himself looking over his shoulder more than once.

At last, the stairway spilled into a round chamber, bare stone and arched windows carved deep into the tower wall. Wind whistled through the open panes. Calla sat in one of the windows, framed in moonlight, her copper curls tousled by the breeze.

"I should've guessed you'd track me here," she said without turning. "Old habits die hard."

"You were the only student who dared enter this tower," Fane replied.

She gave a wry smile. "The haunted tower. Some things never change."

"But the stories aren't true, are they?" Niko asked, his voice tinged with unease.

This time, she did turn. "Oh, very true. The last battle of the Reckoning was fought here. More than ten thousand sorcia died… and double that number of gaol. Dragonmasters fought and fell within these very walls."

Niko paled. "But that was ages ago."

Calla laid a hand lightly against cool stone wall. "Time means very little to stone and mortar, and less to the dead."

Fane's voice was gentler. "The tower stands as a monument to darker times."

Caius frowned. "The Reckoning? I thought that was just legend. Something for talebearers."

Calla exhaled heavily. "They're so young," she muttered, as if to herself. "They don't even know."

"Then teach them," Fane urged.

"Them? I have *one* charge," she snapped, suddenly sharp. "One."

"The Triad knows what they ask of you," Fane said calmly. "It's an enormous request."

"Enormous?" Calla whirled on him, her voice rising. "This is more than enormous!" She was pacing now, a dragon in a cage, fury in her every step. "No dragonmaster has ever had more than one charge! And while I may look like an adult to them..." she threw a hand toward the boys "...there's never been a counsel my age. Ever."

Fane didn't flinch. "Much has always been asked of you, Calla. And you've always risen."

"Not always," she muttered bitterly.

Fane stepped forward and placed a hand on her shoulder. She stiffened but didn't pull away.

"You've faced more than most. And each time, you emerged stronger. This will be your greatest test and the one with the most at stake."

She clenched her fists. "I could refuse."

"You could," he agreed. "But I cannot take them into Tegora-daysol. The City of Dragons requires a dragonmaster."

"There are other dragonmasters."

"There are," Fane acknowledged. "But is that truly what you want?"

Calla didn't reply. Her jaw was tight, her fingers twitching with restrained energy. She turned away and began pacing again, muttering under her breath.

Finally, she stopped. "This is my responsibility," she said. "I'll take them."

Fane nodded solemnly.

Footsteps echoed from below, and moments later Dak entered, followed by Gan, whose usual swagger was dulled by confusion. A second orb hovered behind them before winking out in the presence of torchlight.

Gan glanced around the chamber, scowling. "Why was I brought here? I thought this tower was off-limits."

"These are unusual times," Fane said.

Gan's gaze landed on Calla and lingered there, but he said nothing.

Calla didn't return the courtesy. "And how am I expected to guide a charge that shows nothing but contempt for what he is?"

"He doesn't know what he is," Fane said gently.

Niko's head snapped toward Gan, eyes wide. "Wait...Gan is your charge?!"

Gan bristled. "What are you going on about?"

But Calla ignored him. She stepped in front of Niko, her amber eyes searching his face. "Gan is not my charge, Niko," she said quietly. "You are."

Niko blinked, the color draining from his face. "Me?" he croaked. "No. That… that can't be right."

"I cannot lie," she reminded him. "You are what you are: a dragonmaster. A descendant of Rait."

Caius turned toward his friend and punched him lightly on the arm. "Hey… that's actually kind of amazing."

But Niko was too stunned to reply.

"There's more," Fane said, his voice solemn. "Niko is not the only one. Tangor was meant to counsel Caius. Madoral was to guide Gan."

Gan shook his head. "No. You're wrong."

"I wish we were," Calla muttered.

Fane stepped closer. "You're all dragonmasters. The last of this generation. The smallest generation ever born. You bring the number to seven."

Caius swallowed. "And the other three?"

"In Tegoradaysol," Calla replied. "I hope."

Dak fixed a look of astonishment on the three boys. "Three here...together?"

"Yes." Calla drug her hand through her already tousled curls. "Niko, Caius and Gan are the last dragonmasters to be born."

Dak furrowed his brow. "That doesn't sound right. Shouldn't there be more?"

"Until this generation." she replied. "We *are* the last."

Gan stepped back, shaking his head. "No. I'm not part of this. You made a mistake."

Calla snapped, "You think I can't recognize my own? You were raised to hate what you are!"

"It's in the bloodline," Fane said, more softly.

"What bloodline?" Niko asked.

"You are all third-generation descendants of Diate," Fane said. "A dali-daub. A shape-shifting fairy. She fell in love with Balak, your great-grandfather, and bore him seven sons."

Niko blinked. "Wait… a fairy?"

"She transformed to appear human," Calla said bitterly. "But when he found out, Balak cast her out. Daisthai's witch swore revenge."

"And sold her children to Daiesthai," Fane added. "The Destroyer."

Even the initiates knew that name. Caius felt a chill.

"And this… has to do with us?" Gan said slowly.

Calla nodded. "We're their descendants. And we are the last generation. Supposedly the generation of the prophecy."

"Does that mean… no more dragonmasters? Are we going to die?" Niko asked softly.

Calla placed a hand on his shoulder. "Everything dies, Niko. But I don't plan to go easily. If we're truly meant to face this Reckoning, I mean to win."

Gan took a shaky step backward. "You're all insane. I'm not some dragon-chosen freak like him." He jabbed a finger toward Niko.

Caius opened his mouth to defend his friend, but Calla raised her hand, silencing them all. Her voice was calm, dangerously calm. "You are what you are, Gan. Whether you accept it or not doesn't change that."

"I'm not what you say!" he snapped. "I don't believe any of this." Gan's shoulders slumped, and for a moment, he looked much younger than his years. "I'm not part of this." He turned abruptly and plunged into the darkness, out of sight, his footsteps echoing off the walls.

"Let him go." Calla instructed. "He needs a moment."

"What if he tells someone?" worried Niko.

"I don't think he will." Calla told him. "He doesn't even want to know himself."

"I know how he feels." Caius said, sighing loudly.

"There's an interesting fact about dali daubs that might help you understand what you're feeling." Master Fane said, moving towards the doorway. "No matter what shape they take, a dali daub can never deceive a dragonmaster."

"Which is why they hate dragonmasters." Calla rolled her eyes. "The Omnipotents might find the irony amusing, but I fail to see the humor."

"Why didn't anyone ever tell us?" Niko wanted to know.

Calla frowned. "From our mothers lineage, we are all descendants of Rait. Our dragonmaster bloodline. Our father's carry the bloodline of Diate, and she taught her sons to hate dragonmasters. Balak managed to hide his sons away before they were claimed by Daiesthai but they never forgot those lessons and they passed it on. Until the day your peril stones arrived, I doubt your father's knew they had bonded into the dragonmasters bloodline."

"And we have peril stones?" Caius asked.

"You do."

"Could our parents have destroyed them?"

"A peril stone cannot be destroyed, Niko." Calla assured him. "They probably hid them away, but it won't matter."

Caius was shaking his head solemnly. "They wouldn't have done that." he said. "My mother...she would have told me."

"I'm sure she was only trying to protect you, Caius." She turned away, facing Fane, suddenly all business. "Ackley's is not safe for us any longer and our being here puts the other students in danger. We need to go...tonight."

>

Calla sent Caius and Niko to their dorm with strict instructions. Pack one bag with necessities, get their heaviest travel cloak and speak to no one. They would meet behind the stables in one hour.

Her no-nonsense tone made them follow her direction to the letter without question. The festival was still going on making it easy to avoid speaking to anyone. Most of the students and faculty were still on the watch wall, unaware of what was taking place inside the school.

With a pack in one hand and their wool cloaks slung over their shoulders, they headed out of their dorm room and were stopped abruptly in their tracks at the top of the stairs by Gan's shouts.

"You're wrong!" he raged. "Leave me alone."

"I'm not wrong." Calla said calmly.

Niko motioned to Caius and they crept across the corridor to the room Gan shared with eleven other students.

"Yes you are!" Gan was backed against the far wall, his face drawn, his eyes flashing.

"You know I'm not, Gan."

Niko was amazed at how relaxed the sorcia master seemed. Gan, on the other hand, was as tense as a cat crouching to spring.

"My father will not have this!"

Calla chuckled softly. "I fully expect him to resist. My father did, for all the good it did him." She sat down on the end of a sturdy wooden trunk. "Our fathers were raised to believe dragonmasters were their enemies. That's the dali-daub in us. The two have never gotten on. Until we received our peril stones, they were unaware that their mates were part of the dragonmaster bloodline. It was not an idea any of them welcomed."

Gan gave a vigorous shake of his head. "They will never let you take me to this...City of Dragons."

"You might be surprised."

He regarded her warily. "My father won't be manipulated."

Calla leaned forward, her arms resting on her knees. "Gan, you have my word, I will say or do nothing that might sway your parents. All I'm asking is that you accompany us to Daul Andora."

"How do you know that's where I'm from?"

Calla got to her feet. "You may not have known before tonight what you are but Camalaron has known since you were an infant."

He looked suspicious, but relaxed his stance slightly. "As far as Daul Andora then."

She gave him an impish grin. "That's all I ask."

Niko seized Caius by the arm, dragging him away from the door. "I don't know how I feel about traveling with Gan." he hissed in Caius' ear.

"Me either." Caius agreed as they hurried down the stairs.

>

The hour passed in a blur.

Dak led the boys through hidden corridors beneath the school, the same tunnels used by kitchen hands, staff, and on occasion, troublemakers. They moved quickly and in silence, cloaks tucked tight, eyes wide with anticipation and fear.

At the west stables, the hercudons awaited them.

They were even more magnificent than the illustrations in the spellbooks. Each beast stood at least twelve hands high, with sinewy bodies covered in short, shimmering fur that pulsed faintly with color gold, violet, deep azure. Their elongated heads resembled those of antelopes, but their eyes held eerie intelligence, and their hooves barely made a sound on the stone floor.

"Whoa…" Niko breathed, walking around them and looking awed.

"I think I should go along." Dak told Fane.

"You cannot enter the City of Dragons."

"Then as far as Mim Tor."

"Dak, this is not something we can do, not in this moment."

The elements master was still not ready to concede. "Master Fane, it's not safe for Calla and three boys to be traveling so far alone."

"I expect it is not safe for these four dragonmasters, regardless of the distance." Fane said grimly.

"That's my point."

"Shall we let Calla decide?" the Sage Master suggested.

Dak's expression soured. "She's too stubborn to see reason."

Fane fought back a smile. "Yes, she's quite a determined young woman. Camalaron assures me that she will be able to face whatever she must, and he is not one to give praise easily. In his words, Calla is the most powerful dragonmaster ever born, more powerful than even she knows."

Calla arrived at that moment and if she suspected they were speaking about her, she gave no sign.

"Choose a mount quickly," she said. "We don't have much time."

Caius approached a golden hercudon, who snorted and nudged his shoulder with surprising gentleness. He smiled. "I like you too."

Gan, to everyone's surprise, walked straight to the largest hercudon, a jet-black one with silver-streaked flanks. The beast tossed its head, but Gan stood firm.

Calla watched silently, then nodded in approval.

They mounted swiftly. The hercudons, trained for stealth, padded into the shadows beyond the stable gates.

"There are six wagons from the troupe heading out." Fane told them. "They'll came through here and you can join up with them. Hopefully no one will realize you're gone for some time."

Calla nodded. "We can stay with them to the far edge of Darbin's Wood. Then we can cross the moors into Daul Andora."

"Use care in Daul Andora," Fane cautioned her. "It is no place for dragonmasters."

"Right now, there is no place for dragonmasters...except Tegoradaysol."

The City of Dragons, though Calla thought the idea of calling Tegoradaysol a city was laughable. More like a village, and not a large one at that. Not anymore. Calla gave a shake of her head, pushing those thoughts away. Too much else to worry about to concern herself with things she couldn't change.

Wearing a simple wool cloak instead of her dragonmasters cloak, Calla let her hand rest on the silver cord wrapped around her sword hilt. The wagons of the troupe came into view and she coaxed her mount forward. Wordlessly, the three boys followed. Around them, fairy lights twinkled as the terra fairies went about the business of putting nature to bed before winter.

"Did you see her sword?" Niko whispered when they were a short distance away.

"Yes." Caius replied in a low voice. "What was on the hilt?"

Niko shrugged, then grabbed for the saddle as he felt he was losing his balance. "I don't know."

"It's a swordknot." Gan said brusquely. "Marks the sword of a master wielder. The color marks the house the wielder is loyal to. Silver is the House Mim." he make a sound of disapproval.

Niko nodded. "I've seen some in Cenna Siem now that I think on it. But they were blue, not silver."

"House Dea." Gan said knowingly.

Caius looked perplexed. "But, I thought the entire realm was ruled by King Balin and House Mim."

"The middlings, maybe, but the sorcia..." Gan shrugged and gave a harsh laugh. "The king is a middling, after all."

Caius scowled at him. "He's human, Gan, and so are we."

"No." the other boy disagrees vehemently. "We're sorcia."

Niko gave a slow shake of his head. "Maybe not anymore."

Calla turned in her saddle. "Can you three decide what you are later. The troupe is just ahead."

Caius and Niko exchanged sheepish looks and Gan made a harsh sound in his throat but they all fell silent as they came up alongside the lead wagon.

Behind them, Ackley's towers watched in silence unaware that three of its youngest were slipping into legend.

>

The hercudons moved like shadows, their gait smooth and eerily silent over the frost-kissed woodland. The troupe kept to narrow paths where trees bent low and wind howled through twisted branches like voices from forgotten days.

Niko rode just behind Calla, stealing glances at her whenever the road straightened. He wasn't sure what unnerved him more; what she had revealed, or how little she seemed fazed by it. Dragonmaster. Descendant of a fairy and a warrior. It was impossible, wasn't it?

Caius rode to his right, his golden hercudon practically prancing with each step. "You okay?"

"I don't feel any different," Niko muttered.

"Should you?" Caius asked, offering a half-smile.

"I mean… I didn't grow wings or breathe fire."

"Well, *yet,*" Caius teased. "Give it a few days."

Niko snorted softly, the tension in his shoulders loosening.

Behind them, Gan kept his distance, his hood pulled low, arms crossed tight over his chest. He hadn't said a word since leaving the stables. Every time Niko glanced back, he saw only narrowed eyes and clenched jaw.

Calla rode ahead, alongside the troupe's lead rider, a large man astride a bay, large for a horse, but dwarfed by the hercudon. They seemed to be engaged in conversation.

"Now what would Ackley students be doing traveling in the company of the Genesi Ney?"

Caius and Niko turned in surprise to the driver of the wagon. The talebearer from the Festival grinned at them and pushed back the hood of his cloak.

"The Genesi Ney?" Niko inquired, determined to finally learn what that meant.

"The Language of the Old Age." the talebearer explained. "Your dragondaughter speaks it. I heard her tonight with the dragon." He chuckled. "I am Paun Tal. I believe I saw you earlier outside my tents."

They nodded, looking at each other uneasily.

"Genesi Ney means the firstling."

Niko couldn't help himself. "What's a firstling?"

"Not *a* firstling...*the* firstling." the talebearer laughed. "It's a story I only heard recently, but I did not tell it today. Not with the dragondaughter on the grounds." He looked towards Calla and nodded. "Her birth portends the coming of a reckoning." He leaned back on the bench seat, nodding thoughtfully. "Yes...it might very well be time for another. The last was in Ackley's day." Seeing he had their attention, he slipped into the role of his trade.

"The Omnipotents, Deius and Daiesthai, are the only true immortals. The rest of us are merely playing pieces. The Creator and the Destroyer are constantly battling one another for control of the game...and each one has his time. As the game plays out, there comes a time for a reckoning...as the end draws near."

Niko's eyes were on the talebearer, fascinated and horrified at the same time. "But...if Daiesthai wins..."

"What happens to people?" Caius concluded, just as intrigued by the story.

"Wars, disease, famine…" The talebearer gave a dramatic shrug. "One way or another they cease to exist until Deius creates again and a new game begins." His gaze swept over them and he gave them a sly grin. "They always give omens and put seers into the game. Keeps it lively I should imagine, but the outcome is ultimately in our hands."

"It doesn't sound like it." grumbled Niko.

"But it is." Paun Tal insisted. "Have his creations becomes so corrupted that the Destroyer has the greater power, or are they strong and righteous enough to win the reckoning."

"What a lot of nonsense." Gan said sharply, honey colored eyes narrowing.

"And you believe the time is coming?" Caius asked. He didn't agree with Gan but he certainly wanted to. The idea of being nothing more than a game piece was humbling.

"There is supposed to be a prophecy about the Genesi Ney. Of course, it could be a long time coming. The dragondaughter is young yet."

Niko looked at Caius, his expression grim. "Have you ever heard any of this?"

Caius shook his head slowly. He wished he wasn't hearing it now.

"Quite a story you weave." Calla said amiably.

She had slipped up behind them without being noticed and the boys all looked over at her in surprise, the talebearer looking pleased with himself.

"You can change into a common cloak, dragonmaster, but you cannot change what you are." Paun Tal said, his voice almost reverent. "You travel to the City of Dragons?"

"Eventually." Calla said, keeping her tone light. "First I am delivering these students to their homes."

The talebearer was thinking furiously, a frown creasing his already well lined face. "Then you are not taking them with you?"

"Only a dragonmaster can open the gates of Tegoradaysol." she replied, giving him a scolding look. "You should know that much at least, talebearer. And I know you looked into their faces, yet you did not see the eyes of a dragonmaster."

The old man shook his head but his expression betrayed his suspicion. It was clear he was trying to remember something he had heard that might help him puzzle this out.

Unconcerned, Calla motioned to the boys. "Come on you three. We're entering the heavy woodlands and I want to keep you close." She urged her mount forward.

"He thinks you're lying." Gan said as he rode up alongside.

"He knows that isn't possible."

"But you did." Caius argued, keeping his voice down.

Calla looked over at him, her eyes bright. "Did I Caius?" she queried. "Are you sure?"

"You said you were taking us home."

"I am." Calla said with a grin. "I already told you that. We have to go to your homes for you to retrieve your peril stones."

"You said we weren't going to the City of Dragons."

"I said that only a dragonmaster can open the passageway. That's absolutely true."

"Riddles!" Gan spat crossly. "The language of the dragonmasters. Don't lie, but don't really tell the truth."

"The truth could put him in danger." Calla said, meeting Gan's hostile gaze. "The man has done nothing to me...why would I put him in harms way?"

Gan had no reply, but he continued to look petulant as he shifted his gaze to the road in front of him.

"Master Calla…" Caius began then hesitated. She looked at him expectantly. "Are you what he said...the Genesi Ney?"

She didn't answer right away, her attention on the woods closing around them Finally, she looked over at him and her eyes had a haunted look in them. "Time will tell."

None of them found any comfort in that answer.

Chapter 7: Gathering Stones

The forest gave way slowly, as if reluctant to release them. Bare trees stood like crooked sentinels in the morning haze, their branches dripping with dew. Calla rode at the front, her face set, her cloak pulled close against the chill. The boys followed in silence, though silence didn't last long with Caius.

He guided his hercudon closer to Niko. "Do you think we'll see him again?"

Niko frowned. "Who?"

"The old talebearer. Kind of a creepy fellow, but… he knew a lot."

Gan snorted from the rear. "He knew how to scare children, that's all. Half his talk was nonsense."

"It wasn't nonsense," Niko said quietly, remembering the weight in the old man's voice. "He knew about us. About dragonmasters."

Gan rolled his eyes. "He knew what Calla told him, nothing more."

"Enough." Calla didn't raise her voice, but the word cut through the mist. "He knew more than most. You'd be wise to listen to the warnings of those who've lived long enough to give them."

No one argued after that.

The mist thickened as they left the treeline. Rolling moorland stretched ahead, gray and uneven, with tufts of grass poking through wet earth. Their hercudons' hooves squelched as they moved. Fog curled in low swirls, thickening in dips and valleys.

"It smells like old boots out here," Caius muttered, tugging his cloak tighter. "Do we really have to cross this whole thing?"

They rode in uneasy quiet, broken only by the sucking of hooves in the mud and the occasional caw of unseen birds. Strange stone pillars jutted up at intervals, carved with half-worn runes. Some looked like claws reaching from the earth. Niko's eyes lingered on one that bore a dragon's eye, the detail worn but still eerily sharp.

He shivered. "Do you think the land remembers?"

Caius tilted his head. "Remembers what?"

"Everything. The battles, the people who lived here."

"Stones don't remember," Gan said flatly. "They just sit there."

Niko didn't answer, but he wasn't so sure.

Hours passed in a blur of gray. The moors stretched on, endless, the fog closing in so tight at times that even Calla's figure blurred at the front. Gan's complaints, though less frequent, slipped out in mutters. Caius filled the silence with chatter when he could, but even he grew quieter as the land pressed on them, heavy and watchful.

By midday, the fog thickened until it was difficult to see more than a few paces ahead. The hercudons stamped nervously, their ears flicking at sounds only they seemed to hear.

Then came the clang.

Sharp and metallic, it rang through the mist like a bell struck too close. The hercudons froze. Niko felt his stomach drop.

"Hold," Calla ordered, raising her hand.

A second clang followed, then the sound of voices muffled, indistinct, but urgent. Shouting, perhaps.

Gan gripped his reins tightly. "What now?"

"Quiet," Calla said.

They waited, breath held, until the sounds faded back into the mist. Only then did she motion them forward, slower this time, more cautious.

The ground began to rise beneath their hooves, the slope gradual at first, then steeper. The fog shifted with the incline, thinning slightly, until at last shapes loomed ahead dark towers, jagged walls, and the faint gleam of iron gates.

"Daul Andora," Gan said.

The city rose stark from the mist, built into a cliffside of black stone. Its walls were high, its gates spiked and forbidding. Watchfires burned faintly along the ramparts, casting shadows that stretched like talons through the haze.

"Charming place," Caius muttered.

Calla halted at the base of the slope. "Listen carefully. This city is not Ackley's. It is not your homeland, and no one here is your friend. Do not speak unless spoken to. Do not draw attention. We're here for Gan's family, nothing more."

Gan shifted uncomfortably in his saddle but didn't argue.

They approached the gates in silence. Two guards stepped forward, their faces shadowed beneath helms, halberds crossed.

"Halt." The taller one's voice was rough. "State your business."

"We're seeking shelter," Calla said evenly, her hood drawn low. "And trade."

The guard's gaze lingered on her, then shifted to the boys. His eyes narrowed. "Students?"

"Travelers," Calla corrected, her tone calm but sharp enough to cut. "Passing through to Cenna Siem."

The guard studied them for a long moment, the silence heavy. Then, with a grunt, he raised his halberd. "Very well. But keep to yourselves. Daul Andora doesn't welcome strangers."

The gates groaned as they opened, iron grinding against stone. The group rode through, the air colder inside the walls than out.

The city was a maze of narrow streets and looming buildings of black stone. Smoke curled from chimneys, mixing with the mist, until the whole place smelled of soot and damp. Faces peered from doorways and windows as they passed; pale, suspicious, quick to vanish again.

Niko shifted uneasily. "Why do they all look like they want to slit our throats?"

"Because they probably do," Caius muttered.

"Enough," Calla warned. "Eyes down. No chatter."

They wound their way through twisting streets until Calla stopped before a heavy wooden door set in a tall house of gray stone. She turned to Gan.

"This is it?"

Gan nodded, his face pale. "Yes."

She rapped on the door. A moment passed, then it creaked open.

A woman stood in the doorway, her face framed by dark hair streaked with silver. Her eyes widened as they fell on Gan, then softened with relief.

"Gan." Her voice trembled. "By the stones… it's you."

"Mother." Gan slid from his saddle and stepped forward, awkward but earnest. She embraced him tightly, holding on longer than he seemed comfortable with, but he didn't pull away.

When she released him, her gaze moved to Calla. Recognition flashed in her eyes. "You."

Calla inclined her head. "Soolia."

The woman's lips pressed thin, but she stepped aside. "Come in, all of you. Quickly, before anyone sees."

They entered, leaving the cold stone streets behind. The house was warmer, the air filled with the scent of herbs and baking bread. For the first time that day, the boys let their shoulders relax.

But Calla did not. Her eyes stayed sharp, scanning every shadow.

Soolia's gaze lingered on her son as she shut the door. "You shouldn't have come."

Gan frowned. "I don't think we had a choice."

"There's always a choice," she whispered. Then she looked at Calla again, her expression caught between fear and memory. "Especially with you."

The house was narrow but tall, its walls lined with shelves stacked high with jars and bundles of dried herbs. The air smelled faintly of sage and smoke, warm after the damp streets outside.

Soolia ushered them into a sitting room where a fire burned low, the flames throwing shifting light against stone walls.

Gan sank into a chair, his shoulders dropping for the first time since they'd left Ackley's. Caius and Niko hovered awkwardly, unsure if they should sit, until Soolia waved them toward the benches near the fire.

"You must be exhausted," she said, her voice softer now. "Hungry too, no doubt. I'll fetch something."

"Please don't trouble yourself," Calla began, but Soolia was already gone, her skirts whispering down the hall.

"She seems… kind," Caius said, his voice hushed.

Gan frowned. "She's strong."

Moments later, Soolia returned with a tray; bread still warm, cheese, and a pot of steaming tea. The boys fell on it gratefully, though Calla remained standing, her back to the wall, watching.

Soolia's gaze kept straying to her son, as if reassuring herself that he was really there. But every so often, her eyes flicked to Calla, and a shadow passed across her face.

"You shouldn't have come," she said finally, her voice barely above the crackle of the fire.

Gan set down his cup. "We didn't have a choice. The slayers..."

Her hand twitched. "Don't speak of them here."

"They're already after us," Gan insisted.

"They're always after you," she said. "Because of who you are. Because of who *she* is."

Calla's gaze didn't waver. "Because of who Gan is becoming."

Soolia's lips pressed together, but before she could reply, the door slammed open. Heavy footsteps shook the floorboards.

A man filled the doorway, tall and broad-shouldered, his beard streaked with gray. His eyes burned like coals under heavy brows.

"Karak," Calla said evenly.

"Dragonmaster." His voice was a growl, each syllable heavy with disdain. He strode into the room, his presence making the space suddenly smaller.

Gan stood quickly. "Father."

Karak's glare silenced him. "What is she doing here?" He turned on Calla. "How dare you bring my son into this madness?"

"I didn't bring him," Calla said calmly. "He was chosen."

"He's a boy," Karak snapped. "He doesn't know anything about all that."

"He knows enough," Calla replied.

Karak's face darkened, his fists clenched at his sides. "I will not have my son dragged into your cursed legacy. Haven't you ruined enough lives already?"

"Father!" Gan's voice broke. "I'm not a child! You don't get to decide this for me!"

"You're my son," Karak thundered. "That means I do."

The room crackled with tension, the fire seeming to flare with every shouted word. Soolia stood silently in the corner, her hands clasped tight, eyes shining with unshed tears.

Calla's voice cut through the storm, steady and commanding. "Enough. This isn't about your hatred of dragonmasters, Karak. It's about the truth of your son's blood."

Karak sneered. "Blood means nothing."

"Then let him prove it. If he has no stone, if the blood means nothing, then you'll have your answer."

Gan froze. His throat went dry. "I… I don't know if I can."

"You can," Calla said firmly. "Ask the question most pressing to you at this moment."

Karak crossed his arms, his expression daring his son to try.

Gan swallowed hard. He closed his eyes, his palms damp, his breath shallow. He thought of the Tribunal, of the fire, of Calla's command, of every moment that had led him here against his will. And under all of it, like a drumbeat in his chest, something waited.

The air thickened. The fire bent toward him as if drawn. Voices echoed in his head. His hands trembled, then glowed faintly. A spark burst between his palms then solidified.

A stone lay in his hand. Black as obsidian, streaked with veins of silver light that pulsed like a heartbeat. His eyes flared the same color for a moment, the room bathed in an eerie glow.

Caius gasped. Niko's mouth fell open. Soolia covered her lips with her hand, tears spilling silently down her cheeks.

Karak stared, his face caught between rage and disbelief. "No…"

Gan blinked his eyes, the glow fading slightly. He looked at the stone in his palm, awe and terror mingling on his face. "I… I did it."

Calla stepped forward, her voice quiet but fierce. "You didn't *do* it. You *are* it. This is who you are."

Gan looked up at his father, searching for something approval, denial, anything.

But Karak turned away, his jaw tight. "It changes nothing," he muttered. "You're still my son. And I'll not let her kind destroy you."

The stone in Gan's hand pulsed once, as if in defiance.

The glow of Gan's stone faded at last, leaving only the steady crackle of the fire and the weight of silence. Caius leaned forward, eyes still wide. "By the stars... that was incredible."

Gan stared at his hands as if they belonged to someone else. "I didn't mean to. I didn't even…" He trailed off, words failing.

"You are what you are Gan." Calla said quietly. "A dragonmaster. But it's up to you what you do now...whether or not you accept the binding."

Karak stared at the stone and then to Calla, angrily, as if they were responsible for all the grief in his life.

The tension between them was a living thing, pressing down on the room until Gan could hardly breathe. He shoved his stone into his cloak and stood abruptly. "I need air."

Before either parent could stop him, he strode to the door and yanked it open. The cold air of Daul Andora rushed in, carrying the smell of soot and damp stone. Niko and Caius exchanged a glance, then hurried after him.

The three boys found themselves wandering the narrow streets, the city's gloom heavy even at dusk. Lanterns flickered faintly from doorways, casting meager light across cobblestones slick with mist.

"Your father's terrifying," Caius said finally.

"You don't say," Gan muttered.

"But you did it," Niko said. "You called your stone. That means..."

"It means nothing," Gan snapped. Then, seeing Niko's expression, he sighed. "I don't know what it means. I didn't ask for this."

"Neither did I," Niko admitted. "But we can't pretend it isn't happening."

Gan scowled at the ground. "Maybe I need to try."

Caius kicked at a loose stone, sending it skittering. "Try all you want, but I can see those glowing eyes. You can't un-glow them."

Despite himself, Gan barked a short laugh. "You're an idiot."

"True," Caius said cheerfully. "But at least I'm a useful idiot."

Niko managed a smile, though it faded quickly as he glanced back toward the looming house they'd left. He couldn't shake the image of Karak's face when the stone appeared equal parts rage and fear. If his own parents looked at him like that… he wasn't sure he could stand it.

>

Later that night, Calla found Gan outside, leaning against the shadowed wall of the inn they had taken refuge in. The Wandering Man stood at the far edge of Daul Andora, a tavern with a crooked sign and a reputation for asking no questions. Its rooms were cramped, its air thick with smoke and ale, but it offered anonymity something Calla valued more than comfort.

Gan didn't turn when she approached. "You made me do it."

"You did it yourself," Calla replied.

"You pushed me."

"I opened the door. You walked through it."

He finally faced her, his eyes storm-dark. "What if I don't want to walk that path?"

Calla's expression softened, though her voice remained steady. "Every dragonmaster has felt the same. Choice is an illusion in some things. You didn't choose the stone. The stone chose you."

Gan looked away. "That's no choice at all."

"Perhaps not," Calla agreed quietly. "But what you do with it, that will always be your choice."

For a moment, neither spoke. The sounds of laughter and clattering mugs drifted from the inn, a strange counterpoint to the weight of their words.

Finally, Gan muttered, "My father will never forgive you."

Calla's gaze didn't waver. "I don't need his forgiveness. Only yours."

Gan blinked, caught off guard. He didn't answer, only pulled his cloak tighter and slipped back inside.

The next morning dawned gray and heavy with fog. The group departed Daul Andora with little ceremony. Soolia pressed a kiss to Gan's forehead, her eyes lingering on him with unspoken fear. Karak did not appear to see them off.

The city gates closed behind them with a clang that seemed to echo too long. Calla kept them moving quickly, her eyes scanning the horizon, her hand never far from her cloak.

"Why so tense?" Caius asked after a while. "We made it out. Shouldn't we be celebrating?"

"We're not out," Calla said. "We're only deeper in."

The road wound through low hills, their slopes dotted with sparse pines. The air carried a biting chill, and the fog clung stubbornly to every dip.

Niko rode close to Caius, his thoughts heavy. "Do you feel different?" he asked suddenly.

"Different how?"

"After… you know. After hearing that you were a dragonmaster. Or when Gan called his stone. Do you feel… changed?"

Caius shrugged. "Maybe. Or maybe I just feel hungrier. Hard to tell."

Gan snorted. "You'd feel hungrier if you'd skipped two meals. Doesn't mean you're special."

Caius frowned. "I don't mean hungry. I mean..." He broke off, frustrated. "Never mind."

Calla glanced back at them. "You'll feel it when the time comes. Don't waste energy trying to force it."

Gan muttered something under his breath, but Calla ignored him.

The road grew steeper as they climbed into the hills. The air thinned, carrying a sharpness that made their hercudons restless.

"These lands aren't safe," Calla murmured.

"Safer than Daul Andora?" Caius asked.

"Different dangers," She replied.

The boys exchanged uneasy looks but said no more.

That night, they camped in a narrow ravine where the wind howled overhead but couldn't reach them below. The fire burned low, its light flickering against the stone walls.

Gan sat apart from the others, his back to the rock, his stone turning slowly in his hands. Its silver veins pulsed faintly in rhythm with his breath.

Niko lay awake, watching him. Part of him wanted to ask what it felt like, to hold something that seemed to hum with life. Another part feared the answer.

Instead, he rolled onto his side and stared at his own empty hands, wondering if a stone would ever answer him.

By the second day, the hills gave way to a broad plain dotted with scattered villages. Smoke rose in the distance, thin spirals against the pale sky. Calla slowed the pace.

"We're near Cenna Siem," she said. "Stay alert."

Gan stiffened at the name, his stone tucked tightly into his cloak. Niko felt his stomach twist. This was his turn. His home. His parents.

Caius nudged him with an elbow. "Ready for the family reunion?"

Niko tried to smile, but his throat was dry. "Not even close."

Cenna Siem appeared at last, a settlement nestled in the shadow of a broad ridge. Smoke curled from chimneys, and the smell of bread drifted faintly on the wind. The hercudons shifted uneasily as they entered the outskirts, their hooves clopping against the cobbled streets.

Niko's chest tightened with every step. He knew these streets, these crooked fences, the faint creak of the well in the square. Every detail was familiar, yet it all felt strange now as if he had returned wearing someone else's skin.

"Which house?" Calla asked quietly.

Niko pointed, his hand trembling. "There."

It was a modest stone house, ivy climbing its walls. The door was painted blue, though the paint had chipped with age. His throat constricted as he slid from his saddle.

The door opened before he could knock. His mother, Rea, stood in the doorway, her hands still dusted with flour. For a heartbeat she stared at him as if he were a ghost. Then she cried his name.

"Niko!"

She rushed forward, wrapping him in her arms. The scent of bread and lavender filled his senses, and for a moment he felt like a boy again, safe and small. His father, Dario, appeared behind her, his expression harder, his arms crossed.

"You're supposed to be at Ackley's," Dario said, his voice clipped.

"We had to leave," Niko said, still clinging to his mother.

Dario's eyes flicked to Calla, narrowing. "Because of her."

Calla met his gaze steadily. "Because the time has come, as you knew it would."

Rea gasped, pulling Niko closer. "Not yet. Why? He's just a boy!"

"He's more than that," Calla said quietly.

Niko pulled back, his heart pounding. "I didn't want to come home like this. But I have to know."

"Ask your question, Niko." Calla urged him gently.

He lifted his hands. The air thickened. A faint glow shimmered between his palms, growing brighter, sharper. His parents' eyes widened as a stone materialized, deep scarlet, pulsing with a soft inner light. Its surface shimmered with faint, shifting colors, like trapped starlight.

Rea clapped her hands to her mouth. Tears streamed down her cheeks. "No… it's too soon."

Dario's face twisted with anger. "Put it away. Now."

"I can't," Niko whispered. The stone thrummed in his hand as though alive, answering only to him.

Calla stepped forward, her voice low but firm. "It's a spirit stone. Rare, powerful. Only one dragonmaster in fifty possesses a spirit stone. Usually one in a generation."

"And our generation has two?" Caius asked, remembering Calla also had a spirit stone.

"Three." she informed him. "Tau also has one."

Rea sobbed, clutching Niko's arm. "Please, don't go with her. Stay here, stay safe. We'll hide you. We'll find a way."

Niko's throat burned. He wanted nothing more than to say yes, to sink into the warmth of his home and let the world spin on without him. But the stone pulsed in his hand, demanding a response.

Rea's tears streaked her face. "Please, Niko. Please stay."

His stone pulsed harder, the glow spilling over the ground, reflecting in their eyes. He felt torn in half between his parents' desperate love and the inexorable pull of destiny. The call of the peril stone.

"I can't," he said at last, his voice breaking. "I wish I could, but I can't."

Rea sobbed openly, collapsing into Dario's arms. Dario held her tightly, his jaw rigid, his eyes burning with fury at Calla.

Niko slipped the stone into his cloak, his hands trembling. He turned to his parents one last time. "I love you. Always."

Rea reached for him, but Dario pulled her back, his face a mask of grief and rage.

"Go," he said harshly. "If you must."

The words struck like a blow. Niko stumbled toward the gate, his legs heavy, his chest aching. Nearby, Caius and Gan waited, their faces somber.

"You okay?" Caius asked softly.

Niko shook his head. "No. But I will be."

Calla laid a hand on his shoulder. For once, she had no words of command, only quiet solidarity.

Together, they turned from the blue door as it shut behind them. The sound echoed in Niko's chest like finality.

As they mounted their hercudons and rode from Cenna Siem, the mist closed in once more, swallowing the village, the house, and the life Niko had known. The spirit stone pressed against his chest, warm and insistent.

The path ahead was uncertain, heavy with sacrifice. But it was his now.

Chapter 8: Sai'al Sodonu

The lowlands at the base of the Hills of Deception were a stark contrast to the farms surrounding Cenna Siem. Caius could feel where the fertile grazing lands ended and where the corruption of the hill lands began. The air grew heavier, the ground beneath the horses' hooves harder.

Niko had once told him the livestock would never cross into the land that fell under the shadows of the hills. Stepping from pasture into the Grip, as it was known, Caius understood why. A gloom settled over him an aura of death and devastation that clung to everything.

Since leaving his home, Niko had been unusually quiet. Caius knew the peril stone was tucked inside his tunic, the eerie blue glow still haunting his eyes. Niko had accepted whatever call the summoning had offered him, but he seemed changed far more than Gan after his own summoning.

Caius had tried to start conversation once, but Niko's silence soon drove him to give up. Gan quickly rode up beside him, offering distraction, which Caius appreciated, though his thoughts remained heavy with worry. His best friend had never shut him out before.

A short distance from the first sloping hills, Calla reined her charcoal stallion, Risk, to a halt. She liked the frisky hercudon and she thought the name suited him well.

"We will camp here," she announced, swinging down from the saddle.

The others followed.

"We should tether the mounts," she added. "They won't care for the Grip and may bolt."

Gan helped her secure the animals while Caius built a fire ring and spread their bedrolls. Niko sat a little apart, staring back in the direction of Cenna Siem.

When the horses were settled, Calla crouched near the fire ring. With a sweep of her hand over Caius's kindling, she murmured, *"Flammus."* A bright flame leapt up, startling Caius.

"Handy," he muttered.

Calla smirked faintly. "Efficient."

The fire's warmth did little to lift the heaviness in the air. Caius glanced at Niko again. His friend hadn't moved, his gaze fixed on the horizon as though he could see through the hills back to his family.

"Let him be," Calla said quietly, reading Caius's concern. "The summoning can be overwhelming. Niko just needs time."

Gan dropped onto his bedroll with a grunt. "He's not the only one who's changed. This place does things to you."

Caius shuddered. "Like make you talk less and brood more? Because I don't like it."

Calla allowed the faintest smile, though her eyes never left the flames.

Night deepened, heavy and restless. The boys lay down but sleep came fitfully. The air itself seemed charged, whispering with voices just beyond hearing. More than once, Caius sat up, convinced someone was moving at the edge of camp, but nothing stirred beyond the firelight.

When dawn broke gray and cold, Calla roused them quickly. "We push deeper into the hills today. Stay alert."

Niko mounted silently, his jaw tight. Caius longed to say something to pull him back from whatever storm raged inside, but the words stuck in his throat.

The hills rose steeper as they advanced, their slopes barren and scarred. The ground was littered with jagged stone, and the air smelled faintly of sulfur. Even the hercudons grew uneasy, tossing their heads and snorting at shadows.

Caius muttered, "Cheerful place. Should've packed a picnic."

Gan ignored him, eyes scanning the slopes. "Feels like something's watching us."

Calla said nothing, but her hand never strayed far from her cloak.

By midday, they reached a ridge where the ground fell away into a narrow pass. Mist pooled thick and low, obscuring the path ahead. Calla dismounted, leading Risk carefully into the fog. The boys followed suit, their steps cautious on the slick stone.

Niko lagged a little, his gaze distant.

Caius nudged him. "Still with us?"

Niko blinked, then nodded. "Just… listening."

"To what?" Gan asked.

Niko hesitated. "I don't know. But it doesn't sound friendly."

As if to prove him right, the mist swirled violently. A chill swept through the pass, carrying whispers that clawed at their ears. Shapes flickered within the fog too tall, too twisted to be human.

Caius's stomach dropped. "Oh no…what's happening?"

"Stay close," Calla commanded, drawing her blade.

The shapes surged, voices wailing like broken glass. The boys pressed shoulder to shoulder, their fear palpable. Calla stood before them, her eyes blazing as she slashed through the mist. The forms recoiled but pressed again, their whispers digging into the boys' minds.

"Don't listen!" Calla barked. "They feed on doubt. Hold fast to each other."

Caius clenched his fists. "Easier said than done!"

Gan grabbed his arm. "Shut up and focus!"

Niko shut his eyes, forcing his breath steady. The pulse of his spirit stone throbbed against his chest, faint but steady, a lifeline amid the storm. He clung to it, anchoring himself. Slowly, the voices dulled.

Calla drove her blade through the last of the mist-born phantoms. The fog hissed and thinned, the shapes scattering like smoke. Silence crashed back over the pass, deafening in its suddenness.

The boys stood trembling, their breaths ragged.

"Well," Caius said hoarsely, "that was… refreshing."

Gan shot him a look, but his own hands shook.

Calla sheathed her blade, her expression unreadable. "That was only the beginning. Remember that."

They pressed on, shaken but determined. The land grew no kinder. Every hill seemed to lean closer, every shadow stretched too long. By the time they made camp again, their nerves were frayed.

Gan dropped onto his bedroll with a grunt. "If this is only the beginning, I don't want to see the end."

Caius lay back, staring at the darkening sky. "Still beats cleaning stables at Ackley's."

"Barely," Gan muttered.

Niko sat apart again, staring into the distance. The stone beneath his tunic pulsed faintly, each beat a reminder of what he carried now. He hugged his knees to his chest, feeling farther from home than ever.

Calla watched him silently, then crossed over to join him. She knew the weight he bore because she bore her own.

"Put Caius' mind at ease. We will need a good night's rest before our trip through the hill lands tomorrow."

Niko hesitated, watching Calla with trepidation. It was unsettling enough to be planning a trip across the Hills of Deception, but Calla's own unease made him more anxious. He had lived his entire life in the valley below those hills and had never once heard of anyone venturing beyond the Grip.

"Go on now." Calla gave him a gentle push. "I'll be along after I check on the horses."

Nodding, he returned to camp, while Calla gave the hills one last lingering look before heading toward the tethered animals.

>

Gan woke suddenly, pushing himself up on an elbow and peering into the darkness. Since the summoning of his peril stone, he had been astonished at how much better he could see in the dark. Tonight was no different.

Nothing looked amiss. Two blanketed mounds lay where Caius and Niko slept, and the hercudons, secured to a pitiful scrub tree, stood restless but calm enough. They had been reluctant to enter the Grip, but Calla's murmured words had coaxed them along. Gan wondered what she had said. The language had been strange, fluid and ancient. He realized then it was the Language of the Old Age, one he didn't understand at all.

Before they had settled into their bedrolls, Calla had warned them.

"They are not called the Hills of Deception without reason," she had said gravely. "We call them *Sai'al Sodonu* the hills that deceive."

"In Cenna Siem," Niko had added, "they claim the land belongs to Daiesthai."

Gan had expected her to laugh at that, dismissing it as superstition. Instead, she had frowned thoughtfully, as if considering the possibility.

"Just remember," she had said, "you cannot trust what you see in the hills. And we must not get separated."

Gan hadn't admitted it aloud, but he had no intention of letting himself be separated. Just being in the Grip had already set off alarms inside him. He decided it must have been that unease that had woken him.

He lay back again, pulling the blanket around his shoulders. The whispering started slowly, a faint rustle at the edge of his hearing. At first he thought it was the wind, but the sound sharpened, the voices clearer. He tensed, scanning the darkness, but no figures appeared.

The whispers slithered closer. Gan pressed his hands over his ears. Still, the words bled through: *You don't belong here… you'll never survive…*

He sat bolt upright, heart hammering. Beside him, Caius stirred.

"Gan? What's wrong?"

"Do you hear that?" Gan whispered.

Caius blinked blearily. "Hear what?"

"The voices. They're everywhere."

Caius sat up, listening. The night was still, save for the faint shuffle of the hercudons. "I don't hear anything."

Gan shook his head, frustrated. "They're there. I swear it."

Caius was about to reply when Niko suddenly sat upright, his eyes glowing faintly in the firelight. "He's right. I hear them too."

Calla appeared almost instantly, as though she had been awake the whole time. "Stay together." Her voice was sharp, commanding. She moved to the edge of the firelight, scanning the misty darkness.

The whispers grew louder now, curling around them like smoke. Shapes flickered in the shadows tall, formless, bending unnaturally.

Caius swore. "Not again. I hate this place."

"Don't listen," Calla ordered. "Whatever they say, ignore them."

"I'm trying!" Caius hissed, clutching his blanket like a shield.

Niko pressed a hand to his chest, feeling the pulse of his spirit stone. Its steady rhythm anchored him. "She's right. Block them out."

Gan tried, but the voices clawed inside his head, whispering every fear he hadn't dared to speak aloud. *You're weak. You'll fail them. You'll be the first to die.*

"No!" he shouted, clutching his stone.

The shapes lunged forward. Calla drew her blade in a swift motion, its steel gleaming red from the firelight. She slashed into the shadows, and they recoiled with a hiss.

"Stay behind me!" she barked.

The boys clustered together as Calla cut through the phantoms, each strike sending them scattering. But more surged forward, their whispers becoming shrieks.

Caius squeezed his eyes shut. "This is like a nightmare!"

"Hold!" Calla commanded. "Hold on to one another."

Gan grabbed Caius's arm; Niko clutched his other side. The three pressed together, trembling but united. The connection steadied them, dulled the whispers just enough.

With a final cry, Calla plunged her blade through the thickest knot of mist. The shadows ripped apart, dissolving into nothing. Silence fell, sharp and absolute.

The fire sputtered but held.

The boys collapsed onto the ground, panting.

"Well," Caius croaked, "that was...different."

Gan rolled his eyes, but even he let out a shaky laugh.

Calla wiped her blade clean, her face unreadable. "That was only a test. The hills will throw worse at us yet I suspect."

The next morning, the boys woke drained. None had truly slept after the attack.

As they packed camp, Caius muttered, "I don't know how much more of this I can take."

"You'll take as much as you must," Calla said, tightening Risk's reins.

Caius frowned. "You really don't sugarcoat things, do you?"

"No," she replied flatly. "That would serve no one."

Niko gave Caius a weary look. "She's right. We can't turn back."

"Doesn't mean I have to like it," Caius grumbled, but he climbed onto his mount.

The trail that day wound deeper through the hills, the landscape twisting unnaturally. Paths doubled back on themselves; gullies appeared where none had been before. The land itself seemed alive, intent on confusing them.

Gan kept a wary eye on every shadow. "How do we know we're even going the right way?"

"Instinct." Calla replied.

They made slow progress, and when they finally camped again, exhaustion weighed on them all. The firelight flickered against their strained faces.

Niko broke the silence. "Why do these lands even exist?"

"Perhaps to help you appreciate the lands outside of the Sai'al'Sodonu." Calla suggested. They considered that and decided it made sense.

"Why do people hate the dragonmasters...the real reason." Gan wanted to know.

"Because fear breeds hate." Calla told him, nudging the kindling into a more substantial fire. "The dragonmasters have been in seclusion for a long time...the sorcia don't know much about us."

"But it wasn't always like that." Caius recalled.

Calla drew her knees up and sighed. "Over the centuries, the roll of the dragonmaster has changed...or been changed. We are the protectors of all things created by Deius. That is ingrained in our binding. But at the last reckoning, Lord Ackley managed convince a significant number of sorcia and gaol that the dragonmasters were a threat. That with our power, we could overthrow the existing order and conquer the realm. Nonsense, of course. We have the power to do it, but our binding makes it impossible. But the sorcia doesn't truly understand about our binding. They can't imagine not being able to lie or break a vow." She looked towards the hills somberly. "The dragonmasters were nearly destroyed before they came to understand that the people they were sworn to protect were rising up against them. That's the reason Tegoradaysol was built. Secluded away in the Mountains of the Condemned."

"And seven of us are expected to get through this next reckoning?"

"No...not just the seven of us. There are other dragonmasters at Tegoradaysol. And other enchanted beings." she answered.

"Doesn't sound like promising odds." Gan grumbled.

She gave him a faint smile. "No it doesn't, but nothing is accomplished if we don't try at all."

The next day, there was no light-hearted banter, no question-and-answer session; very little conversation at all. Niko found the silence almost as unsettling as the trees looming over them. His stomach rumbled, and he considered asking about a meal break. Likely they would not stop, but he could eat and ride.

To his left, he spotted a narrow path that wound its way up a steeper hill. It didn't look well-traveled, but it was unmistakably a road. He frowned. The path they had been following had vanished some time earlier.

"Master Calla," he called, reining his gelding in. "There is a road over there."

Calla shook her head, not looking back. "We are going this way."

"But… a road." He frowned uncertainly. "You can see it too, right?" he asked Caius, suddenly realizing it might be one of the hill lands' tricks.

"I see it," Caius replied.

"Why not take the path?" Gan asked.

Calla dragged her fingers through her hair. "Have you noticed anything significant about the path I have chosen?"

The boys exchanged puzzled looks. Then Caius glanced back the way they had come, searching for an answer. Suddenly, it clicked. "We are going around them!" he exclaimed, turning back in the saddle. "You have not gone over a single hill, just around them!"

Calla's expression was grim. "Exactly. That road leads to a hill-top."

Gan eyed it warily. "What is up there?"

"I don't know," Calla confessed. "But I have heard the hilltops are the cores of Sai'al Sodonu's power. Whatever magic flows through here, it is strongest at the cores. Maybe it's only a legend, but I have no wish to find out."

The wind picked up a short time later, gusts at first, then steadily stronger. The hercudons kept their heads low, ears twitching, steps labored. To make matters worse, the light dimmed unnaturally fast.

"We have not been here long enough for it to be nightfall, have we?" Gan asked, perplexed.

"No, we have not," Calla replied tersely.

They pressed forward as the winds howled louder, driving grit into their faces. The sky darkened, as though a storm were swallowing the day whole.

"If we don't stop, the hercs will collapse," Niko shouted over the roar.

"We can't stop here," Calla insisted. Her cloak whipped violently, her hair lashing across her face. "We need shelter...there!"

Through the dimness, they spotted a hollow between two ridges. Struggling against the gale, they guided their mounts into the shallow shelter. The moment they entered, the wind died almost completely.

Caius gasped. "Okay, that is creepy."

Gan dismounted, brushing dust from his face. "It's better than being blown off a cliff."

Calla didn't relax. She scanned the ridges, her expression taut. "Stay close. This could be another trick."

The air inside the hollow grew heavy, pressing on their chests. Caius rubbed his arms. "Feels like someone piled rocks on me."

"That's because we're not alone," Niko whispered.

They all turned. From the shadows at the far end of the hollow, a figure emerged tall, cloaked, its face obscured. It didn't move like a man, its steps gliding rather than walking.

Caius's voice shook. "Uh… anyone want to guess friendly or not?"

"Not," Gan said flatly, drawing his blade.

The figure raised a hand, and the shadows deepened around them. Whispered words slithered through the hollow, thick with malice.

Calla stepped forward, sword in hand. "Stay back."

The figure ignored her, its head tilting unnaturally as if studying the boys. Its voice was a rasp. "Three newlings… and a dragonmaster. How quaint."

Niko's stomach lurched. "It knows…"

"Of course it does," Calla snapped. "Stand behind me."

The shadows lunged like living things. The boys stumbled back as Calla slashed through them, her blade glowing faintly as it cut. The figure hissed, retreating into the darkness as its conjured shadows dissipated.

For a long moment, silence hung heavy.

Caius let out a breath he hadn't realized he'd been holding. "Anyone else vote we never camp here again?"

Gan sheathed his blade reluctantly. "Seconded."

Calla kept staring at the spot where the figure had vanished. "It grows bolder."

They did not sleep well that night. Every flicker of shadow seemed alive. Every gust of wind carried whispers. But nothing else came.

By dawn, all were hollow-eyed with exhaustion.

As they set out again, Caius muttered, "If this is what the Reckoning thinks is training, I'd rather stick with exams."

"Exams don't kill you," Gan said.

"Speak for yourself," Caius shot back. "Professor Whillan's tests nearly did."

For the first time in days, the edge of humor in his voice drew genuine laughter from Niko. Even Calla's lips twitched faintly, though she quickly hid it.

The hills seemed endless. Days blurred into one another, each trek marked by tricks of the land paths that looped back, horizons that shifted when they blinked. Only Calla's unwavering sense of direction kept them moving forward.

By the fourth day, though the unnatural length made them wonder how long it had truly been, food supplies had dwindled, and tempers ran thin. The hercudons stumbled more often, their ribs visible beneath their hides.

"We need to stop soon," Niko urged.

"Soon." Calla promised. "But not here.   This place feels...wrong."

The boys fell silent at that.

Late that evening, they emerged into a valley floor unlike any they had seen. Black stone jutted from the ground like jagged teeth, forming a circle around a central rise. Atop it stood a single tree gnarled, leafless, glowing faintly with a sickly light.

Caius swallowed hard. "I don't care for the looks of that."

Gan frowned. "What is it?"

Calla's voice was low. "I don't know. "

The boys stiffened.

"We avoid it," she said firmly. "No matter what you see, no matter what you hear, do not step inside that circle."

Her eyes lingered on each of them, making sure the warning sank in.

>

Just as the sun had behaved oddly during the day, it vanished abruptly, replaced by a pale, full moon. The change happened so quickly they were all too startled to react for a moment.

Calla was the first to find her tongue. "Well...at least there's a moon."

Gan and Niko had already rolled out their bedrolls and wolfed down their last rations, but Caius, not bound yet to his peril stone lacked their eye shine and found the darkness made him uncomfortable.

"Why don't you try to get some sleep." Calla suggested. "I'll take the watch."

He didn't think sleep would be possible but he unrolled his bedding and laid down, his arms folded under his head. He tried staring up at the sky, but the too pale moon and starless sky was unsettling, and the craggy rocks in the distance took on strange and frightening forms.

To block the unpleasant sights, Caius closed his eyes and before he knew it, sleep overtook him.

He woke what felt like only minutes later, a peculiar tickling against the back of his neck. He panicked briefly, scrambling to his feet and brushing at his neck. A faint glowing inside the ring of black stones made him frown and Caius took a step back. "I am the logical one," he muttered under his breath, trying to steady his nerves. "I can figure this out."

"Come, come, newling."

The voice slithered through the air, drawing Caius's gaze toward the stone circle. A figure materialized within the jagged ring; a man, yet not entirely human. He towered above Caius, wrapped in flowing crimson robes that twisted and swirled as though caught in an unseen storm. His eyes were so dark they seemed bottomless, and the smile that spread across his pale face was anything but kind.

Caius froze, his throat dry. Everything about the figure, from the hem of his blood-red robes to the rough stubble on his head, radiated menace.

"You are not real," Caius whispered hoarsely, retreating a step.

The figure laughed, a deep, thunderous sound that shook the ground. "I am quite real, newling. I am Nefario."

He pointed a long, skeletal finger at Caius. "Spare your life, newling. Deny what you are and live."

"Deny…" Caius swallowed, hands slick with sweat. "I don't understand."

Nefario's eyes burned. "Deny what you are and live!" he roared, the earth trembling underfoot. He bent low, his shadow engulfing Caius, and his voice dropped to a gravelly whisper. "Embrace it, dragonmaster, and die by a slayer's sword."

The words coiled around Caius like chains.

Nefario straightened, his form looming impossibly tall. Caius fought the urge to collapse, forcing himself to remain standing though every instinct screamed to run.

"Deny it and live… embrace it and die." Nefario's voice thundered one final time as his image began to fade, leaving only echoes of his malice behind.

Caius stood alone beside the circle, fear boiling inside him until he could no longer contain it. He threw back his head and screamed.

A hand clamped around his arm. Caius jolted awake, his scream still echoing in the night air.

Calla crouched beside him, her expression taut with worry. Nearby, Niko and Gan sat up on their bedrolls, wide-eyed. Clearly, his cries had woken them too.

"A nightmare," Calla said quietly. "Nothing more."

Caius shook his head violently, his chest heaving. "It wasn't just a dream. He was here. Nefario. He spoke to me."

Gan frowned. "You were thrashing in your sleep. That's all."

"No!" Caius snapped, louder than he intended. His voice cracked. "He was real. He knew about me, about us. He said if I deny what I am I'll live but if I embrace it…" His words faltered. "…I'll die by a slayer's sword."

The others exchanged uneasy glances.

Calla's hand tightened on his arm. "The hills deceive, Caius. That is their nature. They twist your fears and show you what you dread most. Do not give them power."

"He knew my name," Caius insisted, his voice desperate. "He knew."

Silence fell. The fire crackled, filling the space where none of them dared speak. The night promised to be long.

>

Gan woke to the sound of a fife, piping a cheerful tune and with a groan of protest, he raised his head, blinking against the glare of the sun. The instrument was hovering in the center of the stone ring, bouncing about as if it time to the music it played.

Gan looked around to see if the others were seeing what he was seeing and discovered he was alone. Surprise gave way quickly to anger. How could they have left him?

"It is not yet your time to perform, newling." A voice rasped harshly and Gan turned back towards the ring, his tawny eyes taking in the figure standing inside holding the fife. It continued to play as the bony fingers gave it a twirl.

Eyes blacker than coal stared down at Gan. "Your puppet-master will pull your strings when she has a need of you newling."

Gan climbed to his feet, anger giving him a surge of courage. "I am no one's puppet!"

The man's laughter made the hair on the back of Gan's neck raise and a shiver ran down his spine. "I am Nefario, newling. I can help you with your puppet-master if you like." The flute left his hand, drifting closer to Gan. The melody was no longer bright and cheerful. Now it sounded as if it was mocking him.

Gan stared at it, frowning. "I am not a puppet." he insisted, but his voice lacked conviction.

"She will take you to your death, newling." Nefario cautioned him. "Unless you cut your puppet strings, she will guide you to a slayers sword."

The fife hovered at the edge of the ring, piping so shrilly now that Gan was forced to cover his ears. "Stop!"

Nefario and the fife faded out of sight and Gan lowered his hands cautiously, his ears still ringing.

"I am not a puppet." he whispered fiercely.

"Gan." Niko's voice sounded far off.

Opening his eyes, Gan found himself staring into Niko's bright blue eyes. He jerked away, fully awake. "What's wrong?" he demanded, struggling into a sitting position.

"You're talking in your sleep."

Gan drew his knees to his chest, frowning, pretending not to notice the looks of concern on everyone's face. "I'll take a watch now." he said quietly.

Niko had already burrowed down into his bedding and Calla stretched out as well, hoping to get a short nap if nothing else.

She woke soon after, not feeling rested in the least and was surprised to find the sun up. Niko was stretching a few feet away but there was no sign of the other two.

Getting to her feet, Calla strapped on her swordbelt and scanned their surroundings.

"Where are they?" Niko asked worriedly. His eyes fell on the stone ring and he furrowed his brow, uncertain of what he was seeing. A shimmering perhaps. Or an odd glow. But something was definitely happening inside the ring.

"Master Calla?"

"I see it." she said softly.

The thing began to take shape, becoming clearer and Niko shuddered from a feeling like icy fingers moving down his spine.

Robes the color of blood whipped around the figure towering over them, a startling contrast to the pale skin of the bony hands folded together across his chest. His black eyes came to rest on Niko and a smile stretched across his pasty face.

"Yet another newling." The voice reminded Niko of the rustle of dead leaves and he shivered again, staring up at the man that wasn't truly a man. "A newling controlled by his heart." The man chuckled in delight. "I am always intrigued by those that follow their hearts. So strong. So reckless." His voice dropped to a raspy whisper. "They are the hardest to break, and the most satisfying."

Niko never hear Calla's sword leave the sheath but she was standing between him and the figure in the stone ring, weapon in hand.

The black eyes shifted to her, the smile widening. "Genesi Ney." he rumbled softly. "I am Nefario, ruler of Sai'al Sodonu. You would draw a sword as easily as that, dragonmaster? A sword against words?"

Calla stood firmly, sword in hand. "I do when those words are a threat."

The sword didn't appear to concern Nefario. "You are not what I expected, Genesi Ney. You are young...and quite lovely." His eyes swept over her and she had to struggle not to shiver under his cold, black gaze. "The reckoning comes, dragonmaster."

Calla's eyes narrowed and she flexed her grip on the sword hilt.

Nefario laughed, leaning down and studying her with an intense stare. "Defiance...and courage as well as a pretty face. You impress me, dragonmaster, and I am not easily impressed by humans." He expended a pale hand. "Come to me Genesi Ney and I will see that you live through the reckoning."

Calla shook her head. "I will see myself through the reckoning." she said determinedly.

Nefario's smile vanished and his eyes flashed with fury. "Come willingly and I will make you a queen." he barked harshly. "Resist and I will make you my pet. Either way...you will belong to me."

Niko stepped forward angrily, his hands clenched. "Master Calla will never belong to you!"

Nefario's grin returned. "Your heart is already tangled with the Genesi Ney, is it newling? When I tether my pet, your heart will be broken." He gave a triumphant laugh, meeting Calla's gaze again. "Come, Genesi Ney." he said coaxingly, his hand still out to her. "Come and be a queen with all the world laid at your feet. Resist me and I will see you tethered."

Calla's breath caught, a tremor shooting through her but she stared up at him defiantly.

Nefario's voice was a soft rumble. "You fear being tethered, Genesi Ney, and well you should. You will watch the others die and you will envy them for it."

Calla shook her head. "I will not yield."

Nefario snatched his hand back and straightened, dark eyes betraying his rage. "As you wish, dragonmaster."

His image shimmer, wavering slightly and he faded out of sight.

Niko reeled towards Calla, his eyes wide. "What was he?!"

Calla frowned, staring at the place where Nefario had stood. "A dream, I think." She thrust her sword back into the sheath. "Or a nightmare might be a more accurate description."

"Then...it wasn't real?"

"It was real." she replied grimly. "We were obviously brought her to be shown these dreams. Now that we have, I suspect we'll be out of Sai'al Sodonu at last."

>

They set out at dawn, the tension between them heavier than the packs on their shoulders. Caius lagged behind, still shaken by the encounter. Every shadow felt like Nefario's eyes watching him.

As they descended into another barren valley, Calla slowed her pace until she was riding beside him.

"You are stronger than you think," she said quietly.

Caius kept his eyes on the ground. "I certainly hope so."

By midday, they stumbled upon another ridge that overlooked the plains beyond. For the first time in days, they saw the horizon stretch open, the land no longer twisted and deceptive.

Gan let out a shaky laugh. "We made it."

Niko sat straighter in his saddle, relief flooding his face. "Finally."

Caius didn't speak, but his shoulders eased slightly. The grip of Nefario's words lingered, but the open air reminded him the nightmare hadn't claimed him.

Calla dismounted, leading Risk to the ridge's edge. She stared long at the plains below. "Do not grow careless. The hills have let us pass, but our path is not finished."

The boys groaned in unison, and for a fleeting moment, a hint of humor lightened their hearts.

But as the wind shifted and carried a faint, unnatural chill up from the plains, even Caius felt it, that they had only crossed one threshold, and the true trial lay ahead.

Chapter 9: Reunion

By midday, they had left the hill lands behind, riding across open prairie towards the township of Mandirube. Calla opted to stay west of the road, and no one complained. The riding was easy even at the brisk pace she set. Mostly, they were just grateful to be putting as much distance as possible between themselves and Sai'al Sodonu.

When they stopped to rest the horses and eat the meager food Calla had conjured for their meal, Caius broached the subject of their dreams.

"What happened last night, Master Calla?"

"I wish I knew, Caius," she replied hesitantly. "I have heard of spectral rings, some call them dream circles, but I have never seen one. I do believe that was what we experienced."

"Whatever it was…" Niko said with a shudder. "I hope I never see one again."

Caius was in complete agreement. "My dreams have never felt so… real."

"Because dreams are not real, Caius." Finished with her meal, Calla got to her feet. "But a spectral ring is said to be a link between the world of reality and the world of the subconscious. If that is the case, then what we saw last night was real. We were on the dream plane."

Gan regarded her narrowly. "What did *you* see?"

"Nothing I would like to see again," she replied vaguely, moving to Risk's side and checking his cinch.

Annoyed, Gan stood. "That tells us nothing!" he snapped at her.

She met his gaze squarely. "What did *you* see, Gan?"

"A man," he told her without hesitation. "A man that called himself Nefario." Caius's eyes widened. "But… he is not really a man," Gan added in a hushed tone.

"I saw him too."

Caius and Gan turned towards Niko, who nodded uneasily. "He was inside the stone ring, wearing red robes. Master Calla and I saw him."

Puzzled, Caius frowned. "You and Master Calla? Together?"

"Yes," Niko nodded in Calla's direction. "We were both there… but not either of you. We thought you had gone into the ring."

"I was alone when I saw him."

Gan nodded. "So was I." He moved to Calla's stallion, grabbing the reins and stepping between mount and rider. "He called me your puppet!"

Calla arched a brow, their eyes locking. "Are you a puppet, Gan?"

"No!" he snapped, "and I do not plan to be!"

She gave a casual shrug. "And I have no desire to make you one, so what does it matter what he said?"

Caius and Niko rose, worried by the look in Gan's eyes. He stood eye to eye with her, matching her in height but broader and more muscular. But between her magic and the sword, Gan was no match for their counsel. They thought his impudence might well earn him serious consequences.

"He manipulated you, Gan," the sorcia master said quietly. "He knew what you feared, and he used it to his advantage."

"He did that with me as well," Caius put in. "You know that Master Calla is telling you the truth."

Releasing the stallion's reins, Gan continued to meet her gaze. "And what did he use to try to manipulate *you*?"

She looked away, shaking her head. "It makes no difference," she whispered. "I will never allow it to happen."

"We should probably be going," Caius interjected, desperate to keep the peace. "Mandirube is only a few more hours' ride."

Niko caught his gelding and moved closer to Gan. "You should not challenge her that way, Gan," he murmured so that only the older boy could hear. "You know that."

"What if the dream was right?!" Gan hissed angrily, giving the cinch a sharp tug. The hercudon looked over at him with disapproval, and he gave it an apologetic pat. "Sorry, boy," he assured his mount. He looked back at Niko. "I only know that in my dream, I was warned that staying with her could get me killed!"

Niko sighed. "Me too, but how long do you think we can survive without her?"

Gan shot a dark look in Calla's direction. "You hesitated, Niko. I was there… remember? You were not sure you wanted this commitment."

"But I *did* accept… and I have no regrets. Besides…" he added, looking worriedly in Calla's direction. "…I think there are things worse than death."

Gan was in the process of mounting his gelding, but he eased himself back to the ground, facing Niko. "What do you mean?"

Niko gave him a solemn look. "He threatened us with death… probably Caius as well, because we cannot imagine anything worse." His bright blue eyes met Gan's tawny ones. "He threatened Master Calla with something else. Something he said would make her envy the ones who died."

Gan licked his lips nervously, glancing at Calla, who was making a final check of the campsite from the stallion's back. Niko and Gan mounted their horses and fell in behind Caius and Calla.

"What was the threat?" Gan asked quietly.

Niko frowned, remembering Calla's reaction. "He said he would see her tethered."

Gan's brow creased. "What does that mean?"

"I do not know," Niko answered with a shrug. "But I can tell you this… when he said it… just for a moment… she was afraid."

That made Gan's eyes widen. "We could just ask her."

Niko shook his head. "She is not going to tell us… not before Caius has his stone… maybe not even afterwards."

Calla looked over her shoulder at them, her expression impossible to read. "Keep up, you two," she called, heeling her mount to a gallop.

Knowing their counsel wanted to put an end to their conversation, Gan and Niko exchanged looks and urged their horses forward.

>

The four riders entered the township of Mandirube in the late afternoon. A town even smaller than Cenna Siem, its guard wall was more of a deference to tradition than a deterrent to invaders. It was a mere five feet high, and as far as Caius knew, the heavy wooden gate had always stood open.

He felt a rush of familiarity as they rode up the narrow lane that was the town's main street. He had played many long afternoons on this very street in front of his mother's shop.

As she had in Daul Andora and Cenna Siem, Calla seemed to know her way around. She led them past the shops and markets, most already closed for the day, and into the quieter residential area. The weather was cool enough for people to give little notice to the cloaked and hooded riders, but in a town this small, it was impossible to go completely unnoticed.

Caius kept his head down. He did not want to be recognized and draw attention to their group.

They passed the schoolhouse and an orchard of apple and pear trees, the bare limbs making it possible for him to see the small but homey cottage he had grown up in. It might not have looked like much to the others, but Caius thought it was the most beautiful sight in the realm. He slipped from his saddle before his mare came to a stop at the front gate.

"Wait," Calla called out to him.

Caius halted, looking at her in surprise. With a sigh, she dropped to the ground, tossing her stallion's reins over the crumbling stone wall surrounding the yard. "I know that you are anxious to see your parents, but we stay together."

He nodded silently and waited for the others, then led the way up the narrow stone path to the door. Calla hesitated for a fraction of a second, but it was enough for Niko to notice. He wondered if these confrontations with their parents were more difficult for her than she let on. Certainly, his own parents had been unpleasant, and Gan's had been worse, or at least as bad.

The door opened with a creak of protest, and Caius beamed at his mother.

Dark-haired and dark-eyed like her son, Saya was a handsome woman with a warm and inviting smile. She greeted Caius with a hug and a kiss on each cheek, then stepped aside to usher them inside.

Calla was the last one in, closing the door softly and turning to give Saya an uneasy smile.

The older woman stepped forward and pulled the dragonmaster into a tight embrace, laughing, "Calla!" She stepped back, giving the sorcia master an appraising look. "Deius bless you, child, I never thought I would find you on my doorstep again." She reached out and touched Calla's cheek lightly. "You have grown into a lovely young woman. I have sorely missed you."

"Me too," Calla said sincerely.

The boys were staring in astonishment. This was not the welcome any of them had expected. Until now, Calla had been received as warmly as a plague of rats. Saya's behavior came as a surprise.

"You bring Caius yourself." She gave Caius another hug. "I am pleased, of course, to see you, Calla… but we were expecting Tangor."

Calla gave her a solemn nod. "Last-minute changes had to be made."

Saya took a seat near the hearth. "Sit and warm yourselves, all of you," she urged, laying a hand on her son's shoulder as he settled himself at her feet. Gan and Niko settled on a bench near the hearth, but Calla remained on her feet.

Niko had been in Caius's home before and found it practical and cozy, but Gan was shocked by the lack of comfort he took for granted in his own home. The windows were curtain-less, heavy wooden shutters closing out the world, and the wood floor was bare but clean. The furnishings were sparse, and there were none of the homey touches to make the place more personable.

Saya leaned towards Calla. "We knew things were happening," she confessed, smoothing the crisp white apron she wore over her simple cotton dress. "Less than a fortnight ago, an encampment was set up on the road between here and Soronu. There are rumors that it is occupied by slayers." She looked perplexed. "However did you manage to get past them?"

"We have stayed off the roads," Calla replied, and she looked relieved. She had made the right decision not to take the roads. The hill lands might have been unpleasant, but an encampment of slayers would have been fatal. She was grateful to have confirmation that her instincts had been correct.

"They were in town just before that… but they do not wear their cloaks now except in battle, we hear, so it is not always easy to recognize them."

Calla glanced down at her own woolen cloak. "This is not a time to wear your colors, it would seem."

"And a slayer's cloak is as telling as a dragonmaster's," Saya put in.

"Do you make them, Mum?" Caius inquired.

She smiled. "I have made a few. The fabric is difficult to work with, and I have always found them to be a bit tricky. But nothing compared to a dragonmaster's cloak." She and Calla exchanged grins. "Now that was a chore."

"But I treasure it," Calla said with feeling.

Caius's eyes widened. "You made Master Calla's cloak?"

"I asked her to," Calla answered. "Your mother is the best cloak maker in the realm."

Looking proudly at his mother, Caius nodded.

"I would have been proud to make a cloak for any dragonmaster, but especially Calla. And now you." Her hand tightened on his shoulder. "My only son and the girl who was like a daughter to me. I feel very blessed."

Niko and Gan shared another look of amazement. Not many people openly admitted fondness for a dragonmaster… even if it should be their own child.

"I suppose you wonder why we never told you."

Caius shook his head slowly. "No… I know the reason."

Saya managed a weak smile. "Your father is a good man, Caius, but raised with very strong opinions about dragonmasters. We had given up hope of ever having a child, and when we found out we were expecting you, it was the most wonderful news." She ran her fingers gently through his dark hair. "The morning that we found the peril stone in your cradle…" She shook her head, sighing. "…he was so angry… he had no idea I was of the bloodline. Then he decided to put it away as if it had never happened, and we never mentioned it again. I knew it was inevitable… that this day would come… but I let him pretend." She looked over at Calla. "He is not going to be pleased."

"I can imagine," the dragonmaster said drily.

Saya regarded her sadly. "I wish you could forgive Liab."

Calla gave a resolute shake of her head. "I do not see that happening, Saya."

"It is just…" the older woman sighed softly. "…you two were so close. He adored you, Calla."

Amber eyes flashed, and Calla jerked her cloak off impatiently. "That was before!"

Caius got to his feet. "How do you know my parents?"

"It was a long time ago," she replied, avoiding his gaze. "A great deal has changed since then."

Caius turned to his mother. "You said you were close. That she was like a daughter to you."

Saya nodded. "When Calla was a child, she spent more time here than at her own home." Calla started to interrupt, but Saya held up a hand. "He should know."

Frowning sullenly, Calla crossed to stand in front of the fire, her back to the rest of the room. Saya gave her a look of tolerant compassion and returned her attention to her son. "Calla's father, Harith, and your father were cousins. All your fathers are cousins," she added, smiling at Gan and Niko. "Harith and his wife, Bian, lived in Soronu… with Lucan, a son from Harith's first mate, and Calla, eight years younger than her brother."

Calla made a harsh sound, still standing tensely, staring into the flames.

"Harith and Liab were not close, but we did see them from time to time. Soronu is only a half day's ride from here, after all. Not far for most of us, but quite a trek for a six-year-old girl on a pony in the dark. That was the first time she ran away from home, but hardly the last, am I right, Calla?"

"This is your story, Saya," Calla said curtly.

Saya smiled indulgently. "Very well. Calla began to show up here whenever she had a disagreement with her father or her brother. Eventually, she was here as much as she was in her own home. Not that we minded." She reached for Caius's hand. "This was years before we were blessed with you. We had no children and thought we never would. Calla was sassy and spirited and an adorable child. She had Liab wrapped around her little finger."

"What happened?" Caius wondered, though he suspected he already knew the answer.

Calla spun around quickly. "He learned that I was a dragonmaster!" There was no mistaking the venom in her voice.

Saya nodded. "Unfortunately, this is true."

"And you would ask me to forgive him?!"

"He does not understand what you are, Calla," Saya said placidly. "He was raised knowing only the very worst things… never the truth."

Calla's cheeks were flushed, and she ran her fingers through her hair in agitation. "He knew me! He knew me better than my own father did!" she exclaimed. "I was a bloody fool to trust him!"

This was an argument Saya had had too many times with Liab, and she saw no reason to push the matter. Some hurts went too deep, she realized.

"So, have you and the boys traveled all this way from Ackley's?"

The dragonmaster nodded wearily. "Yes. We left the night of Festival."

"What is *she* doing here!?" a voice thundered from the doorway.

Everyone had been so intent on the drama unfolding in the room that no one had noticed Liab entering the house. He slammed the door and stomped over to Saya. "Why is she here?!" he demanded again.

Saya remained composed. "I believe you *know* why she is here, Liab."

His eyes raked over the three boys, then returned to Saya. "Where is Tangor? I thought he was supposed to be here for this foolishness!"

"Tangor is not coming," Calla said between clenched teeth.

Liab gave her a cold look. "Why is that? I was told he was to be here for some nonsense about a binding!"

"You were told that he would be Caius's counsel, but that is no longer true. Caius is my charge, and now that you have arrived, we can begin." She looked to Caius, standing dumbstruck in the center of the room. "Summon your stone."

"No!" snapped Liab.

Calla's eyes narrowed. "Do not interfere with my charge, Liab. This is out of your hands."

"This is my son, and I bloody well intend to know what you have planned before I allow it!"

"*Allow* it?" Calla's voice rose slightly, but she was managing to remain composed. "I can assure you, Liab, that I do not need your permission. As much as it may pain you to hear it, Caius is a drag-onmaster, with or without the binding, and you can do nothing to alter that fact!"

Saya stood quickly, slipping past them and pushing Caius towards the bench where Niko and Gan were sitting in stunned silence. Each of them had witnessed their own parents' resistance to their sons' fate, but this confrontation had a much more intense feel to it.

Patting Caius's shoulder, Saya looked somber. "I knew he was going to react badly… if only it had not been Calla."

"But why does he hate her so much?" Caius asked.

"It is so complicated," Saya replied. "Because he loved her, and he feels betrayed. Calla had no idea what she was either, and somewhere in his heart, Liab knows this… but he just cannot allow himself to get past that feeling of betrayal."

"Is he going to hate me too?" There was a catch in Caius's voice, and he looked imploringly at his mother.

She took his face in her hands. "I pray to Deius that his heart is not that hard," she told him.

Caius looked back at his father. Liab was a well-respected paymaster, a perfectionist and a stickler for detail. He liked things orderly, and he liked them simple. He had never been an affectionate man, that Caius could recall, but he had always been composed and proper. Until this very moment.

Liab was pacing in front of Calla with a murderous expression on his face, his hair falling into his face, his hands clenched.

"Do not think you will come into my house and tell me what is best for my son!" he said angrily.

Calla had remained, in the boys' opinion, dangerously calm. She watched Liab stalk back and forth, her arms folded in front of her, looking as if she fully intended to wait out his tirade. But her charges knew that she would not let him interfere with her duty. The calm could well be hiding the storm to come.

Saya sensed the same thing. "Caius," she whispered worriedly. "…if you know what Calla wants you to do, son, I think you should do it."

Caius looked at his companions.

"Go ahead," Niko urged.

Gan nodded in agreement. "Just remember to focus on the question foremost in your mind."

While his father continued to rant and Calla stood watching him in silence, Caius made up his mind. He held out his right hand, palm up, and closed his eyes. *The question foremost in your mind,* he told himself. That was not as easy as he had imagined it would be. No need to ask if he truly was a dragonmaster; he sensed that he was, and recent events only confirmed that. And there was no need to ask why his parents had kept the truth from him. He knew the answer to that.

The one question that came to him, one he thought he did not want to know the answer to… was his father going to hate him the way he hated Calla?

Visions of dragons, swords, and mountains flashed in his head. He saw Ackley's not as a school but as a bloody battlefield. He saw small villages ravaged by fire, bodies littering the ground. And along with all the visions, a voice was speaking clearly to him, but inside his head.

A dragonmaster must bind to his stone. The voice was soft, silky-smooth, a purr inside his head, but with strength. He felt the weight of the stone as it settled into his hand, warm and solid, and the voice flowed on. *Only in binding willingly are you able to fulfill your destiny, dragonmaster. Bind willingly and vow to be loyal to your brothers, devoted to your counsel. Bind willingly and vow to be honest and trustworthy. Bind willingly to serve as only a drag-*

onmaster can serve, even unto your death. Bind willingly to accept your destiny and your fate, surrendering your past life as you know it. Bind willingly to uphold centuries of tradition and service, to face challenges in the name of honor and truth. Bind willingly with the knowledge that these vows are your bond, not to be taken lightly, not to be set aside. Bind willingly with heart, mind, and soul. Once bound, you are bound until death. This choice is yours to make, dragonmaster. Bind or deny. Choose, dragonmaster.

Caius swallowed hard, his eyes still closed, the pictures continuing through his head. He had no idea if he was seeing the past, the present, or the future, or perhaps some of each. But he began to understand the power of the dragonmaster bound to the peril stone. It was the catalyst that activated the part of him that was truly a dragonmaster, not just in name, but in his very soul. And it was asking him to pledge himself to a cause and a way of life that was foreign to him.

No wonder Niko had been so troubled, he realized. But he did have a choice, just as Calla had promised. Everything she said was truth. Everything she did was in service to a binding she had already accepted, a vow she was honoring. The same vow he was now being asked to make.

His mother was proud; she had told him so. His father was another matter. Liab would never be proud if he accepted the binding. But Liab did not understand. He could not feel the strength of the stone pulsing in his hand or the sense of loyalty of the other three dragonmasters in the room. They would die for him, he knew that as surely as he knew he would give his life for any of them.

He was a dragonmaster, he told himself, chosen for this life. His fingers closed around the peril stone as he silently accepted the binding.

When he opened his eyes, Niko and Gan were wearing their familiar, goofy grins, and Saya was giving him a look of approval. He turned his attention to Calla and his father.

The sorcia master was still holding her temper in check, but it was requiring a great deal of effort on her part. Liab had stopped pacing and was towering over her, his outrage still being vented.

"I made this perfectly clear to Tangor!"

"Papa," Caius broke in quietly.

"And I told him…"

Calla was no longer listening. She turned to Caius, taking in the glow of his dark eyes and the blue crystal in his palm. A smile tugged at the corners of her mouth. "It would seem that you truly are the logical one," she said with a nod.

Liab fell silent, staring at his son.

"I hope you can forgive me someday, Papa," Caius said as he faced his father.

The color drained from Liab's face. "What have you done, Caius?"

"I accepted what I am."

Liab shook his head. "No… you cannot do this. You cannot understand what they are!"

"I *do* understand," Caius said, amazed by his own confidence.

Liab whirled back towards Calla. "This is some of your magic!" he accused furiously. "You have done something to him!"

"I cannot interfere with the binding," she shot back.

Liab let out a roar of fury. "How dare you use your sorcery on my son!" His right hand shot out and delivered an open-handed blow that sent Calla staggering back several steps.

Instinctively, Calla caught her balance, reeling back towards him and unsheathing her sword in a single motion. The room was completely silent, Calla standing ready to fight, Liab fuming in front of her, Saya watching anxiously, wringing her hands.

Wordlessly, the boys moved forward, taking positions in front of Calla. The message was clear. They would defend their own.

Liab stared at each of them with barely contained fury. "Get out!" he finally rasped harshly, glaring at Calla and avoiding his son's eyes. "Get out and do not come back! Any of you!"

Calla sheathed her weapon, grabbed her cloak, and crossed to the door, her charges following. The tension was so heavy no one dared to speak as they left the house.

Saya followed them into the yard, pushing a package into Caius's hands and giving him a tight hug. "Do not hate him, Caius. He just cannot understand."

Caius nodded, but his expression was grim.

Saya turned to Calla with a worried frown, touching the bright red handprint on the dragonmaster's cheek. "I am so sorry, Calla."

"I ask no apology from you, Saya. You have always been a true friend to me."

"I wish…" Saya dropped her gaze. "…he is just so angry."

"He is more like my father than I realized," Calla said softly. "Do not stay in Mandirube, Saya. Tangor should have told you."

"He did," Saya assured her. "We will go straight away." She gave Calla a hug. "He will not wish to, but we will."

Satisfied, Calla climbed into the saddle, and when they were all mounted, she looked down at Saya, holding out her hand. "You were like a mother to me, Saya. I should have told you that before now."

"You never had to, child," Saya said, taking her hand. "*Sar sei 'al*, dragonmaster."

Smiling, Calla nodded and withdrew her hand, guiding Risk back towards the road. Saya gave her son's hand a squeeze and watched the foursome ride away.

Beyond the orchard, Calla glanced over to find Caius watching her intently.

"I am sorry about your father," she told him.

"He should not have struck you," Caius said, an edge in his voice.

"He was protecting you."

Caius looked annoyed. "I did not ask for it." His eyes searched her face. Even in the dim light of nightfall, he could see her clearly, see the impression his father's hand left on her cheek. He was furious that his father had reacted with violence. "I made my decision... and he has made his."

"Any regrets?"

"Not for me." He glanced back at his parents' house, barely visible in the distance. "I wonder if he can say the same?"

Gan and Niko moved closer.

"You were right about the road," Gan said ruefully. "It was better that we crossed the hill lands."

"I was doubting myself until Saya told us about the encampment," she admitted.

"You were?"

She nodded. "I acted on an instinct… that usually serves me well… but it is hardly infallible. I may have more years as a dragonmaster than you three, but I am still not much more than a newling myself. You will see when we reach Tegoradaysol… the other dragonmasters still see me as a child."

"Great…" Gan muttered. "…they will see us as babes!"

Calla laughed. "I have no doubt you will soon set them straight."

>

Only a sliver of a moon hung in the night sky, and the air was cool and crisp. Calla rode a short distance ahead of her charges, her wool cloak pulled tight, her hood up. Amber eyes moved watchfully from side to side. She had debated briefly with herself after leaving Mandirube, wondering if it was better to continue riding or make camp and give them all a much-needed rest. In the end, she opted to ride. There would be time to rest when they reached Mim Tor. She would prefer not to run the risk of encountering slayers on the way to the city.

Besides, she told herself, stopping would give her more time to contemplate, and she was doing enough of that as it was. She had known since leaving Ackley's that the stop in Mandirube would be more difficult than the others. She had tried to prepare herself for the confrontation with Liab, but if she was honest with herself, she knew that she was almost as much a novice as her young charges. Controlling her emotions was still a challenge she had yet to master, though she knew she put little effort into doing so. Hadn't Master Camalaron and Varzi repeatedly said as much?

Unconsciously, her gloved hand raised to her cheek. Liab's blow had caught her completely by surprise, but not her reaction to it. Her defenses were immediate and potentially deadly. But she had been trained to be deadly. A dragonmaster did not wield their weapon in jest.

She never would have used her sword against an unarmed man; she had been trained better than that. But it said something that she instinctively saw him as an enemy. And it said even more that her three charges had been prepared to intercede. It was true that a dragonmaster's loyalty was first to their own, but she had never known of a binding sealing itself so completely in so short a time. Niko, also linked to a spirit stone and being a sensitive, was less of a surprise. Gan, her skeptic, she expected would take longer to embrace his binding, and she would never have asked Caius to stand up to his father. But they had done so willingly, almost instinctively. This last generation was proving to be stronger than she imagined.

Frowning, Calla realized she was dwelling again on things she preferred not to be. She gave herself a mental shake and looked over her shoulder. Her gaze met Caius's, and he urged his mount up alongside hers.

"You did very well tonight," she said quietly. "You summoned your stone on your own."

"Gan and Niko helped."

Calla fought back a smile. It would be better not to encourage them to be too self-sufficient. There were risks to being a dragonmaster that they did not yet know. They were following instincts that could lead them into trouble. Calla was all too familiar with that path.

"One step at a time, Caius," she cautioned. "You three still have a great deal to learn."

"I know," he assured her. "The voice I heard… that offered the binding… who was it?"

"Most think it is Pa-dai-ti, the dragon fairy that forged the original binding."

"Did she really use dragon's blood to heal?"

Calla chuckled. "Rait's story has changed a great deal over the centuries… no one is exactly certain what happened at the first binding. But do you not have any questions for yourself?"

Caius shook his head. "Not… not that I can put into words," he replied. "Except… I would like to know about you and my father."

Calla sighed heavily. "That is quite complicated."

"My mother told us part of it."

Her relationship with Liab was the last thing she wished to discuss, but it seemed important for Caius to know. Wearily, she rubbed her temple. "I have no wish to speak against your father, Caius."

"Just tell me the truth."

It had been years since she allowed herself to think about the events of her past, and the wounds had already been exposed several times since they began their journey.

It is only a story, she told herself. She had to separate herself from the events and the emotions.

"As Saya already told you… whenever I had a disagreement with my father or brother, I ran away from home. Looking back, it was a cowardly reaction, but I was just a child… and your mother was always so warm and welcoming. Liab too. I was closer to them than to my own parents."

That was certainly true enough. Harith had always treated his daughter with contempt, and Bian deferred to her mate in every situation, always uneasy around her headstrong daughter.

"I could not understand why my parents had such a strong dislike for me… until the night of my binding. Like your father, mine was raised to hate dragonmasters. He had known the truth since I was an infant. I found out only a fortnight before I was to attend Ackley's. Tangor thought it would be better for me to continue living with the sorcia and keep what I was a secret. My father agreed; after all, he had no wish to see his son's life ruined by my tainted blood."

"So I went to Ackley's and managed to keep my secret for three terms."

"Until the fencing tournament," Gan put in.

Calla glanced over at him, nodding. She had seen the other boys ride up to join them a few moments earlier and reasoned that it would be better to reveal her story once and be done with it.

"Yes," she continued. "I betrayed what I was and got myself expelled from school. I had no idea what the repercussions would be at the time." She was staring straight ahead, her face lost in the folds and shadows of her hood. "I met Karak and Dario when Tangor brought me back to Soronu after I was expelled. We were going to Tegoradaysol. Liab was there as well, and others… most of them I had never met before."

"Why were they there?"

Calla was silent for a moment, searching for the right words. "They were all cousins... all linked by the same bloodline. Camalaron thought it was time they knew the truth. That there was a female dragonmaster and a possibility that a prophecy was going to be fulfilled. He and Darmon summoned them to my parents' home."

"Darmon?" Gan repeated, clearly impressed.

"Who is Darmon?" Niko wanted to know.

Gan gave him an incredulous look. "He's a member of the Sorcia Tribunal. Do you not follow politics at all?"

Niko made a face. "Too boring."

Calla rewarded him with a wry grin. "I agree with you, Niko, but you will find that, like it or not, dragonmasters are deeply involved in the politics of the realm. It will become important for you to learn at least some of the politics involved. Most of that, fortunately, is between the Tribunal and the Triad at Tegoradaysol."

"So what did they tell our fathers?" Caius wondered.

"As it turned out, they told them very little. Master Camalaron told them what he knew of the prophecy, and everyone started yelling. Darmon was angry with the dragonmasters for keeping my birth and binding a secret from the Tribunal. The Tribunal was angry with my father for not revealing that his daughter was a dragonmaster. Then everyone else just seemed angry because they thought the others knew more than they did." Her gaze dropped to her hand, tightly clutching the saddle's pommel. "My father was expelled from the Tribunal, and he publicly disowned me. Everyone was shouting, calling names, making accusations... it was unbelievable. I was only sixteen... and quite honestly, I understood very little of what was happening."

"When I saw Liab across the room, I believed he would protect me from what was happening. We had always been close… I did not realize then that he shared my father's contempt for dragonmasters. But when I reached out to him, he was not the same man I knew and loved." Her voice caught, and she fell silent for a moment, determined not to give in to the emotions she could feel welling up. When she spoke again, her voice was weary. "So, I ran away. Just as I always did when my home was the last place I could bear. I went out to the Dari San River and waited." She shrugged. "I have no idea what I was waiting for. Maybe for everyone to go. Maybe for Liab to come and explain why he had behaved as he had. Maybe for Tangor to come and tell me what was happening. When no one came… I went home. I had nowhere else to go. I had never been to Tegoradaysol; I had no idea how to reach the city of Dragons. So, I went home. And everyone was gone."

"The house had been destroyed. Every piece of furniture was destroyed, every pillow and cushion slashed, every glass and dish smashed. Nothing had been spared. I truthfully had no concern for my father, but my mother… she was so timid for a Soroni. I was worried about her. I went upstairs."

Calla remembered being brought to an abrupt halt by a large red handprint on the door to her parents' bedroom. She had no idea at that time what it meant, but she understood at her very core that it was a bad omen.

"I knew they were dead before I opened the door, but I suppose I had to see for myself." She shook her head somberly. "I never looked any further… I just left the house. Tangor found me in the yard the following morning."

Again, silence fell over them, Calla still focused on the way ahead, the boys exchanging solemn looks.

"Liab and Karak returned with Darmon, and they both blamed me. Not," she added quickly, seeing they were about to object, "for my parents' murder… at least not directly. People had seen me at the river for most of the night. But they blamed me because by revealing myself at school, they believed I set things in motion."

"That makes no sense," Niko argued.

Calla lapsed into a recitation of the prophecy in an emotionless tone. "*In the days that follow the revelation of the Genesi Ney, sorcerer will rise against sorcerer, man against man, brother against brother. The reckoning will be at hand. Blood will spill, kingdoms will fall and nations will cease to be.*" She shifted in her saddle, frowning. "As they saw it, I had brought the prophecy to life."

"Is that all there is?" Gan asked. "I mean… I thought the last generation was mentioned."

"The prophecy goes on for a bit… very confusing, really. I only know bits of it, and possibly it has been jumbled over time." Again, she began to recite. "*Those born of like blood, descendants of Rait and heirs of the deceiver will inherit the fate of man and the establishment of a new bloodline.*"

Gan was the first to speak, his voice tinged with doubt. "What kind of prophecy is that? It says nothing about what we need to do!"

"Prophecies are not all that accommodating, it would seem," Calla stated flatly.

"Not this one," Caius had to admit. "But… if there is to be a new bloodline, it seems to imply that we succeed."

"The new bloodline exists only if we *do* survive," Calla pointed out. "The outcome is put into our hands… but not all outcomes are good."

"So, the revelation of the Genesi Ney is believed to be when you exposed that you were a dragonmaster at school… fulfilling the first part of the prophecy," Gan concluded.

"That was what many believed, and why I was blamed for my parents' murder. I suppose in that respect, I am guilty."

Caius gave her a quick look. "No, you are not!"

"You had no way of knowing what would happen," Niko put in.

Gan was nodding. "That was not your responsibility. If you had been told the truth, you might well have done things differently. You could have made other choices."

"You think of Karak," Calla said knowingly. "But do you believe that you would have been better off had you known the truth as a child?"

"Yes," Gan said with certainty.

"Tangor once told me that most families send their children to Tegoradaysol the moment they receive the peril stone. But all of us were allowed to live among the sorcia as children, not knowing what waited. Perhaps that gives us an advantage in dealing with the sorcia. Whatever the reason, what is done cannot be undone."

"Did they find out who murdered your parents?" Niko asked quietly.

"I was certain that same day. So were others, I believe. The house being destroyed was very personal."

Caius frowned thoughtfully. "That would likely have been done by someone who took the truth very personally."

"Lucan," she murmured.

"Your brother?!" Niko said in disbelief. "Your brother is a slayer?"

"He was training as a slayer when I was a child, but that was before anyone knew that they were changing. Lucan may even have heard of the Genesi Ney. Master Camalaron believes they have known for some time… they just did not know who it was." Her voice dropped to a harsh growl. "He might have been furious that our father never told him that I was a dragonmaster! How many times had he stood within inches of the Genesi Ney and never known?!"

"If the slayers know… should you be away from Tegoradaysol?" Niko asked anxiously.

"I can assure you; Master Camalaron met with a great deal of resistance when he named me as Niko's counsel. As I said, most still consider me little more than a newling."

"Newling?" Caius furrowed his brow. "Nefario called me that."

"Me too," Niko added.

"A newling is someone new to the binding, though in reality, you will be considered a newling until you are promoted by your counsel."

"How long does that take?" Gan wondered.

"That depends on the charge and their counsel," she replied. "The shortest time was fourteen years, and that was Andorran. The longest…" A grin crossed her face. "…well… I hear it was more than forty… but that may only have been a rumor meant to keep us on our toes."

"Fourteen years!?" Caius exclaimed in disbelief. "You call that short?!"

"That's practically another lifetime for us!" Gan realized, a look of displeasure on his face.

"A dragonmaster's life span is two to three hundred years… providing, of course, he dies a natural death. The time under your counsel will go by quickly… there is a great deal to learn."

"How long did it take you, Master Calla?" Niko inquired. "You… you were promoted, right?"

She laughed softly. "Of course. As much as Master Camalaron wished me to be a counsel to Niko, I could never have done so if I were still under Tangor's charge. He released me after sixteen years… that was only a year ago." Her bright eyes danced mischievously. "Most of the other dragonmasters objected to my release, but that decision belongs to the counsel."

"Why would they object?"

Calla shrugged her shoulders. "You will see for yourself soon enough."

"Master Calla," Caius said earnestly, his expression thoughtful. "…you said something about the heirs of the deceivers. What does that mean?"

"Diate," she said as if the name left an unpleasant taste in her mouth.

"The fairy that could shapeshift," he recalled.

Gan rubbed his jaw. "Master Fane called them… assimilators."

Their counsel nodded. "Yes, though that is a name given them by the sorcia, not their true name. They are *dali-daubs*… tricksters in the Language of the Old Age. A *dali-daub* will avoid a dragonmaster. We can see their true form unless we are eclipsed."

"Then… we are part *dali-daub*… yes?"

Calla sighed. "From our father's bloodline… yes… we are."

"Can we shapeshift, Master Calla?" Gan asked wonderingly.

Calla frowned deeply and looked away. "I think it is time for you to stop calling me Master Calla. I am no longer your sorcia master. Calla will be fine," she said quietly.

"But… you are my counsel," Niko said uncertainly. "I thought that was like a teacher."

"It is… but few counsels bother with titles. Master Camalaron, of course, is the head of the Triad and the leading authority in Tego-radaysol, but he is the only one addressed as Master. He is a Sage and very powerful."

"You did not answer my question, *Calla,*" Gan reminded her, placing an emphasis on her name to make a point. Niko and Caius gave him apprehensive looks. If Calla was choosing not to answer his question, they suspected his goading her was not going to yield positive results.

"Can we?" pressed Gan.

Calla leveled a stern gaze on him. "You do not wish to. I believe it is a very… unpleasant experience."

For a moment, he met her gaze, wanting to prove that he could not be intimidated, and for that same moment, she wished that he could be. "The skeptic," she murmured, more to herself than the others. With a faint smile, she looked away first, and Gan discovered, to his annoyance, that he had been holding his breath. He let it out slowly, hoping that no one else had noticed.

"Before we arrive in Mim Tor," Calla went on casually, "you need to learn to eclipse."

Niko looked surprised. "I thought that was rare?"

"It is. At the moment, there are only a handful capable of eclipsing, but Andorran, Tau, and Tiean can, so it is, hopefully, a skill all the last generation possesses." She slipped easily back into the role of instructor. "Sorcia and gaol identify us by our cloaks most of the time, but also by our eye shine. But there are times when it is better not to be recognized. The cloak is a simple matter to remedy, but the eye shine, for most, is another matter. No one other than a dragonmaster knows that some of us have the ability to eclipse. For that reason, you can never do it in front of sorcia or gaol who know you to be a dragonmaster." Her right hand moved across her face casually. "*Eclipsi*," she murmured.

When she opened her eyes, the eye shine was gone. She repeated the motion, speaking softly again, "*Ocular*." Her bright amber eyes regarded them once again.

Caius was eager to try. Imitating her motions, he whispered, "*Eclipsi*." He had only had his eye shine for a short time, but he already found it awkward to be without it. Everything had been clearer to him before eclipsing, not bright, but distinct. Now, it felt as if he had been plunged into darkness. Even his companions nearby were nothing more than shadowy figures.

Raising his hands back to his face, he reversed the spell, and his eye shine returned. He looked over at Calla and smiled. "I think I prefer it this way."

She gave him a look that told him she agreed and nodded to Gan. "You try now. This should be easy for you, seeing how you care little for the eye shine."

Resisting the urge to roll his eyes, Gan did as Calla and Caius had done with no difficulty. And, like Caius, he realized that he felt suddenly vulnerable. He lost no time using the spell to return the eye shine.

Niko, however, encountered difficulties. Though he did just as the others had, the eye shine remained, and when Calla laughed at his frustrated expression, he threw her a reproachful look.

"Why can I not do it? That is most unfair!"

"And it is most unlikely that you cannot, Niko. But you saw how Gan and Caius reacted to being eclipsed, even for a moment. You are reluctant to try."

"But I *did* try!" he insisted. "You saw me!"

"You said the words," she pointed out gently. "There is no magic in speaking words." Holding her hand out, she spoke clearly. "*Flammus.*" Nothing happened, though the boys had all been braced for something… anything. She grinned and cocked an eyebrow. "Intent is everything in spellcasting," she told them, then whispered, "*Flammus.*"

Brilliant flames shot up from her hand, dancing in the darkness. Chuckling, she lowered her hand, and the flames flickered out of sight.

"The words mean nothing without the intent, Niko."

Nodding, Niko took a deep breath and passed his hand over his face. "*Eclipsi.*" He opened his eyes slowly, and his frown deepened. Everything around him seemed to be nothing but murky shadows, and while he knew that this was how he had seen in the dark before his binding, he was completely unnerved by it now. "*Ocular,*" he murmured, passing his hand in front of his face. With a relieved sigh, he looked back at Calla. "Good, that worked."

She smiled. "I wish all of your lessons could be this easy."

Chapter 10: The Palace of Mim Tor

They were still miles from Mim Tor when the first homes, most of them small farmhouses, began to dot the landscape. Many of the people working on the farms stopped to watch the four riders pass. Some waved, and a few even ventured forward to engage in conversation.

Calla managed to give the impression they were simple laborers looking for work in a city with more opportunities. Gan was quickly adapting to the art of bending words to suit his meaning, but Niko and Caius found it much more difficult. When they opened their mouths to speak, likely as not, too much truth spilled out. It was decided that Calla and Gan would do the talking for the group.

Gan, on the other hand, had to improve his attitude towards the gaol. It was no secret that much of the sorcia considered the gaol inferior, and Gan had been raised to believe that. Calla had to admit, she often had a difficult time understanding the gaol, but her binding called her to protect all of Deius' creatures, and the gaol fell under her protection.

The city walls, smooth white structures some twenty feet high with watchtowers scattered along their length, loomed before them. Calla reined her stallion in. As much as she would have preferred to avoid the city, her instructions were to stop in Mim Tor before continuing to Tegoradaysol.

"From here, we must do our best to blend with the gaol," she told them. "No spellcasting, no eyeshine." Her gaze fell on her tunic, and she sighed. "And no more comfortable clothes." She waved a hand from her shoulders down to her waist. "*Apparelum*."

Her tunic and leggings were replaced by a velvet dress, the dark gray skirt full and deeply pleated. The bodice fit snugly with a modest square neckline, the long sleeves wide and flowing to her fingertips. Rising in her stirrups, she swung one leg over in a most unladylike fashion and settled herself sidesaddle with a look of disgust.

"Use your own names," she continued, choosing not to notice the way they were staring at the dress. "When role-playing, the more truth, the better. Especially for us. The people of Mim Tor know me as Lady Calla. The gaol put a great deal of stock in title and position. Darmon thought it better to give me a title, as I am often at the palace when I come to Mim Tor." She looked over at them and gave a sheepish smile. "You do not have to call me Lady Calla. In truth, I would rather you did not. Bloody nonsense, if you ask me."

Caius raised an eyebrow. "Strong talk for a lady," he noted.

She laughed. "True enough. I must be on guard as well. This is not a role I play willingly, but we do what we must. I will introduce you as my cousins to anyone who requires an introduction. Deius willing, that will not be many." Her gaze rested on them thoughtfully. "Seeing how that will make young lords of the three of you, you will need to be more suitably wardrobed."

Before any of them could voice an objection, she murmured the necessary words. The new dragonmasters found themselves staring at each other in astonishment. Niko fingered the laces of the white silk shirt he was wearing, grimacing. He had never cared much about what he wore, but this was something else altogether.

"Hang me for a fool, I cannot be seen like this!"

Caius laughed but gave his own clothes a dubious look. "Are you sure this is how lords dress?" he wondered.

Calla shrugged. "I am not a bloody tailor, Caius," she grumbled. "It will do."

Niko tugged on the fine wool coat, shaking his head. It might offer protection against the evening chill, but it was shorter than the tunic he was accustomed to, and the black trousers were snug, tucked into knee-high riding boots.

Gan regarded his deep green coat with disapproval. "If the middlings know about the sorcia, why the charade?"

"Mim Tor is the home of the king," she pointed out. "Certain formalities must be observed. Besides, we do not pretend to be goal, unlikely I could ever manage that, but even the sorcia here conform to gaol tradition."

"I know bloody little about the customs of gaol royalty."

"Then say as little as possible," she advised, "and be grateful that you are not the one in the bloody dress."

Niko stifled a laugh, knowing it was probably a hardship for Calla to be clad in such restricting clothing. Still, he had to admit, clad in the riding dress with her curls neatly arranged, she looked noble-born.

They continued riding, arriving at a long section of the road where caravans were set up.

"Refugees," Calla said in a low voice. "Try not to make eye contact."

They rode in silence past the campsites and makeshift structures, listening to the sounds of children playing, women chatting, and men grumbling.

"This situation is not ideal," Calla muttered as they passed the last of the refugees. "I wonder if Darmon has sent word of this to Master Camalaron."

"Do the sorcia and the gaol get along?" Niko wondered. In Cenna Siem, there were very few gaol, and they seemed unconcerned with being surrounded by sorcia. But Mim Tor was much larger.

"The gaol are understandably anxious about the sorcia," she explained. "For that reason, the dragonmasters put a protection spell on the city and a second on the palace itself. No magic is allowed in the city by decree, but the protection spell ensures it is followed. Any sorcerer casting inside the city wall would be hit by a counter-spell that would strip them of their magic." She gave a slight shudder. "Not a pleasant prospect. Few sorcia choose to live within the walls for obvious reasons, but a fair few have businesses and the like."

"Do they know about dragonmasters?" Caius asked.

"They know as much as most, which is very little. Only two know that I am a dragonmaster: Darmon and the Commander of the Guard, Armat. Remember, if anyone knows the prophecy, it will not take them long to deduce its meaning. It is better that few people know."

"But some people do know," Niko reminded her. "The talebearer knew... and Nefario."

"And the gnome at Festival," Caius recalled.

Calla nodded. "Perhaps the dragonmasters have not guarded the secret as well as they had hoped."

"The middlings surely do not know the prophecy," Gan said.

Calla fixed a level look on him. "We can be sure of nothing, not the way things have begun to unfold. And you had best get familiar with calling them gaol, not middlings."

Gan colored slightly, his lips pressed tightly together. Niko wondered if he was embarrassed at being reprimanded or frustrated at the idea of treating gaol as equals. Either way, it seemed a good time to change the subject.

"What about all the refugees?" he wondered. "Where do you suppose they come from?"

Calla frowned and shook her head. "I have no idea, but those we passed are gaol. It would take something severe to put them on the move this time of year. Drought... famine... war."

"War?" Caius echoed worriedly.

"As a reckoning draws near, war is inevitable," Calla sighed, looking somber. "Daiesthai feeds on war. A reckoning would likely be a feast."

Niko looked over his shoulder at the refugee camps they had left behind and felt a deep sorrow. War was coming to the realm, and with it, death and destruction. And for the moment, there was little they could do to stop it.

Another gathering of refugees was situated closer to the city's gates. A few spoke, but most just shuffled out of the way of the well-dressed riders. Calla forced herself not to look at them or show any emotion and cautioned the boys to do the same. No one would expect a noble-born to give more than a passing glance to refugees, but it was difficult. Calla was overwhelmed by the sheer numbers and the fact that many were elderly or young children clinging fearfully to their mothers' skirts.

They looked as if they had come a long distance, perhaps hoping to reach the city before winter set in. In that, they had been successful, but Calla suspected their situation was no better now. The city could not possibly accommodate so many people, and the temporary shelters outside the walls would offer little protection when winter arrived in earnest.

At the gates, they were stopped by an armored guard with a scowl etched on his face. Clearly, he had seen more than enough refugees to make him resentful, but he recognized Calla almost immediately and lowered the lance in his hand.

"Lady Calla." He made an awkward bow in his heavy metal garb, his left hand fisted to his chest. "We were told to watch for you, m'lady, but we did not expect you for several days yet. With all of these..." He cast a dark look at the refugees, then remembered himself. "...it has been necessary to hold the gate firmly, m'lady. I will see that you have an escort to the palace."

Calla hid a smile. "That will not be necessary, I assure you. My companions are quite capable."

The guard opened his mouth to object, but Calla was already nudging her mount towards the gates being opened for them. The other guards bowed their heads, fists to breastplates as they passed, and she led her charges into the city.

"I thought we could not lie," Niko grumbled in a low voice once the gates had closed behind them and they were making their way along the cobblestone path.

The road split, the left leading into the city itself, the right leading to the palace gates. Calla reined right.

"I said that you were capable," Calla threw him a grin. "I did not say of what."

Niko shook his head doubtfully, and Gan snickered.

Caius's dark eyes tried to take in everything at once. Mim Tor was more spectacular than he had been told, the palace casting a shadow in the setting sun that blanketed most of the city.

The homes and shops were not built of stone and wood as in other townships. This was a city of brick and mortar, with slate roofs and cobblestone roads. The palace rivaled Ackley's in size and surpassed it in splendor. Banners waved from the turrets, most red with a silver sun, moon, and star the Coat of Arms for the House of Mim. One or two others were unfamiliar, but one in particular caught his attention.

"I have seen that before."

Looking in the direction of his gaze, Calla nodded. The banner had a blue background with an inverted red heart clutched in the black talon of a dragon. "The dragonsheart," she told him. "The Coat of Arms of the dragonmasters. You would have seen it during your binding."

"We have a Coat of Arms?"

"Like I said, in some things, we concede to gaol traditions."

As they rode upwards, they could look back and see the city. Even Gan was awed by Mim Tor. The city was laid out in a perfect grid, every line straight and precise. The refugees outside clearly made no impact on the well-organized life within the walls.

Calla continued towards the palace. "Darmon has rooms in the palace, but his home is in Dari San. The king gave him the title of Lord and set him up as an advisor, mainly on issues regarding the sorcia." She nodded towards the massive structure. "The palace has stood for nearly three thousand years, through two reckonings that we know of."

At the palace gates, Calla was greeted with more bows and fists to chests and was ushered quickly onto the grounds. This time, she was not offered an escort so much as given one. Stable hands rushed forward to lead the hercudons through the arched opening into the courtyard, eyeing the beasts warily, and they were all assisted from their saddles. Guards not in armor stood watchfully, waiting until the mounts were led away, then dutifully led Calla and her party through the courtyard and up the wide marble steps into the palace.

They took positions at the top of the stairs, lances at the ready. Servants rushed forward to take charge of their belongings, which Gan was reluctant to hand over until Calla gave him a nod. She stood with her jaw clenched as a woman began to brush the dust and dirt from her skirts with a small, ivory-handled brush. She moved away before the woman was satisfied.

Gan and Niko had managed to evade a brushing, but Caius was not so fortunate and endured a motherly woman making 'tsk-tsk' sounds as she whisked away a layer of dirt.

Gan caught Caius's coat sleeve and pulled him away, muttering under his breath about 'bloody middling servants.'

They were then escorted by two guards and several servants into the receiving hall.

Polished marble floors glittered in the flickering light of more than three dozen candles in the chandelier high above. From one end of the room to the other, everything sparkled gold, silver, and crystal. Two more women in full-length aprons over plain linen frocks, the coat of arms embroidered on their collars, dropped deep curtsies as they faced Calla.

"Lady Calla." The older of the two said demurely. "Lord Dar-mon asked that we bring you straight away to his quarters." She gave their traveling clothes a worried look, clearly thinking that time to freshen up was in order, but she kept that to herself. "I'm Silay, m'lady," she continued. "I tended to you on your last visit."

"Yes, I remember," Calla said politely. She had never understood the gaol willingness to be subservient due to birth status, but in her experience, the staff was generally a better source of information than the nobles, and more reliable. Calla was always careful to maintain a proper but pleasant attitude towards the palace servants. Their help was invaluable, and she usually found their company more tolerable. "Much has changed since I was last here," she noted.

"Yes, m'lady. The refugees have been coming for weeks now. They make their camps outside the walls, and His Grace sends out what food he can."

This came as no surprise to Calla. She was actually quite fond of the king. He had a genuine concern for his people and was an admirable leader. Kings in the past had not always been so agreeable, and though few knew it, there had been times when the dragonmasters had been forced to take action. Subtly, but with results.

"His Grace cannot mean for them to winter in the camps."

Silay's expression sobered. "Troops have been sent to Dari San to try to reestablish the peace, m'lady, but we have had no word of their progress."

That news made Calla frown. "How many? When did they go?"

"A force, m'lady, nearly a fortnight ago now."

A thousand men and no word. Calla's mind raced. Dari San was only a two-day ride from Mim Tor, a small enough town that a force should have had no difficulty securing it, providing they were only dealing with gaol.

"What word do you hear from the refugees?"

Silay looked over at the other woman accompanying them up the stairs and grimaced. "We have heard many rumors, m'lady." She turned and led the way up a narrower flight of stairs. "Most say that sorcerers have taken control of the city."

Niko missed his footing and stumbled into Caius. The two women glanced back, but Calla continued to climb.

"There have always been sorcia in Dari San," she said calmly.

"They say these are different, m'lady. It is said that they hold the city as they hold Soronu."

At the top of the stairs, a high-ceilinged corridor led out to a terrace overlooking the mountains to the north. Perched on the stone railing, staring off as if daydreaming, was the tribunal's liaison to the king. Gan knew him on sight.

Darmon wore his silver-gray hair in a braid hanging down his back, secured with a strip of leather. He was tall, broad-shouldered, and fit for a man his age, which Calla knew to be well past the century mark.

His ruby red coat with the crest of the House of Mim on the shoulder was draped over the back of a nearby chair, his crisp white shirt tucked into loose-fitting breeches.

"I did not expect you for several days," he said in a low voice. "You made good time."

Calla stared at his back, glowering. She never liked being treated with casual indifference, and Darmon did it so well.

"Some tea for my guests," he said brusquely.

The two women curtsied hastily before leaving.

"You seem quite comfortable giving orders in the palace," Calla observed drily.

Darmon finally turned to them, smiling pleasantly. "We do what we must, eh, Calla?" His dark eyes swept over all of them, coming back to rest on her. "You look every bit a noble yourself, child. Tell me, does that dress still wear like a halter and bit on you?"

Her fingers unconsciously brushed her hip, seeking a sword that was not there.

Darmon did not miss the move, and he chuckled softly. "I see nothing has tamed that temper of yours yet."

"What is happening in Dari San?" she asked flatly.

Darmon arched a brow, a smile fixed on his still-handsome face. "No time for pleasantries, Calla? Very well. The slayers have control of Dari San." He studied her briefly. "But you already suspected this. I can see it in your eyes."

"You let the king's men march to face slayers?" she asked sharply. "Do you imagine they have any chance at all?"

"Of course not, but the king dispatched them before I got word." Darmon leaned casually against the railing. "Do not give me that look, child," he admonished her, sounding like an overly patient uncle. "I sent word to the troops to hold their positions outside the city and instructed them not to advance. They are merely an inconvenience for the moment. The slayers will not be bothered with them."

Calla looked visibly relieved.

Darmon laughed. "Fane warned me that you still carry a grudge, but you have no reason not to trust me, Calla."

Rolling her eyes, Calla seated herself on the edge of a stone terrace chair, her fingers moving to her curls before she remembered not to muss them. With a growl, she snatched her hand away. "What of Mandirube? I hear gossip that concerns me."

Caius took an unconscious step forward, and Darmon looked over at him curiously. "You are the son of Liab and Saya?"

Caius nodded.

"The township is close enough to Soronu that it is being watched, but the slayers have made no move on Mandirube as of yet."

"Have you had word from their parents?"

"Dario and Rea reached Viera So Sar last night, Karak and Soolia early this morning. He is most unhappy with you, it would seem." Darmon regarded her thoughtfully. "Whatever have you done to vex the man so?"

Calla made a harsh sound that may have been a laugh. "I was born a dragonmaster and then practically stole his only child from him!" she drawled sardonically. "I cannot imagine why he should dislike me." She waved that away with an impatient gesture. "What of Saya?"

"I expect they will arrive late tonight or in the morning," Darmon replied. "They must go around Soronu and Dari San."

Calla nodded and turned to Caius. "We can wait here until we have word from them if you like."

He gave her a grateful look, nodding. He noticed that she only inquired about Saya, not Liab, but with the bruise still on her cheek, he understood.

The two women returned with trays, one laden with an elegant silver teapot and five porcelain cups with saucers, the other bearing pastries, lemon slices, cubed sugar, and tiny pots of cream and honey. They placed the trays on the table near Calla's seat.

"Shall we pour, m'lady?" Silay asked.

"Thank you, no. I will attend to it."

The women bobbed curtsies and left without another word.

Calla returned to the matters at hand without missing a beat. "What is the purpose of holding Soronu and Dari San?"

Darmon sighed. "We do not know. They also have a strong presence in Kambor Tine."

Calla considered for a moment. "They surround Mim Tor?"

"Or Tegoradaysol."

She looked stunned. "But what would be the point? They know they cannot cross the mountains into Tegoradaysol, only a dragonmaster can open the passage and Mim Tor is under a protection spell. They cannot conjure so much as an orb here without severe consequences."

"Perhaps they do not intend to use magic. The slayers are excellent sword-wielders."

"As are the king's guard," Calla pointed out. "That would be a fight they could not be certain of. Too much of a risk to take this early. Would you not agree?"

Darmon gave that some thought, then sighed. "Well, who can know what is in the mind of a slayer?" He crossed to the table and poured himself a cup of tea, adding a dash of cream. Grinning, he looked over at the boys. "You may as well help yourselves. Calla may have told Silay that she would tend to the serving, but that means only that she will tell you to get it for yourselves."

"They are quite capable of getting it for themselves," Calla stated. "As are you."

Darmon looked amused. "You have the serving staff at the palace so confused they do not know up from down when you are here, Calla."

"You may be comfortable being waited on, but I am not! And I will not have my charges grow lazy and over-indulged." She threw them a look that told them she was not bluffing. "Help yourselves," she urged.

They did not need a second invitation.

"Lazy?" Darmon said with a laugh. "The last time you were here, you created a virtual scandal when you offered to wield with the king's guard."

"That is not what happened," she said curtly. "I walked through the practice yard, and that idiot captain tried to bully me. Said only wielders were allowed inside. But when I offered to wield, he got all red in the face and ordered me back inside."

Caius grinned and swallowed a gulp of tea. "What did you do?"

"Tangor made me come inside," she replied with a sigh of regret. "The gaol do not allow women to wield."

Gan looked surprised. "Why not?"

"I can no more explain the gaol than I can explain the Aminites," she said with a shrug. "Bloody confusing lot, the both of them." Her expression softened. "Well, not Tau," she added.

She was referring to the people of Pur Amin, who refused to use their magic for anything other than healing. They knew it was because of a law passed after the Battle at Ackley's, but they had no idea the reason for it, or how they managed to enforce it.

"You have a little time to freshen up before dinner," Darmon said casually, taking a sip from his cup.

Calla gave him a wary look. "Dinner?"

"Well, naturally, the king is expecting..."

Calla set her cup down with a clatter, her eyes wide. "Are you mad?!" she demanded, jumping to her feet. "We are supposed to be traveling to Tegoradaysol, not dining with the bloody nobles!"

Darmon held up a hand to calm her. "You were planning to remain until you had word from Saya, and you cannot decline an invitation from the king, Calla." He looked confident the matter was settled. "I have had your rooms made ready and had rooms prepared for the boys as well."

"Where?" she asked suspiciously.

"Adjoining yours, of course."

She nodded her approval but was still scowling at Darmon.

"Relax," he said soothingly. "It is not a formal dinner."

"And Gadin?"

Darmon's smile widened. "If you have the servants thinking up is down, you have the poor prince thinking day is night. That young man is quite smitten with you."

Calla looked ready to commit mayhem. "You were supposed to find him a mate, Darmon! You promised that you would!"

"I tried," he insisted, "but he is not... cooperative."

"Try harder!"

Darmon shook his head. "I could parade every woman in the realm before him, he has eyes only for you."

Gan choked on a laugh, and Calla gave him a reproachful look. "You find this amusing, do you, Gan?"

"A little," he admitted with a grin. "I am trying to imagine you with a mid..." He caught himself. "a gaol prince." He chuckled. "Princess Calla."

Niko and Caius were laughing as well, and Calla gave them each a wry look. "Very amusing," she chided. "Almost as amusing as three more goats sleeping in the goat pen tonight."

Caius winced and straightened his face, but Gan and Niko were laughing so hard they were forced to put their cups down or risk spilling the contents.

"You should go to your rooms and ready yourselves for dinner," Darmon suggested, laughing as well. "I will send Silay along for you shortly."

Grumbling about 'bloody gaol traditions' and 'self-indulgent princes,' Calla moved to the stairs, the boys hurrying after her. She seemed to know her way around the castle, turning left at the foot of the stairs, her skirts sweeping along with more energy than they should have. Her brisk pace made the household servants pause after they bowed or curtsied, watching her pass. More than once, the boys caught a whispered 'Lady Calla' in disapproving tones. They wondered if it was because of her unladylike pace, the muttering under her breath, or something else altogether.

She took several more turns, climbed more stairs, and finally came to an abrupt stop in front of an ornate door in the center of a well-lit corridor.

"I am never going to find my way out of here," Niko declared, panting slightly.

"You will be with me," Calla reminded him. "I will leave you to sort out the sleeping arrangements. The rooms on the left and the right are prepared for you, and knowing Darmon, the wardrobes will be filled with appropriate attire. Just remember" She gave them a rueful smile. "no casting. We do this the gaol way."

>

Calla had only one bit of advice for them about managing dinner. "I just watch what they do and mimic it," she confessed in a low voice as they followed Silay from their rooms. She gave her skirt a tug.

Caius eyed her curiously. "Are you certain that is how that is worn?"

Calla frowned down at the silver-blue dress. "I am not certain of anything. It was a complicated contraption to get into, but every dress in the wardrobe seemed more peculiar than the next. This one was the only one that..." Her cheeks colored slightly. "...well, looked as if it covered everything." She shrugged. "Silay helped me into it, so it must be correct."

Niko chuckled. "It certainly is... different."

The silver-blue fabric clung to her seductively, and Calla was grateful for the shift worn underneath. Satin lacings wove their way down the sleeves, leaving a bare strip of skin from her shoulders to her wrists, and another wound up the front of the bodice, tying off a bit lower than Calla would have preferred.

Gan was tugging at his velvet coat with a growl. "How do they bear wearing all this? Three layers! I am wearing three layers of clothing!" And worse, though he opted not to mention it, was the young valet who had come in to help them dress. Fortunate that he had, as none of them had the first idea what they were doing, but it had been a long time since any of them had required assistance dressing. "I am going to suffocate in all of this!"

"All of what?" Calla hissed at him crossly. "I freeze in too little clothing, and you swelter in too much!" She gave the neckline another fruitless tug in an attempt to raise it. "Do the gaol enjoy being enigmas?!"

"I think you look very nice," Niko told her. "Of course," he added with a grin, "I am not accustomed to seeing quite so much of you."

She rolled her eyes. "I am not accustomed to having quite so much of me seen," she assured him grimly.

"At least we now know why the prince is so taken with you," Gan said with a chuckle.

"That is not amusing, Gan," she scowled. "Darmon may well think the match a good one, but I do not intend to bridge that gap."

"Is that what he had in mind?"

"An idea he considered, according to Tangor. Bloody Aminites!" she grumbled, trying again to adjust the neckline. "I just know that is where Darmon acquired this ridiculous dress!"

"He cannot seriously expect you to take a gaol for a mate, even if he is a prince."

"The new bloodline," she reminded him. "The sorcia and the royal family. Darmon considers that a possibility."

"Is he so awful?" Niko wondered.

Calla considered for a moment. "No, he has a certain charm," she allowed, then shook her head. "But he is the future king. I have no wish to spend my life in a gaol court in a city where I cannot cast."

Silay reached a set of wide double doors and pushed them open, dropping into a deep curtsy. Calla muttered a hasty last-minute warning against casting and followed.

Unlike the formal dining room where the king held elaborate dinner parties, the smaller dining room was meant for more intimate meals, but Calla still found it overdone. The long table could easily seat twenty, and silver and crystal gleamed at each place setting. No less than half a dozen attendants stood ready to serve.

Darmon was already seated at the table, just to the left of the head. He stood when Calla and the boys entered, as did the two men sitting across from him. At the head of the table, a distinguished-looking man with mocha colored skin, graying hair and a warm smile motioned them forward.

Calla dropped into a curtsy, muttering "bow" out of the corner of her mouth. Gan executed an admirable bow, deep from the waist, his head lowered. Caius and Niko did their best to imitate him, but they suspected they looked awkward at best. Neither had ever had an occasion to bow until now.

"Come in, come in," the king urged them, not seeming concerned in the least with how well bows were performed.

"Your Grace," Darmon smoothly made introductions. Niko watched Gan, Caius watched Niko, and Calla murmured instructions as subtly as possible. Across from Darmon was the prince, Gadin, and at his right, an older man who looked less enthusiastic about their arrival, a scowl set on his face. The king's cousin and advisor, Thuras.

Calla was seated on Darmon's left, and Gadin sat back down, smiling across the table at her.

"You look lovely, Lady Calla. That color suits you."

Calla offered a demure smile. "Thank you, Your Highness, though I rarely find myself comfortable in the fashions of Pur Amin." She shot a meaningful sideways look at Darmon.

The tribunal member gave her a smile. "Some cultures see fit to display beauty rather than conceal it."

"Some cultures see fit to eat insects, Lord Darmon," she retorted evenly. "I would not wish to embrace that custom either."

Gadin laughed appreciatively. "I would have to agree with Lady Calla on eating insects, but I see no reason why a beautiful woman should feel the need to conceal her beauty."

Small talk ruled the first part of the meal, the servants busy filling plates and goblets, seeing to every need before it was realized. Caius and Niko watched everyone and copied their moves, as Calla had recommended, and Gan had enough experience in formal dining to manage.

Gan had been seated on Calla's left, Niko and Caius across from him. They were grateful for the food and drink to keep them busy and out of the conversation.

Lord Thuras also remained silent for most of the casual conversation, but after the dinner plates were whisked away and replaced by a decadent-looking pastry with cream, he spoke up, directing the talk to matters of state.

"How much longer do you intend the troops to hold outside of Dari San?" he asked Darmon coolly. "I cannot think they are happy with that arrangement."

"I cannot think they would be happier engaging in battle with slayers," Darmon returned.

"And why is it the dragonmasters are not intervening?" Gadin pressed.

Calla hastily shoved a large bite of pastry into her mouth to keep herself from speaking. Women were not expected to have an opinion on political matters, and if they did, they were not encouraged to voice them.

"The dragonmasters are mediators, Gadin," his father pointed out. "They will not step in until it becomes absolutely necessary."

Gadin's dark eyes rested on Darmon. "And what will it take for them to decide that it is necessary?"

"I would not presume to speak for the dragonmasters, Your Highness," Darmon said placidly. "Camalaron tells me only what he feels I need to know."

Gadin made a scoffing sound, and Calla tensed. Beside her, Gan sensed she was rapidly losing the battle to hold her tongue. "I suppose they will wait until there are slayers inside the walls of Mim Tor!"

Calla's hands closed into fists. "If you think that they are not already inside the walls, you delude yourself!" she said tightly, only reluctantly adding, "...Your Highness."

Gadin looked at her in surprise. "How could you know such a thing, Lady Calla? You have only just arrived."

Darmon laid a hand on her arm to restrain her, but Calla shook him off, meeting the prince's gaze determinedly. "Because it would be foolish not to have eyes and ears inside the city, and the slayers are not foolish!" she answered. "They will want to know everything that goes on in Mim Tor, and inside the palace as well."

The king was regarding her with quiet interest, and when Darmon made another attempt to silence her, he shook his head, leaning forward in his chair. "Let her speak, Darmon," he said in a quiet but authoritative tone. "Tell me, Calla, where would you have heard these things? Spies in the city, I concede the possibility, but within the palace?"

"This is not a topic for young women to indulge in," Thuras said sharply.

"You might be surprised to learn what young women discuss, Lord Thuras," Calla said in a polite but firm voice.

"Indeed?" King Balin lifted a brow. "Spies and slayers... and do you have battle strategies as well, Calla?"

"I am not ignorant on the subject," she assured him.

The king looked over at Darmon, who was doing an admirable job of appearing bored with the entire conversation, but the boys were not fooled.

"An interesting development, Darmon," the king said. "I had no idea women were so well versed on these matters in other cities."

"Calla more than most, I should think," Darmon said, disapproval in his tone.

Thuras looked more than disapproving. He gave Calla a hard look. "Perhaps you would enlighten us, Lady Calla, on the matter of slayers you think might be in the palace. How would you root them out?"

Calla frowned. She had never liked the king's cousin, and it was no secret that he had no fondness for her. She could not understand why King Balin had made the man an advisor. Calla did not believe the man was honest or dependable. He even looked deceitful, in her opinion, with his small, wiry frame and beady black eyes. Worse, Calla despised the condescending tone he used with her.

"First," she said pointedly, "I would be very careful who I discussed strategy with."

"Surely there is no one in this room that you cannot trust."

This time it was Gan who gave Calla a warning nudge under the table and out of sight. She nodded and sat back in her chair. "In the short time that we have been here," she went on softly, "...we have learned that you have a full force outside of Dari San, another preparing to move towards Soronu. Two of your army's commanders are at odds with one another over a girl from the kitchen, as I understand it, and many citizens are concerned that the refugee numbers will grow to present a threat." Gadin started to speak, but she did not give him the chance. "These are things I have learned without making an effort in a very short time. Imagine what I could discover if I tried."

Thuras dismissed her concerns with a wave of his hand. "The staff likely speaks more freely in front of a lady than..."

Calla slammed her hands down on the table and glowered at the king's cousin. "That might be your greatest error yet!" she snapped.

Dessert forgotten, the boys watched their counsel anxiously. Surely there was some law against glaring at an advisor to the king, and more for raising your voice to him. If Calla was aware of their concerns, she gave no indication.

"You underestimate more than half of your population, but I can assure you... the slayers do not!"

Gadin looked perplexed. "Are you saying that you believe they would use women?"

"I am telling you that they absolutely do!"

"Women!" Thuras scoffed.

Calla's laughter rang through the room. "Women that could best you, I would wager, Lord Thuras. The slayers are very well trained to wield a sword, men and women alike."

A knock at the door silenced everyone for a moment. The king motioned to the footman, who bowed and opened the door. A tall, dark-haired, and stern-looking man entered the room, clad in a charcoal gray uniform with silver trim. The coat of arms was embroidered on the right shoulder of his uniform, and the silver and red braided sword knot marked him not only as a master wielder but as the king's Commander of the Guard.

"Your Grace," he said gruffly, dropping to his left knee, his right hand on his sword hilt, his left hand fisted to his breast. He lowered his head until his chin touched his collar.

Calla's face drained of color, and she was the only one at the table not looking towards the newcomer.

"Commander Armat," King Balin regarded him. "You needed to speak with me?"

"A man has arrived at the gate, Your Grace, insisting on seeing *Lady* Calla." The emphasis he placed on her name made Calla stare hard at her plate.

"Bloody charade," she grumbled, frustrated. "...I knew this was going to happen eventually."

Darmon touched her arm. "Who knows that you are here?"

Armat's words began to register, and she frowned, looking over at Darmon. Who indeed? she wondered. No one outside of Tegoradaysol other than Darmon and Master Fane knew that Lady Calla would be at the palace.

"No one who should be looking for me," she replied in a low voice.

Darmon turned back to the commander, now back on his feet and standing stiffly.

"Who does he say that he is, Commander?"

"Master Dak, from Ackley's School, your lordship."

Calla's head jerked up, and she looked at the boys, all of them looking back in astonishment.

"That is it!" Calla declared, shoving her chair back and rising. She pointed a finger at the boys. "You three, do not budge from those chairs and do not open your mouths except to put food in them!" Turning, she jabbed a finger in Darmon's direction. "You... come with me!"

Everyone was staring at her in shock as she completely took control of the situation, no one knowing exactly what to say.

She laid a hand on Gan's shoulder. "I will be back as quickly as possible," she murmured. "Sit tight."

He nodded, watching Calla approach the commander. This turn of events had him worried, and he had no idea why. The looks on Caius and Niko's faces told him they were just as baffled.

Fighting her growing frustration, Calla stopped in front of the commander, keeping her eyes lowered. Commander Armat knew her as a dragonmaster. It was no wonder he had used her title questioningly.

Armat had given her the silver sword knot, though he had made her earn it. He was the only person aside from Darmon to know who she really was, though as Lady Calla, she had been careful to avoid him.

"Commander Armat, please allow me to explain when I return," she said somberly, making sure not to meet his gaze. Eclipsed and unable to cast to remedy that, she could not let him see her eyes.

"As you wish, Lady Calla," he said quietly. He might not understand what was happening, but he knew enough about dragonmasters to know the explanation would be interesting.

"And would you please have Master Dak brought here?"

"Yes, m'lady." There was no mistaking the mocking tone, and she winced. She had that coming, she supposed, but Darmon had plenty coming as well, and she intended to see that he got every bit of it.

Darmon followed her as she hurried out of the room. "What are you up to, Calla?"

"Up to?!" She was moving as fast as her dress would allow. "I am not up to anything! And I have no intention of discussing my plans in this den of vipers!"

Darmon looked around curiously. "You were serious about that?"

Her reply was a withering look. Servants scampered out of the way as she passed, remembering to bow or curtsy but looking indignant. Calla paid no attention, making her way out of the palace and into the courtyard.

"Where are you going?" Darmon demanded.

"Where do you think?" she shot back. "I cannot cast within the city walls!"

"What are you planning to do?"

Never slowing her pace, Calla rounded the stables. "What I should have done from the beginning! Be what I am!"

"Calla... you cannot!"

"Do not tell me what I can and cannot do, Darmon! I never liked playing this role, and I will not continue to do it. And I will not ask it of Niko, Gan, and Caius!"

Darmon reached for her arm. "You are overreacting."

Eyes narrowing, Calla jerked her arm free. "You are not talking me out of this!"

"I could make it an order," he reminded her.

Calla gave a harsh laugh. "You could," she conceded, "...but you will not."

"What makes you so certain?"

She spun to face him. "Because you know that I am right! I am a dragonmaster, not a bloody noble! With Tangor, I could manage this charade, barely. He was able to keep me from falling on my face! You are only concerned with a union between the royals and the sorcia, and I refuse to be part of that!"

Darmon looked insulted. "I never said that."

She rolled her eyes. "You never had to! Tangor saw it long ago!"

He nodded, frowning. "Very well, I had considered the possibility. Gadin is a good man, like his father. He will make a good king."

"I have no doubt he will," Calla agreed, "...but that has nothing to do with me except in regard to my vow to the gaol!"

"It could be a good match, Calla," Darmon insisted.

She stopped, folding her arms across her chest. "Do you think so, Darmon? Do you think that he will be willing to put a dragon-master on the throne beside him?"

Darmon heaved a sigh. "As you wish. Come with me."

Suspicious, Calla followed him. He went around the far end of the barn and stepped into a small shed with gardening supplies.

"Only three people know this, so I do not have to tell you to keep this a secret." He looked around warily. "This is the only place inside the walls of Mim Tor where you can use magic."

Her eyebrows shot up, and she gave the shed a doubtful look. "I thought the protection spell covered all of Mim Tor?"

"It does, with the exception of this storage building," Darmon assured her. "When Sharda put the original spell in place, he left this place exempt, just in case. Only Fane, Camalaron, and I know."

She frowned, resting her hands on her hips. "Cast a spell."

A startled look crossed his face, then he laughed. "You really are suspicious of everyone! And we thought Gan was the skeptic." She continued to regard him expectantly, and he grinned. "Very well, then. *Iridesci.*" A softly glowing orb appeared hovering between them.

Satisfied, Calla cast her own spell, replacing the dress with her leggings and tunic. Her slippers were exchanged for her soft, calf-high boots, and she stretched slightly, savoring the comfort of her own clothes. Her right hand rested on her sword hilt, then moved to the dagger sheathed at her waist. Another murmured spell, and she was looking again through bright, glowing eyes, her silver cloak settled around her shoulders.

"You intend to go through with this?"

"I do." She started to step out of the shed, then paused and smiled. "*Apparelum*." Three bundles appeared in her hands, and she handed them to Darmon. "My charges will never forgive me if I forget about them," she explained with a grin, dragging her fingers through her tousled curls.

Darmon looked at the bundles, then at her retreating back, and he sighed. Camalaron had once told him there was little to compare to the pride of a dragonmaster. He was seeing for himself exactly what that meant.

Pushing the double doors wide, Calla strode several steps into the room before dropping to one knee, her right hand on her sword hilt, her left fisted and pressed to her breast. A stunned silence fell over the room.

"Your Grace," she said respectfully, lowering her head.

The king rose slowly, looking over at Darmon, who bowed, looking grim.

"You assume the hail of a soldier," King Balin said with a glance in the commander's direction. "What is the meaning of this?"

Calla rose, her bright eyes meeting the king's gaze. "I am a dragonmaster, Your Grace; therefore, a soldier."

Gadin was staring in astonishment. "A female dragonmaster?"

"There are no female dragonmasters!" Thuras said contemptuously. "And even if there were, dragonmasters cannot lie! This woman has done nothing but lie!"

Darmon shook his head. "She never lied," he said in her defense. "She only played a role that was created for her, and she was never a willing participant." He noticed the three boys grinning from ear to ear, beaming at Calla. More than pride, he realized; this generation had an unusual and powerful bond.

"A dragonmaster," the king repeated, shaking his head in disbelief. He looked again to Armat. "You knew of this?"

Armat nodded. "I knew Calla was a dragonmaster, Your Grace. Camalaron sent her to earn her sword knot some time back, as he does with all dragonmasters when they are ready."

All eyes moved to Calla's sword and scabbard, Gadin's eyes huge in his dark face. "A master wielder?"

Armat's mouth twitched slightly, and if it had been anyone else, Calla would have sworn he was masking a smile. "She earned it, Your Highness. I do not give them easily, as His Highness is aware. I would put Calla up against my best man."

High praise coming from the Commander of the Guard, and Calla fought the urge to grin. It would not look good to be too full of herself. She suspected she was already on precarious ground.

King Balin eased himself back into his chair. "And the reason for the deception?"

"To protect Calla," Darmon replied. Calla almost envied his ability to lie with such ease. "She had to come to earn her sword knot. We had to find a way she could do so without rousing suspicion."

"I heard a rumor years ago about a female dragonmaster," Gadin said, still staring at Calla as if he expected her to suddenly grow wings and fly around the room. If not for the protection spell, Calla would have been tempted to do something at least as dramatic.

"...but they were just nonsense. Something about her turning all her classmates into sheep and being banished. But they were... you know... just nonsense."

Gadin's expression and the laughter in Niko, Gan, and Caius's eyes did nothing to improve her mood. "It was one classmate," she grumbled, "and it was a goat, not a sheep. It was barely worth noting." She looked back to the king. "I apologize, Your Grace, for my part in the deception. To say it was not my choice is not an excuse. I could have refused." Her gaze moved to Armat. "But I desperately wanted the sword knot."

Calla did not particularly care how Thuras, Gadin, or even King Balin took her admission, but she was concerned with Armat's reaction. She had the utmost respect for the commander. She faced him, her expression impassive, and he met her gaze stoically.

"And you earned it," he said flatly. "I do not understand your actions, dragonmaster, but I know you as a commander knows his soldiers, and I know that you are loyal to the palace and to the king. The rest is none of my concern."

Calla could not have been more relieved if he had beamed at her and patted her on the head. Turning back towards the table, she squared her shoulders, preparing herself for whatever came next.

"This is most unsettling," Thuras said with a frown. "Why is it the dragonmasters would not want us to know what you were?"

Darmon started to speak, but Calla waved him to silence. "As I said before, information is much too available in the palace."

The king looked thoughtful. "Surely you can trust the few of us assembled here."

"Your Grace, please do not misunderstand me. I mean no disrespect, but there are only three in this room I would trust with my secrets, and they are the three that accompanied me here."

Gadin looked shocked. "You cannot mean to say that you do not trust the king?!"

Calla managed a tight smile. "I would no more share my secrets with His Majesty than I would expect him to share his with me," she said bluntly. "It is not a matter of trust alone. It is also who needs to know." She turned to the boys, and her mouth relaxed into a genuine smile. "And on the matter of trust, I hope you know that I would never allow myself to be comfortable and forget about you." She took the bundles from Darmon and handed them to her charges.

Looking past them, her gaze fell on Dak, and her smile vanished. "Deius help me, I had forgotten about you," she grumbled in irritation.

Darmon sighed wearily. "I think it is time we were returning to our rooms," he suggested.

Calla shook her head. "Under the circumstances, it might be better if we find accommodations in the city."

"Nonsense," the king said amiably. "This has been a peculiar evening, to be sure, but dragonmasters have always been welcome at the palace."

Calla accepted the offer gratefully, took a knee asking to be excused, and ushered Dak and the three boys out of the room.

In the corridor, Calla raked her fingers through her hair, chuckling softly. "I expect Darmon will be some time trying to smooth this over. And it will only be half of what he deserves." Back in her own clothes, the charade of Lady Calla behind her, she felt more relaxed. "You can change in your rooms," she told the boys, indicating the bundles they carried.

Niko nodded enthusiastically. "Anything will be an improvement."

Calla rounded on Dak, her expression suddenly menacing. "You have some explaining to do!"

Silver cloak billowing, she strode along the shadowy corridors, attendants and servants darting out of her way with startled looks. They knew what the cloak meant. Most were too surprised to bother bowing, not that Calla took any notice.

Gan, Caius, and Niko each gave their elements master a sympathetic look as they followed. They had a feeling Master Dak was in for a severe dressing down.

>

Calla's room was spacious and well furnished, a large canopy bed occupying one end along with a massive wardrobe, a dressing table, and a washstand. At the other end, double doors opened onto a terrace, a comfortable sitting area arranged just inside. The doors stood open, letting in the night air, but the room still felt too small and too warm.

Caius suspected it had a great deal to do with his counsel, pacing furiously, her amber eyes flashing. "Aside from the fact that I specifically asked you not to come," she was saying harshly, "...you left Master Fane with who knows what sort of trouble!"

Dak sat in the high-backed chair closest to the door, trying to look contrite but failing. "I said I was sorry, Calla," he said for the fourth time.

Gan, now clad in his tunic and leggings, sat leaning casually against the arm of the chaise lounge across from Dak. Niko was on the other end, his legs stretched out. Caius sat between them, the only one who looked tense, his gaze following Calla as she stalked the room. None of them had spoken since entering after changing, not that Calla had given them a chance.

"Not that I regret the king knowing the truth, but this was not the way I intended for him to hear it!" she continued. "This is the palace of the king! You had no right to come here demanding to see me! A fine impression you made! The gaol already think the sorcia cannot behave in a civilized manner!" She paused to throw him another scathing look, her fingers fretting through her curls. "Deius help me, I am not looking forward to seeing Darmon again! He is probably taking a scourging from the king and likely planning one for me!"

"I was worried," he stated simply.

She frowned at him. "I told you not to worry! We made it here, did we not?!"

Chewing on his lower lip thoughtfully, Caius had been listening. A thought occurred to him, and he sat up straighter. "How did you keep up with us?" he wondered. "We made it here sooner than we were expected."

Calla stopped in her tracks, her fists on her hips. "Caius has a point," she realized. "How did you keep up?"

Dak shrugged. "I wanted to be here before you left for Tegora-daysol."

She shook her head. "Now you resort to dragonspeak?! I thought you disapproved of the dragonmasters' evasive answers! You should be at least four days behind us!"

"That's right," Niko put in, puzzled. "We saved time by crossing the hill lands."

"You crossed the hill lands?" Dak eyed them each in turn, clearly surprised. "That explains a lot. I thought I was the only one fool enough to risk that."

Calla's eyes widened. "You crossed Sai'al Sodonu?"

He frowned. "I would appreciate it if you would say that with a bit less amazement," he said dryly. "After all, the four of you did it."

Gan stifled a chuckle. "Master Dak, did you see anything... odd?"

"Everything in the hill lands looked odd," Dak replied. "Did you?"

Calla stepped forward. "What did you see?"

He shrugged. "Nothing worth mentioning, really. Just... illusions... but I was expecting that."

A knock at the door made Calla groan. "Now what?" she muttered, crossing to the door and throwing it open.

Prince Gadin stood in the corridor, his dark eyes regarding her uncertainly.

Calla's expression was far from welcoming, but she bowed her head and raised her left fist to her chest. "Your Highness."

He brushed past her, looking agitated. "I do not..." His gaze fell on Dak, and he broke off abruptly. The elements master regarded him questioningly, still slouched in the armchair, and Calla rolled her eyes.

"Dak, would you have Prince Gadin believe the sorcia have no manners?" she asked, giving him a hard look.

Reluctantly, Dak hauled himself to his feet and managed a less-than-convincing bow. The boys, she was relieved to see, had not required prompting and were on their feet bowing with more sincerity. Not a great deal more, but more.

Gadin seemed indifferent to all of them, his attention on Calla. "I cannot understand why you did not tell us the truth before now."

She frowned. "I was trapped by Darmon's introductions. He introduced me as Lady Calla, and Tangor went along. What was I supposed to do?"

"So you lied."

"I did not lie!" she broke in sharply.

Gadin gave a disapproving grunt. "Perhaps not directly, but you were not honest."

Calla had no argument for that and decided the wisest course was to say nothing.

Gadin folded his arms across his chest, standing more than a head taller, regarding her intently. "I do not recall that your eyes were so... bright."

"People see what they expect to see," she said evasively.

He was unconvinced but did not pursue it. "Why are you in Mim Tor?" he asked. "Darmon would not give my father a satisfactory answer."

Calla was pacing again. "Darmon is suddenly worried about saying too much?" she said crossly. "Where was that sound judgement before tonight?!"

"Dragonmasters have always been well received in Mim Tor, Calla. You had no reason to keep who you were a secret."

She raised a brow. "How many female dragonmasters have you received?"

Gadin shook his head slowly. "There..." His expression grew solemn. "...none, I suppose."

"I have the privilege of being the first," she said quietly. "And because I am, I have been... overprotected... to some degree anyway." She heaved a sigh. "As for why I am in Mim Tor, I was told to stop here on my way to Tegoradaysol. Dragonmasters have an interest in what happens here."

"So, you are a spy."

Gan bristled, getting to his feet, but Calla only laughed. "Not by choice. Master Camalaron is a man who seizes an opportunity when he sees it."

The prince finally looked over at the others. "Darmon said that they were your cousins."

"They are," Calla assured him. "Except Dak, of course. He is a teacher at Ackley's." She shot the elements master a stern look. "Or he used to be."

Dak forced a smile. "Very amusing."

Gadin dismissed Dak with a cool look. "You are here then because of Dari San?" he asked Calla.

"No," she insisted. "Until we arrived, I had no idea what was happening in Dari San. I travel to Tegoradaysol. The recent activity of the slayers is a surprise to me."

"Now that you know, what do you intend to do?"

Calla was surprised by the question. "Do? What would you have me do?"

"You are a dragonmaster," he said bluntly.

She tipped her head to one side. "A dragonmaster, yes, but I can do nothing for Dari San or any other city on my own. I suspect that Darmon has already sent word to Tegoradaysol, and Master Camalaron will decide what steps the dragonmasters take, if any."

"I thought you were protectors of the sorcia and gaol! What do you mean, if any?"

Calla struggled to maintain a tone appropriate for the heir to the throne, but it was getting difficult. Gadin may have been smitten by Lady Calla, but he seemed to have reservations about Calla the dragonmaster.

"I mean that I have been away for some time and do not know what Master Camalaron may have planned," she said tersely. "I will be certain to convey your concerns to him."

Gadin looked over at the boys. "What of these cousins? Why do they travel with you?"

She abandoned all pretense of cordiality, folding her arms across her chest and meeting his gaze defiantly. "They are none of your concern, Your Highness."

Gan cringed. Even a dragonmaster was probably not encouraged to use such a tone with the prince, he thought, and Dak looked as if the same concern was crossing his mind. He made a gesture designed to get Calla's attention.

She waved him off indignantly. "I am handling this, Dak!" she snapped.

"I do not know that handling it is the way I would put it," Niko said in a whisper meant to be heard.

"I suppose they really cannot behead her," Gan whispered back. "She is a dragonmaster, after all."

"Not the most tactful dragonmaster, to be sure, but a dragonmaster just the same."

Caius frowned at his companions. "If you two would kindly hold your tongues," he admonished them in an equally audible whisper, "I, for one, do not wish to spend my night as a goat!"

Calla gave them a quick glance, her eyes sparkling, then turned back to Gadin.

"No one is going to be beheaded," Gadin informed them frankly. His eyes swept over Calla calculatingly. "Especially not a dragonmaster, even if her tongue is as sharp as her sword blade."

Calla's brows shot up, and Dak laughed out loud.

Crossing to the door, Gadin sighed. "Good night, Calla." He did not wait to see if she would kneel or even bow her head.

When the door closed, Gan dropped back onto the chaise, laughing. "It would seem you have found the way to cool the prince's ardor!"

Calla chuckled softly. "I suppose there should be some comfort in that."

Dak rolled his eyes. "Being a woman or a dragonmaster does not hobble you as much as your tongue."

"Sharp as a sword blade!" Niko chortled, laughing so hard he toppled off the end of the chaise. Gan roared with laughter, slapping his thigh, and even Caius was having difficulty keeping a straight face.

"I am so glad that you all find this entertaining," Calla drawled, moving to the door that adjoined their rooms and opening it. "Quite frankly, I have had all the entertainment I can bear for one night, so if you three will take yourselves off, you may laugh all night if it pleases you."

Still laughing, they filed through the door.

"Do not leave the room without me and no casting," she added as she closed the door.

She turned her attention to Dak. "You need to return to Ackley's at first light, but stay on the southern road. There is a slayers camp somewhere along the road between Soronu and Mandirube." She crossed to the door Gadin had taken. "You can see that we have made it this far safely, and you can go no further with us." Opening the door, she pointed into the corridor. "The boys have the rooms to the left. I am sure they will be happy to accommodate you tonight."

He looked ready to argue, but she held up a hand to stop him and shook her head. Annoyed, he stomped out, slamming the door.

Wearily, Calla crossed to the terrace and stared out at the city. Unable to use magic in Mim Tor, she would not sleep this night. Away from Tegoradaysol, she always slept under a protection spell, but unable to cast, she would remain awake.

Besides, she told herself, she had plenty to think about. Darmon would likely want to talk in the morning, and it would not be an amiable conversation. It was just as likely that he had sent word to Master Camalaron that she had revealed herself as a dragonmaster at the palace. She did not like to think what consequences lay ahead for that decision, but she was convinced that she had done the right thing. She only hoped that she could convince the Triad of that as well.

Chapter 11: Tegoradaysol

Calla and the boys went with Dak the next morning to the stables. The dragonmaster was determined to see that Dak was on his way back to Ackley's and had him escorted to the city gates. As Calla and the boys returned to their rooms, Darmon caught up with them.

"Word has arrived from Viera So Sar," he told them. "Liab and Saya arrived safely."

Caius sighed in relief.

"Good," Calla said briskly. "We can be on our way."

"On your way?" Darmon shook his head. "The king wants to see you before you leave."

Calla gave a firm shake of her head as she started up the stairs to their rooms. "You will have to make my excuses, Darmon. The boys and I will be leaving as soon as we gather our belongings."

"Calla!" Darmon called after her. "This is not how things are done!"

"I am a dragonmaster," she replied with a dismissive wave. "Let that be your excuse for my poor manners."

They quickly collected their meager belongings and returned to the stables. Darmon was noticeably absent as they mounted fresh horses and rode out through the palace gates.

By nightfall, they had reached the foothills of the Mountains of the Condemned. On this side of Mim Tor, there were no refugees, no farms, no signs of life. Few dared to travel this close to the mountains.

Snowcapped and rugged, the mountains were far from inviting. The first signs of winter greeted them: a cold wind accompanied by small flakes of snow. Eyeing the steep, craggy slopes, the boys felt doubt begin to creep back in.

Calla moved forward confidently, her silver cloak trailing gently behind her, her hood pushed back so she could savor the feel of the snowflakes melting against her skin. Winter had always delighted her and she was going home. True, her home would be a very different place without Tangor. But she had Tau and Tiean, and she was eager to see them again.

She could sense the boys' trepidation, knowing it was likely very similar to her own the first time Tangor had brought her to the City of Dragons, sometimes called Dragon's Lair. The mountains looked daunting, almost impassable. And they nearly were… at least on foot. Even without the spells woven by the dragonmasters, the terrain was unforgiving. Dragons were the most dangerous creatures one might encounter, but they were not the only ones.

There were no roads or marked paths. The ground was steep and treacherous.

The horses began to climb, weaving their way through large rocks and past boulders big enough to fill a room. Finally, Calla pulled her stallion to a stop before a rock wall.

"Rendus," she murmured, laying a hand against the cold gray stone.

A faint rumble echoed. The ground beneath the horses quaked, and the wall shimmered. Moments later, a doorway large enough for a horse and rider opened in the stone.

"A tunnel!" Niko exclaimed in amazement.

Gan looked up at the mountains. "But I thought…"

"You never said there was a tunnel through the mountains," Caius pointed out.

"It's supposed to be a secret," she reminded them lightly. "Iridesci."

At her word, a glowing orb appeared and drifted into the opening. She motioned for them to enter.

Once they were all inside the tunnel, the doorway sealed behind them.

"Why not just materialize there?" Caius asked.

"A dematerializing and rematerializing spell is very difficult and very limiting. A sorcerer can only go short distances, and they must know exactly where they will appear. Some of the missteps have had gruesome results, or so I've been told. And it is exhausting. It takes a great deal of power to do it even once."

Gan frowned. "My father said the sorcia no longer had the ability to do that."

Calla shrugged. "Most do not. Many spells and powers were lost after the last reckoning."

"But… you can do it," Niko said, remembering their first day of sorcia class.

Calla chuckled. "Yes… but I rarely do. Only when I think I need to prove a point to my students."

Niko and Caius exchanged embarrassed grins, while Gan shook his head.

"I have no idea what that means… but… you can dematerialize?" he asked.

"Most dragonmasters are able to," Calla explained. "It can be a handy spell to know when you're trapped by a particularly stubborn dragon."

That made Caius shiver slightly. "We're not going to… you know… face any dragons, are we?"

Calla's laughter echoed off the rock walls. "Caius, you are a dragonmaster. I think it's safe to assume you will be facing dragons. But to begin, you'll only work with those we already have relationships with."

"But you mentioned… stubborn dragons," Niko pressed.

"There are some species we've never been able to manage. Most commonly the fire-breathers; crimson drakes and golden draxons. Some spiketails can be contrary, and only one in three angrondoras are ever truly managed. But they are rarely aggressive." Calla smiled reassuringly at them. "You'll find that you have a gift for this, so there's no need to worry. And the dragons settled in Tegoradaysol are all reasonably disciplined."

"Reasonably?" Gan echoed doubtfully.

"We are talking about dragons," she pointed out.

"There are no fire-breathers here, though… right?" Caius asked nervously.

Calla smiled at him. "No. Even if they were more manageable, the climate here is too cold for them. They live south of Fala Do Sol, in the Mountains of Fire."

Caius looked relieved.

The trip through the gateway into Tegoradaysol was fairly easy, though with only the glowing orb to light the way, it was impossible to know the time of day. They passed the time asking about dragons, Tegoradaysol, and more of the history of the dragonmasters. Occasionally, they stopped at places created along the passage to stretch stiff muscles, answer nature's call, and eat. Despite their weariness, they all agreed to press on rather than stop to sleep.

At last, they emerged from the mountain passageway. Morning was dawning, the ground touched here and there with lacy patches of snow. The sun was just peeking over the eastern mountains, and the clear sky overhead promised a beautiful day.

The valley stretched out before them, nestled snugly among the surrounding peaks. A lazily winding river, no more than a hundred yards at its widest, cut through the center. Majestic trees grew thick along its banks.

"Welcome to Tegoradaysol," Calla said brightly.

Gan stared in astonishment. *This* was the City of Dragons? It was barely more than a village. On the far side of the river stood several single-level stone structures with thatched roofs. A narrow stone bridge spanned the river, and a single dirt path wound its way through the small settlement.

"This is it?" Niko said, trying not to sound disappointed.

Calla chuckled. "Primitive compared to what you're used to, perhaps. But Tegoradaysol is the most self-sufficient community in the realm."

They followed the path down into the valley, the boys taking in every detail. There were no more than forty buildings, all similar in size and style, scattered randomly across the clearing. Each one was large enough to house a dozen or more people.

Clean, clear water rolled gently under the bridge as they crossed into the village, lapping at the grassy banks with a soothing sound.

After their initial surprise, the boys began to realize how beautiful and inviting the place was.

"We have the last building on the left," Calla told them. "Tau, Tiean, and Andorran are probably still asleep, but you'll meet them soon. Master Camalaron thought it best for the seven of us to share quarters, but we each have our own room."

Though it was still early, the village was already bustling with activity. At the forge, flames roared as bellows pumped, three horses waiting in the paddock to be shod. Several men stood near the livery in animated conversation, while the warm, enticing smell of fresh bread drifted from the bakery.

Calla led them toward the livery.

"Calla!" a deep voice called out. She smiled and nodded.

"Imrac."

The aged man brushed straw from his gray hair and returned her smile. "I knew you must be close. Valor has been as giddy as a young maiden."

"He arrived safely then," Calla said in relief, her gaze flicking toward the mountains beyond the valley.

Imrac took the reins as she dismounted. "You'll see him soon enough, child. Master Camalaron put out word that you were to be sent to him as soon as you arrived."

Calla nodded. "I expected he would."

The boys swung down from their saddles, and Imrac gathered their reins as well. "I'll see to your mounts," he told them. "Best you tidy up at the rain barrel."

Calla made a face, grabbing her pack as the boys did the same.

"You mind yourself, child," Imrac warned.

"I'll do my best," she replied, heading up the dirt lane with the boys at her heels.

They washed quickly, then made their way to the central building of the village. A tall, gangly man answered their knock and ushered them inside.

"Welcome back, Calla," he said stiffly.

She nodded. "Thank you, Vien."

He led them through a bare entryway into a large, high-ceilinged room. Once they were all inside, he glanced at Calla.

"The Sovereign Master will be with you shortly."

Closing the door behind him, he left the four of them alone in the room.

The room was anything but inviting. A massive stone hearth stood at one end, filled with cold ash and charred kindling. The furniture, sparse though it was, had been carved from dark wood, cumbersome and unwelcoming. Two pairs of high-backed chairs with flat seats faced each other before the hearth. Dragons were etched across the crown pieces of the backrests.

Beyond the chairs stood a huge desk with similar carvings across its front, facing the hearth. Its legs were fashioned like dragons' feet, resting heavily on the bare wooden floor. But the most impressive piece of all was the chair behind the desk. Made of the same dark wood, it was easily the size of a throne. Set into the crown of the backrest was an inlaid silver dragon, reared up on its hind legs, wings outstretched, fangs bared. A glittering ruby served as its eye.

Niko stared at it for a moment, then quickly looked away with a faint feeling of unease. His gaze shifted to Calla, standing at the window and staring out toward the mountains. She looked ready to collapse, a heavy sadness clinging to her.

Caius silently hoped the Sovereign Master would notice her exhaustion and send them on their way, leaving conversation for later.

"I suppose we'll get food and a bath soon," Gan said hopefully. "I could do with both."

"You will find life here much different from the outside," Calla said quietly. She was still gazing out the window, and the boys exchanged wary looks, uncertain whether she was speaking to them or simply thinking aloud.

"Different… how?" Gan asked.

"Just… different," she replied, dragging her fingers through her hair. "There are no schedules here. You eat when you're hungry, sleep when you're tired."

The door opened, and a young man with dark eyes and even darker hair entered the room. He looked only a few years older than Calla though Niko was quickly learning that it was difficult to guess the age of a dragonmaster.

His tunic fit him well, accentuating his build without restricting movement. Compared to their own rumpled, travel-worn clothes, his looked fresh and crisp. He wore soft-skin knee boots like Calla's, and a scabbard hung from his waist belt, its polished hilt fashioned in an elaborate design of twisting ivy.

Caius suspected most women would find him handsome, with his well-defined features and intelligent eyes, but Calla seemed indifferent to his arrival. The man gave the boys a curious once-over, then smiled reassuringly before moving to stand beside her.

"We were worried," he said quietly.

"Who is *we*, Tau?" she asked. "Tiean, perhaps. But not you. I have never known you to be a worrier."

Tau shrugged. "I have no need to worry about you, Calla. You can take care of yourself. But bringing three charges across Sai 'al Sodonu…" He shook his head, his dark hair falling over his shoulders. "…that gave me a moment's concern."

"There were slayers camped along the main road," she told him. "I did what I had to do. I suppose Andorran is prepared to lecture me."

"He has been in Kambor Tine," Tau said.

She drew a deep breath and nodded. "That is one stroke of luck."

"It is very good to have you home."

To the boys' surprise, Calla turned and allowed Tau to pull her into an embrace. She rested her head against his chest while his hand stroked her tangled curls.

"It is good to be home," she said wearily.

The door opened again. This time a much older man stepped into the room. His shoulder-length hair and neatly trimmed beard were gray, though his bright blue eyes were sharp and alert. Clearly, this was the Sovereign Master. If his quiet self-assurance and regal bearing were not proof enough, Tau's immediate bowing his head, both hands resting on the hilt of his sword left no doubt. At Tau's gentle nudge, Calla lowered her head as well.

The older man seemed not to notice as he crossed the room and laid a gnarled hand upon each of them.

"Deius protect you, children," he said in a voice surprisingly strong for one so aged.

Calla had already told the boys of the ritual, and they lowered their heads, waiting to receive the blessing. When it was done, they watched as the Sovereign Master stepped back to look them over.

"I expect this has been a trying few days for you."

The boys glanced at each other, uncertain how to respond.

"I am Camalaron, Sovereign Master," the man continued. He turned to Gan first. "And you must be Gan. Our skeptic and with no ties to Mim Tor. Still, I suspect you will learn tolerance for the gaol in time."

Then he moved to Caius. "Our logician. Caius, son of Liab, though you favor your mother with your dark hair."

Niko darted a quick look at Calla, catching her watching with keen interest. Then Camalaron stood before him.

Until that moment, Niko had believed Master Fane to be the oldest sorcerer he had ever met. But Camalaron was ancient. Deep lines etched his face, and a slight stoop bent his frame. Yet he radiated undeniable power.

"Niko, our sensitive," the Sovereign Master said warmly. "I sense you are not pleased with this gift."

Feeling the color burn in his cheeks, Niko dropped his gaze. "Well…"

Camalaron patted him on the shoulder. "Not to worry. You will soon learn to embrace your nature. It is a gift not many possess."

"Have you chosen a counsel for Gan and Caius, Master Camalaron?" Calla asked.

Camalaron looked puzzled. "They have a counsel."

Calla looked up abruptly. "But… how can… I mean…"

"You are already part of their binding, Calla," the Sovereign Master pointed out. "It would be better for you to retain that link than for us to try to reestablish it with another."

Calla opened her mouth to object, but Camalaron shook his head. "It is asking a great deal, I understand that. But I believe it is for the best. Tau, Tiean, and Andorran will assist you with their training."

Calla looked as if she disagreed entirely, but she held her tongue.

"I understand Niko also possesses a spirit stone."

Calla nodded, still looking put out.

"There have not been three in a generation, not in my lifetime. Perhaps that is a good omen." His intense gaze rested on Calla. "And on the subject of the peril stone…"

"No!" she broke in harshly.

"It is your duty, Calla."

Shaking her head adamantly, Calla stepped away from the window. "I cannot!"

"Calla," Tau said gently, putting a hand on her arm, "you know that you must."

"No." Her eyes shone brighter than usual, and Niko realized she was fighting back tears. "I cannot do this." She backed away slowly, then turned and headed for the door.

"Calla." Camalaron's voice was not loud, but it cracked like a whip, halting her in her tracks. "You have a duty, and you must fulfill it."

"I know this is difficult," Tau said, moving to stand before her. "I had to do it as well, though Madoral and I were not as close as you and Tangor."

She looked at him solemnly. "You were able to summon it then?"

He nodded.

Her gaze dropped. "I had hoped…" she whispered, shaking her head sadly.

Tau touched her cheek lightly. "I know."

With a defeated look, Calla held out her hand and closed her eyes. A pained expression crossed her face, and a single tear rolled down her cheek.

"What is she doing?" Caius whispered, edging closer to Gan and Niko.

"She is summoning a peril stone," Camalaron told them. Seeing their confusion, he smiled faintly. "A dragonmaster and his counsel share a binding to the stone. Calla can summon your stones as easily as you can. But once released as a charge, that is no longer true unless, Deius forbid, one of you were to die. Counsel and charge may then summon the other's peril stone."

Caius' dark eyes lingered on Calla. "Tangor was her counsel," he said softly, beginning to understand. "If she can summon his stone…"

Camalaron nodded. "A fact she does not wish to accept. Until now, she has been focused on getting the three of you here safely. Now… she must face her loss."

A blue stone appeared in Calla's hand amid a bright glow. As though the last of her strength had been drained, she sank to her knees, choking on a sob. Tau caught her in his arms, murmuring consolations as he eased the peril stone gently from her grasp.

"If this is so difficult, why do it?" Niko asked quietly.

"Because the circle must be closed," Camalaron explained, crossing to where Tau held Calla. Without looking up, Tau handed him the stone. The Sovereign Master carried it to his desk. "When a dragonmaster has fallen, his stone is always retrieved. It has been that way since the beginning."

Opening a drawer out of their sight, Camalaron placed the stone inside and sighed. "In the morning, it will be gone. No one knows how or where. It has just always been."

"Much of what we do is because it has always been," Calla said gruffly, pushing herself back to her feet.

Tau caught her arm. "Tradition is important." He gave her a meaningful look. "You are tired, and this has upset you."

Camalaron nodded. "Tau is right. You should go to your quarters. I will see that food and water for bathing are sent. Then you must get some much-needed rest." He stepped out from behind his desk, regarding her earnestly. "I expect you will behave more appropriately after you are rested," he added pointedly.

"Yes, Master Camalaron," she murmured.

After the Sovereign Master departed, Tau rounded on Calla with an exasperated look.

"Have you taken leave of your bloody senses!?" he demanded. "First you defy him, and then you treat him as if he were the bloody gaol! That was outrageous even for you!"

She scowled, swiping angrily at her damp cheek. "Caius, Niko, Gan… follow me."

Suddenly she was the Calla they knew again, and the three boys scrambled after her, brushing past a stunned Tau without a word.

>

In the week that followed, the boys were overwhelmed by life at Tegoradaysol. At first, they had assumed Calla was exaggerating when she told them that she and the others of the last generation were treated like children. But her words proved true. Compared to the other dragonmasters in Tegoradaysol, they *were* children.

And they soon learned what she meant when she said life in the City of Dragons was very different. Calla, the dragonmaster they had seen command power and respect behaved more like a rebellious child than a stern sorcia master. If anything, it only made her more likable.

At the moment, however, she looked anything but childlike. Sword in hand, she and Tau were sparring on the grassy banks of the Tegora Dari San, the River of Dragon's Tears, as they were told. Calla was the only one of the them to have earned her sword knot, but Tau was proving himself a worthy opponent.

"You have grown soft, teacher," he drawled as he dodged a parry, arcing his blade around to meet hers with a resounding clang.

These were no training blades, and neither of them was holding back. Despite the cool day, sweat glistened on their faces, and damp strands of hair clung to their skin.

Tiean, older than Calla by two years, and three years Tau's junior, lounged with the boys, watching the swordplay. Blond-haired and blue-eyed, Tiean's features were almost pretty, with long lashes, a wide mouth, and a sprinkling of freckles across his nose.

"Tau is a bloody fool to provoke her," he said in amusement. Sprawled beneath an enormous oak, he gave the others a knowing smile. "He's never beaten her."

Gan and Niko exchanged grins, their eyes fixed on Calla as she feinted left, spun on the ball of her foot, and brought her sword around with startling speed. Tau barely managed to swing his blade into position in time to block, and the force of the strike drove him back a step. Calla seized the opening, sliding her weapon smoothly along his and bringing the tip to rest lightly against his chest.

He raised his blade to his forehead in salute, conceding the victory.

"You still think me soft?" she teased, grinning impishly. "I wager this teacher could still teach you a thing or two."

"No doubt about that," he laughed and with a mischievous flick, swung his blade to give her a swat across the backside.

She yelped, eyes wide, and Tau wisely darted out of reach, sheathing his sword. "Your turn," he called to Tiean.

Tiean shook his head. "I think not. Not with swords."

The newlings already knew Tiean preferred a stave to a blade. His hometown of Baldar'tine hosted one of the largest jousting matches in the realm each spring, and until his calling as a dragonmaster, he had trained for the joust. He could handle a sword well enough, but his real talent lay with the stave.

Calla smiled disarmingly. "Come on, Tiean. Come wield with me."

He laughed, shaking his head harder. "I believe I'll pass."

Tau collapsed onto the grass beside him, wiping his face with his sleeve. "You should teach them your poles, Tiean."

"I might at that." Tiean gave Tau a scolding look. "And stop calling them that. They're staves, and you know it." He rested a hand on the polished blackwood staff lying beside him. "And one of them might take to it quite nicely."

Calla's charges regarded the staff doubtfully. To them, it looked like nothing more than a stick. How could it be of any use in combat?

Tau grinned. "I do believe all your newlings are skeptics, Calla," he said mockingly. "Perhaps you should show them how it's done."

Tiean rose smoothly to his feet. "Yes, Calla. We can show them."

Grabbing his stave, he tossed it toward her. Calla caught it deftly in one hand.

"I'll find something suitable," he said, scanning the branches overhead. He grasped one limb, frowned, and moved on until he found another. "This will do."

Tau unstrapped the small hatchet at his belt and lopped the branch cleanly, stripping away bark and twigs before tossing it back to Tiean.

Meanwhile, Calla tested the weight of the stave in her hands, giving it a few experimental swings. Tiean hefted his own branch, spinning it with practiced ease.

Calla gave him a hard look. "I am not one of your Baldar'tine jousters, Tiean," she reminded him.

He grinned. "You hold your own."

The two faced each other, Tiean relaxed and confident with his weapon, Calla looking as though she wondered how she had let herself be talked into this. She swiped the back of her hand across her brow, then gripped the stave with both hands, a foot of space between them.

Both dropped into ready stances feet apart, knees bent, weight balanced on the balls of their feet. Loose, yet tense.

Calla was quick. But Tiean was quicker. He blocked her strikes with casual confidence born of long practice, slipping in several sharp blows to her ribs that made her grunt aloud. The boys exchanged glances, certain their counsel would be nursing bruises before the day was through.

Caius winced as Calla took a particularly hard rap on her forearm. He wondered how long they would keep at it. As she had once told Arrio back in school, she did not wield a weapon for sport.

"When do we begin classes?" Gan asked, cringing as Calla barely dodged a blow meant for her shoulder. Her stave whipped up to meet Tiean's with a loud crack.

Leaning back on his elbows, Tau shot him a questioning look. "Classes?"

Niko and Caius both nodded, and Tau grinned. "Ah... Calla mentioned lessons, so you thought... classes. But here, you learn by doing and by living." He gestured toward Calla and Tiean. "You're learning right now. Learning that Calla is no match for Tiean with the staves."

The boys exchanged surprised looks. No classes? It sounded too good to be true.

"This looks interesting," a gruff voice declared.

Calla glanced over just as Tiean's stave cracked against her jaw. With a sharp cry, she instinctively swung back and struck him on the temple.

Caius, Niko, and Gan stared in horror, but Tau collapsed in a fit of laughter.

Gingerly testing her throbbing jaw, Calla turned a scowl on the newcomer. "You did that deliberately!"

Stepping into the clearing, the man dismissed her accusation with a look. "Do not blame me if you are so easily distracted." He laughed.

Rubbing the red welt rising on his temple, Tiean frowned. "You have an odd sense of humor, Andorran."

The newlings studied the man. Andorran the oldest of the last generation, and certainly the largest. Strength was clearly his gift. He looked as if he could toss a hercudon with ease. Standing well over six feet tall, with broad shoulders and large work-roughened hands, he radiated raw power. His coal-black hair was shaved at the sides, the rest plaited into a long braid that reached nearly to his waist. The grin he wore seemed chiseled in granite, never touching the sharp green-blue of his eyes. He looked the group over calculatingly.

"You intend to teach them the staves?" he asked.

"Why not?" Tiean shrugged. "The stave is as good a weapon as the sword when used properly."

"At knocking out a tooth, perhaps."

Calla's hand dropped to her side. In truth, she had been checking to see whether Tiean had loosened a tooth, but she had no intention of letting Andorran know that.

"Their only experience so far has been in school, with sporting rapiers," Tau explained from his place beneath the oak.

"Who is to be their counsel?" Andorran wanted to know.

"I am," Calla replied flatly, handing Tiean back his stave.

Andorran's brow rose. "All three of them?"

She nodded. Tiean spoke up. "Master Camalaron decided it would be difficult to transfer them to another counsel. He asked us to help her with their training."

"Help?" Andorran echoed, frowning. "I should think so."

"Tau and Tiean are helping," Calla informed him coolly. "Your help I do not need."

His gaze swept over her. "You say that as if you have a choice."

She folded her arms across her chest. "I have managed quite nicely, thank you. We are working on wielding… or have you improved since last I saw you wield?"

Her gaze dropped to his sword. "Decorus," she murmured, barely loud enough for anyone to hear.

Tau and Tiean howled with laughter at the sight of the large pink bow that appeared on the hilt of Andorran's sword. Tau toppled over backward, while Tiean clutched his ribs. Even the boys chuckled, though they were careful to avoid Andorran's eyes.

Andorran's expression darkened. He tore the ribbon from his blade and flung it to the ground. "It is time you were put in your place, Genesi Ney," he said ominously. His gaze raked over her. "Apparelum."

In an instant, Calla's tunic and leggings vanished, replaced by an emerald-green gown of silk and lace. The low-cut dress clung to her curves and left the newlings blushing furiously.

Calla stared at herself for only a heartbeat, then her shock melted into a smile. Tau and Tiean exchanged worried looks. They knew she was up to something.

Raising her eyes to Andorran, Calla clasped her hands demurely behind her back and stepped toward him. "Is this how you see me, Andorran?" she drawled in a husky voice.

Tau's eyebrows shot up. He started to speak, but Tiean slapped a hand over his mouth, shaking his head.

The three newlings watched wide-eyed as Calla moved closer. There was a sway in her walk that could not be explained by the clinging dress alone. Her eyes glittered with mischievous fire.

She laid a hand on his broad chest, looking up at him coquettishly. "You put me in a dress fit for a tavern wench." Slowly, her fingers trailed across his chest. His narrowed eyes never left her, his expression unreadable.

Tau's face was easy to read his jaw hung open and his eyes were huge. Tiean alternated between amazement at Calla's audacity and apprehension at Andorran's reaction.

Andorran caught her wrist in a powerful grip. "You play a dangerous game, Genesi Ney," he rumbled.

"Hardly a game, Jomm de Gola."

Tau groaned under his breath. "Stop talking, Calla."

Niko leaned toward him anxiously. "What is Jomm de Gola?" he whispered.

"It means 'Strength of the Mountains,'" Tau whispered back. "A nickname… more or less. But only Calla would have the nerve to use it."

Andorran twisted Calla's arm behind her back, pulling her against his solid frame. "You wield a woman's weapon well, Calla," he said menacingly. "I would not have thought you knew how."

"Actually," Tiean said quietly, "I'm a bit surprised myself."

Tau nodded in agreement.

"I use the weapon you gave me. You would prefer steel?" Calla asked. "I have no objection. Just return my clothes."

The dress vanished, replaced by her tunic and leggings, and Andorran released her arm. Stepping back, Calla unsheathed her sword, her eyes sharp and watchful.

Tau sat up straight, his expression grim. "This is a bad idea."

Tiean nodded. "Agreed. Do you intend to stop them?"

"Not a bloody chance," Tau said vehemently.

Steel met steel with a reverberating clang. Calla moved with agility and confidence, wielding her blade with both hands. She was a master, assured in her ability but Andorran had the advantage of sheer strength.

If the boys had thought Calla and Tau's sparring had made defense class at Ackley's look like child's play, this felt like *true combat*. There was nothing casual about the way the two wielded their weapons.

Swords whistled through the air with sharp slicing sounds, each strike ending in the crash of steel against steel. Calla moved constantly, her motions fluid, graceful. Andorran never let his eyes leave her face, watching her gaze as closely as her blade.

"I know she's good…" Caius said worriedly. "But this…"

"If this were for points, Calla would win hands down," Tau told them. "Her technique and skill are far superior to Andorran's. But his strength makes him dangerous. I won't wield with him."

"Calla would challenge Daiesthai himself if he roused her temper," Tiean grumbled, pushing himself to his feet. "We should stop this, Tau."

"And how do you propose to do that?"

"From a distance, I assure you," Tiean muttered, eyeing the duel warily.

Sweat beaded on both combatants' faces. Calla poured every ounce of strength into meeting the force of Andorran's blows, while he focused on countering her relentless advances. The five onlookers knew only her skill had kept her standing. A single slip, and she would be vulnerable.

Calla blocked a left-side parry that rattled her teeth, then jerked her sword upward with all her strength, throwing his slice off balance. In the same motion, she swung back around and nicked his forearm with her blade. The cut wasn't elegant, but it forced him back a step. The sleeve of his tunic split, crimson seeping through.

"She's drawn blood," Niko breathed.

Gan exhaled in relief. "Thank Deius."

Andorran didn't even flinch. His strength remained undiminished as he swung hard. Calla dodged easily, shifted left, and crouched with her sword raised, prepared for the blow she knew was coming. His moves were predictable, brute strength was his advantage, not skill and she knew his weaknesses as well as he knew hers.

Gan frowned. "Why do they go on? She drew first blood."

"This is not fencing, Gan," Tiean said quietly. "They duel until one yields."

Gan groaned. "And how bloody likely is that? He'll part her head from her shoulders before she yields!"

"Could you make their swords disappear?" Caius suggested.

Tiean sighed. "We could... but they'd only arm themselves again."

"And likely give us a thumping for our trouble," Tau added.

"There's that to consider," Tiean conceded.

Before they could decide what to do, the two wielders were suddenly plucked up by unseen hands and dropped unceremoniously into the icy waters of the Tegora Dari San.

"Master Camalaron," Tau muttered warningly. Though he had yet to see the Sovereign Master, he recognized his handiwork.

Niko, Gan, and Caius quickly lowered their heads, right hands resting on their sword hilts, left hands covering their right. After their first meeting with Camalaron, Tau had made certain the newlings knew the proper way to behave in his presence. Left to Calla, he had warned, they might suffer for her stubborn pride.

Coughing and sputtering, Calla and Andorran waded out of the river and back onto the bank. The others glanced at them quickly, struggling to hide their smiles. If the dunking had been intended to humble them, it had failed. Neither looked humbled. But both looked furious.

Andorran sheathed his sword and lowered his head, though his jaw clenched and unclenched furiously. Calla still held her weapon. She lowered her head as well, but her stance was defiant.

"Not a very good example to set for our newlings," Camalaron said calmly, settling onto a smooth wooden stool that seemed to appear from nowhere. Vien, his young aide, stood silently at his side.

"I did not start this," Andorran said tightly, then quickly added, "...Sovereign Master."

"You were not going to finish it either!" Calla snarled, swiping her dripping hair from her face.

To everyone's surprise, Camalaron chuckled softly. "The other five of the last generation carry a responsibility few would envy, keeping these two stubborn dragonmasters from killing each other."

Tau groaned, and Niko was tempted to join him. From what he had seen so far, that task was not unenviable... it was impossible.

Calla's head jerked up, her eyes flashing. "I have nothing to fear from him!" she snapped.

"Nor I from you!" Andorran shot back.

"That will do," Camalaron said sternly. "Another word from either of you, and I will deal with you more severely."

When neither flinched, he gave a satisfied nod. "Much better. The seven of you must learn to work together. You come from vastly different cultural, political, and social backgrounds, with a wide range of talents and abilities. You are the future, all seven of you and I dislike finding two of your number behaving like ruffians. You give a poor accounting of yourselves to the newest members of your group."

He turned to his aide. "What do you think, Vien? Have our young wielders cooled their tempers sufficiently?"

Vien regarded Calla and Andorran doubtfully. They certainly looked cold, but their tempers were another matter. Niko was almost surprised not to see steam rising from both of them.

"No?" Camalaron shrugged. "Perhaps not. It has always taken time for either of them to rein their tempers back in. The rest of you may sit. Our sword wielders will remain on their feet."

Calla shoved her sword into its sheath and folded her arms across her chest. Dripping wet, she fought against shivering, though it was little comfort that Andorran must have been just as cold.

Camalaron's gaze shifted to the newlings. "I trust you are settling in?"

"Yes, Sovereign Master," Gan replied.

"Calla is your counsel, but the others are here to assist as well. No counsel has ever held three charges at the same time, but Calla is an exceptional dragonmaster. I have no doubt she is up to the task."

If Calla was flattered, she gave no sign. Her arms folded tighter across her chest, and her jaw flexed in irritation.

"And if you have questions the four cannot answer, come to any of us. We are here to help."

Tiean looked reluctant, but Camalaron smiled at him. "I have confidence in you, Tiean. And our newlings are quick studies. It is an honor to be a dragonmaster. Rait was the first, sworn to protect the dragons from needless destruction. Only his descendants can forge the binding and make the commitment to be dragonmasters... and not all of them. Only those born with dragonsong."

The boys exchanged baffled looks.

"It is one of the gifts passed down from Rait," the Sovereign Master explained. "When a child is born destined to be a dragonmaster, a dragonsong goes out, letting the fairies know where to find them. It continues until the peril stone is delivered. The binding begins then, though most children are unaware of it. They cannot tell lies and have a strong affection for animals, but nothing that distinctly marks them. The final binding comes later, as yours did when the dragonmaster makes the decision whether or not to accept the fate he is born to."

Calla made a small murmur of protest, and Camalaron inclined his head.

"My apologies. The fate that he *or she* is born to." His eyes swept over them. "Do you have questions?"

Gan glanced at Niko and nodded. Frowning, Niko looked up at the Sovereign Master. He and Gan had spoken before about the dreams they'd had in the hill lands, and one detail still puzzled him.

"I was wondering, Master Camalaron," he said, "what it means to be tethered?"

Tau's head snapped toward him in shock. Tiean made a strangled sound.

"What do you know of tethering?" Camalaron asked quietly.

"Nothing," Niko said quickly. He wished now that Gan had asked instead. "I heard it in a dream… in the Hills of Deception."

Andorran's head shot up, his eyes narrowing. *"Sai'al Sodonu?!* You went into Sai'al Sodonu?"

Niko swallowed nervously. He did not want to be on the wrong side of Andorran. From now on, he decided, all difficult questions could be asked by Gan.

"We crossed the hill lands on our way to Mandirube," Calla said flatly.

"There is a road to Mandirube!" Andorran reminded her.

"As it happens, there was a slayers' camp on that road," Calla shot back.

"And you knew that before crossing the hill lands?!" Andorran challenged.

Calla shifted her gaze away. "No. But the point is… they were there. My decision was a sound one."

Andorran folded his arms with a scoffing sound. "Sound or not, the real reason you crossed the hill lands was to avoid Soronu! You will run from your girlhood nightmares, yet you do not hesitate to venture into the nightmares of Sai'al Sodonu!"

Calla drew herself up indignantly. "If you think..." She broke off with a gasp, staring down at herself in shock.

The dress Andorran had conjured for her earlier seemed modest compared to what she now found herself wearing. Her sword hand grasped frantically at thin air.

"What is the meaning of this?!" she demanded, stomping her slipper-clad foot angrily. The movement revealed a bare leg through the long slit of the filmy fabric, and she winced, tugging the skirt back into place.

Camalaron regarded her with interest. "I do not recall where I saw such a dress, but the young lady wearing it did not seem to have the difficulties you are having."

Calla doubted any lady had *ever* worn such an impossible garment. Blushing furiously from the tips of her ears, she hardly dared move. Worse, she could feel everyone's eyes on her, though she carefully avoided looking at anyone.

"Master Camalaron," she said in a strained voice, "…may I please have my own clothes back?"

Camalaron stood, smiling pleasantly. "You see, Calla, you can rein that temper of yours in when it suits you. As for you, Andorran," His gaze shifted to the well-muscled young man, who was very deliberately not looking at Calla. "A week on the watch should help you remember to think before you speak."

Andorran's frown made it plain he was displeased, but he nodded, avoiding the Sovereign Master's eyes. Calla was equally careful, straightening her tunic and touching her sword as if for reassurance.

Camalaron turned back to Niko. "You were asking about tethering. That is a word we do not use often, a word only a few know."

He smoothed the folds of his crisp white robe, his expression distant in thought.

"At your binding, you likely realized that your powers are closely tied to the peril stone. With it, you are bound to your counsel and granted abilities few others possess. In a sense, the peril stone is what makes you a dragonmaster. Unfortunately, this bond can leave you vulnerable to those who understand it. If your stone were to be surrendered into another's hands, someone not your counsel, who knows its power, it could be used against you. The possessor would control the power… and control the dragonmaster. That is what is known as tethering."

Calla's hand tightened on her sword hilt, and Niko knew he had not imagined her fear that night in the Hills of Deception.

"Who did you dream of that mentioned tethering?" Camalaron asked, his eyes fixed on Calla. "Did all of you dream this?"

Calla shook her head slowly. "Niko and I had a shared dream, but Gan and Caius each had their own."

The Sovereign Master had them recount their dreams Niko and Calla together telling every detail of the vision they had shared.

"You have made a powerful enemy, Genesi Ney," Camalaron said softly. "Nefario is a stygian… a being created by Daiesthai himself. The gaol call them demons, I believe."

"But Daiesthai is the destroyer. He does not create," Tiean said, looking apprehensive.

"He does not create as Deius creates, true… but he does create," Camalaron assured them. "He creates the things that destroy. The stygian, the banedars, the wraiths...all of these were made by Daiesthai."

"He was in a spectral ring," Calla recalled. "I think he was confined there."

"There are ways, Calla. For the moment, he may be trapped… but you know part of the prophecy. *The minions shall rise again, unbegotten in the land of the begotten, unman, seeking to recreate himself in the image of man.*'"

Camalaron laid a hand on her shoulder. "The spectral rings may not hold him for long. He tested you, and you stood up to him. That marks you as his enemy, and the stygian take pleasure in breaking their enemies. He will see you as a challenge now and he will be even more eager to claim you." His eyes searched her face. "We do not need a prophecy to know what will happen if you are tethered by one of Daiesthai's creatures."

Her eyes narrowed. "That will not happen."

"Deius willing, it does not." He patted her shoulder. "Let us concern ourselves with more pleasant matters, for now." Forcing a more cheerful expression, he added, "You should call Valor down. It is time for the newlings to discover the first gift of the dragonmaster."

Suspicious of his sudden change in tone, Calla gave a curt nod, bowed her head slightly in his direction, and strolled out of the clearing.

Camalaron turned back to the others, his mood sobering again. "Calla's powers are strong… very strong. Imagine that power in the hands of a stygian. He could force her to destroy every one of you, and she could do nothing to stop him. And he would do it for no other reason than to break her. You must keep a watchful eye."

"Calla is not going to appreciate that," Andorran said grimly.

"If only she were not so stubborn," Tiean sighed.

Camalaron smiled faintly. "Calla relies a great deal on her resolve… and it has served her well at times." He looked at each of them in turn, his expression thoughtful. "I sometimes worry, Vien, that I reveal too much and at other times, not enough. It is difficult to know where to draw the line."

Vien nodded slowly. "Yes, Sovereign Master. And sometimes there is not the luxury of time for leisurely lessons."

"Very true." Camalaron rubbed his jaw between forefinger and thumb. "So, I will be direct, if you will indulge me. All of you possess admirable traits meant to aid you in the days ahead some stronger than others, but that is as it should be. Andorran, you have the strength of two men, yet also courage and passion. Tiean is fervently loyal, but I do not doubt his logic or his courage. Gan, our skeptic, is nearly as tenacious as Calla and fiercely loyal. But you all have traits that can be as much vice as virtue. Calla has her temper. Andorran suffers from impatience. Tau can be… tactless."

Tau felt his face redden. How was it, he wondered, that this had begun with an argument between Andorran and Calla, and yet somehow *he* was being called tactless?

"Tiean," Camalaron continued, "you and Tau are closer to Calla than most. Would you doubt her courage, strength, or loyalty?"

Tiean shook his head vehemently. "Of course not, Master Camalaron! I would call out anyone who said such a thing!" His blue eyes shone with indignation.

"You would be calling out Calla," Camalaron told him. "She doubts her strength because she has backed down. She doubts her courage because she has run away. And she fights those doubts with the one thing that has never failed her...her temper."

Tau looked baffled. "When did Calla ever back down or run from anything?"

Niko clenched his fists tightly. "The night her parents were killed," he said quietly. "She was overwhelmed that night… and ran away. She told us that."

The others turned to stare at him, curiosity sharpening their expressions. Flushing at being the center of attention, he felt his face burn. But the Sovereign Master nodded for him to go on.

"Well… I mean… she believes that if she had acted differently, she might have saved her mother."

Camalaron inclined his head. "Niko is correct. Calla is the Genesi Ney the first of her kind, as far as we know and she is feeling her way blindly into an uncertain future. You all are. But much

responsibility has been placed on her shoulders, and she fears fail-
ure. I would not ask you to indulge her, that would be a disservice
but I ask you to understand. Her anger is sometimes a mask for
other emotions."

He smiled faintly. "Now, you should probably go and join Calla.
She will not wait patiently."

Chapter 12: Lessons

Burrowing under the heavy wool blankets, Caius heaved a weary sigh. Since their arrival in Tegoradaysol, he and Niko had chosen to share a room. Neither of them was quite ready to be alone with all the changes that had taken place, but they agreed not to tell anyone else. The last thing they wanted was to give the others something to tease them about.

Tonight was Caius' turn on the settee. The small divan was far too short for him to stretch out, though that hardly mattered; every muscle in his body ached. They had endured a particularly grueling workout with swords, followed by staves. The latter had left a nasty bruise on his collarbone.

Tiean had offered to heal it, struggling to keep a grin under control, but Caius had scowled and refused. Now, lying stiff and sore, he regretted his stubborn pride. Sometimes, he thought Calla's attitude was rubbing off on him.

"I do not believe Tau likes me much," he grumbled, flopping over in search of comfort.

From the bed, Niko chuckled. "It was an accident, Caius. I saw it… it really was."

Punching his pillow, Caius frowned and looked over at him. "It might have felt more like an accident if everyone hadn't laughed."

Niko sat up, grinning. "Sorry, Caius, but it was funny."

If he was being honest, Caius knew that had it happened to anyone else, he probably would have laughed too. And if he hadn't been so frustrated, he might have laughed at himself. As it was, he could see no humor in the incident.

Tau had apologized right away, quick to offer him a hand up. But it was hard to be gracious when his face was burning and everyone else was laughing. Well… everyone except Calla. She had been too annoyed to laugh.

"You should have let Tiean help you when he offered," Niko said, settling back against his pillow. "He really is a very good healer."

Caius rolled his eyes. "I do not want to talk about it!"

"Tiean thinks you have a gift for healing as well."

Caius sat up so suddenly he nearly toppled off the settee. "This was all Andorran's fault!" he said heatedly. "He had to make a comment about Master Dak!"

Niko thought his friend was doing a great deal of talking for someone who didn't want to talk. "That certainly got a reaction."

"It sure got Calla's attention. And then Tau had to go tripping over his own feet." Caius glanced at his aching shoulder. "You'd have thought the remark was meant for him."

"I think Calla and Master Dak might have been more than just friends back in their school days."

Caius raised a brow. "They don't seem all that friendly now."

Niko gave him a knowing look. "I think she still cares about him. But trusting him is another matter. Do you remember what she said at school that his feelings for her changed after he found out she was a dragonmaster?"

"You may be right," Caius admitted. "She must still care about him… otherwise why would she have bristled the way she did today?"

Niko scrunched his brow. "Did you notice anything odd about what Andorran said?"

"Other than the fact that it got me thumped?" Caius asked dryly, laying back down. "No, I can't say I did."

"He sounded jealous," Niko said quietly.

Slowly, Caius sat back up. "Jealous?" He stared at Niko in disbelief. "Andorran… and Calla?"

"Have you not noticed that he always gives Tau the worst possible tasks and glares at him whenever he gets too familiar with Calla?"

Caius shook his head. "No… not really. Tau and Calla, I can see. He obviously adores her. But Andorran?" He made a face. "They're positively volatile together."

Niko yawned, pulling the blankets up to his chin. "Perhaps. But Calla has strong feelings of some kind for Andorran. Women are confusing to understand. I do know she has no romantic feelings for Tau. She adores him, but more like a brother." He grimaced. "Well… that may not be the best comparison, given her brother… but you know what I mean."

"How?" Caius demanded. "How can you know these things?"

"I have no idea," Niko admitted. "I just… sense them. Gan, for example"

Caius' eyes widened. "Gan?! You don't mean to say he fancies Calla?!"

"Deius forbid!" Niko said in mock horror. "But he has developed a rather unexpected protective attitude toward her."

"I think it's not only Gan that feels that way."

"No," Niko agreed. "We all feel protective of Calla. Perhaps because of what Master Camalaron said in the clearing that day."

Whatever the reason, Caius realized Niko was right. Gan was not the only one who felt protective of Calla.

>

Gan vaulted out of bed, eyes wide. The scream that had jerked him from sleep still echoed around him and it was definitely not human.

Darting into the corridor in only his leggings, he collided with Niko, who was coming out of his room with Caius right behind him.

"What is that?!" Niko demanded, alarmed.

"No idea," Gan muttered.

Another savage scream led them down the dimly lit corridor to Calla's room. Her door stood partly open, and they could hear Tau inside.

"Are you sure you have her?"

"I have her!" Andorran sounded winded.

Peering in, the boys froze at the sight. Andorran stood in the middle of Calla's room, bare from the waist up, his powerful arms locked around a majestic-looking snow leopard. One hand clamped its muzzle shut, while bloody scratches across his chest and shoulder made clear that the struggle had been fierce.

Tau stood a safe distance away with a blanket in his hands, and Tiean hovered anxiously at the head of Calla's empty bed.

The boys gaped in astonishment. The creature was beautiful, white fur patterned with ebony markings, golden eyes burning bright. They had never even heard of a snow leopard in the realm, let alone expected to see one inside their quarters.

"Do not get too close," Tau warned grimly.

Andorran tore his gaze from the animal long enough to shoot them a pained look, but the leopard's struggles demanded his attention.

Gan's eyes darted to Calla's bed. "Where is she?"

Tiean looked pale, as if he might be sick. Tau sighed heavily. "Calla is right here."

The boys looked around in confusion. The room was far too small to conceal anyone. Like their own, it held only a narrow bed, a small settee, a bureau, a desk and chair, and a washstand with a basin and pitcher.

Caius opened his mouth to ask what Tau meant but the words died on his lips as the leopard ripped free of Andorran's grip and let out another ear-splitting scream. Everyone but Andorran clapped hands over their ears.

Before their eyes, the creature's body began to shift. Its twitching tail shrank away, paws stretched into slender fingers, fur retreating into smooth, creamy flesh. The transformation took less than two minutes and when it was done, the three newlings stood in shocked silence.

Where the leopard had been, Calla now lay in Andorran's grasp, breathing hard, groaning in pain, and as bare as the day she was born. Tau stepped forward quickly, wrapping the blanket around her, while Andorran lowered her gently onto the bed.

"Check her, Tiean."

"But you are bleed…"

"Her first," Andorran cut him off gruffly.

Casting a fretful look at the bloody gashes, Tiean turned his attention to Calla. Her breathing was still ragged, blood smeared across her mouth, chin, and hands. After a quick examination, he shook his head.

"The blood isn't hers," he reported. "…and I'd prefer not to know where it came from. She does have a few broken ribs."

"I told you, you were holding her too tightly," Tau grumbled.

Andorran shot him a dark look. "Do you want to hold her when she changes back next time?"

Tau ignored the barb, looking back at Tiean. "Seems she did some hunting."

Tiean grimaced, waving the comment away. He glanced at the newlings, who still stood frozen. "Come and help me, Caius," he urged.

Shaken from his shock, Caius stepped forward only to have Andorran catch his arm.

"No," Andorran said sharply. His expression softened as he looked at Caius. "Nothing personal. But Tiean has experience."

"And how do you expect him to get any if you never let him try?" Tiean countered, giving Andorran a look that, for him, was positively stern. "Come on, Caius."

Reluctantly, Andorran released him. With one last hesitant glance, Caius joined Tiean at Calla's side.

"You have good instincts," Tiean told him. Taking Caius' hands, he guided them under the blanket, pressing them gently against Calla's ribs. Her skin was warm and soft, and Caius felt his face heat instantly not just from touching a naked woman, though that was enough, but also because he could feel Andorran's gaze burning into him.

He wanted to learn more about healing, but with Calla as the patient, he half-feared he might soon need healing himself.

Calla groaned, and Caius instinctively tried to pull his hands away. Tiean pressed them firmly back in place.

"Sometimes healing requires a little discomfort," he said logically. "Concentrate on the injury."

Gan and Niko edged closer, still bewildered.

"She is… a shapeshifter?" Niko croaked.

Tau nodded wearily. "A *dali daub*," he clarified. "We all descend from Diate… but none of us has ever shown the ability to assimilate. Not until Calla."

Gan furrowed his brow anxiously. "Shape-shifting," he whispered, still trying to convince himself of what he had seen.

"That is why we have these quarters to ourselves, just the seven of us," Tau explained somberly. "Master Camalaron does not want the others to know she can assimilate." His eyes lingered on Calla. "It has only happened since you three received your peril stones as children."

"And she has no control over it," Tiean added. "It only happens when she sleeps."

Caius was only half listening. The fact that Calla could assimilate intrigued rather than surprised him. They were, after all, descendants of a *dali daub*. It was only natural that one of them might inherit some of the ancient skills. If she could learn to control it…

His thoughts were broken by the sudden warmth spreading beneath his hands.

Calla drew in a sharp breath, her eyes fluttering open. Tau laid a hand on her shoulder. "Be still," he cautioned.

She nodded faintly. Her thoughts were hazy, but as she looked around the room, realization began to settle in. She frowned.

"Do you remember anything?" Tau asked.

She nodded. "Some," she replied. "I was a cat this time."

"That's right," Andorran spoke up. "What else do you remember?"

Her eyes widened as she looked at him. "Andorran… you're hurt!"

"It's nothing."

Calla's frown deepened. She started to sit up, then squealed, grabbing at the blanket as her face reddened. "Forgot about that part," she muttered, wrapping it more tightly around herself and struggling into a sitting position. Tau and Tiean each offered a hand, helping her settle on the edge of the bed.

"Tiean, see to those, would you?" she said.

"Maybe now he will be more cooperative," Tiean grumbled.

Andorran's expression hardened, but he allowed Tiean to turn his attention to the bloody gashes. Within minutes, only faint traces of the wounds remained. Andorran flexed his shoulder experimentally.

"Good as new," he declared with a nod.

Calla gave him an apologetic look. "I really am sorry, Andorran... I don't..."

He waved the apology away. "No need, Calla. Just tell us what you can remember."

Calla sighed. "I... was in the mountains, I think..."

Andorran turned to the washbasin, wringing out a cloth and offering it to her. She stared at it a moment, then caught sight of her bloody hands and winced. Taking the cloth, she wiped her face and hands before handing it back.

"Now... what can you recall?" he pressed, dropping the cloth into the basin and leaning against the wall near the head of the bed.

"The mountains," she repeated. "...I was chasing something. A rabbit, I think." She made a face. "I really need to eat more at dinner. Going to bed hungry is a bad idea."

Tiean raised a hand in protest. "Please, no details. Suffice it to say you had a snack. Leave it at that, shall we?"

"But you don't remember changing?" Tau asked.

She sighed softly. "No... nothing."

"Were you dreaming?"

"Not that I can recall."

"What happened after the rabbit?" Andorran pressed.

Calla hugged the blanket tighter around herself, staring down at the floor. This ritual after each transformation was meant to jog her memory, in hopes that something might help them understand her ability to assimilate. But as usual, what she remembered were only fragments; disconnected pieces that made little sense.

She could never recall the moment of changing out of her own form. But she always remembered the return. The pain of it muscles straining, tendons stretching, her body twisted into unlikely positions until she resumed her true form. Without Tiean's healing, she could be in agony for days.

"I remember… I was tracking… something…"

Tiean looked uneasy. "Uh… what kind of something?"

"No, not like that," she assured him quickly. Tiean never had the stomach for the details of her peculiar eating habits while transformed. She didn't blame him. The first few times, when she realized what she had eaten, she had retched until nothing remained in her stomach. Even now, if she thought about it too much, she felt queasy. Over time, she had either grown accustomed to the idea… or developed a taste for it. She preferred to think it was the former.

"There was something odd," she said at last. "…I remember thinking it didn't belong." Her expression shifted to frustration. "This gets us nowhere!" she snapped. "Are you doing what I asked, Tiean?"

He frowned, shaking his head. "I cannot. I don't think…" He threw up his hands in defeat. "I don't think it's possible, Calla."

"Have you tried?"

Andorran gave her a stern look. "Calla, he cannot heal what is not an illness. You know that."

"This is a curse!" Calla declared, though in her present condition, her anger was far from intimidating. "There has to be a counter-curse!"

Tiean sat on the edge of the bed, his expression earnest. "I know that's how it must feel to you… but it is not a curse. I investigated this. It's not something I can heal any more than I can heal your being a dragonmaster. It's simply who you are."

Tears glistened in her eyes and her lower lip trembled a clear sign to Tiean that she was exhausted. He patted her hand lightly. "You should get some rest."

"What happens if I do not come back?" she whispered.

"You always do, Calla," Tau reminded her. "You were pacing outside our quarters tonight when Andorran found you."

"I think it's like a homing instinct," Tiean added. "You always come back here before you return to your true form."

Calla shook her head slowly. "I don't mean come back here. I mean… come back to *myself*."

Tau and Tiean exchanged worried looks. The boys suspected this was not the first time they had discussed the matter. But Andorran gave a firm shake of his head.

"Dali daubs always revert to their true form," he said with authority. "You have nothing to fear." He caught her chin gently in his hand. "You are the Genesi Ney. This is your true form, and you will always come back to it."

She sighed softly and nodded.

Releasing her, Andorran motioned toward the door. "We'll leave you to get some sleep."

Calla slipped wordlessly down into her bed. Within moments, she was asleep, and the others filed out quietly. Andorran eased the door closed behind them.

Gan turned on him. "Why did no one tell us about this?" he hissed angrily.

"You found out the same way we did," Tau said with a shrug. "You really have to see it to believe it."

"And Master Camalaron wants to be sure none of the others know," Tiean added. "A sorcerer with the ability to assimilate… it has been a point of great concern. No one has ever shown even a hint of the ability until Calla."

"And her ability is limited," Tau pointed out. "We cannot determine the trigger, but it always happens while she sleeps. When she is away from Tegoradaysol, she shields herself at night to prevent assimilation. Only here can she sleep without it."

"In Mim Tor, she cannot cast, so she does not sleep at all." Tiean looked miserable. "I am not sure she believes I cannot heal her of this."

"She believes you," Andorran said matter-of-factly. "She does not want to believe it cannot be healed, but she knows that if you could, you would."

"And if you could… would Master Camalaron allow it?" Caius wondered.

Tiean shook his head. "Unlikely. I chose not to tell him I was even trying to see if it was possible."

"He would like her to learn to control it," Tau said. "He believes that if she has this ability, she must be meant to use it."

"But… it cannot be good for her." Niko scrubbed his hands over his face, stifling a yawn. "She was in a great deal of pain… and she really hates having this ability."

Andorran folded his arms. "She hates anything she cannot control. The pain is an inconvenience to her. The real problem is that the ability to assimilate links her to Diate and she very much hates that idea."

"That is an understatement," Tau said with a grin.

Caius smiled faintly. "She called her Daiesthai's witch back at school."

Andorran chuckled. "One of the nicer things she has called her."

"All we can do is try to help her understand how it works," Tiean reasoned. "And get her through the transformations when they happen."

"And what about her fears of not returning to herself?" Gan asked. "Is that a real possibility?"

"I think not," Tiean replied. "Nothing I've found suggests a dali daub can be 'stuck,' as it were, in a transformation."

Gan looked relieved.

Niko closed his eyes, reaching out with his sensitivity. Calla was sleeping soundly, her pain and anxiety only faint glimmers at the edge of her mind. Curious, he brushed against Andorran's emotions and nearly staggered under the whirlwind he encountered. He pulled back quickly, opening his eyes. Andorran was watching him with a suspicious look, and Niko forced a grin. His abilities as a sensitive were growing, but for now only Caius knew. He thought it wise to keep it that way.

>

The mountains offered more classrooms than a hundred schools, and the newlings were beginning to understand what the others meant by *learning by living*. Everything around them seemed to provide a lesson, and they devoured their training hungrily.

For the most part, the dragonmasters of the last generation were left to themselves, and they were nearly always together. They came and went throughout the mountains as they pleased, ate and slept when it suited them, and paid little mind to the elder dragonmasters, who kept a discreet watch from a distance.

They had fallen into a comfortable rhythm: spells, charms, and other magical skills in the mornings; wielding practice with swords and staves after lunch; and most evenings spent in the mountains with the dragons.

The dragons of Tegoradaysol had their lairs built into the sides of the mountains surrounding the valley. By day, they could often be seen soaring in the skies or lounging by the far banks of the river. But as darkness fell, each returned to his own lair.

Valor's lair was one of the closest to the valley floor, making it more accessible than most. Tau and Tiean insisted that the spiketail was the best teacher for the newlings. Raised among dragonmasters, he understood the fumbling ways of novices. For a dragon, he was remarkably patient.

Gan, however, had a very different opinion. Caius and Niko seemed to be making progress with Valor, but Gan was struggling to get the dragon to even acknowledge his presence.

Wrapped in his cloak against the cool night air, Gan scowled toward the mouth of the den. "He is deliberately ignoring me!" he grumbled for the tenth time that evening.

"Of course he is," Tiean agreed. "Dragons are notoriously stubborn." He laid a hand on Gan's shoulder. "Valor will not listen to you until you listen to him."

"Dragons like to have the first and last word," Tau added. "Rather like women that way."

Perched on a massive stone just outside Valor's lair, Calla sat with Niko and Caius on either side of her. She pulled a face at Tau. "Gan is every bit as stubborn as Valor," she declared. "Call him again, Gan."

"I see no point!" Gan said crossly. They had been there nearly an hour, and the spiketail had shown no interest in coming out for him.

"I think Valor truly is ignoring Gan… though I cannot understand why he is being so obstinate."

"Valor is very selective," Andorran said. He was seated on another large rock opposite Calla, watching the lair's entrance. "Let her call to him, and he will trample the rest of us underfoot to get to her."

Tau chuckled. "True enough. If he were a sorcerer, or she a dragon, I think he would have her as his mate."

"I think he sees her that way regardless of species," Andorran muttered.

Calla grinned. "Jealous?" she drawled.

He rolled his eyes but stayed silent.

Calla nodded toward Caius. "You call him out."

Thinking of Andorran's warning about being trampled, Caius slid off the rock, keeping well to the side of the lair's opening. Taking a deep breath, he centered himself. Calling a dragon was not like calling a dog, it required him to reach into the peril stone he carried in a small pouch beneath his tunic, draw from it, and listen carefully.

He could hear Valor's heart beating, slow and steady, deep inside the mountain. In his mind, he called the dragon's name softly… and felt Valor stir in response.

It was not difficult. Caius could not understand why Gan struggled so much.

A moment later, Valor's head emerged from the shadows of the den. Gan's scowl deepened.

"Well done, Caius," Tau said with a smile.

"It would probably help if Gan liked him," Niko murmured, more to himself than anyone else.

Calla looked over at him, brows knitted. "What do you mean… *if he liked him*?"

"Not Valor specifically," Niko clarified quickly, regretting having spoken aloud. "Gan just… does not like dragons."

All eyes turned to Gan, and his face flushed red. "I never said I didn't like dragons," he protested defensively. "I said I didn't completely trust them."

"Deius help us," Andorran muttered, giving a slow shake of his head. "A dragonmaster who does not like dragons."

Calla dropped gracefully to the ground, her expression thoughtful as her gaze shifted from Gan to Valor. She had been so sure about Gan's ability with dragons, though she had kept her suspicions to herself. Being such a skeptic, Gan often made her task difficult but she was convinced she was right about him.

A grin spread across her face, and she motioned for him to join her. "Come on."

Gan eyed her suspiciously, but slid off the rock where he was perched, landing at her side.

"What are you up to, Calla?" Andorran asked.

"Teaching my charge," she replied, grasping Gan's hand and tugging him forward.

"Hey!" he protested, digging his heels into the rocky ground. "Where are we going?"

"Aldurus," she murmured.

Valor straightened at the word, stepping further out of his lair. A dragon saddle was already strapped to his back, and he lowered his head to regard Calla expectantly. She smiled and patted his scaled neck.

"I am no..." Gan began to object, but Calla pulled him toward the mounting ladder.

"Yes, you are," she interrupted smoothly. "On your own or with my help it makes no difference to me."

Having Calla physically place him in the saddle would be more humiliating than Gan could stand, so with great reluctance, he climbed the ladder himself and settled into the large leather saddle. Calla scrambled up nimbly, taking her seat behind him.

"Calla, you had better not get that boy hurt," Andorran called sternly.

"Hurt?" Gan echoed, just as Calla chuckled.

"Valor would never hurt you," she assured him, her hands closing lightly around his wrists. "Take the reins."

Gan gathered the reins, looping them around his gloved hands, and took a deep breath.

"It's much like reining a horse," she explained. "And Valor will respond to verbal commands as well. To get him in the air, you simply give the command: *Sor'ingol.* It means *to the air.*"

Gan swallowed hard. Sitting on the dragon's back was one thing. Flying was another. "Sor'ingol," he croaked.

Valor strode forward a few steps, extending his powerful wings. His neck arched, head rising as his wings beat with a steady, powerful sweep. Muscles rippled beneath the saddle, and Gan tightened his hold on the reins as the ground fell away. The wind ruffled his dark-blond hair and cloak as the dragon lifted them into the sky.

He was flying.

Ascending above the mountains in the pink and orange glow of sunset, perched on a dragon's back, he was *truly* flying. Valor moved with a grace and speed Gan had never imagined, banking slightly to the left.

Calla gave his wrist a gentle squeeze. "You're at the rein," she reminded him with a laugh. "Mind where you take us."

"This is fabulous!" he exclaimed.

To his surprise, Calla hugged him impulsively from behind. "I knew you were a flier!"

Gan turned Valor to the right, delighting in how easily the enormous dragon responded. "A flier?" he asked.

"A dragon flier," she told him. "Only about one in fifteen ever truly fly dragons. It takes a certain daring. Tau and Tiean will only ride as passengers and only when absolutely necessary."

"And Andorran?"

"Probably the best flier in Tegoradaysol," she replied. "He has to be, to manage a eudraco. They're the largest dragons here, difficult to fly. Master Camalaron says fliers have a brashness that goes beyond bravery. He also says we're a bit suicidal."

"I prefer not to think that true."

She rested her chin lightly on his shoulder. "Of course it isn't. Flying is dangerous, yes...dragons can be unpredictable. There are other risks: the weather, a fall, slayers, even other dragons. Actually…" she laughed softly. "I suppose that does seem like a long list. But none of it compares to the thrill of flying."

With the wind rushing past him and the ground racing far below, Gan realized she was right. The risks seemed insignificant against the exhilaration of flight.

"But why does Valor dislike me?" he asked.

"He likes you," Calla said with amusement. "You wouldn't be here otherwise. But trust is very important to dragons… especially Valor."

"What made him change his mind?"

"Valor trusts me. And he trusts the people I trust." Her hands rested gently on his waist.

Valor dipped lower, skimming across the surface of the river. Calla threw her head back, curls flying wildly in the wind. Glancing back at her, Gan chuckled. He could suddenly understand why Master Camalaron thought fliers were brash.

Then she sat up straighter, eyes narrowing as she pointed to their right.

Leaning forward, Gan followed her gaze and frowned.

"Valor, *sor'interra*," she commanded in a low voice.

"Gan, take him toward the bank but stay low. And quiet."

Gan did as she instructed, guiding Valor to the ground. They dismounted quickly, Calla sliding down the ladder first.

"Who is it?" Gan whispered.

She shrugged, motioning for Valor to wait. Moving silently toward a clump of trees a few hundred yards away, they spotted a small fire glowing beyond. Shadows flickered over three figures gathered around it.

Gan recognized the Sovereign Master immediately. The other two he knew only by sight the remaining members of the Triad Tau had told them about.

Calla slipped into the shadows, Gan close at her heels. Her eyes were bright and suspicious as she listened to the conversation drifting from the clearing beyond the trees. When Gan slid his hand into hers and tugged gently, she shook her head.

For several long minutes, they crouched in silence, straining to hear. Only when Calla finally allowed him to lead her away did they exchange grim looks, making their way back to Valor in silence.

"I suspect that information was not meant for our ears," Gan said once they were airborne again. "I hope they did not know we were there."

"You would be surprised how much I learn eavesdropping in places where I am not supposed to be," she confessed. "I have a knack for it, actually. Niko and Caius do as well. We seem to stumble into the right places at the right times."

"Should we tell the others?"

"Do you think we should?"

Gan frowned irritably. "I suppose… but…" He broke off, shaking his head.

"I know," she said softly. "But really, Gan… it is hardly our fault we are related to slayers. Of course… we will have to admit we were eavesdropping. Andorran will have something to say about that."

"I think he'll understand."

"That will not stop him from lecturing," she said flatly.

"He does get a bit overprotective."

"He likes being in charge." she grumbled.

Gan laughed, unable to help himself. "Niko is absolutely right."

"About what?" Calla asked, suspicious.

Gan shook his head, still laughing. "Never mind."

She gave him a long look, then murmured, "Sometimes, Gan, I wonder which of us is the charge, and which is the counsel."

Andorran looked extremely annoyed when Valor landed back on the ledge of his lair. Calla and Gan climbed down from the saddle, and with a muttered word from Calla, it vanished.

The spiketail rumbled softly and gave her a solemn look; she patted his side before he lumbered back into the shadowy depths of his den.

"We were getting worried," Tau said, though he did not look worried in the least.

Tiean gave Gan an appraising look. "Our newling does not look any worse for his lesson."

"There was no need to worry," Calla said with a wave of her hand. "I would not have let anything happen. Besides, he hardly needed me at all. Gan is a flier."

Andorran, Tau, and Tiean had already reached that conclusion. Gan had looked far too comfortable in the saddle when they returned. Caius and Niko, however, were visibly impressed. Having received a short lesson in dragon flight themselves, they knew exactly what it meant to be a flier.

"It's dark, Calla," Andorran said quietly. "You should not have stayed away so long. It is dangerous flying after dark… especially for a first-time flier."

To everyone's surprise, Calla simply nodded. "We lost track of time."

They started down the path leading into the valley.

"Gan and I saw the Triad," Calla said casually.

"What did they say about you flying after dark?" Andorran asked at once.

"Nothing," she assured him. "Of course, they didn't see us or they might have spoken. They were on the far side of the river. Po-lam-ti was with them."

"I thought she had been banished?"

"No one ever actually said as much. It was just a rumor… probably started by Vien."

The newlings had learned that not all the residents of Tegora-daysol were dragonmasters. Many, like Vien, were sorcia who supported them. Of the population, nearly three-quarters were not dragonmasters. They were craftsmen; blacksmiths, weavers, bakers, candlemakers; most with some tie to a dragonmaster. They were content to live in the village with their families and were steadfast in their devotion.

Yet their role went beyond simple trades. Unlike dragonmasters, they were able to lie and rumors spread easily from their tongues. The last generation often suspected that some of those untruths were supported, if not outright encouraged, by the Triad.

"Where do you suppose she was?" Tiean asked.

Calla's fingers sifted through her hair. "Probably spying."

The seven of them instinctively gathered into a circle, crouching low with arms resting on bent knees a stance that had become second nature.

"For Camalaron?"

"Or the Triad," Calla said flatly.

"Where was this?" Andorran pressed.

Calla sighed, her gaze fixed on the ground. "We landed near the blue clearing. They were gathered there."

"You were eavesdropping," Andorran said disapprovingly. "Calla."

"Are you sure you weren't seen?" Tiean interrupted anxiously.

"You know she wasn't. She never is," Tau reminded him.

"Po-lam-ti said she had come from Mim Tor," Calla continued. "She said a dragonslayer had been brought to the palace asking to see the king, and wanting to send a message here as well."

"It has been decades since the slayers reached out to Tegora-daysol," Tiean breathed softly.

"What was the message?"

"According to the slayer, all are being forced to swear an oath to Daiesthai. Those who refuse are killed outright. The one in Mim Tor died. He was nearly dead when he arrived."

Andorran frowned. "What killed him?"

She shook her head. "They don't know. Po-lam-ti suggested a curse."

Andorran's contempt rumbled deep in his chest. "How do we know this is not a trap of the slayers?"

"Po-lam-ti suggested that too," Calla said. She glanced at Gan, whose expression was as grim as her own. "If it isn't a trap, then we are not facing slayers. We are facing Daiesthai's army."

Tiean grimaced. "But… I thought the Omnipotents did not get directly involved."

"Likely he is not now," Andorran said logically. "The oath to Daiesthai is probably given through another. But the last six reckonings have been Deius' triumphs. Barely at times, but a victory is a victory."

Caius looked stunned. "Wait...are you saying the sorcia have survived the last six reckonings?"

"Yes." Tau sounded matter-of-fact. "Actually, according to history, they have survived since the creation of the dragonmasters."

Caius raked his fingers through his hair a habit he had clearly picked up from Calla. "Seven dragonmasters for a seventh reckoning," he said gravely. "Perhaps Daiesthai holds the dragonmasters responsible for his defeats."

"But… he could just eliminate us from the equation if he wanted to!" Tiean declared. "Why bother with the rest?"

"Because that is not how the game is played," Calla said quietly. "His desire is to win, and he will manipulate the game to his purpose… but he cannot just smash the pieces and be done with it."

"I agree," Andorran put in. "Daiesthai would never be allowed to destroy one of Deius' creations personally. He must use his playing pieces. Even the Omnipotents have rules."

Calla raised her eyes to the dark sky above. "I only hope Deius also plans to manipulate the game in his favor, as well."

"I think we should not count on that," Andorran said with a frown. "Did Po-lam-ti say anything else?"

Calla looked down at her hands, her body tensing.

"Lucan is in Soronu," Gan said quietly. "He heads the band of slayers holding that city."

He reached out and laid a hand on Calla's arm. "Your brother and my uncle… whatever they were, or are now… this is our family." He nodded toward the others.

She gave a small nod. "You are right."

"I think this stays between us for now," Andorran decided. "We will wait and see what Camalaron does and what he chooses to tell us."

They all nodded solemnly. Calla could almost feel the gap between themselves and the rest of the dragonmasters widening further. Rising, they continued toward the village.

But there was one thing Calla had not mentioned, something that gnawed at Gan. Perhaps she thought it unimportant, or perhaps she was simply unwilling to share. Gan, however, could not be so cavalier. Someone needed to know. But who?

The oldest of them and the unofficial head of their group, Andorran was the logical choice. Calla bristled at every attempt he made to rein her in, but she usually acknowledged his authority as leader of the seven.

Gan moved up beside the larger man, wishing he felt on more even footing. Approaching Andorran was like approaching an untamed wolf: you were never quite sure how close you could get, or how much danger you were in.

"Andorran," he called softly.

Andorran glanced over casually, then frowned when Gan motioned for him to fall back. For a moment, Gan thought he might refuse, irritation prickling at him. It was frustrating, always being the *newling*.

But Andorran slowed his pace, letting the others move ahead until he fell into step beside Gan. "There is something she did not tell us," he said flatly.

Gan blinked. "How did you know?"

"I know Calla," Andorran replied simply. "What did she leave out?"

Gan sighed, glancing toward Calla walking ahead with Tau on one side and Niko on the other. "I don't want her to feel I betrayed her."

"Did she ask you not to tell me?"

Gan shook his head.

"Then it isn't a betrayal."

Gan wasn't so sure Calla would agree, but he had already decided someone needed to know. He squared his shoulders. "The fairy told Master Camalaron that Lucan has offered a reward for Calla. She didn't say what the reward was, but she did say it was only valid if Calla was taken alive."

A muscle twitched in Andorran's jaw, and his fingers curled tightly around his sword hilt. His blue-green eyes fixed on Calla's back, gaze intense. "That can only mean he plans to tether her. He would have no use for her alive otherwise."

"But… she would never allow that to happen."

"We will see that he never gets the chance," Andorran said darkly, determination hardening his voice. His eyes never left Calla. "And this stays between us, Gan."

The younger man nodded. He had already expected as much. Still, his mind reeled as he fell a step further behind. He was grateful for the day's end, but a gnawing unease settled deep in his chest. What, he wondered, did the days ahead hold for them?

Chapter 13: Earning and Sword Knot

The rift between the last generation of dragonmasters and the others in Tegoradaysol widened with each passing day, though the seven themselves seemed unconcerned. They stayed busy from sunup to sundown often later pushing themselves relentlessly.

Camalaron kept a watchful eye from a distance, but it was becoming increasingly difficult. They seemed to know they were being observed and behaved accordingly, yet he suspected more was going on than he was allowed to see.

Niko, though diligent, had limited skill with the sword and doubted he would ever master it enough to earn his sword knot. Gan, however, was rapidly rivaling Tau in his wielding, while Niko had found his own strength in the staves, mastering them with surprising ease.

Through the winter, on the banks of the river, they wielded tirelessly until even Andorran was convinced that some were ready to test for their sword knots. Calla agreed. Niko, Caius, and Tiean would likely never be master wielders, but the other three were more than ready. Calla herself had not bested Andorran in weeks, and Gan and Tau were pushing her harder than ever.

Crouched on the riverbank, they discussed plans for their trip into the palace city. Calla was unusually quiet, listening while the others spoke. She knew it would take a week perhaps longer before Commander Armat was convinced enough of their skill to grant the silver sword knot. And she knew she could not possibly endure that long in Mim Tor without sleep.

"I suppose we should send a message to Darmon," Tau said.

Andorran nodded. "I am sure Camalaron will agree. But we still have to present this to him."

"That should not be a problem," Tiean said. Though he, Niko, and Caius would not be testing for sword knots, they looked forward to seeing their companions earn theirs. "Things have been quiet in the realm, no word of further activity from the slayers. And we always go to Mim Tor for sword knots."

A shadow crossed Andorran's face. "And the counsel always accompanies their charge."

"Not this time," Calla said softly, shaking her head. "You will have to stand for me, Andorran."

Gan's tawny eyes widened. "You must come, Calla! You're the one who trained me!"

She forced a smile. "I'll be with you in spirit, Gan. You know that. But I cannot stay a week or more in Mim Tor."

Caius thumped his palm against his forehead. "The shielding," he realized. "You cannot cast your shielding spell to sleep."

"So we stay outside the city as you did when you earned your sword knot," Andorran decided.

She arched a brow at him. "But there were no refugees outside the city then," she reminded him.

"Then we will hardly be noticed… will we?"

Calla chuckled. "I appreciate the thought…"

"No, Calla," Gan broke in determinedly. "I want you there."

She gave him a grin. "You're willing to camp with the gaol?"

"If I must, so be it."

That settled it. Together, they continued making their plans for the trip to Mim Tor.

>

Camalaron regarded the seven young dragonmasters with interest as they entered his study. They rarely came to him of their own accord, preferring to keep to themselves, so their presence intrigued him.

Vien had announced them with more than a trace of apprehension and disapproval. No one came before the Sovereign Master without summons or an appointment. Vien, always rigid about protocol, saw this as further proof that they were out of control.

He was not the only one saying such things. Many of the other dragonmasters had complained to Camalaron of the seven's aloofness and disregard for rules, insisting he do something to bring them back under his authority. Secretly, Camalaron wondered if he had ever truly held authority over them at all.

Looking across his desk, he gave them a polite smile. "What brings you to see me?"

"We want to go to Mim Tor, Master Camalaron," Andorran announced.

He and Calla sat in the two chairs nearest the desk. Tau and Tiean occupied the others, while the three boys sat cross-legged at Calla's feet.

"Mim Tor?" Camalaron echoed, puzzled. "The city is in crisis. I understand there are more than five thousand refugees gathered outside its walls."

"We want to earn our sword knots, Master Camalaron," Tau said.

The Sovereign Master looked at Andorran. "All of you?"

Andorran shook his head. "Tau, Gan, and I."

"You are certain you are ready?"

"They are, Master Camalaron," Calla assured him.

"The newling?" Camalaron asked doubtfully.

"Gan is a quick study and a powerful wielder, Sovereign Master. I am certain Commander Armat will find him worthy of the sword knot." She touched her sword hilt lightly. "I was not much older when I earned mine."

"But you studied under the Commander," Camalaron reminded her. "And it took you several months."

"It will not take long this time. I had only a little training before going to Mim Tor. Gan is already trained. A week… maybe a fortnight. Commander Armat is not easy to please. He will make them work for it… but I cannot imagine it taking longer than that."

The mention of Commander Armat always gave Gan a pang of apprehension. The man was strict, demanding, and not easily impressed. But if Calla believed him ready, he would trust her confidence. She knew the Commander better than anyone in Tegoradaysol.

With no one in the valley willing to teach the Genesi Ney, Calla had been forced to learn directly under Armat after mastering the basics. He had not been enthusiastic, he had never trained a woman to wield, but Calla had stubbornly persisted. She spent hours watching the guards, studying their techniques, learning their moves.

Tangor had taught her the fundamentals, but as only a fair wielder himself, he could offer little more than encouragement.

Calla had needed a master, and eventually, even the reluctant Commander had been forced to acknowledge her determination.

No matter how many times the Commander chased her off, Calla had always returned, defiant and determined. In the end, he had convinced himself she would either lose interest or get hurt badly enough to quit. She had surprised him.

"Perhaps in the summer," Camalaron suggested.

"The situation in Mim Tor may be less tolerable by summer," Calla countered. "The weather is holding now. This is a good time to go."

The Sovereign Master studied her in silence, wondering if there was more to their request than they admitted. It was true Mim Tor might soon become more difficult to enter. His spies had not agreed on what was happening beyond the Mountains of the Condemned.

He shifted his gaze to Gan. "Are you willing to pledge to the House of Mim? I know your father supported House Argoran."

"I am not my father, Master Camalaron," Gan said quietly.

"And you all intend to go?"

Andorran nodded. "Yes, Master Camalaron. Calla is Gan's counsel she should be there. Niko and Caius are her charges, and they should be with her."

"And I do not wish to stay here alone, Sovereign Master," Tiean added with a faint smile.

Camalaron frowned at that. He found it telling that Tiean should think of himself as *alone* when there were more than three hundred people around him. His eyes returned to Calla. "You said a week to a fortnight? That is a long time in a city where you cannot shield."

"We have considered that, Master Camalaron," Andorran replied evenly. "We have already made plans to address the problem."

Camalaron had suspected as much. He was torn between admiration and concern for their independence. Under ordinary circumstances, he would not hesitate to send a dragonmaster to Mim Tor for a sword knot. It was a tradition older than he was. But circumstances were far from ordinary and neither were these seven.

He saw only two options: grant permission, maintaining at least the appearance of authority, or refuse, and risk them defying him outright, revealing how little control he actually held.

"When would you leave?" he asked at last.

>

Andorran's steel-gray stallion led the way out of the mountain passage, Calla the last one through, sealing the opening behind her. Ahead, the city of Mim Tor glittered under a blanket of fresh snow. After months in the seclusion of the mountain village, the city's garish sprawl looked almost overwhelming, even from a distance.

"Spring is late on this side of the mountain," Tau observed, urging his strawberry roan beside Calla and her mount. "Are you sure Darmon will not tell the king we are coming?"

"I was very clear in my message," Calla replied. "I told him we had no time for the foolishness of palace summons. He was only to inform Commander Armat of our coming and our purpose."

"And Commander Armat will say nothing?"

Calla chuckled softly. "King Balin gives his Commander of the Guard a free hand. Armat has no need to report every detail. He certainly never told the king about me during all those months I trained under him."

"But Darmon did," Andorran reminded her.

"Yes. And I doubt he will be eager to repeat that mistake."

"Besides," Gan added, "you cannot even see the practice yard from the palace."

"It would be best to slip into camp late," Calla suggested. "The gaol are likely wary of the sorcia after a long winter."

"A good idea," Andorran agreed. "We should not attract too much attention. And we limit our casting no serious magic, except for Calla's shielding at night."

All nodded solemnly. None envied Calla the burden of shielding. It was a useful spell, protecting the one shielded from outside forces, but it also prevented casting from within. Some shields merely repelled magic, but stronger ones could block even physical contact. To prevent assimilation in her sleep, Calla always shielded outside Tegoradaysol.

At her insistence, the newlings had also learned shielding spells, though all hoped they would never need them. They were competent casters, but had quickly discovered that casting was not at all what they had expected. It was not as simple as wishing something into existence. Spells had consequences. A charm cast for a honey cake might seem harmless enough, but somewhere, it left someone fruitlessly searching for a missing honey cake that no longer existed.

Counter-casting, undoing a spell, was even more complicated. Often only the original caster could undo their work. Tau had explained by reminding them of the day Andorran had replaced Calla's tunic with the gown by the river. Without knowing exactly what spell he had used, Calla could not reverse it. She could conjure a fresh tunic, yes but only Andorran knew where her original clothes had gone.

The newlings had been amazed at how complex spellcasting truly was. Yet they were also discovering that, especially those with spirit stones, they possessed a gift for it. Together, they had even rediscovered spells long thought lost among them, a fusing spell.

According to legend, there were only two ways a dragonmaster could be parted from their peril stone: death, which allowed the bonded dragonmaster to summon it, or voluntary relinquishment. To anyone's knowledge, the latter had never been done.

The last generation took precautions nonetheless. They could not be sure how much of the legend was true, but the fusing spell gave them assurance that if they were ever incapacitated, no one could steal their peril stones.

By the time darkness settled, they had reached the eastern wall and could see fires glowing before the makeshift shelters of the refugees. Andorran chose a spot some distance from the sprawling camp, uneasy about having the gaol too close.

They set up camp with minimal magic: an unimpressive tent that would do little more than keep snow off their heads and shield them from prying eyes, a temporary corral for the horses, and a small cleared circle for fire. A single spell for flame, another to shield their mounts that was all Andorran would allow. They were too cold to wait for a natural blaze, and none of them wanted to see one of their horses stolen to feed starving refugees.

Once their modest camp was in place, they shared a quick meal and outlined their plans. Calla and Tau would ride into the city to meet with Darmon and arrange the testing with Commander Armat. The others would move quietly through the refugee encampment, listening, watching, and learning what they could.

Theirs was the last fire visible from the watch wall. When at last it was extinguished, they slipped into their cramped tent. Eclipsed by the dark, they had to feel their way to bedrolls, settling in as best they could. After two long days of riding, they were asleep almost at once.

\>

Perched on the top rail of the practice yard fence, Calla watched Tau and Gan wield with a look of satisfaction. Andorran had earned his sword knot several days earlier, and now the Commander was testing the other two. Calla was not concerned. That morning they had bested two of Armat's top wielders, and the Commander had seemed pleased.

Beside her, Niko sighed. "I am never going to earn a sword knot," he muttered, shaking his head. "I will never wield as they do."

Taking her eyes from the practice yard, Calla smiled at him. "Sword wielding is not your greatest strength, true, but you are formidable with the stave." She tugged playfully at his chestnut locks. "And who knows what other skills you will uncover, newling? You will surprise us all."

Niko grinned, his blue eyes bright. "You think so?"

"I am certain of it," she replied warmly.

Commander Armat's boots crunched on the snow as he crossed the yard, his gaze lingering briefly on Tau and Gan before turning to Calla. She dropped lightly to the ground, Niko landing beside her.

"You have taught your charge well," the Commander said gruffly.

High praise indeed from Armat, and Calla fought to keep her grin from widening. "Gan is a natural, Commander."

"So he is," Armat agreed. "Like you. He shares your temperament as well." His dark eyes shifted to Niko. "Andorran tells me two of your number prefer the stave, and one has yet to find his weapon of choice."

"Niko and Tiean favor the stave, that's true. As for Caius…" she smiled faintly. "…he is more healer than warrior."

Armat gave a curt nod. "Warriors are often in need of healing. It is wise to have one among you." His eyes hardened. "You take a great risk coming to Mim Tor."

"As few risks as possible, Commander," Calla assured him. "As far as most know, we are only seven more refugees. We avoid the city itself, and the refugees are too burdened with their own survival to trouble themselves with us."

Armat's scowl shifted toward the refugee camps. "They endured a harsh winter. They came ill-prepared for the lives they now lead. Some have already turned to thieving, and my men have little patience for them."

"Things will only grow worse," Calla said, dragging her fingers through her hair.

"Likely." Armat's tone was grim. "Darmon tells me a few have moved on, but most refuse. They believe themselves safer here, close to the palace."

Calla frowned. "They must know the city's protection spell does not extend beyond the walls. Surely Darmon told them that much."

Armat's scowl deepened. "No telling what he told them. The man forgets his place."

Calla chuckled. "That is what most say about me."

To Niko's surprise, genuine affection flickered in the Commander's dark eyes. "You never forgot your place, dragonmaster. You simply refused to be held to it." His gaze dropped critically to her worn tunic, and the corners of his mouth twitched. "You still do."

Turning back to Tau and Gan, still wielding though with less intensity now, he asked, "Have they bested you yet?"

"Not yet."

"But Andorran has."

Calla grimaced, looking away. "Yes," she admitted reluctantly.

"I thought as much." Armat gave her a sideways look. "Unusual for a Kamborian. They rarely take interest in the sword."

"Andorran's father is a merchant ship captain. I doubt he ever held a sword before arriving in Tegoradaysol."

"I suspect you are right. Kamborians favor daggers and cloak knives. Andorran is handy with both."

Niko noticed the faint flush creeping into Calla's cheeks and bit back a grin. Her feelings for Andorran were confusing and dangerous to tease about. He wondered whether the Commander was aware of that… or deliberately pressing her.

"Andorran is handy with many things, from what I hear," Calla said flatly.

Niko nearly choked on a laugh. The jealousy in her tone was unmistakable.

Realizing she had revealed too much, Calla drew in a deep breath, forcing her focus back to the practice yard.

Armat seemed to sense her discomfort. "Those two have earned their sword knots," he said quietly, drawing two silver cords from the pouch at his waist. "I suppose I should let them know."

Calla and Niko followed Commander Armat across the yard to where Tau and Gan were sheathing their swords. Both young men nodded respectfully, though their reactions were very different from Andorran's quiet acceptance days earlier. The two were pounding each other's backs in triumph, grinning ear to ear. Tau even caught Calla in a one-armed hug, planting a quick kiss on her cheek.

She rolled her eyes and muttered, "Bloody Aminites," under her breath, but she was smiling proudly as they fastened the silver cords to their sword hilts.

Armat returned their salutes and, with his usual briskness, excused himself. The new masters laughed and talked as the Commander strode away, their spirits soaring.

"I was certain he would make us wait a few more days," Tau said, grinning from ear to ear.

Calla shook her head. "Not after this morning. I told you he was impressed." She beamed at Gan. "I am not so sure I'll be willing to wield with you in the future, newling."

Gan's face reddened at the praise, though his grin was irrepressible. "I'm not a bloody Aminite, but…" Leaning forward, he kissed Calla on her other cheek. She gave him a firm pat, eyes bright with pride.

They left the practice yard together, laughter still bubbling among them until Calla spotted two figures approaching. Her smile vanished. A low, displeased sound rumbled in her throat.

"He really *does* forget his place," she muttered. Dropping to one knee, she lowered her head, left fist pressed to her chest, right hand on her sword hilt. The others followed suit, heedless of the snow.

"Rise," Prince Gadin muttered, his tone edged with annoyance. His eyes fixed on Calla. "I did not expect to see you in Mim Tor."

She grinned wryly. "Nor I you, Your Highness." Her gaze darted to Darmon. "And certainly, I was not supposed to."

Darmon bristled. "I did not tell him you were here!"

"He did not," Gadin admitted. "But with all his comings and goings, I suspected he was up to something."

Gan and Niko flanked Calla, Tau close at her back, all of them watching warily.

"I was hoping to speak with Andorran," Darmon said, scanning the practice ground.

"He is not with us." Calla folded her arms. "What do you wish to speak with him about?"

The Tribunal Master frowned. "When will he be coming into the city again?"

"He will not be," Calla answered flatly. "Tau and Gan have been awarded their sword knots. We leave in the morning."

Gadin's eyes narrowed in surprise. "This boy has earned a sword knot?"

Amber eyes flashing, Calla glared at him. Prince or not, she did not appreciate the dismissal. At fifteen, Gan was no longer a boy. "That is the problem with the gaol," she snapped. "You always underestimate half your population!"

Gadin began to retort but stopped himself, shaking his head slowly instead.

"Where are you staying? Darmon tells me you've been here nearly a fortnight."

"We are camped outside the walls," Calla replied.

The prince looked horrified. "With the refugees?!" He turned to Darmon. "You knew this?!"

Darmon's expression soured. "I tried to talk them out of it, Your Highness. But one only gets so far reasoning with dragonmasters."

Calla ignored the barb. "Whatever you wished to discuss with Andorran, you may tell us."

Darmon hesitated. "It was a matter he and I had already been discussing."

Calla stiffened. Niko saw the flash of anger in her eyes; anger she barely contained. Andorran had not mentioned speaking with Darmon at all.

"You can tell us," Tau said calmly. "We do not keep secrets from one another."

"We are not supposed to, anyway," Calla added pointedly. Niko exchanged a glance with Gan; neither missed the storm beneath her voice.

"Well…" Darmon began uneasily, "it was something Camalaron and I had considered. A man here in the city is in danger. We thought he might be safer in Tegoradaysol. Since you are returning, it makes sense for him to accompany you.”

“You want us to take someone to Tegoradaysol?!” Gan asked incredulously.

Calla’s eyes narrowed. “Andorran agreed to this?”

“He did not disagree,” Darmon said quickly.

Calla laughed harshly. “You should know by now, Darmon Andorran’s silence is as good as refusal. He would never consent without consulting the rest of us.”

Darmon scowled. “I do not see the problem. Camalaron thought it a logical solution.”

“Then let him escort the man himself,” Calla shot back.

Tau tilted his head. “Who is it you wish us to take?”

Darmon’s gaze shifted uneasily. “Just a refugee. A man who came to Mim Tor some months ago.”

Calla’s eyes widened. “You are talking about that dragon-slayer!” she accused.

“Not so loud,” Darmon hissed, glancing nervously around. “That is not a word to shout these days.”

Her glare was withering, fists on her hips. Gadin wisely stepped aside, leaving Darmon to bear the brunt of her fury.

“If Andorran even considers such a notion, I will..”

“I thought that man was dead,” Tau interrupted hastily, sparing them from hearing what Calla would do to Andorran.

“That is what Po-lam-ti said,” Gan added grimly.

Darmon's eyes flickered with surprise. "You spoke to Po-lam-ti?"

"You and Camalaron are not the only ones with spies," Calla retorted coldly. "So his death was a ruse?"

Darmon glanced about uneasily. "Yes. It was."

"And you would ask us to take him to Tegoradaysol?"

Tau laid a restraining hand on Calla's shoulder. "Relax, Calla," he said soothingly.

She shot him a fiery look over her shoulder. "I will not take a dragonslayer into Tegoradaysol!"

Niko and Gan both nodded in agreement. The last place a dragonslayer belonged was in their mountain sanctuary, and they did not blame Calla for her indignation.

"Calla, the man is quite ill," Darmon explained. "He will not cause trouble. And he may die if we do not get him somewhere safe."

Her expression did not soften. "That is not my concern."

Prince Gadin stepped forward. "I have seen this man myself, Calla. Whatever he once was, he is no threat now."

"We have kept him hidden and spread the story of his death," Darmon pressed. "But his life is in danger here."

Gan thought the man would be in just as much danger with Calla, judging by the murderous look on her face. She spun on her heel and stomped out of the practice yard, muttering furiously under her breath.

"We are not equipped to deal with prisoners," Tau said, watching her go.

"He is not a prisoner," Darmon replied wearily. He had already fought this argument with Andorran. Camalaron himself had warned him the seven dragonmasters rarely did anything they did not wish to do.

"Maybe he should be," Gan suggested. He pressed his left fist to his chest and nodded at Gadin. "If you'll excuse me, Your Highness, I should go after Calla." Without waiting, he trotted out.

Tau sighed and glanced at Niko. "How angry is she?"

"Very," Niko answered grimly. "She's gone to find Andorran."

Tau brushed his dark hair out of his face. "We should probably be there."

"I suppose," Niko said reluctantly.

Darmon frowned. "Do not make a decision until you've seen the man. Promise me at least that much."

The two exchanged doubtful looks. "We can suggest it," Tau allowed. "That's about all we can promise."

It was better than nothing. As he watched them leave, Darmon sighed. These seven would not be led into the reckoning as he and Camalaron had once hoped. They fully intended to lead.

>

Calla was pacing furiously at the campsite when Tau and Niko arrived. Gan crouched silently at the fire ring, watching her prowl back and forth. They squatted down beside him.

"I take it they've not returned yet," Tau murmured.

Gan shook his head. "Thank Deius. Maybe she'll cool off before they do."

Niko doubted that. Her anger was blazing too brightly for him to risk probing her thoughts since she often sensed when he did, and this was not the time to test her temper.

"Darmon wants us to see the man before deciding," Tau reported.

Gan scowled. "I don't see the point."

"If Master Camalaron supports it, he must have a reason," Niko said cautiously.

Gan rounded on him. "Camalaron hasn't seen the man. He's taking Darmon at his word and I wouldn't trust Darmon as far as I could throw him!"

"You really are a skeptic, Gan," Niko sighed.

Gan's tawny eyes narrowed. "Not the only one." He jerked his chin toward Calla.

She had stopped pacing, standing rigid with her hands on her hips, glaring toward the refugee camp. Caius spotted her from a distance and felt the waves of her anger even before seeing her face.

"Uh oh," Tiean murmured. "One of us is in trouble."

Andorran had no doubt who. Calla looked angrier than he had seen her in some time. The explanation was obvious: she had spoken to Darmon.

To her credit, she waited until they were all gathered around the fire before speaking. Her voice was taut, though level. "Tell me you are not considering Darmon's request."

Andorran removed his gloves, tucking them into his sword belt. "Request?" he echoed. "I didn't get the impression it was a request."

"He is a dragonslayer!" she burst out. "How can they even ask this of us?!"

Andorran rested his arms on his knees. "Darmon is not a dragonmaster. He does not see this as we do."

"And Camalaron?" she demanded.

He shook his head slowly. "I don't understand his purpose…but it is safe to assume he has one."

Calla clenched her fists. "Then he should have told us! I do not like this, Andorran. Why do they keep secrets from us, spy on us, feed us half-truths? How are we supposed to trust them when clearly they do not trust us?"

"We don't need them to trust us, Calla," Andorran said quietly. "We only need to trust each other."

"You didn't tell us Darmon spoke of this with you," she reminded him sharply.

"You had other things to focus on." His eyes flicked toward Gan and Tau. "They needed to earn their sword knots. You needed to be there to support them. I meant to tell you as soon as that was accomplished." His blue-green eyes locked on hers. "Do you trust me, Calla?"

Her fists relaxed. She nodded. "I trust you."

"Then we go see this man ourselves and decide," Andorran declared. "Without Darmon."

"Can we?" Tau asked skeptically.

Caius grinned. "Not a problem. We've just been there."

"I thought this man's whereabouts were supposed to be a secret," Gan muttered.

"Try keeping a secret from one of our eavesdroppers," Tiean chuckled. "Caius is every bit as good as Calla though it does prick his conscience."

Caius blushed faintly. "I overheard talk of a sick refugee in quarantine. I mentioned it to Andorran, and he told us about Darmon's plan. We thought it might be the same man."

"Better for us, actually." Andorran rose to his feet. "We can cast if we need to."

Calla scrubbed her hands over her face. "It is madness to even consider taking a dragonslayer into the village. And what about the story of the pact? Is that true? Shouldn't he be dead if he broke it?"

"I'd like to find out more about that," Andorran replied. "I think we should go tonight, after dark."

"I agree," Tau said at once.

Calla shook her head firmly. "I don't care if he's half-dead...he is still a dragonslayer."

"And what we know of dragonslayers now tells us not to trust them," Gan added grimly.

Tiean sighed wearily. "I thought we agreed we'd cooperate with the Triad as much as possible."

"Cooperate, yes," Calla said sharply. "That does not mean I intend to bare my throat and let it be slit at their request."

Niko gave her a small grin. "I don't think it will come to that. And once we reach Tegoradaysol, he'll be Master Camalaron's problem."

"I'm not sure that makes me feel any better," Calla muttered.

"We vote," Andorran said. "I say, unless we see an obvious threat, we take him."

Tau, Caius, Tiean, and Niko quickly voiced their agreement. Calla and Gan exchanged grim looks. Outnumbered, they refused to vote in favor.

"If this man gets us killed someday," Calla said dryly, "I'll be glad I voted against it."

Tau laughed. "If that happens, I'm sure you'll remind us."

"So…who goes tonight?" Tiean asked. "We can't all go."

"It should be Calla and Andorran," Niko suggested. "One from each side of the vote."

"Not to mention the strongest of us," Tau agreed.

Calla rested her chin in her hands, frowning into the fire. What was supposed to be a straightforward trip to Mim Tor for sword knots had just grown far more complicated.

>

The refugee camp was chaos. Filth littered the ground, the air stank, and Calla wrinkled her nose in disgust.

Pulling her hood lower to shadow her face, she groaned. "How long can people live like this?"

"They don't really have a choice, do they?" Andorran said.

She shrugged. "Perhaps not. But I should think life in Dari San would be better than this."

From what they'd heard, the slayers held the city but with little real force. Their presence alone kept most people subdued. For now, Dari San was little more than a place to hole up.

"These people are starving and freezing," Calla said solemnly. "And there's little the king can do. Let them inside the walls, and they'll overrun the city."

Andorran shot her a warning look. "Don't get ideas, Calla. We're not here to help the refugees."

"I know," she grumbled. But she did not have to like it.

"That's the tent," Andorran said at last, nodding toward a shabby shelter.

Calla blinked. "One guard?"

"Darmon's spell is on it. Not very strong, but I don't know the counter."

Closing her eyes briefly, Calla reached out, feeling the faint tingle of the barrier even from several yards away. The guard, one of Darmon's, she was sure, watched them narrowly. Andorran took her hand, and together they strolled past, feigning the easy closeness of a couple out for an evening walk.

Once safely beyond the tent, Calla stopped, facing him. "It's not a shield, just a warning barrier. We only need to get inside without crossing it."

"Dematerialize," he sighed. "Tricky, when we don't know what's inside. We could land on top of him."

"The shadows show he's near the front. If we aim just inside the opening, we'll have to hope for the best."

They clasped hands tightly. Andorran gave her a final caution. "Be ready for anything."

She nodded, closing her eyes and picturing the tent, herself standing just inside the guarded flap. A tingling started in her stomach, sharp enough to make her clench her jaw. Her fingers squeezed Andorran's. Then, as suddenly as it came, the sensation was gone.

Calla opened her eyes cautiously. She and Andorran stood inside a cold, cramped space, still holding hands. A low cot and its lone occupant took up most of the room. The canvas ceiling brushed Andorran's head, and he gave it a reproachful glance before turning his attention to the man.

Freeing her hand, Calla stepped forward, whispering, "Inaudus."

Andorran raised a brow.

She shrugged. "We don't want to be overheard."

His frown deepened. "How long have you been able to do that?"

A sly grin tugged at her mouth. "A while," she answered vaguely. She flicked her hand, and the blankets peeled back.

On the cot lay a man who looked barely alive. He was not much older than Calla, but his skin was a sickly gray, his eyes sunken, his white-blond hair dull and limp. Only the shallow rasp of his breathing proved he still lived.

"He certainly doesn't look very intimidating, does he?" she murmured.

"Neither do you, most of the time," Andorran replied quietly. "Looks can be deceiving."

Calla shot him a scolding look, then turned back to the dragon-slayer. "I'm sure they've already checked him for weapons…but if you don't mind ."

Andorran grinned. "You're sure you don't want to do that your-self?"

"I'm sure," she assured him.

The man stirred faintly as Andorran searched him, but did not wake. Once Andorran was satisfied, Calla laid her fingers gently against the man's temple. She gave a light jolt just enough to shock him awake. His eyes flew open, and he instinctively raised a hand to strike. Andorran caught his wrist easily.

"Who…who are you?" the dragonslayer croaked, pale blue eyes darting from Calla to Andorran. The larger man released him and folded his arms across his broad chest.

Calla forced a smile. "Who are you?"

The man's eyes bulged, and for a moment he looked ready to faint. "I…I am not…what you think." He struggled to prop himself up. "There's a guard just outside."

"We saw him," Andorran said flatly.

"What is your name, dragonslayer?" Calla pressed.

He gulped, shaking his head, stringy hair falling across one eye. "K…Kodar. But why…why do you think…"

"That you're a dragonslayer?" Calla finished for him. "Darmon told us."

Confusion clouded his gaunt features. "Where is he?"

She dismissed the question with a wave of her hand. "Were you in Dari San when the slayers took the city?"

"No…" he whispered. "…Soronu."

"What do they want in Dari San and Soronu?"

He frowned, shaking his head weakly. "They never told us."

"Tell us about the pact," Andorran demanded.

Kodar's hands clenched together, his face turning even paler. "I only know we were to be asked to swear a pact. Those who refused were executed on the spot." He gave them a pleading look. "I trained to be a dragonslayer, not a mercenary. I wanted no part of that pact."

"So you didn't swear it?"

"No. I managed to slip out of the city."

"And you came to Mim Tor?"

He nodded. "I thought the dragonmasters should know."

"Are they looking for you?"

"Possibly." Kodar winced, shaking his head. "The leader of the band in Soronu…he's been involved in something dark for a long time, I think."

"Lucan?" Calla asked sharply.

At the name, Kodar closed his eyes in defeat. "You're here to kill me?"

"I haven't ruled it out," Calla said flatly. She glanced at Andorran. "What do you think?"

He shrugged. "I think he's no threat... at least, not at the moment. What do you think?"

Calla raked her fingers through her hair. "I still don't like it. But you won the vote. We take him."

>

Before sunup, eight riders moved north along Mim Tor's eastern wall. Darmon had been quick to find Kodar a horse and seemed relieved that they were taking him. He never asked what had changed their minds.

Kodar stayed silent, obeying every order. He knew well enough they were not pleased to have him along, and none offered him more than the barest instructions. He had not learned their names, nor where they were headed, but Darmon had assured him he was in good hands. Kodar only hoped the Tribunal Master was right.

The woman watched him with open suspicion, and the young blond boy with tawny eyes did the same. Kodar tried hard not to provoke them further. Weak and ill, he doubted he could defend himself against even the smallest of them.

They said little as they rode, heading toward the Mountains of the Condemned. Kodar took the chance to study them. The oldest, with his ebony braid and piercing blue-green eyes, was clearly Kamborian. The boy with the stave across his back golden-blond hair tied at the nape, wide sapphire eyes looked southern, Baldar'tine or Fala Do Sol perhaps. The darker-skinned youth was likely western.

Four bore the silver sword knot of Mim, including the woman. She intrigued him most of all. Somehow she had slipped past Darmon's guard and into his tent without being seen. She had known of Lucan and of the slayers' pact. Younger than him, he guessed, but powerful and striking, with her riot of red-gold curls, amber eyes, and the thin scar cutting across one porcelain cheek. Petite, lithe, yet radiating strength.

An unusual company, yet they thought and moved as one. The three boys stayed close to the woman, speaking with her in low voices. The others rotated near him ostensibly to steady him in the saddle, though Kodar knew they were watching him. Trust went both ways, and there was none here.

The woman reined in her dark stallion and frowned back at him. "Blindfold him."

He had been warned of this, but reluctance still surged in him. The Kamborian's hard stare told him there would be no choice.

"How is he supposed to ride blindfolded?" one of the boys asked. Kodar wondered the same.

The woman sighed. "Lead his horse, then. Or let him ride with one of you."

"You're the smallest," the dark-haired man said. "He rides with you. More room in your saddle."

She gave him a sharp look but wheeled her stallion around. Kodar considered protesting, but her expression silenced him. He slid off his mare, handing the reins to the Kamborian. With surprising strength, the woman hauled him up behind her.

The Kamborian leaned close, knotting the blindfold tight. "Don't try anything foolish, dragonslayer. We'll be watching. Any move we think suspicious we kill you. If she doesn't get to you first."

Kodar didn't doubt him.

The woman chuckled, her curls brushing against his cheek. "Time to go home," she declared.

>

Crouched in a circle, the seven dragonmasters finished their meal, deliberately ignoring Kodar, who sat apart with his own food. He had been brought along only to appease the Triad, not because any of them wanted his company. He was a dragonslayer trained to kill the very creatures they were bound to protect. Necessary, perhaps, but who willingly chose such a life?

They had kept him from knowing who they were or where they were headed, but now, more than halfway through the mountain passageway, secrecy no longer mattered. Kodar was effectively a captive, unable to leave the mountains on his own.

Calla shoved the last bite of bread into her mouth, rose, and stretched. "A few more hours now, I should think."

Tau rolled his shoulders with a groan. "I'm looking forward to sleeping in my bed tonight."

Gan flicked a glance toward Kodar. "I'll be glad to be rid of him," he muttered.

"He's caused no trouble," Tiean pointed out.

Kodar shot them a sour look. "Are you going to tell me where we're going?" He swept a hand at the cavernous passage. "What are you...trolls?"

Calla grinned. "Do we look like trolls?"

"I'm not sure what you look like," he admitted, climbing to his feet. "You're not gaol, but I don't think you're sorcia either."

Andorran passed a hand over his face, his eyes glowing faintly in the gloom. "If I told you we were going to Tegoradaysol, would that answer your question?"

Kodar's eyes widened. "Dragonmasters? Which of you ?"

"We all are," Tau replied.

Kodar's gaze darted from face to face until it fixed on Calla. "You? You're a dragonmaster?"

The seven passed their hands over their faces, dispelling the eclipsing spell. Kodar shook his head slowly. "Then it's true…there is a female dragonmaster."

Calla swung easily into the saddle. "Time to finish this trip."

When they were mounted again, Kodar tried to ride alongside her, only for Gan to cut him off with a fierce glare.

"I only want to talk," Kodar said defensively.

"You can talk from there," Gan growled.

Calla smiled faintly. "What is it you wish to talk about, dragon-slayer?"

"All that talk I've heard about the reckoning…and the Genesi Ney. Is it true?"

"I don't know what you've heard," she replied smoothly. "What about the pact you were asked to take? Was it to the Destroyer?"

Kodar sighed heavily. "I told you I didn't make the pact. I don't know all the details." His pale eyes searched hers. "Are you the Genesi Ney?"

"Does it matter?"

"I think it does. If you are, Lucan has offered a reward for you."

"I heard." Her voice was calm, but her amber eyes sharpened. "Is it your intention to collect that reward from my brother?"

Kodar's face twisted in shock. "Brother? Lucan is…your brother?"

"We're not a close family," she said dryly.

Kodar gave a bitter laugh. "And I'll see no reward. Unless you count a knife between the ribs."

"Just as well. You won't be leaving Tegoradaysol."

His brow arched. "I'm a prisoner?"

"As far as I'm concerned." She wrapped the reins around her hands and urged her stallion forward, ending the conversation. If Kodar thought to follow, Gan's warning glare quickly dissuaded him. Shoulders slumping, Kodar fell back into silence.

>

When Camalaron entered his study, he found Andorran and Calla waiting, heads bowed, hands resting on sword hilts. Between them stood a bewildered young man who looked ready to collapse.

"Deius protect you, dragonmasters," the Sovereign Master said. They straightened as he lowered himself into his chair and gestured for them to sit. Calla and Andorran took their seats across from Kodar, both deliberately ignoring him.

"I see you returned with the sword knots you sought?" Camalaron began.

"And a few things we did not seek, Sovereign Master," Calla said curtly.

"I'm certain Darmon explained that his life is in danger."

"He mentioned it," Andorran replied, his tone nearly as sharp as Calla's. "We couldn't imagine why you'd want a dragonslayer in Tegoradaysol, but we brought him as you requested."

Calla's chin lifted, her expression hard. Andorran might call it a *request*, but they all knew it had been closer to a command.

"We weren't sure what you wanted done with him," Andorran went on. "Vien didn't seem to know either."

Camalaron turned his gaze to Kodar. "You'll understand that you won't be allowed your weapon. Darmon sent it along, I presume?"

Andorran gave a curt nod.

"You cannot leave Tegoradaysol for now, at least," Camalaron continued. "But consider yourself a guest. Our healers will see you restored to health, and I'll arrange quarters. Vien will be happy to show you around, acquaint you with what you need to know."

Calla doubted Vien would be *happy* to do any such thing.

"Andorran, Calla, and the others can help you get settled as well," Camalaron added.

That was too much. Calla shot to her feet, outrage flashing in her eyes. "I've spent as much time with your guest as I care to, Master Camalaron! Let someone else settle your dragonslayer. If it's left to me, he may not like how he's settled!"

Andorran rose quickly, planting himself between her and the Sovereign Master, irritation clear in his voice. "I think the dragonslayer would prefer to spend his time elsewhere, Sovereign Master. As for Calla and myself we've had a long journey and we're tired. Perhaps the details can wait for another time."

Camalaron nodded, intrigued. Calla fumed silently, held in place by Andorran's firm grip on her arm.

"You're excused, then," the Sovereign Master said mildly. "Take Kodar with you. Vien will collect him once his quarters are ready."

Andorran lowered his head respectfully, then practically hauled Calla out of the Sovereign Master's study, Kodar trailing at a cautious distance.

Once they stepped into the crisp night air, Calla exploded. "Do you realize what he's asking?! I knew this wasn't going to be a simple matter of dropping him off for the Triad to deal with!" She tried to yank free, but Andorran's grip on her arm held firm.

"You're overreacting," he said calmly.

She stared at him in disbelief. "Overreacting? You heard him! He practically ordered us to look after him as if it was *our idea* to bring him here!"

"It wasn't an order, Calla."

"Well, it didn't sound like a request!"

Andorran dragged her along at a brisk pace, more concerned with getting her away from Camalaron's quarters than whether Kodar kept up. Only when they reached their own did he release her. She rubbed her arm and glared at him.

"I'm not going to be responsible for him, Andorran! I didn't want to bring him here in the first place!"

"Will you, for once in your life, stop reacting like a wounded bear!" he barked. "I don't like this any more than you do, but yelling at Camalaron isn't the answer and neither is shouting at me!"

Calla snapped her mouth shut, visibly offended. A few feet away, Kodar froze, uncertain whether to stay or flee.

Andorran sighed and set his hands on her shoulders. "I know how you feel about dragonslayers. You have more reason than most to distrust them. But he isn't going to be a problem." The look he shot Kodar made it clear what he meant.

"He knew we were coming, Andorran," she said more quietly. "And he knew we were bringing him. So why didn't he have quarters prepared already?"

"I don't know," Andorran admitted. "But we agreed, didn't we? For now, it has to look like the Triad is still in power."

Sullenly, she nodded. "I remember. But I don't like being manipulated."

To her surprise, Andorran chuckled, folding his arms across his chest. "I wouldn't think so. You prefer to do the manipulating."

"That's not very nice, Andorran." She didn't deny it, though, and a reluctant smile tugged at her lips. Turning, she crooked a finger at Kodar. "Come along, dragonslayer. I won't have you getting into trouble before Vien comes to collect you."

Inside their quarters, the others looked up in surprise when Kodar followed Calla and Andorran into the main room.

"Is there a problem?" Tiean asked with a frown.

"He's not staying here, is he?" Gan growled, rising from the hearth.

Andorran shook his head. "He's here only until Vien comes for him. But we may have a problem. Master Camalaron *suggested* that we help him get settled."

"Suggested?" Niko echoed warily.

"How are we defining suggested?" Tau wanted to know.

"I'd say…just short of an order," Andorran replied. "He's careful with his wording."

"How long are we going to play this game?" Gan asked in disgust.

"As long as it takes, I suppose," Calla said wearily, squatting by the fire.

"We agreed it had to *seem* as though the Triad was still in control," Andorran reminded them.

"And the orders that aren't quite orders?" Tau pressed.

"We'll comply as best we can," Andorran said flatly. "We don't have much choice. We're not ready to openly take control, not yet."

"What about him?" Niko asked, nodding toward Kodar.

"His sword marks him a master wielder, but he won't have it. Camalaron has it for now," Andorran explained.

"And his casting?"

"He'll remain shielded," Calla said with a shrug.

"Camalaron might not like that," Caius warned.

"If he asks, we'll remind him that we have dragons to protect."

"There's a chance he won't ask," Andorran added. "He's being careful with us. That gives us some room so long as we're not careless."

Niko chuckled. "Who knows…we may even find some use for him."

Caius studied Kodar thoughtfully, then nodded. "Niko might be right. Keeping him close could be in our best interest."

"Close?" Calla didn't like the sound of it. "How close?"

Grinning, Caius stood. "Very close. Calla, I know you don't even want him in Tegoradaysol, but he's here and I think there's a reason."

"Deius hedging his bet?" Tiean suggested.

"Maybe," Caius agreed.

Gan frowned. "How close?"

Caius shrugged lightly. "We have room here."

Gan's eyes widened, and he turned to Calla.

She grimaced. "Closer than I'd like…but he has a point. Best to keep our enemies where we can see them."

Andorran watched their reactions carefully. Calla had taken it better than expected. Gan looked as though it would take convincing, but that was in his nature. Tau and Tiean seemed to be weighing the idea, and Niko stared at Caius in open-mouthed shock.

"It'll mean more spells," Andorran said at last. "Shielding him won't be enough."

Tau nodded. "And we'll have to be careful what we say in front of him until we know his intentions."

"We don't know that he *has* intentions," Tiean reasoned.

"And we don't know that he doesn't!" Gan snapped. "At the very least, he's a dragonslayer and a wanted one at that! At worst, he's a spy. If so who for? The slayers? The Tribunal? The Triad?"

Calla set a hand on Gan's shoulder. "You're right. As a wanted dragonslayer, he's dangerous. As a spy, he could be fatal. But keeping him where we can watch him might be the best way to protect ourselves."

Tau tugged at his dark hair, frowning. "Caius is right. We've got the sound shield, we can set barrier spells on our rooms. We're better equipped to handle him than anyone else."

Niko sat heavily on the hearth. "I don't think he's a spy. Not for the slayers, anyway," he said quietly. All eyes turned to him. He shrugged. "I just don't get that from him. He's afraid and with the looks Calla and Gan have been giving him, I can't blame him. Honestly…I'm a little afraid for him myself."

Andorran's mouth twitched as he met Calla's gaze. She cocked her head and grinned faintly.

"He's angry too," Niko went on, "but with himself, I think. Maybe for getting into this mess at all. And he's curious."

"Curious about what?" Gan demanded.

"All of us," Niko said simply. "Calla most of all. He didn't believe in the reckoning or the Genesi Ney until now."

Calla glanced at Kodar. He couldn't hear them through the sound shield, but he could certainly see.

"So…is he staying?" Andorran asked into the silence.

One by one, they gave their consent. Gan was the last, offering only a curt nod.

Chapter 14: Mystic Dragonsheart

The door at the end of the corridor eased open without a sound, and Kodar slipped into the hall. A single flickering torch threw just enough light for him to make his way past the rows of doors toward the one he sought.

Pausing, he placed his hand against it. The room wasn't shielded, but a barrier spell shimmered faintly in the air. The ward they had placed on him prevented casting, not sensing, and he could feel its hum beneath his palm. He had protested, of course, but his objections fell on deaf ears. These seven took no chances with him.

The seven of the last generation. The thought still rattled him. He had never believed there was truth to the tale. He'd dismissed it as the ravings of a madman. Lucan's ravings. And Lucan was a madman, at least in Kodar's estimation. Brilliant, cunning, deadly…but a madman all the same.

Kodar turned the handle, opening the door with care, and braced himself. If she wasn't asleep, Calla would likely thrash him before he could speak. But the glow of the torchlight fell over her form lying on the bed. She was sleeping soundly, flat on her back, one hand resting across her stomach, the other tucked beneath her head.

He took a step forward then stopped. Crossing the barrier would wake her, and if she saw him here, she might not ask questions before striking him down. Kodar wasn't ready to die.

Why they had changed their minds and given him a room among them, he still didn't understand. Vien had been shocked when told and more than relieved. The aide had practically tripped over his own feet in his hurry to carry their decision back to the Sovereign Master. In the fortnight since his arrival, Kodar had realized Vien wasn't the only one keeping a safe distance. The people of Tegoradaysol were wary of these young dragonmasters, not because of him, but because of their power.

He'd grown up hearing stories about dragonmasters that they were violent, manipulative, dangerous. He'd discovered they were all those things, but also…more.

His gaze lingered on Calla, coming to rest on her face. In sleep, she looked almost harmless. Vulnerable, even. But he already knew better than to call her either.

The Genesi Ney. The woman Lucan claimed would determine the outcome of the reckoning. Kodar had scoffed at the prophecy, but somewhere in his mind he had imagined what such a figure might look like. The fiery young dragonmaster before him with her crown of red-gold curls, impish grin, and lightning temper was not what he had pictured.

Leaning against the doorframe, he scolded himself. Night after night, he felt this same pull, an irresistible urge to come here. Drawn to her like a moth to flame, with consequences just as deadly. If Andorran or Gan found him in her room, they would cut him down without hesitation. And he doubted the others would treat him much better.

He forced himself back, easing the door closed before slumping against the wall. This calling, this strange compulsion, was going to get him killed if he didn't find a way to resist it. He hated the helplessness of it, hated the thought that some unseen power could strip away his will and drive him to such recklessness.

Casting a wary glance up and down the corridor, he slipped back to his own room. As always, now that he'd gone to her door, he would sleep deeply, waking stronger and healthier and dreading the next night's summoning.

>

Along the shores of the Tegora Dara Mai, a mystic raced beneath the full moon, silver mane and tail streaming like banners in the wind. Its hooves thundered against the ground, tearing up tufts of turf, while the spiraling silver horn on its brow gleamed brilliantly in the moonlight.

The slender legs stretched in long, smooth strides, carrying it away from the village and deeper into the mountains. At a narrowing of the river, the mystic plunged into the dark waters, swimming with powerful strokes across to the far bank. Emerging, it shook itself vigorously, sending a rain of droplets from its pristine white coat and shimmering mane.

Then it continued on, tail swishing proudly, as though guided by instinct alone. For nearly an hour it pressed forward, tireless, its path unerring though it had never walked this way before.

At last it reached the place it sought: a clearing where an icy lake lay nestled among the peaks, fed by a roaring spring, the headwaters of the Tegora Dara Mai.

Flowering trees and lush green pastures surrounded the lake, an oasis of spring hidden within the wintry peaks. The mystic did not seem to find the strangeness unusual. Lowering its head, it stepped to the water's edge and drank deeply.

From across the lake, a glowing mist began to rise, drifting slowly over the surface until it gathered near the mystic. The shape shifted, the brilliance dimming as the glow softened and dissolved.

A woman stood in its place. Her shimmering hair, pale as moonlight, fell in a silken curtain to her feet, cloaking her body entirely. Her eyes an impossible, luminous silver were filled with compassion.

She stretched out her hand to the nervously prancing mystic. "Come, child," she coaxed in a lilting, musical voice. "You have nothing to fear."

The mystic reared, letting out a sharp whinny of protest before coming down hard on its forelegs, retreating several steps. Its silver mane whipped as it shook its head vigorously.

"Come, child," the woman urged again, hand still outstretched. "I am Shiran Aku, Mistress of Mystics. Look the others come to greet you."

The mystic sidestepped, wary, as three figures entered the clearing: a stallion and two mares, pure white with silver that glistened in the moonlight. They studied the newcomer with keen interest. The stallion stepped forward first, whickering, bobbing his head. One of the mares mimicked him with perfect precision.

"They know you are not truly a mystic," Shiran Aku continued gently, gliding closer. "Come, child. I may have the answers you seek."

The mystic lowered its head, pawing at the earth with one forehoof. Tentative, but yielding. Shiran Aku reached forward and stroked its forelock.

"Quite incredible," she murmured in admiration.

But the creature shuddered, throwing its head back. A peculiar sound rose from its throat a long, anguished wail that sharpened into a shriek of agony. Its legs buckled, its body convulsed, and it crashed to its knees, teeth bared, eyes rolling back.

Moments later, the mystic was gone. Calla was left kneeling in its place, on hands and knees, her body drenched in sweat, breath coming in ragged gasps.

Shiran Aku knelt beside her, brushing tangled curls from her face. "This pain comes because you resist, child," she whispered. Calla lifted her head, eyes full of anguish, and the woman caressed her cheek. "That you found your way into our valley tells me much, for only a mystic can cross into the Valley of Mystics."

Shivering, naked, her muscles screaming, Calla curled into a ball. The Mistress of Mystics sighed softly, the sound melodic. "You are the Genesi Ney. You must embrace your destiny." Rising, she extended her hands. "Come, child. On your feet."

Calla groaned miserably. "I want to go home."

"In good time, child...in good time." Shiran Aku wiggled her fingers playfully. "Come now up, up."

Calla wanted to refuse, yet somehow found herself standing. Her legs trembled beneath her, the pain of transformation still clawing at her, but she stood. Never before had she reverted to her true form away from her quarters, away from Tiean's healing. And now she realized she had no idea how to return home. That thought alone nearly broke her resolve.

Shiran Aku smoothed the curls from Calla's damp forehead, smiling warmly. Her beauty seemed to illuminate the clearing. She cupped Calla's face tenderly.

"You are very strong, child," she said. "And pure of heart, to have taken the form of a mystic. They are creatures of strength and purity as well. Pride may be their only fault." Her gaze drifted affectionately toward the trio nearby. "But given what magnificent beings they are, even that can be forgiven."

The stallion snorted, tossing his head before galloping off. The mares followed at once, graceful and obedient.

Heat spread across Calla's cheeks beneath Shiran Aku's touch. That warmth traveled through her, soothing every ache, easing her pain until she felt whole again stronger, even. She gasped at the sudden relief, then quickly crossed her arms over herself, flushing at her nakedness.

Instinctively, she tried to cast for her clothes. Nothing happened.

"You cannot cast here, child," Shiran Aku told her with a musical laugh. "I forget how modest your kind can be." With a graceful wave, she conjured a gown of sheer silk and satin, white as moonlight, draping Calla's body. It was not what she would have chosen, flimsy and too fine, but she was grateful to be clothed.

"How…how did I get here?" Calla asked.

"There is magic in the world beyond even my knowledge," the Mistress of Mystics replied.

"You said you had answers for me?"

Shiran Aku's smile returned. "Yes…some."

"What answers?"

"What are your questions?"

Calla frowned, raking her fingers through her curls. "I have to know the questions before you'll give me the answers?"

"Naturally, child." The Mistress regarded her as if she were slow-witted. "Answers follow questions. I must hear the question before I can provide the answer."

Calla doubted it would make more sense even if she were still in mystic form. "Well… I have so many questions, I hardly know where to start." She hesitated, then asked, "…Did the slayers make a pact with Daiesthai?"

"Not with the Destroyer himself, but with one who serves him. They chose a dark path…a path that can only end in destruction."

"But we *can* defeat them?"

"Of course you can, child." Shiran Aku's silver eyes gleamed. "That does not mean that you will."

Calla thought grimly that this woman would have made a formidable dragonmaster. She was skilled at answering questions while giving away very little. "So…what do we have to do?"

"Stay strong. Stay loyal. Follow your heart. And trust only those who share your dragon's heart."

"My…what?" Calla frowned.

"Genesi Ney, you have made powerful enemies."

"Yes," Calla replied grimly. "That much I do know."

The Mistress of Mystics leaned closer, her silver eyes hardening like tempered steel. "You will be betrayed by one you once counted as a friend."

"Who?" Calla demanded.

"I do not know, child." Shiran Aku extended her right hand and pressed it lightly against Calla's left collarbone. "You have been brought to me to forge your new binding, Genesi Ney. From this day forward, you will bear the mark of a new bloodline, the heritage you will pass on to future generations, should you choose the correct path and walk it well. You must build upon this new binding. Hold strong to your convictions, remain steadfast in your beliefs, and trust those who will be sent to aid you in your quest."

"Quest?" Calla was overwhelmed. "What binding? What convictions? How do I…" Her words broke into a strangled gasp as white-hot pain seared beneath Shiran Aku's touch. She dropped to her knees with a howl, tears streaming down her cheeks.

Just as suddenly as it had begun, the pain ended. Calla scrambled backward, glaring reproachfully at the woman who had hurt her without warning.

"You will know whom to trust," Shiran Aku told her serenely, "those who share your mystic dragon's heart. Those who bind with you in body, mind, heart, and spirit."

Exhausted, Calla staggered to her feet. "What did you do to me?" she rasped.

"I gave you the power that is rightfully yours, Genesi Ney, the power to forge." Shiran Aku held out her hands.

Calla regarded her warily, then stepped forward and placed her own hands in the woman's with hesitation.

"Follow your heart, child." Shiran Aku leaned in and kissed Calla on each cheek. "You possess a mystic dragon's heart to guide you. You need only listen."

As she released her, a faint glow began to halo Shiran Aku's form. The warmth of her smile made Calla want to believe every word, even though she understood so little.

The glow intensified until her outline grew hazy. Calla stumbled back several steps.

"Deius bless you, Genesi Ney," the Mistress of Mystics called as her shimmering form drifted away over the water.

"But " Calla stepped toward the lake, alarm tightening her chest. "How do I get back? I don't even know where..." She spun around, breath catching in her throat. "...I am," she finished in a whisper.

Because she knew. She was standing in the corridor, facing the door to her own room. She was home.

Suddenly drained, Calla sank to the hardwood floor, staring at the closed door. For the first time, she clearly remembered her time in another form. She still had no memory of the transformation itself, nor of how she had returned but everything in between was sharp and vivid.

She wondered if it had been a dream. But the filmy white gown she still wore proved otherwise. If Shiran Aku thought her answers had been helpful, Calla would have to disagree. She was more confused than ever.

A door opened behind her. She didn't need to turn. Andorran's quarters were across from her own.

"Calla?" His voice was confused but alert.

She drew a deep breath and nodded, her shoulders slumping.

Andorran knelt beside her, concern etched across his face. He gently tipped her chin upward. "Are you all right? What are you doing out here?"

Calla stared at him, distracted by details she had never noticed before his blue-green eyes flecked with gold, framed by thick lashes. Almost pretty. His hair, no longer shaved in the traditional Kamborian style, hung in a braid down his back, the loose mane around his face curling slightly at the ends. It softened his sculpted features in a way that unsettled her.

"Calla? Are you all right?" he pressed.

She blinked, shook herself, and wondered again what Shiran Aku had done to her. "I…I'm fine," she stammered, attempting to rise. Her legs buckled, and she would have fallen had Andorran not caught her.

Ignoring her protests, he half-led, half-carried her into his room and set her down on the settee. Then he strode back out, leaving the door open. She heard him pounding on doors, calling for the others. Calla wanted to object there was no need to wake everyone but she was too weary. More than anything, she wanted her own bed.

Andorran returned, his sharp eyes sweeping over her as though to confirm she hadn't vanished. He pulled a blanket from his bed and handed it to her.

"I've never seen you wear anything like that before," he said gruffly.

Calla looked down at herself, remembering Shiran Aku's gauzy gown, and flushed scarlet. She wrapped the blanket tightly around her, grateful for the cover. Too tired to cast new clothes, she let it suffice.

The others arrived soon after, rumpled and bleary-eyed but concerned. At Andorran's gesture, they formed their usual circle around her.

"I suspect Calla has assimilated again," he told them.

She nodded. "Yes. Andorran is right."

"Do you need healing?" Tiean asked, studying her carefully.

"No…I don't think so."

Andorran made a harsh sound, folding his arms across his bare chest. "What about that mark on your shoulder?"

Puzzled, Calla tugged the blanket aside to look and gasped, the cover sliding down into her lap. "What did she do to me?!"

Branded into her skin, just below her left collarbone, was the dragonmasters' symbol: the dragon's talon clutching an inverted heart. But unlike the others, hers bore a striking difference. At the center of the heart rose a spiraling mystic's horn, gleaming like silver inlay against her flesh.

"Where did that come from?" Niko asked in astonishment.

Calla shook her head, just as stunned as the rest. "The mystic dragon's heart," she murmured, biting her lip as she stared at the marking in dismay.

Andorran rose and gently drew the blanket back over her shoulders. "Tell us what happened, Calla," he urged softly.

She recounted everything she remembered from leaving the village in mystic form until she found herself standing at her own door. "I have no idea how I got back here," she finished wearily.

Tiean leaned forward, intrigued. "You said she told you to forge new bindings?"

"That's what she said." Calla glanced ruefully at the shining mark on her chest. "But I have no idea what she meant. I can't forge a binding. No human has that power."

"It didn't sound as if she made much sense," Tau agreed. "You've never returned to your own form away from here before."

"I think Shiran Aku changed me back," Calla said quietly.

Caius was staring at her in awe, wishing he could have seen her in the form of a mystic. When she caught his look, he smiled brightly. "Calla, I don't think you understand the significance of assimilating into a mystic. Mystics are considered the purest of creatures. I've been reading about dali-daubs. They can't assimilate into beings that are pure and virtuous. Mystics are at the very top of that list." His sapphire eyes shone. "That you can take that form means you don't need to fear your link to Diate. This isn't dali-daub magic."

Andorran gave her shoulder a reassuring squeeze. "He's the logical one. If Caius believes this is something special, I'm inclined to agree."

Caius nodded emphatically. "It is special!"

"I've never heard of the Mistress of Mystics," Tau admitted.

"Neither have I," Tiean added. "Her purpose is to care for them?"

"I suppose," Calla said with a shrug. "We never discussed that."

Gan frowned. "You said she knew who you were, even in mystic form?"

"That's true." Calla raked her fingers through her curls. "I just wish her answers hadn't been so vague. Someone I count as a friend is going to betray me? And I'm supposed to trust those who share my dragon's heart? Everyone I trust shares the dragon's heart. We're all dragonmasters! How does that help me?"

"Maybe she didn't mean dragonmasters," Niko suggested.

"Or maybe she didn't mean the dragonmasters' heart," Caius added thoughtfully.

Andorran studied the gleaming mark on Calla's shoulder. "Or perhaps she was speaking of the mystic dragon's heart." He held her gaze. "What exactly did she do and say?"

Calla closed her eyes, concentrating. "I can't remember the order exactly. She put her hand on my heart…said something about me being brought to her for a new binding…and about holding fast to convictions, trusting those sent to help me on the quest…" Her voice trailed off.

"Are you sure she didn't cast any kind of spell?"

"No…she didn't cast. Her magic was…different." Turning to Andorran, Calla pressed her hand against his chest, just below the collarbone. "She touched me here, and then she was just talking like it was a conversation. Telling me to trust those who would help me on the quest, and then…" Her eyes widened, locking on his.

In her mind, the melodious voice of Shiran Aku echoed.

A pledge of devotion is asked of you. A binding to the Genesi Ney.

Calla's face paled. Horrified, she tried to snatch her hand away, but Andorran held it firmly in place.

"Andorran you can't!" she whispered, panicked.

"Let me hear it all, Calla," he said quietly.

The others, who could not hear, rose uneasily, exchanging worried looks.

Shiran Aku's voice flowed on, silk and steel:

Bind with body, heart, mind, and spirit. Only a pledge freely given, without reservation, will be accepted. A pledge false or deceitful will forfeit your life. Once made, this oath is held even beyond death. It cannot be severed. It is sacred above all vows. Do you so pledge on your life?

Calla's amber eyes filled with terror. "You cannot," she begged.

"I pledge on my life," Andorran said with conviction.

A rush of searing heat burned beneath Calla's hand, biting into his flesh. He clenched his jaw, teeth gritted against the pain. Tears spilled down her cheeks as she whispered frantic protests, shaking her head in defeat.

When the heat faded, she gave him a stricken look.

Andorran released her hand and glanced down. Branded into his chest, just below his collarbone, gleamed an identical silver mystic's dragonheart.

The others gaped in disbelief.

Tau found his voice first. "How…how did you do that?"

"I don't know!" Calla wailed. She struck Andorran's chest with her fist. "Why did you accept?! Why would you pledge to that bloody binding?" She turned desperately to Tiean. "You have to undo this!"

Tiean looked troubled. "Undo…what exactly?"

"The binding!"

"Undo a binding?" Gan's voice rose in shock. "Calla that can't be done!"

She whirled back on Andorran. "Then revoke it! Break the pledge!"

His gaze was calm, steady. "I would not, even if I could. I accepted of my own free will."

"But why?" she cried.

"Because you are the Genosi Ney."

Tears streamed down her cheeks, but her eyes blazed like fire. "I don't know what I'm doing!" she snarled. "I don't know how to face this reckoning, much less survive it! Following me is like following a blind man off a cliff! Revoke it, Andorran!"

He caught her hands, pressing them firmly against the silver mark on his chest. "I'll do anything else you ask of me, Calla," he said quietly. "But not that. We are bound and we will remain bound."

Her anger finally drained away, and Calla let her head fall forward onto Andorran's shoulder. "This is wrong," she sobbed softly. "We are not supposed to have the power of binding."

"It is meant to be," he answered gently. "When a blind man nears the cliff, should he not have someone he can trust to pull him back and keep him safe?"

She lifted her head, studying him with troubled eyes, chewing her lip. He had pledged his life to her without hesitation, binding himself with absolute conviction while she was still plagued by doubt. How could he be so certain of her, when she could not even be certain of herself?

As he wrapped the blanket firmly around her shoulders, Calla sighed. Gan was right: this could not be undone. She and Andorran were bound truly and irrevocably.

Down the corridor, Kodar slipped quietly back to his own room, frowning. At first the muffled commotion had worried him, but when no one came to collect him, relief gave way to curiosity. The seven dragonmasters were gathered in Andorran's chamber, the door ajar. Calla sat pale and spent, wrapped in a blanket, her head against Andorran's shoulder. She appeared asleep though not the peaceful sleep he had witnessed during his nightly compulsions. No, this looked like exhaustion, as though every drop of energy had been drained from her.

His position was precarious enough without being caught lurking, and he had learned quickly that angering them was a mistake only fools made. He spent nearly every waking moment in their company by their choice, not his and more than once had crossed invisible lines he hadn't known existed. Gan was the quickest to put him in his place, though the others could be equally unyielding.

He had gravitated toward Tiean and Caius the slowest to anger, the most inclined to give him second chances. They even called him by his name, where others barked orders or ignored him entirely. Still, in the time he had spent with them, Kodar had learned much.

Three were dragon fliers, able to soar astride the massive beasts of the mountains. Two had the gift of healing. Three carried the coveted spirit stones, though Kodar did not yet understand their true significance. Four bore sword knots as master wielders, while two excelled with the stave. Each was formidable alone, but together they were something more something dangerous. Fierce. Loyal to one another beyond reason.

The villagers called them *Una'savagi* in the Language of the Old Age. Kodar did not know the translation, but judging by the way the seven chuckled whenever they heard it, he suspected it was no compliment.

With thoughts of the last generation heavy in his mind, Kodar finally drifted into uneasy sleep.

>

Less than a week later, he found himself once more at Calla's door in the dead of night but this time with a certainty that chilled and steadied him in equal measure. At last he understood why fate had delivered him into the hands of these seven, and why he had been drawn, night after night, to her.

Now his problem was convincing them, especially Calla. He knew he would need at least four of them to share his vision of his purpose. If even two stood with him, he would be lucky. But none of it mattered if he could not first persuade her. She was the one with the power to bind.

The thought still left him reeling. A human with the ability to bind was unheard of yet he had seen it with his own eyes. For days, the seven had argued, always behind sound shields or in hushed voices. At last, they had reached a decision. From outside their warded common room, Kodar had witnessed the impossible: Calla placing her hand, one by one, upon her companions, leaving each with a silver dragon's heart etched with a mystic's horn. Andorran, it seemed, had been bound already.

Now, certain of his own course, Kodar eased her door open. He felt the familiar hum of the barrier spell. If he crossed it, there would be no turning back. He drew a deep breath and stepped forward. The barrier shuddered then snapped.

Calla bolted upright in her bed, amber eyes burning in the sudden dark. With a whispered incantation, her lantern flared to life. Her gaze locked on him. A harsh sound rumbled in her throat.

She was on her feet in an instant, a cloak dagger flashing in her hand. Kodar had no idea where it came from her simple white shift gave no place to hide such a weapon.

"What are you doing in here?!" she demanded, fury sparking in every syllable.

Seeing murder in her eyes, Kodar lifted his hands quickly. "I am not armed," he said. The dragonmasters' code of honor, he prayed, would prevent her from striking an unarmed man. He hoped it was true.

Her eyes narrowed. "Answer my question, dragonslayer."

"I…I come every night."

Her shock was plain. "What?!"

Nodding, he swallowed hard. "It is the truth. Something…I don't know what…draws me here every night."

Calla's frown deepened. The revelation unsettled her more than she cared to admit. The thought of a dragonslayer drawn into her room made her skin crawl.

"I did not know why," Kodar continued quickly, his gaze fixed warily on the dagger she shifted from hand to hand. He had seen her wield it before fast, precise, deadly and he knew just how accurate she could be. "It just kept happening… and I could do nothing to stop it."

Her glare was unrelenting. "And to what end?"

Kodar shook his head. "I did not know. I was only here for a few minutes each time… I never crossed the barrier. But it seemed like…" His face tightened with uncertainty. "…like I was getting stronger after each visit."

Calla tilted her head, studying him suspiciously. They had all noticed the change: the return of color to his cheeks, the healthy sheen in his once-lifeless white-blonde hair, the brightness in his pale eyes. His gaunt face had filled out, muscle tone returning. They had credited it to fresh air, steady meals, and time to recover yet now his words forced her to reconsider.

"I am not a healer," she snapped curtly.

"I know."

"Then how can you think I had anything to do with your strength returning? Particularly…" Her tone turned scathing. "…if I was asleep?"

Kodar sighed, lifting his shoulders helplessly. "I do not know. I can only tell you what I felt."

Her dagger still in hand, Calla swept her gaze around the room, then fixed him again with a sharp stare. "You said you never crossed the barrier… until tonight. Why now?"

Kodar met her eyes with determination. "Because I think I know what has been drawing me all this time."

She arched a brow, motioning with the dagger for him to go on.

"I want you to forge a binding with me," he blurted.

Calla froze. Shock rippled across her face, as if he had asked her to throw him to a dragon. "You want me to *what*?!"

"I know you can," he pressed, nodding earnestly. "I saw you do it with the others."

She didn't bother denying it. "They are dragonmasters!" she hissed, her grip tightening on the dagger. "I will *not* forge a binding with a dragonslayer!"

She turned sharply, shoving the blade back into its sheath on the headboard. She didn't quite trust herself to keep holding it.

"You *have* to!" Kodar insisted.

A bitter laugh escaped her, harsh and sharp. "*Have to*?" She folded her arms, taking a deliberate step toward him. The strap of her nightshift slipped at her shoulder, revealing the shimmer of silver just below her collarbone. "You put yourself on dangerous ground, dragonslayer. No one would blame me if I dealt with you… severely."

The look in her eyes left no doubt what she meant by *severely*.

Kodar resisted the urge to retreat. He had faced dragons less intimidating than this woman but he would not show fear now. "I think you need me, Calla."

Her scowl deepened. He had never spoken her name before, and hearing it on his lips made her bristle.

"I do not need you for *anything*," she spat.

"You will," he persisted, his pale eyes locked on hers.

Then, with sudden boldness, he caught her hand, pulling her closer, his grip frighteningly strong. "Just do it, Calla."

She tried to yank free, but he captured her hand in both of his, pressing her palm firmly to his chest.

Her eyes blazed. "You are a blood fool if you think to trap me with this, dragonslayer! Do you even understand what you are asking? What will be demanded of you?"

"I have an idea," he said, though his racing heartbeat betrayed his calm tone.

Her voice lowered, sharp as a blade. "Do you know what will happen if you are not completely sincere? If this is some kind of trap?"

A faint smile touched his lips. "Nothing pleasant, I am sure."

"Bind him, Calla," came Andorran's quiet voice from the doorway.

She spun, astonished. "He is a dragonslayer!"

The others were there too, she realized, gathered silently, watching. How long had they been standing there? How much had they heard? Surely, they could not agree with this. "You cannot want me to do this."

Andorran's eyes flashed with fury, but he nodded once. "Bind him."

Her gaze darted to Tiean and Caius both nodding. Tau and Niko, after uneasy glances at one another, gave reluctant nods as well. At last her eyes found Gan.

He frowned, eyes burning, but his voice was soft. "Do it, Calla."

She bit her lip, shaking her head in disbelief. She had been certain they would never agree. Yet here they stood, united. Stunned, she looked back at Kodar. His heart thundered beneath her hand, but his eyes were steady, waiting.

Her breath left her in a sigh. "Dragonslayer… this is your last chance. If the binding is offered and refused, you may walk away. But if you accept, and you are not sincere…" She shuddered. "…I would not want to be in your place."

Kodar said nothing he only waited.

Calla pressed her lips together, closed her eyes, and flexed her fingers against his chest.

And then she heard it; the melodious, silken voice of Shiran Aku, summoning Kodar to pledge himself to the Genesi Ney.

Calla's stomach knotted. If he saw reason, he would decline, and all would remain as it was. But if he accepted… she had no idea what would happen. A false pledge would be punished immediately, she knew. What form those consequences would take, she could not guess.

Kodar's hand held hers firmly against his chest as he accepted the binding in a strong, confident voice. At once, Calla felt the familiar heat flare beneath her palm.

But almost immediately, she realized something was wrong. The heat was far more intense than it should have been. Her heart pounded violently in her chest, her breath came in shallow, ragged pants, and sweat broke out across her skin. With a strangled whimper, Calla crumpled to her knees Kodar collapsing beside her.

Gan started forward, but Andorran's heavy hand clamped down on his shoulder, holding him back. A faint glow surrounded Calla and Kodar, brighter and more volatile than any of the bindings before.

"What is happening?" Tau whispered in alarm.

Andorran shook his head, his eyes narrowed. "I do not know. I think… she is trying to break it off."

Calla clawed at Kodar's hand, desperate to tear herself free, but it wasn't his grip holding her. It was the binding itself, unrelenting, locking them together. Pain surged through her body, sharp and suffocating. Her head throbbed, her stomach churned violently, and she fought for every breath as a whirlpool of darkness spun around her. It was foul, tainted, pressing down on her with suffocating weight.

Kodar was suffering too, his teeth clenched, eyes wide with pain. But he made no attempt to break away. He endured.

Minutes stretched unbearably until, at last, Calla's hand tore free. She collapsed forward, gasping hoarsely for air, then lurched to the chamber pot and retched violently. Kodar dropped flat onto the floor with a guttural groan, the silver mystic dragonsheart now gleaming on his chest. His face was ashen, drained of all color.

Gan rushed to Calla, steadying her trembling body while Niko dipped two cloths in the wash basin.

"What was that?" Calla rasped, her legs weak as water. Gan eased her onto the edge of the bed, and she pressed the cool cloth Niko offered against her face.

Still sprawled on the floor, Kodar lifted his head, his pale eyes filled with awe. "You… you severed the old binding," he gasped, swiping the second cloth across his clammy skin. "My oath as… a dragonslayer."

Andorran's face was grim. "A dragonslayer's oath," he muttered. "No wonder it made you sick."

Calla lifted her head, nodding weakly. "But… how could that even be possible? That was supposed to be unbreakable."

Kodar glanced down at the silver marking etched into his chest. "Maybe this binding… supersedes oaths to the contrary."

A weary moan escaped her lips. "Deius save me, I hope I never have to do that again."

"I am sorry," Kodar said quietly, guilt in his voice. "I had no idea…"

Her gaze met his, and despite her exhaustion, she managed a faint smile. "No, dragonslayer… *Kodar*," she corrected softly. "I owe *you* the apology. I misjudged you."

Tiean moved to help Kodar to his feet, steadying him. Tau gave a single approving nod.

"Tomorrow, your sword will be returned to you," Andorran said firmly.

Calla let out a breathless chuckle, her lips curling wryly. "Welcome to Una'savagi, Kodar. You're one of the 'wild ones' now."

Chapter 15: The Balance of Power

By summer's end, Camalaron was drowning in petitions from the citizens of Tegoradaysol. They wanted something done about the ones they now called *Una'savagi*.

The Sovereign Master had to admit, the name was apt. The seven dragonmasters had become increasingly unruly, and their independence unsettled many. Even more troubling to some was that the dragonslayer, Kodar, had somehow become part of Una'savagi. Camalaron still did not understand how that had come to be.

Uniting these dragonmasters had always been the plan ever since the peril stone had been left with the infant daughter of Harith and Bian in Soronu. He and the other members of the Triad, along with the Tribunal, had known the prophecy was in motion, and that these seven would play a pivotal role in its outcome. But none of them had expected the deep bond the group would form or that a dragonslayer would fit into it. The seven were learning at a staggering rate, and with time perhaps against them, Camalaron had no wish to interfere unless necessary. They needed every advantage.

No one truly knew what powers the young dragonmasters possessed. They were not forthcoming, but it was clear they could cast spells long thought lost. Without his spies, Camalaron would know even less, but even that was becoming difficult. Niko's uncanny ability to sense intruders was foiling attempts at surveillance, and Calla seemed to be rallying animals to her defense. More than once, his agents had returned with absurd tales of being chased off by swarms of bees or flocks of aggressive crown birds.

Yes, Una'savagi knew their own strength. Their confidence bordering on arrogance, had others on edge. They listened politely when required, but Camalaron knew the truth: they answered to no one but themselves.

He was reflecting on all this as he sat at his desk, waiting. Andorran had been summoned, though Camalaron suspected the entire group might come. Preparing for them was no small matter. Too few chairs might suggest he was unprepared; too many, a concession. Vien had suggested no chairs at all, forcing the dragonmasters to stand. Camalaron disliked the idea of being surrounded by all of them on their feet in his own study, but he admitted it was wiser. All chairs but his own were removed.

At the window, Vien looked pale and fretful. "I am not sure this was a good idea, Sovereign Master."

"It was not my idea," Camalaron reminded him. Varzi had sent the summons to Andorran before even informing him. Now all he could do was make the best of it. He cast Vien a dry look. "Move away from there. You look like a condemned man awaiting his execution."

Vien flushed, but obeyed, crossing to the desk. "More tea, Sovereign Master?"

Camalaron glanced at his full cup and shook his head. "No."

Vien whisked the cold tea away anyway, grateful for the task. A knock at the door made him start so violently that the cup clattered noisily onto the silver tray.

Suppressing a sigh, Camalaron rubbed his temples. Vien was a bundle of nerves, nearly useless, but dismissing him would only humiliate the man. Better to hope he managed to compose himself.

"Come," Camalaron called, leaning back in his chair.

The door opened without hesitation. Not the cautious entrance of one summoned, nor the pompous stride of older dragonmasters, but something casual. Controlled.

Andorran entered first, his bow just respectful enough without being deferential. The others followed silently, Kodar among them. Eight in all, they approached his desk with a confidence that stopped just short of insolence.

If they noticed the absence of chairs, they gave no sign. Instead, they formed a line before him like well-drilled soldiers.

Andorran stood in the center, flanked by Calla, Niko, Kodar, and Tiean on his right, with Gan, Caius, and Tau to his left. Camalaron doubted the arrangement was accidental. The newlings were carefully positioned between the more seasoned.

He studied them closely. All had let their hair grow long. Tau, Gan, and Caius tied theirs back with leather cords. Tiean and Niko wore theirs like Kodar, laced and hanging over their shoulders. Andorran still wore his braid down his back, shaggy curls framing his face, a neatly trimmed beard lending him an even fiercer aspect. Calla's tousled curls hung loose, brushing her shoulders, glinting gold in the light.

They were lean, sun-darkened, hardened by mountain air. The newlings had shot up in height Gan and Niko now nearly a head taller than their counsel, and Caius nearly eye-level with her. Each wore leggings, soft-soled boots, and sleeveless tunics of well-tanned deerskin. Swords and daggers hung from their belts, gloves tucked neatly in place. Tiean and Niko bore staves on their backs, while Kodar carried the dragonslayer's leather shield strapped over his shoulder.

They stood with feet slightly apart, hands on hilts, heads inclined but not bowed. Almost the picture of model dragonmasters. Almost.

Camalaron folded his hands and forced a smile he did not feel. "Deius protect you all."

They blinked, silent.

He leaned forward. "Master Varzi and I have heard troubling stories. Of unusual markings… on your shoulders."

Andorran's mouth quirked faintly. "We have markings, Sovereign Master." He tugged his tunic aside, revealing the gleaming silver dragonsheart.

Camalaron had heard the rumors, but seeing it with his own eyes was another matter entirely. It took effort not to gape.

Varzi did not bother hiding his astonishment. His green eyes widened. "Where did they come from?"

"I could not say, Master Varzi," Andorran replied smoothly, releasing his tunic.

Camalaron pursed his lips. Not an answer. The Kamborian was growing more skilled in dragonmaster evasions. Questions would need to be phrased carefully.

"When did it appear?" Varzi pressed.

"After our return from Mim Tor."

"And all of you bear them?" Camalaron asked.

They nodded in unison.

Camalaron's gaze flicked to Tiean. "Have you attempted a healing?"

Tiean's bright blue eyes were steady, though his brow arched slightly. "A healing, Sovereign Master? Why would I heal what is neither sickness nor injury?"

Varzi bristled. "Have you tried or not?"

"I saw nothing that required healing," Tiean answered flatly.

"Perhaps I should try," Varzi suggested, glancing at Camalaron.

Before Camalaron could respond, Varzi strode directly to Calla. The air thickened instantly with tension. His hand rose toward her shoulder only to be caught in a grip like iron.

Andorran's eyes blazed, his voice a low growl. "If you intend to examine one of us… it will be me."

Camalaron made a mental note: never make an uninvited move toward Calla. Not with Andorran present. Judging by the looks in the others' eyes, he was not alone in his fury.

Varzi hesitated, then finally nodded, and Andorran released him. Silence fell as the healer studied the mystic dragonsheart on Andorran's chest. Camalaron took the opportunity to study the others.

They showed no concern for Varzi's inspection. A few glanced his way, but their expressions were more amused than wary. Calla and Gan exchanged grins, and Tiean murmured something to Kodar that made the dragonslayer smile faintly. Camalaron wondered what it would take to rattle these *wild ones*.

"I have never seen anything like this on a human," Varzi muttered at last, his scowl deepening. Stepping back, he glanced at the others. "They are all the same?"

The eight nodded in perfect unison.

Camalaron shook his head, almost whispering in awe. "Most remarkable. A dragonsheart… and a mystic's horn." He turned to Varzi. "What does it mean?"

Varzi continued to glower. "I do not know. It is not a branding more like… part of them." He shook his head, unsettled by his own words. "But that should be impossible. I would like to see all of them."

Calmly, without a hint of protest, the others pulled their tunics down from their left shoulders, revealing identical mystic dragon-shearts. The healer took an instinctive step back, nearly colliding with Camalaron's desk, edging toward the Sovereign Master without turning his back on them. Their expressions suggested they noticed.

"You truly have no idea how these appeared?" Varzi pressed, suspicion sharp in his tone.

"We do not know their origins," Tau replied evenly.

Not the same as not knowing how, Camalaron thought grimly. More dragonmaster evasions.

The door slammed open, crashing against the wall. Vien squeaked, nearly dropping the silver tray in his hands, while Camalaron turned in surprise. Una'savagi didn't so much as flinch.

"Why was I not informed of this summoning?" Gira demanded, stomping into the room.

"It was not a summoning," Camalaron replied quietly.

Dark eyes narrowed, Gira swept his gaze over Varzi, then the *wild ones*, before fixing on Camalaron. "Then what would you call it?"

Varzi bristled. "We merely asked them here to settle a rumor. I am here as a healer, not as a member of the Triad."

"Which of them requires your healing, Varzi?" Gira asked dryly. "They look perfectly fit to me. And Tiean and Caius are more than capable of tending their own."

Camalaron gestured to Andorran. "Would you?"

With indifferent shrugs, the eight bared their markings once more.

Gira stared, incredulous. "Then… I thought… how?" He couldn't finish the thought, but his face said enough. He had dismissed the stories as nonsense, mere hysteria among the villagers. Seeing it for himself left him shaken. "What do you plan to do about this?"

"I am not sure anything *can* be done," Camalaron said grimly. "Varzi insists they are part of them. Not a brand." He looked at Andorran. "You have heard what the people of Tegoradaysol call you?"

"Una'savagi," Andorran answered. "Yes, Sovereign Master, we have heard."

"Does that not concern you?"

"Should it, Sovereign Master?" Tau asked politely.

Camalaron leaned back, steepling his fingers. "If it were me, I would be concerned."

Calla's tone was respectful, her face unreadable, but her words dripped insolence. "Then it is fortunate, Sovereign Master, that they do not call *you* Una'savagi."

Laughter flickered in eight pairs of eyes, though none of them smiled.

Camalaron resisted the urge to shift uneasily in his chair. The last thing he wanted was to confirm what they already suspected, that Una'savagi troubled him greatly. With the fate of the reckoning possibly in their hands, they faced him with the certainty that *they* held control.

"Was there anything else, Sovereign Master?" Andorran asked quietly.

Camalaron frowned. With the Triad present, the last thing he wanted was to make the dragonmasters feel manipulated.

"You are not letting them go?" Varzi protested sharply.

Letting? Camalaron could almost hear Una'savagi echo the word in their heads. He spoke quickly. "They are free to go. Clearly, we have learned all we can about the markings." Certainly all that the *wild ones* intended them to know. He inclined his head. "You are excused."

Together, the eight nodded, turned, and filed out in silence.

As the door closed, Varzi and Gira erupted in protest, but Camalaron silenced them with a gesture. He crossed to the window.

Outside, in the bright sunlight, the eight walked. Not merely walked they strode, with a stride that bordered on arrogance. Niko and Caius had arms slung over each other's shoulders, laughing. Tiean, Gan, and Kodar chatted easily. Calla walked between Andorran and Tau, her hand caught in Tau's, swinging playfully.

"Why did you let them go?" Varzi demanded, joining him at the window. "We are losing control of them!"

Camalaron laughed sharply. "Losing? Did either of you believe, even for a moment, that we had *any* control?"

Gira looked faint, leaning against the wall in lieu of a chair. "Should we try to rein them back in?"

Shaking his head, Camalaron sighed. "It is too late for that."

"They cannot do this alone!" Varzi snapped. "They need the rest of us!"

"They know that," Camalaron said. "Which is why they remain minimally respectful. They are not fools. But they also know they do not need us nearly as much as we need them."

"This is your fault, Camalaron!" Varzi snapped. "I told you months ago that you were giving them too much freedom!"

"They have learned more in months than most dragonmasters learn in years," Camalaron countered. "Uniting them, giving them rein that was our best option. We all agreed when Calla received her peril stone."

Gira tugged his beard with a sigh. "Perhaps. But we did not know then that they would become… Una'savagi. The name fits."

"I agree," Camalaron admitted. "Though I am not pleased by it."

As if to taunt him, Calla looked back over her shoulder and flashed a radiant smile. She *knew* they would be watching. Turning forward again, she extended her hand to Andorran. He caught it leisurely, and together they vanished around the corner of the livery.

>

In the clearing beside *Rait's Tree*, on the banks of the Tegora Dara Mai, the afternoon sun blazed down as Tiean and Niko sparred with their staves while the others practiced their sword work.

"Caius block those!" Andorran barked, his tone sharp. "Tau, you're going too easy on him!"

Caius would have argued if he had a spare breath, but wielding against Tau demanded his full focus. Battling Tau was still preferable to facing Calla or Gan, but even so, it left him exhausted and usually in need of Tiean's healing. Try as he might, Caius simply wasn't the warrior the others were.

Across the clearing, Gan's sword clashed against Calla's with a ringing clang. He swept his blade around in a quick arc, narrowly deflecting her counterstrike. Sweat trickled down his face and shone on his bare chest, his muscles taut, though his breathing was steadier than Caius'. He relished the challenge of wielding certainly more than the staff, where Niko was gaining mastery. Still, what he truly wanted was to be flying.

Calla smacked his elbow with the flat of her blade. "Get your head out of the clouds, flier!" she scolded, sheathing her sword and dragging the back of her hand across her brow.

Gan grinned impishly. "I'll wager you've heard that a time or two."

Andorran, lounging under the massive burr oak known as Rait's Tree, let out a laugh. "That would be a safe bet."

Calla dropped down beside him, accepting the leather water pouch he held out. "You're a flier you know what Gan and I feel."

"I also know that daydreaming can get your throat slit," he countered.

The others drifted over, Niko and Caius climbing into the tree's twin forks above Calla and Andorran while the rest sprawled in the shade. The water pouch passed hand to hand.

Tau studied Andorran. "You haven't said a word about this morning's meeting with the Triad."

"What's there to say? As we suspected they wanted to know about the markings."

Calla grimaced. "This isn't over. Varzi wasn't satisfied."

The subject of their markings had sparked heated debate among them. Calla had argued firmly against telling anyone anything. Let the gossips whisper, she said. She wanted no one to know she could forge a binding or worse, that she could assimilate. Working out in the heat, she was the only one not bare-chested, a deliberate choice.

Niko, ever sensitive to Calla's instincts, had sided with her. Gan argued that since it was *her* gift, it should be *her* choice whether to reveal it. Tau sympathized but thought honesty was wiser. Caius and Tiean reasoned that too many people had already seen the markings to pretend secrecy. Kodar, typically reluctant to weigh in, would have abstained except Calla flatly refused to let him. Pressed, he'd sided with Tau.

Andorran had let them argue until their words grew heated, then finally proposed a compromise: they would reveal the markings if asked, but nothing about Calla's assimilation or binding.

Grudgingly, they had all agreed. They needed to appear united especially in front of the Triad.

"I don't think Master Camalaron sent that summons," Tau said.

"I agree." Caius nodded. "And I don't think Gira was meant to be there."

"So we agree it wasn't meant to be a full Triad summoning," Tau continued, leaning back on his elbows. "I think Varzi sent it."

"And he seemed particularly interested in Calla," Tiean recalled.

Taking the water pouch from Calla, Caius grinned. "Well, hers is the only one others haven't seen."

"Or maybe he just wanted to antagonize her," Niko suggested. "He certainly provoked Andorran."

Calla laughed. "You don't need to protect me from Varzi."

"Perhaps I was protecting *him* from you," Andorran said dryly.

Her grin widened. "Well, you certainly got his attention."

"Vien's as well," Tau chuckled.

One leg dangling from the branch, Niko drained the last drops of water and passed the pouch back down to Andorran. "I don't understand why Vien's so afraid of us. We've never done anything to him."

"Probably afraid Calla will sic her friends on him," Gan said with a smirk. "I heard Dimar was stung six times before the bees turned back."

"He's lucky I sent bees and not bears!" Calla retorted hotly. "I expected spies but not while I was bathing!"

The others burst out laughing. Animals seemed to mirror Calla's moods, often with dramatic results. The more outraged she was, the fiercer their response. Dimar was fortunate indeed that it had been only bees. Calla could just as easily have summoned something far more dangerous.

"I do not think he will make that mistake again," Tiean said firmly.

Calla yawned, resting her chin on her knees and hugging her legs close. "Well...they did not ask as many questions as I expected."

"I do not think they expected all of us," Kodar noted.

"That worked in our favor," Niko added quietly. "We had the advantage right away."

"Master Camalaron knows," he went on after a pause. "He knows we are stronger...and that we are only biding our time."

"I am not surprised," Calla murmured, stifling another yawn. "Tangor always said the Sovereign Master saw more clearly than most."

Above her, Caius covered a yawn of his own. "I do not think he plans to interfere."

Rubbing her eyes, Calla gave a third muffled yawn. "I hope not."

Andorran leaned forward, peering into her face, then glanced up at Niko and Caius, both struggling against wide-mouthed yawns. "What is wrong with you three?"

"I do not know." Calla blinked rapidly, fighting to keep her eyes open. "I can barely stay awake."

"Me either," Caius mumbled, slumping against the tree fork.

"The water," Tiean said suddenly, a worried look crossing his face. "We have all been drinking it."

"It came from the rain barrel," Tau added, fighting his own yawn. "Anyone could have tampered with it."

Calla groaned and sagged back against Andorran. He quickly slipped an arm around her to keep her upright.

"She is the smallest it will take her first," Tiean explained. "Niko and Caius will be next." He nodded towards the two boys, already half-asleep in the tree branches. "Without knowing what was used...I cannot stop it."

Gan muttered through heavy lids, "I am going to be very angry about this when I wake up." He dropped to the ground and surrendered to sleep.

"Calla should be shielded," Tau suggested, his voice thick.

But one by one, the others succumbed Kodar already snoring softly, Tiean's breathing deep and even.

Andorran felt the first wave of drowsiness wash over him, and his arm tightened around Calla. She shifted against him, head on his chest, one arm draped across his stomach. Pressing a kiss to her forehead, he murmured a spell, his blue-green eyes fixed on her pale face.

"They will pay for this," he promised in a low growl, before the drugged sleep claimed him too.

Varzi strolled into the clearing a short time later, two uneasy companions trailing behind. His eyes swept over the eight sleeping *Una'savagi*.

The plan had been simple: pour a draught into the rain barrel, wait for the wild ones to drink, then examine their markings while they slept. But Dimar and Bamal did not like taking chances with these eight. Nothing about *Una'savagi* felt simple.

Up close, the silver-shimmering markings made both men blanch. Dimar, who had already endured an unfortunate run-in with Calla's bees, looked as if he would bolt if given the chance.

Kneeling beside Tiean, Varzi laid a hand over the dragonsheart. The healer stayed silent for several minutes, studying the marking intently.

"Those two in the tree..." he ordered brusquely. "...see what you make of their markings."

Dimar's stomach turned. He had no idea what he was supposed to be "looking for" and he had no desire to climb the great oak. But refusing Varzi seemed even more dangerous.

Bamal boosted his slimmer brother up with a cupped hand. Dimar secured himself among the branches with a grimace.

Varzi had already moved on to Tau. "Check the dragonslayer," he snapped.

Bamal scowled. Varzi always gave him the worst of it. Still, he knelt by Kodar and laid a hand over the dragonsheart etched on his chest. Bracing himself, he waited for something to happen. Nothing did. He exhaled in relief.

"I sense nothing. Maybe it is not what you thought."

From the tree, Dimar called down, "I do not see anything strange either. But then…I am no healer."

"The markings I saw were on a mystic," Varzi muttered tightly. "Each herd bears a unique brand from the Mistress of Mystics. They were silver, like these. That *these eight* have a mystic's horn woven into their mark…" He shook his head. "I intend to know why."

Bamal arched a brow. "What do mystics have to do with dragonmasters?"

"That," Varzi said coldly, "is what I intend to find out."

His gaze shifted to Calla.

Dimar and Bamal exchanged horrified looks. Everyone knew her marking was hidden beneath her tunic. Worse, she slept curled in Andorran's arms. To see it, she would have to be moved.

"She is asleep!" Varzi barked. "She cannot hurt you!"

They hesitated. She was the Genesi Ney. And Andorran furious even in sleep looked more dangerous than Calla ever could.

"Bamal, stop wasting time!"

Scowling, the heavier man stepped closer. First the dragon-slayer, now this. He wished he had taken Dimar's task with the tree instead. Bending, he reached for Calla's shoulder, intending to turn her gently.

A surge of white-hot energy flung him across the clearing. He landed flat on his back, twenty feet from where she slept, the breath knocked from his lungs.

Dimar bolted to his side. "Bamal!"

Varzi cursed furiously, eyes fixed on Calla. "Of course. She is shielded."

Bamal staggered upright with Dimar's help, pale and shaken. He had endured enough. If Varzi wanted Calla's marking, he could damn well take the risk himself.

"Are you well, Bamal?"

The deep voice froze him where he stood. Camalaron had arrived, his face carved with restrained fury.

Lowering his head, Bamal placed his hands on his sword hilt. "I…I am fine, Master Camalaron."

"Attempting to breach a shield can be dangerous," Camalaron said, his tone controlled but heavy with warning. "I suggest you go to the infirmary and have Urra attend you. Dimar go with him."

The two men bowed their heads gratefully and all but fled the clearing, leaving Varzi to face the Sovereign Master alone.

Varzi folded his arms, glaring at the Sovereign Master. "The fact that she is shielded only proves my point!"

"It proves nothing," Camalaron countered sharply.

Varzi's green eyes flared. "I told you my theory about these markings! I told you where I had seen others like them!"

"That may have nothing to do with this." Camalaron's gaze swept uneasily over the sleeping *Una'savagi*. "Do you realize what you've done here? The repercussions could be devastating. They *had* to know something was wrong, no matter how quickly your potion worked!"

"And Calla still took the time to shield herself!" Varzi pressed.

Camalaron frowned. "Would *you* have done any differently? Have you considered how they might react once they realize this? These are not dragonmasters to be trifled with, Varzi. They could retaliate for this *attack*."

"This was not an attack!" Varzi snapped. "I was trying to regain control!"

"You will have *no* control after this," Camalaron warned coldly. "None of us will."

As he spoke, Caius' limp hand slipped from the tree fork above Calla's head. Camalaron caught it and tucked it back against his chest, frowning. He laid one hand lightly on Caius' chest. "His heart beats too slowly." His tone was tight. "How much did you give them?"

Varzi shrugged. "Bamal was supposed to pour the dram into their rain barrel."

Camalaron bent swiftly over Niko, fingers at the boy's neck. He drew in a sharp breath. "His pulse is hardly better. Check the others."

Varzi hurried to Tau and Tiean while Camalaron moved to Gan and Kodar. "The rest seem stable enough," Camalaron muttered, returning to Caius. He pressed two fingers to the boy's jugular, channeling energy into him. Varzi did the same for Niko, and together they strengthened the boys' faltering pulses until their breathing steadied.

"That fool Bamal must not have checked the barrel," Varzi grumbled. "The potion wasn't diluted enough."

Camalaron's frown deepened. "If it was too strong for Caius and Niko…" His gaze shifted to Calla.

For the first time, Varzi's face flickered with concern. "We can do nothing for her while she is shielded."

Camalaron's expression turned grim. If Calla died, the others would be ruled by vengeance, and Tegoradaysol itself might not survive their wrath.

"You must be able to break her shield!" Varzi urged desperately. "It has been done before!"

"If there were a way to undo this mess you've created, I would do it!" Camalaron snapped. "But their spells are not mine and I do not know the counter-casts."

Varzi paled. His panic seemed less for Calla than for himself. His life would be worth nothing if she died by his hand.

"They cast spells unseen for decades...centuries," Camalaron said grimly. "Only *they* know how to undo them."

Calla's breathing grew shallower. Camalaron considered breaching her shield himself, he was stronger than Bamal, but it might drain him too much, and still he might fail.

Andorran's arms tightened around her. Still deep in drugged sleep, his hand rose to rest against her collarbone. He drew a deep breath, pressing his cheek to her curls. Silvery light bloomed around them both.

Camalaron's eyes widened, and Varzi gasped aloud as Calla mirrored Andorran's breath, her chest rising and falling in unison with his. After several long moments, she sighed and nestled closer to him. The glow faded. The danger had passed.

Camalaron was astonished. The bond between them was stronger than he had ever imagined.

Varzi's face darkened. "She was not under *her* shield. *Andorran* is shielding her! Do you still think they are not defying us because of her? Twice in one day he has intervened on her behalf!"

"He is protective," Camalaron argued, though without conviction.

"Do not treat me like a fool!" Varzi snarled.

Camalaron inclined his head, weary. "Very well. I will admit it there is a powerful connection between them. Perhaps it is because they are the last generation."

"Then I say we find out," Varzi declared. "Summon them formally, Una'savagi to the Triad."

Camalaron grimaced. "I do not think it wise to use that name. And after this…they may not even respond to a summoning."

"They will come," Varzi snapped. "And they will answer to *Una'savagi*. It is time to rein them in!"

He stormed away, leaving Camalaron with a sinking dread. This disaster had barely been averted, and Varzi was already sowing the next. Perhaps it was not only *Una'savagi* who needed to be reined in.

>

Later, pacing their common room with the formal summons clenched in her fist, Calla glowered at Vien. His face was ashen, his hands trembling. He clearly wanted to flee, but his orders were to wait for their reply.

"I say we ignore it," Gan said darkly from the hearth. Tau and Niko nodded in agreement.

Andorran shook his head. "We do not want to appear intimidated."

"They cannot think that," Tiean argued.

"We have tried following the rules, as best we can," Caius said reasonably. "I think we should go and hear what they want."

"We already faced them once," Tiean reminded. "As long as we are together, there is little they can do."

Kodar frowned. "We were together this afternoon," he pointed out.

Calla glared at the parchment and it burst into flame in her fist, falling to the floor in sparks and ash. "I have no interest in answering *their* summons. Not after what happened. But we *do* have matters to discuss with them." Her amber eyes swept the circle. "So I say *we* send the summons Una'savagi to the Triad. Let them meet us on *our* terms."

Andorran looked intrigued. "Interesting idea."

"It is perfect!" Gan exclaimed, leaping to his feet. "Calla, you are brilliant!"

She grinned at his enthusiasm.

"What should it say?" Caius asked. "We need to keep it simple. Minimal words have greater impact."

"Simple it is," Tau said with conviction. *"Una'savagi summons the Triad to their quarters."*

As he spoke, Calla lifted her finger, tracing graceful letters in the air. Shimmering symbols hovered briefly before settling onto a roll of parchment that materialized with a faint scratch of quill on paper. She rolled it and crossed to hand it to Vien.

He took it with relief, glad his errand was nearly complete, though dread shadowed his eyes. "They are not going to like this," he muttered aloud before realizing the words had slipped free.

Calla laughed huskily. "No, I suppose they will not. And tell them we will not be expecting refreshments."

Vien blinked in confusion.

"We will prepare our own food and drink from now on."

The baffled look on his face made Andorran chuckle. He motioned Vien to go, and the man hastily obeyed.

When the door closed, Andorran moved to Calla's side. "You are not going to let your temper get the better of you, are you?"

She sobered, meeting his eyes. "Are you not angry about what happened, Andorran?"

"I am furious," he admitted without hesitation.

"I do not want them thinking they can get away with what they did."

Framing her face gently in his hands, he said, "They will not get away with anything." It was a vow he fully intended to keep. Even in his unconscious state, the binding had called him when Calla was in danger. Without it, she might have died and he would never have known she needed him to pull her back. Accident or not, too much potion had been poured into their water. Forgiveness was not in his heart.

Calla, unaware of what had truly happened, showed no memory of it. For now, Andorran thought it best not to tell her. She was angry enough.

"Andorran?"

He released her, surprised by her soft tone.

She patted his jaw playfully. "You are not going to let *your* temper get the better of you, are you?"

His lips curved into a smile. "I hope not."

>

The Triad came, reluctantly, but they came. That, *Una'savagi* counted as a small victory though not nearly enough.

The meeting was held in Una'savagi's common room. It had no furnishings; they had no need of them. The Triad would be forced to conform to *their* rituals instead of the other way around.

Camalaron instantly recognized the message in the setting but made no objection. They were in the "wild ones'" territory now.

Varzi had been livid when Vien returned with the summons, adamant that he would not respond. It had taken Camalaron and Gira threatening everything short of binding and dragging him to force his compliance. Gira, furious, reminded him it was *his fault*

Una'savagi no longer trusted them. Rectifying that was the least he could do.

Now, Varzi sat sulking on the hearth, flanked by his fellow Triad members. Una'savagi crouched in a semi-circle before them.

Andorran began, his tone steady. "Certain spells have been put in place for this meeting."

Varzi sputtered at that, but Camalaron silenced him with a look.

Tau calmly explained: "An anti-spell charm prevents anyone here from casting, and a sound-barrier spell ensures that no one outside this room can hear us."

When the Triad gave curt nods, Andorran wasted no time. "The incident today made us realize we are at risk even from those we should be able to trust."

"We were not all involved in that," Gira said sharply, shooting a pointed glance at Varzi.

"In his defense," Camalaron added carefully, "Master Varzi believed he was acting in your best interests."

Andorran frowned. "We will look out for our *own* best interests, Master Camalaron."

"I realize that," Camalaron acknowledged with a respectful nod. "And you do so admirably beyond imagination, in fact. The shield on Calla prevented us from helping her today, but clearly, you managed on your own."

The subtle glance Calla gave Andorran promised he would be explaining himself to her later.

Camalaron continued. "It did, however, bring an important matter to light."

Varzi's eyes narrowed. "Then ask them straight out...are those markings a binding?"

"Yes," Andorran answered without hesitation.

Gira paled. Varzi sprang to his feet. "I told you!"

In a heartbeat, Una'savagi were on theirs, hands on sword hilts, ready. Camalaron shoved Varzi back down onto the hearth. "Relax! All of you relax!"

Gira eyed them warily. "Who forged this binding?"

Calla stepped forward. "I did."

The Triad stared in stunned silence. Camalaron sank down beside Varzi, who glared at Calla with undisguised loathing. Gira shook his head, words failing him.

Una'savagi exchanged brief looks, then nodded to each other. As one, they crouched back into their semi-circle, arms draped over knees. They looked relaxed but alert.

"We are bound to the Genesi Ney," Tiean explained.

"It is forbidden for humans to possess the power of binding!" Varzi snapped shrilly.

"That was before," Tau said coldly. "We are the new blood. The old ways do not apply to us."

"That is blasphemy!" Varzi cried, face red with outrage.

Andorran's voice cut through like tempered steel. "This is why we were reluctant to tell you. You cannot understand what we are. We are *more* than dragonmasters."

"More?" Camalaron repeated, wary. "What does that mean?"

"We have powers and abilities beyond other sorcerers…beyond other dragonmasters."

"Dark powers from Daiesthai, no doubt," Varzi accused.

Camalaron braced for fury but Una'savagi only chuckled, as if he had told a joke.

Calla's amber eyes glittered dangerously. "You had best hope we never choose that path. Your fate is questionable enough as it is."

Varzi bit back his retort.

"Andorran," Camalaron said gravely, "this claim of being more than dragonmasters will not sit well, least of all with the other dragonmasters."

"We cannot help what we are," Andorran said firmly.

"We cannot change what we are," Tiean added.

Calla's voice was quiet, but resolute. "And we will not tolerate those who expect us to try."

Gira leaned forward, listening intently. Dragonmasters had been the most powerful humans alive for nearly ten thousand years. The idea of something greater was almost unthinkable. But if the Genesi Ney was meant to be the bloodline of a new age…if she survived the reckoning…it stood to reason that she would be *more* than a dragonmaster. Just how much more, he could not yet imagine.

"We will not risk another incident like today," Andorran continued. "We have placed spells around our quarters, and it would be wise to make everyone aware of them. That way, we can avoid any…unpleasant accidents."

"What sort of spells?" Gira asked.

"Spells to guarantee our safety and our privacy," Tau explained evenly. "No one will be able to come within twenty yards of our quarters without an invitation."

Camalaron looked uneasy. "Are the spells harmful?"

"No more than the potion we were given today," Tiean said pointedly, a faint smile tugging at his lips.

Camalaron frowned. That answer left plenty of room for interpretation.

"We will have similar wards around the clearing when we are there," Gan added. "And from now on, we will prepare all of our own food and drink."

Gira looked troubled. "You cannot truly believe anyone here intends you harm?"

Andorran shrugged, though his hard gaze slid deliberately toward Varzi. "What happened today may have been meant well, and the fact that it turned dangerous might have been an accident. But we will err on the side of caution."

"You risk widening the rift between yourselves and the rest of the community," Camalaron warned.

"So be it," Calla said dismissively. "If they choose to fear Una'savagi, that is on them. We have done nothing to create that fear."

"The prys that were previously in place are no longer effective," Niko added. "And we do not advise replacing them."

Tau leaned forward slightly. "Also…we will need to make a few trips."

"Trips?" Camalaron asked, alarm sharpening his tone. "Where do you intend to go?"

"Choran Sa, to start," Calla said firmly. "We need to see if the slayers hold the city."

Gira's jaw dropped, and Varzi's face darkened as if he were about to erupt.

Camalaron spoke before Varzi could. "That is not safe especially for you seven."

"We can eclipse," Tau said reasonably. "And three of us are fliers."

"Dragons?!" Varzi rasped, clutching at his chest. "You mean to take dragons?!"

"Naturally," Calla replied coolly. "But only to the edge of the woodlands. It will save a great deal of time."

"And after Choran Sa?" the Sovereign Master pressed.

"That will depend on what we find there," Caius answered.

"But you cannot simply go running about..." Gira began.

"We can," Andorran interrupted firmly. "And we will."

"To what end?" Camalaron asked, still trying to grasp their intent.

"The theory has been that the slayers surround Mim Tor," Calla explained. "Eventually, they may intend to destroy the ruling house perhaps even to topple the gaol altogether. Without a reigning house, the gaol will panic. It has happened before, and it could happen again." She shook her head. "But Darmon suggested another possibility, that the true target is Tegoradaysol."

Varzi looked outraged. "That is madness! They would never attempt such a thing!"

"If there are no slayers in Choran Sa," Andorran said quietly, "we can focus on protecting Mim Tor and the king. But if slayers *are* there or in any of the northern cities then Darmon is right. Their target must be Tegoradaysol."

Gira tugged anxiously at his beard. "This…this cannot be. Tegoradaysol? How could they even hope to cross the mountains?"

"I would not think it possible either," Camalaron admitted gravely. "But perhaps a visit to Choran Sa will provide us with a clearer picture of what we face."

"You mean to let them go?!" Varzi demanded.

Camalaron gave him a rueful smile. "I do not believe they are asking for our permission, Varzi."

The healer drew a sharp breath, glaring at each of them in turn. "You are fools if you think you can survive a reckoning alone! You are barely more than children some of you *are* still children!"

"We have no intention of going into the reckoning alone, Master Varzi," Caius said pleasantly. "When we need you, we will let you know."

Outraged, Varzi shoved past them and slammed the door on his way out.

Una'savagi exchanged looks of grim satisfaction, while the Sovereign Master sighed heavily. "It is a difficult task, leading people particularly those who do not wish to follow."

Andorran met his gaze levelly. "We will do what needs to be done, Master Camalaron. We do not delude ourselves into thinking it will be easy."

Camalaron nodded. Una'savagi had just stepped into the most powerful position in the realm. Whether intended or not, they were now the ruling force in Tegoradaysol.

Chapter 16: Into Choran Sa

For a flier, there were few thrills to compare with being astride a dragon, high above the ground with the landscape little more than a blur beneath. Calla and Gan lived for the exhilaration of the dragon saddle and though he would never admit it, they all suspected Andorran felt the same.

Caius, however, seated between Calla and Niko, did not share their joy. His eyes were squeezed shut, his body stiff as a board. He liked Valor well enough on the ground but did not enjoy his company in the air. Niko was not as reluctant, but even he was always grateful to feel the earth under his boots again.

Tau and Kodar flew with Andorran, while Tiean paired with Gan, and all three declared themselves devoted land-lovers. Tau had at least taken the time to teach Caius and Niko a spell to help settle their stomachs in flight, a spell they were profoundly grateful for.

Gan's dragon had been chosen for him, not the other way around. Valor, who had chosen Calla as his rider years before, brought his half-brother Finesse to Gan. The young dragonmaster had been delighted to claim a spiketail of his own. Though Gan was fond of Valor, it was clear the older dragon's heart belonged entirely to Calla.

Andorran's mount was a different breed altogether. Ba'tair, his great eudraco, stood more than eighteen feet at the shoulder, his body armored in shimmering blue-gray scales. Eudracos were considered the most intelligent of all dragons, and his name reflected it. In the Language of the Old Age, *Ba'tair* meant wisdom.

Ba'tair made Caius nervous even on the ground. The massive dragon relied on sheer strength. Without the deadly spikes of the spiketails, and with his thick, shorter legs ending in talons less fearsome than other breeds, he still commanded respect. His tail twice as long as a spiketail's was a weapon in itself, capable of sending an enemy flying with a single flick. In the air, despite his immense size, Ba'tair was graceful and agile, his sixty-foot wingspan matching Valor for speed.

Whatever their breed or size, a dragon in flight was impossible to miss. Three together could not go unnoticed. The fliers set their mounts down a safe distance from Choran Sa, just outside the forest, with instructions to return to Tegoradaysol if danger arose or their riders were delayed. Dragonmasters could always find their own way back.

After a good night's rest in the shelter of the woodlands, Una'savagi began their trek toward Choran Sa at first light. This was their first mission but they all knew it would not be their last.

Choran Sa was a city of more gaol than sorcia, only slightly smaller than Daul Andora, with a reputation nearly as notorious. A riverfront hub, it attracted a wild assortment of traders, gamblers, and smugglers, and its taverns kept the streets raucous well into the morning hours.

Andorran was comfortable enough in a city like Choran Sa. Few cutpurses would dare consider him a target. Magic or not, his sheer presence was enough to make most thieves think twice. The others, however, looked far less enthusiastic as they entered the noisy, bustling streets.

Getting into the city was no trouble at all. If the slayers did hold Choran Sa, they did so discreetly. Day-to-day life bustled along as usual. But Una'savagi knew that if the slayers were present, someone would know and when it was safe, someone would talk.

Calla, Niko, and Caius skilled at eavesdropping on conversations not meant for their ears took on the task of listening for rumors. Andorran had not liked the idea of splitting up, but he conceded it was the most efficient way to cover ground. They agreed to meet at the Water Wheel Inn before dark, and if trouble came sooner, their bindings would summon the others.

Well inside the city's walls, among throngs of bustling citizens, Una'savagi divided. Andorran, Niko, and Kodar made their way toward the riverfront. Tau, Tiean, and Caius veered north, where small shops and the residential quarter clustered. Calla and Gan pressed into the heart of Choran Sa.

"Have you been here before?" Gan asked as they wound their way down the dusty, littered street.

Calla shook her head. "I prefer to stay south of the mountains," she replied, eyeing their surroundings with distaste. Choran Sa was loud, dirty, and vulgar. Though only midday, men staggered drunkenly from taverns, some bellowing in protest at being tossed out, others leaning on questionably clad women.

Gan's brows lifted. "I think I know where Master Camalaron saw the design for that dress he put you in."

Calla followed his gaze and grinned. A pretty blonde, not much older than Gan, gave him a dimpled smile as she waved a silk handkerchief to ward off heat and dust. Her gown clung scandalously to her curves, its neckline plunging low to display an impressive bosom on the verge of spilling free, a high slit baring nearly her entire thigh.

Chuckling, Calla jabbed Gan in the ribs. "That little miss would have you for dinner, newling," she teased, "and use your bones to pick her teeth afterward."

Gan shot her a dark look but avoided the blonde's eyes. He had too little experience with women not to take Calla's word as fact. When a brunette winked at him at the next corner, he startled and shook his head in bewilderment. He had seen courtesans before, as his father had called them, but they had never paid him the slightest attention.

"Women are certainly forward here," Gan muttered.

Calla glanced at him and nodded. "Just watch your step. I have a feeling they're not all as harmless as they appear."

Gan did not think they looked harmless in the least, but he wisely kept that thought to himself. For the next several blocks he kept his eyes fixed straight ahead, avoiding eye contact with Choran Sa's courtesans. That was attention he could do without, and he had no doubt Calla would find the whole ordeal immensely entertaining.

When Calla stopped suddenly to peer through a grimy shop window, Gan was grateful for the distraction.

"This looks interesting," she decided, leading the way inside.

The musty-smelling shop was crammed with weapons. Gan's eyes widened at the sight: swords, daggers, shields, staves, beltknives, spears, and a few strange tools he could not identify.

The proprietor, a small round man with only a few hairs clinging stubbornly to his head, bustled forward. His sharp gaze flicked to the blades at their waists, and his crooked smile showed that he had marked them as serious buyers.

"Welcome, young miss, young master," he greeted in a high-pitched voice that startled Gan. Unsure how to address them their simple tunics and leggings gave little clue to rank he seemed to hesitate. In Choran Sa, rank mattered, and Yori was clearly calculating. They looked like smugglers or mercenaries, but something about them suggested more.

"I am Yori. You come for weapons, no?"

"To look," Calla replied. Her gaze swept the room. "You have quite an assortment here, Yori."

He beamed, revealing stained, crooked teeth. "The best in Choran Sa, no?"

Gan's eyes caught on an enormous mace resting on a central table. The head bristled with spikes, each wicked tip at least two inches long. He cringed and turned quickly away, focusing instead on a case of daggers to his right. Some looked well-used, and he cast Yori a questioning glance.

The little man offered a sickly smile. "I do some trading, young master. Mostly for the bow, no? They are the new favorite, no?"

"An archer's bow?" Calla asked with interest.

"Yes, miss." Yori reached across the counter and produced a longbow with a quiver full of arrows. "Many find them intriguing, no? But few have the skill. They think distance gives them an advantage, but…" he licked his lips nervously, "…these are difficult times, no?"

Taking the bow, Calla turned it over curiously. She had heard of such weapons but had never seen one up close. "How is it used?"

Yori grinned and motioned her to follow. He led them through a curtained doorway into a cramped back room, then out into the alley.

"Bal!" he called sharply. "Bal, come here, boy!"

A scrawny boy of seven or eight scrambled down a rickety ladder from the roof. Dressed in clothes far too big for him, he shot Yori a sullen look before turning large, dark eyes toward the dragonmasters.

"Show them the bow," Yori ordered.

Bal accepted the weapon from Calla, plucked an arrow from the quiver, and faced a stack of grain sacks further down the alley. With surprising skill, he nocked the arrow, sighted, and drew the bow taut. The string thrummed, and the arrow streaked forward, thudding into the sack.

Calla walked down the alley, tugged the arrow free, and inspected its steel, three-sided tip. "Very impressive," she said with a nod. "I can see the advantage."

"For some, perhaps," Yori said grimly. "But the Watch has perfect aim, no?"

"The Watch?" Calla echoed, returning to them, still studying the arrow.

"The new guard," Yori explained. "You must have seen them on the wall, no?"

She had noticed the guards, but unarmed, they had seemed unremarkable. The gate guards had carried swords, though even those had not impressed her.

"They use bows," she realized. That explained why no swords had been visible, their weapon allowed them to strike without closing the distance.

"That they do, young miss."

Calla and Gan exchanged a meaningful glance before she turned back to the boy. "Can you teach us to use the bow?"

A slow smile spread across Bal's face, and he nodded eagerly.

Across the city, Caius peered wistfully into the window of a dressmaker's shop. The smell of dyes and bolts of fabric made him think of his mother's shop small, cozy, and familiar.

"Can I be of assistance?" an elderly woman asked as they stepped inside. Her gaze flicked uneasily over their weapons and travel-stained clothes.

"We were looking for a friend," Tiean said amiably. "We thought she might have come in here."

"From outside the city, no?" the woman asked. "You are not Choranites."

"No, we are just passing through," Tiean replied smoothly. "We were told Choran Sa was an interesting place to visit."

Her frown deepened. "I suppose that depends on what interests you, no? You best be on your way. I have seen no outsiders today."

Tau sighed as they stepped back into the dusty street. "We are not having much luck, are we?"

"I am hearing quite a bit," Caius told them. "I do not know if they are slayers, but there's a new guard in the city, and people are unsettled."

"Those guards on the wall?" Tau scoffed. "They're not even armed."

Caius shook his head. "I do not know if they are the same or not, but the people are calling them the Watch and they are truly afraid of them."

Tiean gave him a look of wonder. "I do not know how you, Niko, and Calla can do that."

Tau laughed. "It makes me want to be careful what I say."

"It is not something we try to do," Caius explained. "It just seems to happen."

"Well, I suppose we don't really have secrets from each other."

"I wouldn't go so far as to say that," Tau said meaningfully. "Some of us think we have secrets."

Caius raised a brow. "Are you talking about Niko and me?"

The other two exchanged puzzled looks. "You and Niko?" Tiean asked.

"You have secrets?" Tau added, curious.

"What kind of secrets?"

Caius felt the color creep into his face. "Well…you know…that we are…roommates." He gave an embarrassed shrug. "It's…well…when we first came here..."

"Oh, that!" Tau gave him a playful shove. "We knew all about that."

"We just didn't know it was supposed to be a secret," Tiean added lightly. "Tau and I shared a room for more than five years after we arrived in Tegoradaysol."

"It can be difficult," Tau admitted. "Finding out what you are, accepting the stone, being rejected by your family."

Caius sighed in relief. "I guess Niko and I weren't the only ones overwhelmed."

"Hardly." Tau gave him a look of understanding. "None of us thought anything of it, really."

"So…then who were you speaking about having a secret? Gan?"

"Gan has a secret?" Caius asked in surprise.

He laughed. "That's what I'm asking you."

"Likely our skeptic has his secrets, but nothing we need be concerned with," Tiean decided. "No…we were talking about Calla."

"You mean her feelings for Andorran?"

Tau grinned. "You see? She only thinks it's a secret."

"Niko said something about it…but I thought…" Caius looked at Tau uncertainly. "I mean…you and Calla…"

Tau exploded with laughter, and Tiean grinned broadly. Caius remained perplexed, shaking his head.

"I love Calla madly," Tau confessed, "but not in that way. It'll take a man at least as strong as Andorran to manage our Calla, and I'd just as soon not put my head on that particular chopping block."

"Calla is the only one who cannot see it, and only because she does not want to," Tiean said knowingly. "I've never heard of a match between a Kamborian and a Soroni."

Caius still looked doubtful. "I cannot see it. They're a volatile match."

Looking thoughtful, Tau nodded. "Yes…they are. And it's going to be very interesting when one of them finally surrenders."

>

The riverfront was the heart of Choran Sa's chaos.

Growing up along the banks of the Dari San, Niko thought he knew something of waterfront life, but the Garron Nir River made the Dari San look like little more than a glorified creek. The water here was wide, churning, and busy. He could barely make out the far bank.

The docks swarmed with men. Some bellowed orders, others scrambled to obey. Bare-chested sailors hauled crates, coiled ropes, and scampered like monkeys up tall masts to secure rigging. Despite the disorder, it was a well-practiced rhythm, each man knowing his place in the puzzle.

Niko gawked. He could not imagine how long it had taken to learn which rope controlled which sail. To him, it looked like an impossibly tangled puzzle.

Andorran, however, strode confidently down the center of the furthest dock. He had grown up in Kambor Tine, another city along the Garron Nir, and his father had captained a merchant ship. To him, the bustle of the waterfront was familiar.

"Are you hearing anything?" Kodar asked.

"Plenty," Niko replied. "But I don't know what any of it means."

"Just tell us what you hear," Andorran instructed, "and we'll decide what it means."

Niko nodded and veered right to avoid a mangy dog trotting toward him. Ordinarily, he loved dogs, but those in Choran Sa looked anything but friendly. In fact, he had not seen a single friendly face since entering the city except, perhaps, for a few women at the city gates. And they had been far too friendly. Niko could imagine exactly what his mother would have thought about that.

"People here are tense," he noted.

Andorran glanced back at the city wall. "The guards here look more serious than those on the west end. They're new since the last time I was here. The city used to be run by a civil watch. No uniforms."

These guards wore black tunics and leggings with red piping, black cloaks lined in red. Every one of them kept his hood up, concealing his face.

"I keep hearing people mention the Watch," Niko added.

Kodar frowned. "Black and red…those colors don't belong to any house or tribe I know."

"Maybe Choran Sa formed its own army," Niko suggested, "because of what's been happening in the other cities."

"Perhaps." Andorran's expression was unreadable as he scanned the docks. He moved with purpose, sifting through the cargo and crews until he spotted what he wanted. Motioning for Kodar and Niko to follow, he approached a man in a dark blue coat with gold insignia on his lapels and cuffs, a captain, clearly, who was overseeing the loading of a ketch.

"I haven't seen the *Roue* in some time," Andorran said quietly.

The captain turned, studying him with curiosity. "You're familiar with the *Roue*?"

"When I was a child, she was captained by a friend of my father's."

The man grinned faintly. "And your father? Who might he be?"

"Loam."

Recognition flickered in the captain's eyes. He studied Andorran more closely. "A good man. A good captain. You favor him." His expression hardened slightly.

"Are you taking passengers?"

The captain looked from Andorran to Kodar, then to Niko, and back again. His square jaw flexed as his eyes narrowed. His hair dark, shaved at the sides, the rest gathered in a braid hanging down his back marked him as a Kamborian. But that did not mean he would do a favor for a fellow Kamborian, even if he knew his father.

"Just you three?"

"Five more," Andorran replied.

The man rubbed his beard with stubby fingers and glanced toward the guards at the head of the docks. "You running?"

"Not yet."

That made the captain grin. "Well…I need no trouble with the Watch," he said. "Let me see your hands."

Andorran didn't hesitate. He held out both hands, palms up. The captain turned them over quickly, then did the same with Kodar and Niko. Afterwards, he gave a curt nod.

"You're not with the Watch." His gaze slid back toward the guards. "But a pass is required to leave the city."

"We had no trouble getting in," Niko mentioned.

The man chuckled. "You'll find it's more difficult to get out, trust me, lad. Stay out of their way if you know what's good for you. They have no tolerance for anyone looking to make trouble."

"Who are they?" Kodar asked.

The captain shrugged, looking away. "I don't ask too many questions, and they leave me to my business."

Andorran drew in a deep breath and let it out slowly, scanning the waterfront with a practiced eye. "Waters aren't too bad right now."

"Storms to the north will be on us sometime tomorrow."

Andorran nodded. "Well…we thank you for the advice on the Watch. We'll try not to cause them any trouble."

Niko certainly hoped Andorran meant what he said. He had already heard enough to know they wanted no part in trouble with the black-cloaked Watch.

The man grunted something and spat over the edge of the dock. "If you do find yourself running, Kamborian…I'm scheduled to sail at last bell."

With a nod, Andorran turned and headed back the way he had come.

"We're leaving by boat?" Niko muttered with a frown.

"It's an option," Andorran corrected him. "And not one Calla is likely to vote for. She's a terrible wave rider, but we'll deal with that if we have to."

Back on the cobblestones, they passed through the gates with the carts hauling cargo up from the ships. Niko tried not to look at the Watch guards as they passed, but he could feel their eyes on him. The air was heavy with suspicion, fear, and despair.

"What are you sensing?" Kodar asked in a low voice.

"Enough to know that the sooner we're out of Choran Sa, the better," Niko whispered back.

>

The Water Wheel Inn was one of the less popular gathering places for gamblers and carousers, situated a fair distance from the waterfront. Still, as evening approached, it managed to fill its common room. Tau was grateful he had arrived early enough to secure a table in the far corner.

He, Tiean, and Caius had just been served steaming bowls of mutton stew and mugs of dark ale when they spotted Andorran, Niko, and Kodar at the door. It took them several minutes to weave through the crowded room before Niko slid onto the bench next to Caius with a weary look.

"My mum would have a fit if she saw me in a place like this," Niko confided.

"Mine too," Caius agreed.

"We've heard stories about it being difficult to leave the city," Tau reported, grabbing a thick slice of bread from the basket in the middle of the table. He dipped it into his stew and bit off a generous mouthful.

Andorran motioned for food, seating himself across from Niko and Caius. "We've heard the same. We may encounter problems leaving."

"We may encounter worse if we stay," Tiean said, his usually amiable face twisted into a surly expression. "People here aren't very receptive."

"And we were spotted as strangers straight away," Tau added.

"There's a craft leaving at last bell," Andorran said. "If we have to…we'll be on it."

Tau looked concerned. "Let's hope it doesn't come to that."

"I agree." Andorran fell silent as a woman arrived at their table with a tray of stew and ale for the newcomers. She flashed them a quick smile before moving on.

Niko dug eagerly into his meal, telling Caius about the waterfront while Caius described what he had learned in the city.

"And I know now where Master Camalaron saw that dress he put Calla in," Caius reported with a laugh.

Niko nodded enthusiastically. "I saw them too. My mum would really have a fit over that."

"I cannot imagine Master Camalaron would notice that…sort."

Niko grinned around a mouthful of mutton and potatoes. "I can't imagine he could miss them."

"Any mention of the Watch?" Andorran asked Tau. "Caius says everyone seems to be afraid of them."

"Niko says the same."

"Any chance they're not what we think?"

Andorran shrugged. "I'm not sure what they are…but we don't want to overlook that possibility." He glanced at the door, unsettled. "Where are they?"

Tau didn't need to ask who he meant. "It's only just getting dark. I'm sure they'll be along any time now."

"I told you it was a mistake to pair those two together," Tiean muttered. "They incite each other to trouble."

"They don't need each other for that," Andorran grumbled.

Niko and Caius laughed. Andorran was right. Calla and Gan shared a reckless nature, and neither made much effort to bridle their tongues. Together, they were twice as likely to find trouble.

"They can look after themselves," Tau said confidently, though he gave the door a quick glance. "Besides…how much trouble can they get into in one afternoon?"

"You must be joking!" Tiean rolled his eyes. "That's ten times longer than either of them needs."

"They have a job to do," Tau decided. "They'll stay out of trouble."

Caius mopped up the last of his stew with a slice of bread. "We would have known if they'd gotten into too much trouble," he reasoned.

"Did you hear about a marking of some sort?" Andorran asked, turning the conversation back to business.

Tau grimaced. "We did. An eye branded on the back of the hand. It marks the Watch and their spies."

"So, it would seem that Darmon's theory is not so far-fetched," Kodar said quietly.

Caius shook his head slowly. "No, I don't think it is. I heard Varan Sal Bou is held by the Watch as well."

"And Kambor Tine," Niko added.

"But I don't understand the point," Tau said, perplexed. "They surround the mountains…but to what end? They cannot hope to cross the mountains."

"And a siege seems pointless," Tiean tacked on, pushing his empty bowl aside. "I wonder how difficult it really is to get out?"

"We could go at night?"

Niko and Caius both shook their heads.

"They close the gates at last bell."

"And double the guards," Niko confirmed.

"If we're not out of here by last bell, we could be stuck for the night, at least. It might be better to take the *Roue* while we have the chance."

Tiean shrugged. "I have no problem with that…but you know Calla and water."

"Speaking of Calla…" Caius nodded toward the door, and they all turned.

With a hand on the shoulder of a bedraggled-looking boy, Calla and Gan were weaving their way across the room.

"And you thought they couldn't get into trouble," Tiean said smugly.

Reaching the table, Calla gently pushed the boy onto the bench beside Tau and dropped down next to him.

"This is Bal," she said lightly.

Gan slid in next to Niko, grinning broadly.

Andorran arched a brow at Calla. "A friend of yours?"

Bal's dark eyes regarded Andorran fiercely. "I am Sera Calla's dal'amine."

Calla brushed her hair out of her face, avoiding Andorran's questioning look. "We have a few things to work out…Bal and I."

Tau eyed her suspiciously. "What is a dal'amine?"

Gan chuckled, giving Calla an impish grin. "You can explain that, he's your dal'amine after all."

Calla frowned at him. "He's no one's dal'amine." She looked down at the boy. "You've got to stop saying that."

Bal looked up at her with a smile, clearly unconvinced.

"A dal'amine is a person owned by another person," Andorran explained, his tone stern. "And just how did you come to own a boy?"

"Oh, Andorran." She dismissed his concern with a wave of her hand. "I don't own him, of course. He's merely…confused."

Bal was scowling across the table at Andorran, which did nothing to improve his already drawn features. Niko studied the boy intently. He was underfed and pale, his clothes hanging from his scrawny frame like an old sack. A dirty, old sack. Niko didn't even want to think about when he had last bathed.

His face was thin, his nose a bit too wide, and suspicion and anger burned in his coal-black eyes unless they were fixed on Calla. For her, they shone with adoration.

"Calla…I never thought I'd hear myself say this…but you can't have a pet."

Bal bristled, but Calla gave him a reassuring pat on the back. She met Andorran's gaze squarely. "He's not a pet…he's just a little boy. And it's a bit complicated to explain, but he needs to come with us."

"We don't even know if we're going anywhere," Tau said flatly.

"The Watch." Calla said knowingly, trying to catch the attention of a serving girl. "A person could starve to death around here!" she added in annoyance when she was ignored.

"You saw the Watch too?" Caius asked.

Calla and Gan exchanged a glance, and she nodded. "Up close and personal."

That made Andorran frown. "What does that mean?"

"I warned you," Tiean said again.

"I know!" Andorran barked crossly. He turned back to Calla. "What happened with the Watch?"

"It was nothing really…just a misunderstanding."

Gan chuckled, and Bal looked indignant.

"Sera Calla is a camia'ol," the boy said firmly, his grubby fists clenching.

Calla groaned and slapped her hand over Bal's mouth. "You'd better mind where you speak out, whelp and stop calling me Sera."

His large eyes stared up at her reverently, and she heaved a sigh. Gan was still laughing, and the rest of the group looked confused.

Giving Bal a warning look, Calla released him and tried again to get the serving girl's attention, with no luck. The woman deliberately sauntered past their table to serve a group of men.

"I might have known!" Calla huffed. "I could starve to death for all the attention I'll get in here!"

"Can we discuss this boy?" Andorran said in exasperation.

"But…I'm hungry."

"Me too," Gan chimed in, raising a hand. Almost immediately, a pretty girl appeared with a bowl of stew and a mug of ale. She winked as she set them down and turned to leave.

Gan reached for a spoon just as Calla whisked the mug and bowl away, setting them in front of Bal. The boy dug in eagerly.

"Hey!" Gan protested, ignoring the laughter from the others.

"Just put your hand up she'll bring you another," Calla assured him.

As predicted, another bowl and mug were placed in front of him by the same girl. She touched his shoulder lightly before she left.

"See?" Calla said, sliding the second bowl and mug toward herself.

Gan's tawny eyes flashed. "Will you stop doing that?!"

She gave him a disarming smile. "She'll think you're flirting with her," she teased. "She'll find you cute and irresistible."

Kodar and Tau chuckled, nodding in agreement, while Niko and Caius laughed so hard they clung to each other to keep from falling over.

Gan shook a finger at her scoldingly. "You were the one warning me about getting eaten alive, and now here you are, offering me up as the main course!"

Niko and Caius howled with laughter, and even Tiean smiled, shaking his head. The table was drawing attention from others in the room. Andorran noticed too, giving Calla a reproachful look.

"We have matters to discuss," he reminded her in a low voice, "…if you're finished playing games?"

She smiled sweetly at him, the picture of innocence, and picked up her spoon.

The serving girl returned with another bowl and mug for Gan this time with a brunette at her side.

"This must be the best-looking table in the room, no?" Gan's blonde serving girl purred, twirling a strand of his dark-blonde hair around her finger.

"Certainly the hungriest," the brunette teased.

Both women were clad in similar dresses, the blonde's a deep lilac, the brunette's a vibrant red. The skirts were slit high on the right side, the necklines cut daringly low, and the long sleeves ended at jeweled fingers. Calla and Bal were the only ones too busy eating to pay them any mind.

"I am Dela," the brunette said, resting a hand lightly on Andorran's shoulder.

Calla arched a brow, chewing slowly.

"And this is Sousa."

The blonde giggled. "Mora thought you might wish some…company, no?"

Dela gave a husky laugh and stroked Tau's cheek with one finger. "What brings so many handsome men to the Water Wheel?"

Hunched over his bowl, Bal watched them with a solemn expression.

Dela's hand drifted to Andorran's jaw. "A very strong man…you work the dock, no?"

He shook his head, pulling away from her touch. She laughed and shifted her attention to Tiean.

"This one is pretty, no?"

Tiean blushed furiously, staring down at the table.

"Very pretty," Sousa agreed, running her fingers through Kodar's pale locks. "This one too."

Calla pushed her bowl away. "I think I've lost my appetite."

Dela's smile turned calculating. "Does one of these lovely boys belong to you, pet?" she asked sweetly.

Calla rose to her feet, and Bal jumped up with her, his small fingers twitching against her palm. She gave his hand a squeeze. "I know, Bal," she murmured reassuringly.

Dela's smile stayed fixed in place, though her eyes sharpened. "I would not wish to take one you've already claimed, pet," she purred.

Calla chuckled softly. "Rest assured, *pet,* you couldn't if you tried."

The implied threat hardened Dela's gaze, but Calla had already dismissed her. She turned to Gan, Niko, and Caius. "You three, with me."

They jumped up instantly, knowing better than to argue.

"The rest of you…" She leaned close to whisper in Kodar's ear. "I'd look closely at those pretty hands if I were you."

Turning on her heel, she strode out of the common room, Bal still clinging to her hand, the three newlings at her heels.

Once outside, she whirled on them, fury blazing in her amber eyes.

"You bloody men and your brains that turn to mush when a pretty woman smiles at you will be the death of me!" she snapped.

Caius gaped at her. "We…we did nothing," he protested.

"Were they marked?" Gan asked quietly.

"Bal said they were," Calla replied, still fuming. "The way you behaved, anyone would think they were sirens rather than serving wenches!" She jabbed a finger at Caius before he could speak. "And don't tell me you did nothing...that's the problem! You sat there like lumps of clay waiting to be molded!"

Bal brushed his black hair out of his eyes. "Sera Calla…are you angry because the pretty ladies were making a fuss over them?"

"No, Bal…not exactly," she told him.

He nodded, puzzled. "Is that not what the pretty ladies are supposed to do?"

"Yes, it is."

"But you didn't like it."

"No," Calla said firmly. "I didn't."

"Then why didn't you send them away?"

"Because…I couldn't." She ran her fingers through her curls, exasperated. "It's complicated, Bal."

That seemed enough for him, but the boys still looked baffled as they followed her up the street.

The others caught up moments later, but they hung back, wisely giving her time to cool off.

"What happened with the Watch?" Andorran asked Gan.

"Figures." He muttered, glaring at Calla's back.

"Does it have anything to do with the boy?"

Gan nodded. "Bal has the gift of foresight or something like it anyway. Not strong, but he's only eight."

"Where did he come from?"

"A weaponry shop. He was working for the owner." Gan's expression darkened. "Not working, exactly. He was the shopkeeper's dal'amine."

Niko frowned. "He called himself Calla's dal'amine."

Gan grinned. "I know. He's really attached himself to her."

"We could see that for ourselves," Andorran said curtly. "Could you elaborate?"

Gan sighed dramatically. "Alright. We were in a weaponry shop, and the proprietor, a man named Yori, told us about the Watch. He said some were buying and trading for bows."

Caius' eyes widened. "Bows?"

Gan nodded. "They give the archer the advantage of distance."

"They have an archery competition in Baldar'tine," Tiean said. "It's a tricky-looking weapon."

"That's what Yori said. He's sold quite a few, but most can't manage them. Calla was interested, so he took us into the alley and had Bal show us. The boy's actually pretty good." Gan admitted.

"Did you try?" Niko asked.

Gan looked embarrassed. "Unfortunately. Nearly put my own eye out with the bloody thing." His expression brightened. "But you should've seen Calla! She hit the target eight out of ten times! Bal was so excited I thought he was touched in the head." He paused. "I'm still not sure he isn't. He started calling Calla camia'ol."

"Which is?" Tau prompted.

Gan shrugged, but Andorran answered. "A warrior. A clan of warriors...all archers. The last of them died about three hundred years ago."

Tiean frowned. "How does Bal know about a clan that's been gone for centuries?"

"His parents were chroniclers," Gan explained. "They were recording lost history, according to Bal. They were executed as spies several months ago…and Bal was made Yori's dal'amine to pay their debts. At least, that's how Yori and Bal tell it."

Andorran dragged a hand over his bearded jaw, groaning. "That would've been enough to rile Calla."

Gan nodded reluctantly. "It did. The conversation got a bit…loud…and two members of the Watch came to investigate."

"Deius help us," Tau muttered, shaking his head.

"Bal made up some wild story about Calla being his father's sister, coming to pay his debt and take him away. Yori didn't want to explain to the Watch that he'd been using Bal to teach the bow. All he cared about was money and avoiding trouble. She wasn't happy to part with sixty dobbs, but she paid it."

Andorran grimaced. Sixty dobbs was a steep price for nothing to show but an eight-year-old boy.

"Now…Bal insists he has to stay with her and pay his debt," Gan continued. "He says he's her dal'amine, though she tried to tell him he owes her nothing. More importantly, he swears he must be with her because he saw it in a dream."

"A dream?" Tiean echoed skeptically.

Gan lifted his shoulders in a shrug. "That's what he says and I think he's telling the truth. He seemed to recognize Calla when we first met, and he nearly lost his senses when she asked him to teach her the bow."

"Well…foresight or not, I don't see how we can take a boy with us," Tau stated.

"You're not going to talk her out of it," Gan said with conviction. "I can't explain it, but there's something between them."

"In just an afternoon?"

Gan nodded firmly. "Trust me."

"Besides…" Niko warned. "She's in a mood."

"Just because of some tavern women?" Tiean asked in disbelief. "I can't believe she'd spare a second thought for a couple of serving wenches."

"Oh…it's a lot more than that," Niko muttered darkly as they moved forward to catch up with Calla and Bal.

Andorran reached out and caught Calla's arm. "How did you know?" he demanded, not giving her the chance to speak first.

She pulled away, planting her hands on her hips. "How did I know what? That you were about to make bloody fools of yourselves over a pair of strumpets?"

Niko's brows shot up in surprise, and Gan looked stung.

"I don't think it was difficult to see," she went on.

"But Calla…they came to us, we didn't…"

She smiled at him then, slow and sharp. "Gan," she drawled, cupping his face in her hands, "…pretty little poppet. I wouldn't deny you an education in any subject though in some, you may be in well over your head. Perhaps in such matters, Andorran would be willing to take you under his wing. But I don't relish the idea of plucking you out of the Watch's prison just because you were taken in by a pretty face." She gave his cheek a brisk pat, then turned to Andorran. "As for how I knew they were spies for the Watch I think you might just be grateful I bothered to tell you."

"They were spies?" Tiean whispered, appalled.

Andorran nodded. "I saw the marking under her sleeve after Calla warned us." He fixed Calla with a stern look. "But Calla…you know we're not going to let those women or anyone distract us from what we have to do."

She frowned at him. "I hope not."

"If they bothered you, why didn't you just say something?" Tau asked carefully.

Calla's amber eyes flashed as she snapped her gaze to him. "And what would you have me say, Tau? That yes, in fact, all the lovely boys are mine, though not in the way she thinks?" She shook her head, resolute. "I don't own any of you, and I won't lay claim to such! You are free to do as you please! Just don't expect me to sit and watch!"

She held out her hand. Bal slipped his into it at once, throwing the others a smug look as he melted into the shadows at her side.

Andorran started to follow, then stopped abruptly, dragging in an angry breath. His jaw clenched. "That woman had better make her mind up soon or I'll do it for her, her bloody pride be damned!"

Tau and Kodar looked horrified as Andorran stalked off, his heavy footsteps echoing down the street. Tiean's mouth fell open.

"What?" Niko asked in alarm. "What did that mean?"

"Do you remember Master Camalaron telling us we might have a task no one would envy?" Tiean asked quietly.

The newlings nodded warily.

"I think that task might be at hand," Tau said grimly.

Chapter 17: Wave Rider

It took the others several minutes to realize that it was not Calla but Bal leading them through the alleys and backstreets of Choran Sa. Clasping Calla's hand possessively, the boy moved with confidence, keeping them well out of sight of the Watch. Clearly, he had traveled these paths many times before.

When they reached the wall above the docks, Bal slipped through a narrow doorway. Calla followed, Gan close behind, but Niko hesitated and looked to Andorran.

"If Calla and Gan trust the boy, we should be fine," Andorran decided, nodding for them to move. He had to duck to squeeze through the opening, and once inside the small, damp room, his head brushed the sagging ceiling.

"Where are we?" Tau whispered.

"Bal says this place is safe from the Watch," Calla answered.

The room was empty but for dust and cobwebs. About the size of their common room back in Tegoradaysol, it had likely been a shop once, though now it reeked of rot.

Bal hurried to a far corner, dropped to his hands and knees, and tapped along the wall until he found what he sought. Rocking back, he pried up a section of the floor and reached into the darkness. A sharp click sounded, and a narrow slice of wall swung inward, revealing a crumbling stairwell descending into blackness.

"These old buildings have hidden passages to the river," Bal explained to Calla. "My parents found this one before the Watch took control."

"Why were they built?" Niko asked, peering into the gloom.

"Some were meant as escape routes if the city came under siege," Andorran said. "But most were built by smugglers."

Bal nodded, his dark eyes fixed on Calla. "Most have caved in. This is the only one I know that still leads to the water."

Calla frowned at the stairwell. "No hurry for that," she muttered.

"There's a craft leaving tonight at last bell," Andorran announced. Calla turned on him with disapproval, and he only shrugged. "Just in case."

"Passes are required for boarding any craft leaving Choran Sa," Bal warned. "The Watch checks carefully."

"What is this Watch?" Tau pressed.

"Are they slayers?" Tiean asked.

Calla raked her fingers through her curls. "No," she said softly. "And they're not sorcia either."

Everyone but Gan and Bal stared at her, stunned.

"Well…if they're gaol, leaving the city shouldn't be a problem, right?" Caius ventured.

"They're not gaol," Gan assured him. "Calla and I saw them up close, remember?"

Andorran gave Calla a troubled look. "What are they?"

She sighed. "I think…maybe…they're banedars."

Tau drew in a sharp breath. Tiean groaned.

"Are you sure?" Andorran pressed.

She shook her head. "I've never actually seen one. But they match the descriptions we were taught."

"What are banedars?" Niko asked.

"Hunters," Tau replied grimly.

"Daiesthai's hunters," Tiean corrected.

Kodar tugged nervously on his pale hair. "But banedars are solitary hunters. They don't work in groups."

Andorran rubbed his jaw. "The women at the inn weren't banedars."

Calla's expression hardened at the mention of Dela and Sousa. "I don't think banedars carry the mark, only those working with them."

"But…you never told us how you knew," Tiean reminded her.

Calla gave Bal a smile. "Bal told me. Our young friend has useful talents and some long-forgotten skills, thanks to his parents. He can cue."

Cueing was a skill nearly lost to history. Fewer people could cue than could speak the Language of the Old Age.

"So he told you they were marked?"

Calla nodded. "When he wasn't working for Yori, Bal spent his time exploring the city and avoiding the Watch." She ruffled his hair, and he grinned proudly. "Lucky for us."

"So maybe he can tell us how to get out of the city."

Bal's hands shifted in subtle gestures, even as he spoke aloud. "They don't let sorcia leave."

"Banedars aren't supposed to possess magic," Tiean mused. "Perhaps they're not much of a threat."

"They're hunters," Calla said firmly. "And deadly accurate with those bows, from what I've heard. I don't think we want to underestimate them."

"You are Camia'ol," Bal said earnestly, his right hand cueing as he spoke.

"You were impressive with that bow," Gan admitted, "but I don't think you're ready to face forty or fifty banedars."

"If Andorran has secured passage, I'd rather leave tonight," Tau decided. "Forty or fifty banedars is about forty or fifty too many for me."

Calla looked miserable at the thought, and Andorran's expression softened. His father had taken him aboard trading vessels as soon as he was old enough to handle rigging, and he was as comfortable on water as on land. But Calla…Tangor had sworn he'd rather walk an extra fortnight than put her back on a ship.

"We wouldn't be aboard long," Andorran assured her. "Only as far as Artiga maybe Kambor Tine. Four days."

That sounded like an eternity to Calla. "And the captain? How do you know we can trust him?"

"I don't," Andorran admitted. "But I know the craft. She's up and down the Garron Nir often. I think this captain is only interested in trade and maybe a bit of smuggling. Nothing riskier."

"If he gives us passage and the Watch catches him, he'll be involved in something far riskier than smuggling," Tau pointed out.

Andorran was no more eager than the rest to put innocent lives at risk, but he was practical. People would die whatever path

Una'savagi chose. That was the consequence of a reckoning. Better to die for something you believed in than waste away waiting for safety that would never come. Sacrifices would be necessary…sometimes brutal sacrifices.

"What about passes?" Calla asked.

"We won't board at the dock," Andorran decided. "We'll use this passage to the water."

Tiean glanced at Gan. "You grew up the farthest from the river. Can you swim?"

"Well enough to keep from drowning if the water's calm," Gan admitted. "…and not for too long."

Calla winced inwardly. She wasn't much better. Too much time in the river and the Garron Nir would become her reckoning.

"And how do you plan to keep deckhands from killing us when we climb aboard?"

"We don't climb aboard." Andorran smiled faintly. "We're going to be rescued."

Gan grimaced. "That may not be much of an act for me."

"Or for me," Calla muttered.

"We'll stay close to both of you," Andorran said, meeting Calla's eyes. "Can you do this?"

"Do I have a choice?" she asked wearily.

"If we're going to try, it has to be soon," Kodar pressed. "Last bell's not far off."

Andorran was still watching Calla. Her teeth worried her bottom lip, her gaze fixed on the dark stairwell yawning before them. "Calla?" he pressed gently.

Dragging her fingers through her damp curls, she nodded. She couldn't ask them to risk more just because of her fear of wave-riding. "I'll manage," she said, a defiant edge in her voice. Sometimes she felt like her own worst enemy.

>

Getting plucked from the Garron Nir proved easier than she had feared. The crew of the *Roue* hauled the nine of them from the cold waters quickly, tossing blankets around their dripping shoulders. They'd rescued plenty of desperate souls since the Watch had taken Choran Sa, and likely would rescue plenty more.

Kodar spun a lie as wild as he pleased, weaving the tale of a small craft capsizing. He offered no more, and the crew asked no further questions. Too much truth was dangerous these days.

The captain gave Andorran a sharp look, one of recognition, then introduced himself as Hablig. He welcomed them aboard with a cautious nod. Ordinarily, he would have put such passengers ashore at the first opportunity, but Andorran offered coin for fare and all willingly showed their hands. That, plus a fellow Kamborian among them, seemed to earn them passage at least as far as Artiga.

As Hablig laid out rules for passengers, Calla staggered to the railing, clutching her stomach as it heaved violently. Bal clung to her fretfully, while Gan held her curls out of the way.

Niko rubbed her back in sympathy. "Can Tiean or Caius heal this?" he asked softly.

Calla shook her head, still bent miserably over the rail.

"Not much of a wave rider, your lady," one crewman quipped.

Calla grumbled something unintelligible, her face pale. Niko kept rubbing circles on her back. "Pay them no mind."

Tau joined them, frowning at her condition. "We're going below. Think you can walk, Calla?"

She retched noisily again, and he grimaced, stepping back. "Well…maybe not."

She shot him a resentful glare. "Just go!" she barked hoarsely.

"I'll stay here with her," Gan offered, nodding at Niko. "Go see where we'll be staying and come back."

"I'll stay with Sera Calla too!" Bal piped up stubbornly.

Calla raised a trembling hand to her spinning head. "Go below, Bal," she croaked.

The boy scowled, ready to argue, but Andorran caught his collar and pulled him back firmly. "You heard her. You're coming below."

When the others had gone, Gan stayed by her side, looking sympathetic. "How long does this usually last?"

She moaned softly. "A day…after I'm back on land."

Gan grimaced. "Maybe this wasn't a good idea."

"We had no choice," she muttered, then ducked under the railing, retching again until she was empty.

After a few moments, she straightened weakly, wiping her mouth on her arm. "My stomach must be empty by now. What I need is dry clothes."

"You want to go below?"

She shook her head, frowning. "Not yet. No." She shrugged off the blanket, easing her sodden pack from her back. The thing had nearly dragged her under, but she'd clung to it. Inside she found a rumpled but dry tunic.

Gan lifted the blanket high to shield her as she wriggled out of her wet clothes and tugged the tunic over her head with a sigh of relief. She had no spare leggings, and her boots were still packed at the bottom, safely wrapped against the water. The tunic and her underclothes would have to do. She tied the blanket around her waist, resigned.

Hablig stepped back on deck with Niko at his side. His sharp gaze flicked from the sodden pile of clothes to Calla in her tunic, and one brow arched.

"Feeling any better?"

"Not much," Calla admitted.

"Not a wave rider, eh?"

"Evidently not."

Niko, now in dry clothes and having left his blanket below, gave Gan a pointed look. "You should get out of those wet things too. Caius is waiting at the hatch he'll show you the way. I'll stay with Calla."

Gan hesitated, but when Calla nodded, he relented.

"I see you've changed," Niko noted, glancing curiously around the deck. "Um…where, exactly?"

"Gan held the blanket up for me," Calla told him dryly. "I appreciate your concern for my modesty."

Niko flushed and quickly looked away. Even seasick, Calla could still manage to embarrass him.

The captain produced a silver flask, thrusting it at her. "Take this. It'll help."

She shook her head. "No, thank you."

His scowl deepened. "It will help, girl! Don't be stubborn!"

Girl? she thought irritably.

Hablig twisted the lid off. "He said you wouldn't take it without proof." Before she could ask who *he* was, Hablig tipped the flask to his lips, swallowed, then wiped the rim with the back of his hand. "See? Safe. Not good…but safe."

Niko leaned in. "Andorran sent it. He picked it up this afternoon in case we had to board a craft. He said it'd help your head and stomach."

Still wary, Calla sniffed the contents, wrinkling her nose. "Ugh! What is it?"

"Rum and catspaw root," the captain explained. "Old remedy for wave sickness. The rum cuts the bitterness."

Bracing herself, Calla took a sip. It felt like liquid fire, searing her throat. Her eyes watered and she clutched her chest, glaring at Hablig.

He chuckled, tapping the bottom of the flask. "Drink it down, girl."

"All of it?" she asked incredulously.

"Every drop."

Her amber eyes narrowed. She rarely drank anything stronger than ale, and while the flask was small, it held more rum than she was used to. Yet, to her surprise, the fiery liquid didn't rebound in her stomach. Warmth spread through her instead, the spinning in her head slowing. As vile as it tasted, it was working. Grimacing, she held her breath and drank again.

By the time she drained the flask, Calla felt much improved, *too* improved, Niko thought uneasily. She had shed the heavy wool blanket, her flushed cheeks catching the attention of several crewmen.

The captain left to see to his duties, and Niko quickly realized he didn't cut an intimidating figure on his own. If necessary, he could cast to protect her, but revealing sorcia here would be a last resort.

Gan returned just then, taking in the scene with wide eyes. "What in the name of Deius is going on up here?!" he demanded, storming across the deck and glaring at the crew.

Niko held up the empty flask helplessly. "It must be the rum. Andorran sent it for her."

Calla sighed heavily. "I really do not like the water," she grumbled.

"I know." Niko patted her shoulder, exasperated. "She's said that about fifty times now along with a few other things I'd rather not repeat."

Gan shoved his wet hair back from his face, snatching the discarded blanket from the deck and thrusting it into her hands. "Wrap up in this."

"I'm not cold." She let it drop.

"Fine," Gan growled. "Then we're taking you below." He glanced over at Niko. "I've never seen a little rum do this before."

"Maybe it's the catspaw root," Niko muttered.

"Catspaw root?" Gan echoed.

"That's what he said. Mixed in the rum. It's good for wave sickness, right? She's not sicking-up anymore."

"Yes," Gan admitted reluctantly. "It's good for that but it has…peculiar side effects." Gathering her belongings, he took Calla's hand. "Come on, Calla. Let's find our cabin."

"I don't like the water, Gan," she repeated stubbornly.

"Yes, you've mentioned that." He tugged her toward the hatch.

"We should talk to Andorran," Niko added quickly.

Calla swayed unsteadily, then nodded. "Yes. We should talk to Andorran."

Both boys sighed in relief, steering her down the ladder to the lower deck. Between Gan leading and Niko coaxing from behind, they maneuvered her through the narrow corridor until they reached their cabin.

It was cramped, double berths on either side, a table with four chairs between, a washstand just inside, and a battered sea chest against the far wall.

Tau raised a brow when Calla stumbled inside. Kodar chuckled.

"I see she's feeling better," Andorran observed.

Gan shot him a dark look. "Catspaw root? Was that wise?"

"She'll be fine," Andorran said confidently.

Bal, perched on the upper berth with Caius and swimming in a tunic far too big for him, glared down at the older boy. "What have you done to Sera Calla?"

Andorran groaned inwardly. He had already had his fill of Calla's new shadow. It had taken threats to keep Bal from following Niko back on deck, and Andorran knew it was only a matter of time before the boy pushed too far. When that day came, he had no reservations about putting him in his place.

"Calla is fine," Tau assured the boy.

Between the rum, the catspaw root, and the pitching of the *Roue*, Calla was struggling to stay on her feet and it frustrated her to no end.

"I want off this craft," she declared, her words beginning to slur.

"At the next port, Calla," Andorran told her.

She shook her head regretting it instantly. The motion sent her stumbling backwards, and she landed squarely in Kodar's lap. For a heartbeat both of them froze in mutual shock, then Calla dissolved into an unexpected fit of giggles.

Tiean, sprawled on the berth below Caius and Bal, stared in disbelief. "I've never seen catspaw root do this."

Andorran leaned back on the sea chest, amused. "Men usually get belligerent, pick fights. It lowers their inhibitions. I've never seen it given to a woman before, but clearly the effect is similar."

Kodar shot him a scathing look. "Belligerent I can handle...I bloody well expect it with Calla. But this..." He grimaced as Calla, still chuckling, began plaiting his damp hair with surprising concentration. "...this is another matter." He tried to push her hands away. "Calla...go to bed."

"I am not tired."

The others burst out laughing at Kodar's discomfort. He scowled at them. "A little help here? If you can pull yourselves together long enough."

Tau got up, still chuckling. "Come on, Calla," he coaxed, tugging her gently to her feet. "You're frightening poor Kodar."

The dragonslayer looked relieved. "If she remembers any of this, I'd rather it not be my lap she recalls. Put her in yours and let her play with *your* hair if you find it so amusing."

"I dare you, Tau," Tiean laughed.

Grinning, Tau steered Calla toward the vacant lower bunk but she twisted free and planted herself in front of Andorran instead.

"I do not like the water," she said with solemn intensity.

"I know that, Calla."

"It makes me sick."

He managed not to grin. "You've already proven that."

"I want to get off."

"We will," he promised. "…just a few more days."

She licked her lips nervously. "No. That is too long."

"You can manage a few days," he said softly.

Her gaze dropped. "Watercrafts sink. I cannot be in the water."

Andorran studied her, troubled. He had made sure she and Gan were the first pulled from the river earlier, but her aversion still puzzled him. Raised in Soronu between the two largest rivers in the realm she should have been as at ease with water as he was. Yet her discomfort near deep water was well known in Tegoradaysol. Master Camalaron had not been the only one to use dunking in the Tegora Dara Mai to bring her to heel during training.

"Nothing will happen to the *Roue*," he said quietly. "She's a sound craft."

"Do you promise?"

His expression softened. "I promise I won't let anything happen to you."

"Two days," she relented, pressing her palms against his chest. "I can manage two days."

Amber eyes locked with blue-green ones. Silence stretched. Gan and Niko had already climbed into the opposite upper berth with Caius and Bal, Tau had reclaimed his chair, but Andorran only saw Calla her fingers flexing almost imperceptibly against him, her wide eyes unblinking. His gaze dropped from her eyes to her lips, then back again.

Seconds passed. Then Calla rose on tiptoe and kissed him.

For one glorious moment he let himself savor it, her lips warm and soft, the faint taste of bitter root and sweet rum mingling on her breath. Then, gently, he set her back, his hands firm on her shoulders.

Bal exploded between them like a lightning bolt, his skinny arms wrapped protectively around Calla's waist, glaring up at Andorran with venomous eyes. Startled, Calla glanced down at the boy, then simply smiled, ruffling his hair before hugging him with one arm.

Andorran rose, voice quiet but edged with steel. "Calla, this boy should be in bed. Take that berth." He nodded at the empty lower bunk. "You and Bal."

On the upper berth, Niko sat rigid, wide-eyed. He hadn't meant to probe Andorran in that moment, but what he had glimpsed left him shaken.

Once Calla and Bal were settled, Andorran straightened, his gaze pinning Niko. "You should all sleep. Calla will remember none of this in the morning and I intend to see it stays that way." He spoke to all of them, but his eyes never left Niko's.

Niko swallowed hard and slipped under his blankets. Being a sensitive was proving more dangerous than useful.

>

The next day, Calla's stomach had steadied and her headache had faded, though she still mistrusted the water and refused food. She spent most of the morning with Bal, working on cueing.

If Bal had his way, Calla would be the only one to learn the hand language. He shadowed her obsessively, glaring at anyone who drew her attention for more than a moment. Niko and Caius relieved Andorran first, but were glad enough to hand her off to Kodar.

Kodar picked up the signals quickly though only because Calla was teaching him. Bal made his feelings perfectly clear: he tolerated the others solely because he had no choice. By the time Tau arrived to relieve Kodar, the dragonslayer was seriously considering tossing the boy overboard. It might be worth Calla's wrath just to teach the whelp some manners.

Tau watched Kodar stomp away, then lowered himself to the deck beside Calla. "Did you and Kodar have words?"

She blinked at him curiously. "No…why would you ask that?"

"He looked angry when he left." Tau shrugged.

Calla followed his gaze to Kodar's retreating back, frowning. "I cannot imagine what he has to be angry about." She glanced at Bal. "Did you notice anything?"

The boy shook his head.

"Well, perhaps I am wrong." Tau draped an arm around her shoulders. "You are getting to be quite a wave rider."

She made a face at him but leaned into his embrace. "I will be glad to reach Artiga," she admitted. "That root Andorran gave me helped, but I still do not like the water."

"Have you thought about what we do if the Watch holds Artiga?"

She shook her head. "I prefer not to think about that."

"Well…we have until tomorrow evening. Perhaps fortune will be with us for once."

Calla drew a long breath and let it out slowly. "That would be a nice change."

Bal's fingers flickered quickly. She smiled. "Thank you, Bal."

Tau studied the boy, puzzled. The bond between them unsettled him. "So, I hear you have a talent for cueing," he tried. Bal stared back in silence. "You learned it from your parents, yes?"

The boy gave a single nod, then turned immediately to Calla, hands flying. She cued something back, and he frowned sulkily, looking away toward the water.

"What was that about?" Tau asked.

"I just told him you were my friend," she said. "I think he is a little jealous."

Tau frowned. "So Kodar *was* angry when he left."

"Well, as I told you, I have no idea why," she insisted.

Tau took her hand, noting the way Bal's jaw tightened as he watched from the corner of his eye. "Calla, maybe Bal should spend some time with the others. The newlings, perhaps. They're closer to his age. It might be good for him."

"What are you talking about? He spent most of the morning with Caius and Niko."

"I meant without you," Tau clarified.

Bal whipped around at once. "I stay with Sera Calla!"

"You will do as you are told, boy!" Tau snapped. His tone was stern now. "He is becoming too attached to you, Calla."

She freed her hand from his grasp. "Tau, he lost his parents and was made a dal'amine. Maybe what he needs most right now is the sense that he is safe."

Tau let it go. The conversation could wait until they were off this vessel.

By evening, the wind was rising, lightning flickering in the distant clouds. Calla's unease grew until Tau finally convinced her to go below. At least in the cabin she would not see the flashes. She and Bal followed him down.

Kodar and Caius were at the table with a map spread between them. Both looked up as she entered. Tau flung himself onto his bunk with a sigh.

Leaning over the map, Calla tapped a point with her finger. "What is here?"

"Nothing," Caius explained. "That's the best place to disembark without docking."

"We need to avoid the cities altogether," Kodar told her grimly. "The Watch holds Artiga, Kambor Tine, and Soronu."

Calla rubbed her temples; her headache was returning. "So if we land here…" she tapped again "…we have a clear run across the road between Artiga and Kambor Tine, then into the timberlands to the mountains."

"That is Andorran's thought." Caius nodded.

She liked the sound of being back on land.

The others returned not long after with bread, cheese, and salted fish. Calla winced at the food and climbed into her berth while the rest ate.

When Bal finished his share, he clambered up beside her, already drowsy. Curling close, he slipped into sleep, her arms instinctively wrapping around him. Soon they were both breathing evenly.

Kodar's frown deepened. "That boy needs to be taken in hand," he hissed. "He was lucky not to be treading water this afternoon!"

Niko and Caius grinned; they had thought the same.

"I think we should part company with him," Tiean said. "He'll need more care than we can give."

"That is the problem." Tau's voice softened. His eyes lingered on Calla and Bal. "You must sense it, Niko. Calla was the first person to show him kindness since his parents died. He is not willing to give that up. He is looking for a mother."

"But she is not his mother," Tiean pointed out.

"Then we must find someone else to take him in," Gan suggested. "He is a pitiful sight. Surely someone will care for him."

"Someone already is." Andorran's voice was quiet but firm. "For better or worse, we are his family now. Calla will not abandon him and I am not sure we should ask her to. We will have to manage."

"Well…Tangor managed with Calla," Tiean muttered.

Tau rolled his eyes. "Have you forgotten that first year?"

Caius, brushing crumbs from his face, looked up curiously. "What happened that first year?"

A grin spread across Tau's face. "Tiean and I were newlings when Calla first came to Tegoradaysol. I'd been there only three years, Tiean less than two. Until Calla, we were the youngest dragonmasters. Naturally, we weren't told much."

"We all knew about the Genesi Ney," Tiean continued. "Everyone in the village knew from the day she received her stone. She was the first dragonmaster to be known before ever setting foot in the village. Ordinarily, only the Sovereign Master knows. But Calla was different. Tangor was chosen for her the day her stone was placed."

"Which had never been done before," Tau added. "Ordinarily, a counsel isn't chosen until just before the binding. But Calla was the Genesi Ney, and they wanted her watched closely."

Tiean nodded. "All any of us really knew was what Tangor reported back and he tended to…well, gloss over her more colorful traits."

Tau chuckled. "He was a master at dragonspeak, I'll give him that."

"He didn't want the Triad or the Tribunal insisting she be brought to Tegoradaysol," Andorran added. "He feared they would break her spirit."

Tau looked surprised. "How do you know that?"

Andorran shrugged. "Tangor told me."

"Well, that makes sense. I suppose Master Camalaron agreed."

"He did," Andorran confirmed.

"So she was intentionally kept away from Tegoradaysol?" Gan asked, frowning.

"Yes," Andorran said somberly. "Tangor disliked interference where Calla was concerned. It was even his idea that she attend Ackley's instead of coming to the village after her binding."

"But then came the fencing match, her expulsion, and her parents' deaths…so she was finally brought to the village." Tau grinned faintly. "I don't know what she expected, but she wasn't nearly as surprised by us as we were by her."

Tiean laughed softly. "Absolutely not. We were expecting a grieving, frightened little girl. If she was either of those, she hid it well."

"She was madder than a scalded cat," Tau said. "Tangor had his hands full just trying to keep her out of trouble."

"She made enemies it seems, especially Varzi," Caius noted, shaking his head. "But why?"

Niko sighed. He knew the answer. "Because anger is how Calla hides everything else. Master Camalaron told us that."

Tau nodded thoughtfully. "The wall she built around herself was as difficult to breach as a cast shield."

"But you breached it," Caius pointed out.

"Maybe she admired his persistence," Tiean teased with a grin.

"I think she simply needed a friend too badly," Tau said at last. "She kept me at a safe distance until that fifth round of 'twenty-ones.'"

"Fifth round?" Niko echoed in amazement.

Kodar frowned. "What are 'twenty-ones'?"

"One of the harshest punishments for newlings," Tau explained.

Caius, Niko, and Gan had all heard of them, Gan had even been threatened with them once, until Calla intervened.

The punishment was designed to teach humility and respect to undisciplined newlings: twenty-one lashings given publicly, followed by twenty-one hours in the fourth battle stance before the Sovereign's study sword in hand, arms outstretched, blade skyward, no matter the weather. The newling could not speak or be spoken to. Then came twenty-one days of confinement.

Caius shuddered at the thought. He could not imagine anyone failing to be humbled after such an ordeal.

"In her first year, Calla did five rounds of twenty-ones," Tiean revealed. "A record."

"Beating Andorran's old record by one," Tau added with a laugh.

Andorran scowled. "Not a record I'm proud of, thank you."

The *Roue* suddenly lurched to port, pitching them all sideways. Andorran steadied himself, eyes lifting to the ceiling.

"Looks like the storm's on us." He glanced toward Calla. "Hopefully her shield will keep it from waking her. But if not, don't leave her alone."

The others nodded. Andorran reached for his cloak. "I'll be topside. Hablig asked for help with the crew."

After he left, Una'savagi climbed into their berths to ride out the storm.

With the catspaw root out of her system and the vessel heaving in the rough waters, Calla woke well before dawn, wave sickness forcing her to the chamber pot. Her stomach was empty, but the dry heaves wracked her just the same.

Bal was instantly at her side, patting her shoulder with a worried look in his dark eyes.

"There's more catspaw root if you want it," Tau offered sleepily from his berth.

Calla groaned and shook her head. She'd already lost hours after the last dose and had no desire to risk another gap in her memory.

Her amber gaze swept the dim cabin. "Where is Andorran?"

"Topside," Kodar answered from the shadows. "Helping the crew."

She shivered. "Is that safe?"

"He's weathered worse than this," Tau assured her. "Besides, the worst of the storm is past."

"Are you certain?"

Niko sat up. "You should be able to sense that yourself, Calla."

Perhaps she should. With the others, the binding gave her a steady pulse of reassurance even when they were out of sight. But with Andorran…there was only a faint echo, easily blocked.

"You cannot sense him?" Caius asked.

She shook her head. "Not like the rest of you."

"I wonder why that is," Kodar murmured.

Niko did not wonder. He knew exactly why Andorran shielded himself from Calla, he just didn't know how. Dropping to the floor, he grabbed a damp cloth and laid it across the back of her neck.

"He was just in here," Niko added. "Said the worst had passed."

Calla looked relieved, and Bal fussed over her, readjusting the cloth with a scolding glance at Niko.

"The sooner we're off this cursed craft, the better," she grumbled. "We'll disembark today, won't we?"

"Before the bend in the river, just after midday," Tau replied. "Hablig says he can put us within a few hundred yards of the bluffs."

"Swimming again?"

"Afraid so."

Gan grimaced. He wasn't eager to return to the water either especially not after the storm's turmoil.

Calla sank to the floor, resting her head against the sea chest. Bal nestled close, and she smiled faintly. "Let's hope this is the last time we're forced onto a watercraft. I suspect I'll never be a wave rider."

Chapter 18: Staking Claims

The land stretching between Kambor Tine and the Mountains of the Condemned was a flat expanse of dense timber. From the bluffs where Hablig had left them, it took the rest of the day to reach the woodland's edge. Heavy rains and Calla's lingering wave-sickness slowed their progress.

The dragons, they knew, would have returned to their dens once the dragonmasters failed to return for them, leaving Una'savagi to make the trek on foot. If the rain continued, the journey would be grueling. The thickets grew so tightly in places that a straight course toward the mountains was impossible, and the leafy canopy overhead did little to shield them from the downpour.

By the time they entered the timberland locally known as the *Forest of Whispers* Andorran finally agreed to halt and build a fire. Cold, wet, and weary, they quickly cast a canopying spell, coaxed flames to life, and huddled around the heat.

Calla pushed back her hood, pulled off her gloves, and tucked them into her belt before holding her pale hands out to the fire. Dark circles under her eyes betrayed her fatigue, but the nausea had passed, and her head no longer throbbed. In fact, now that the queasiness had eased, her appetite was slowly returning.

They shared a meager meal of salted fish, hard bread, and flat ale left over from the *Roue*.

Bal huddled close beside Calla under his cloak, gnawing on a heel of bread. He had managed to keep pace so far, but Calla worried how he would fare once their march through the timber grew harsher. More troubling still, she feared that one of Una'savagi would eventually give in to the urge to thrash him for his insolence and that would certainly slow him down.

She could not fathom why Bal was so determined to alienate the others. Even good-natured Caius and Tiean had begun avoiding him. Perhaps bringing him along had been a mistake. Yet Calla remained convinced the boy had a role to play in the reckoning. If only she could explain that to the others, they might show him more tolerance. As it was, she could only hope to keep him from earning a strapping, no easy task.

"How are you feeling, Calla?" Kodar asked.

"Much better," she assured him. "I won't slow us down any longer."

Gan studied her with concern. "Just don't push yourself. We're not in such a hurry that you need to make yourself sick."

She grinned. "There you go, trading roles with me again. I'm beginning to worry about you."

He grinned back. "I learn quickly."

"We only have a few hours of light left," Tau observed. "Do we press on, or make camp here?"

"Press on," Andorran advised. "I'd rather be deeper in the timber before we stop."

The others agreed. They hurriedly finished their meal, doused the fire, pulled their hoods up for all the good it did and trudged deeper into the *Forest of Whispers*.

>

By morning, the downpour had lessened to a steady drizzle, but their rest faded quickly into groans of frustration. Wet, hungry, and weary, they spent half the morning circling a vast tangle of thorn brambles that forced them miles out of their way.

Tau tried to cast a spell to clear a passage, but soon realized the dense thicket was troll magic, likely concealing a doorway. Caius warned them that their sorcia would be useless in such cases.

By midday, discomfort and irritation combined with Bal's dark glares finally pushed Gan's patience past its limit. He turned on the boy with a harsh scolding.

Bal bristled with fury and lunged at him only to be caught by the back of his cloak as Tau hauled him up short. "Hold there, Bal," Tau warned. "You'd come out worse for that, I promise you."

Gan stood watching, half-regretting Tau's interference. He was more than ready to take the insolent boy to task. Bal's defiant look shifted into one of desperation as he turned to Calla, his fingers flying with frantic cues.

Before she could respond, Andorran stepped between them. "Leave him to Tau," he said firmly.

Calla blinked at him, startled. "What?"

"He's becoming too dependent on you," Andorran continued. "It's time you stopped mollycoddling him."

"I am not mollycoddling him!" Calla snapped. "But I don't see the need to bully him either!"

"Andorran is right," Tiean interjected. "If he's thrown his lot in with ours, then he must stop clinging to you and treating the rest of us like enemies."

"What about a little compassion?" she shot back sharply. "The boy's had a miserable few months."

"And they won't get easier if he stays with us," Gan reminded her. "And don't forget you have a responsibility to Niko, Caius, and me. But he won't let us within ten feet of you."

Her gaze flicked to Caius and Niko, standing quietly with uneasy expressions. "Is that how you feel? That I'm neglecting you for Bal?"

"No…not intentionally," Niko admitted, staring at the ground.

"But with him glaring at us whenever we get near you," Caius added glumly, "we'd rather keep our distance."

"But he's just a little possessive," she argued. "That will pass."

"It's more than that, Calla," Andorran countered. "You are not his mother, nor his *Sera*. If he cannot accept all of us…then I don't see how he can stay."

Calla looked from Bal's dark eyes wide with panic as he listened to the turn of the conversation to Andorran, whose face was set with grim determination.

"Maybe I've been lenient," she conceded softly. "…but after all he has been through…"

Andorran's frown deepened. "I don't recall anyone making such allowances for you. A week after your parents died, you were already doing your first set of 'twenty-ones,' as I recall."

"But he is only a boy."

"You were only sixteen," Tau said flatly. "Bal has been managing well enough on his own. He's clever, resourceful…not helpless."

"I agree with Andorran," Kodar added. "He needs to be separated from you for a time."

Calla sighed, shoulders sagging. "Very well, if this is how all of you feel." She turned to Bal. "You'll stay with Tau for now."

His face drained of color. "No, Sera Calla, I have to be with you!"

"You are with me," she assured him, "we are all together. But you need to spend time with the others."

"No!" he shouted, struggling in Tau's grip. "I am your dal'amine!"

Calla's temper snapped. "You are no such thing!" she barked. "Stop saying that and stay with Tau!"

She swept past them, setting a hard pace deeper into the forest.

Bal writhed in Tau's grasp until Andorran's voice cut like steel. "That will be enough, whelp," he said, tone ominous. "You'll do as you're told, or you'll suffer the consequences."

A brooding expression darkened Bal's face as he realized Calla would not bend to him this time.

"That was unpleasant," Niko muttered as they pressed on, Calla well ahead of the group.

"It had to be done," Caius reasoned.

"I suppose…" Niko's voice trailed.

Gan fell into step beside them. "Is she very angry?"

"She is," Niko admitted. "But mostly with herself."

"Why?" Caius asked, puzzled.

"Because bringing Bal along was her idea. She worries she made a mistake."

Gan shook his head. "No she didn't." His tawny eyes hardened with conviction. "I'm as sick of him as the rest of you, but Calla was right to bring him. That day in the weaponry shop…Bal said something. He knows what she is. He called her the *Genesi Ney*.”

The two boys stared at him in shock.

“How?” Niko breathed. “How could he know?”

Gan shrugged. “Maybe it has something to do with his parents being chroniclers. I don’t know. But I think he’s meant to be with us.”

Caius nodded slowly. “Maybe he is.”

>

Calla woke the next morning to a silence that told her the rain had finally stopped. Relief washed over her. Perhaps the break in weather would ease the tension hanging over them all.

She sat up, tugged on her damp boots, and stripped away her sleep-shield. Fingers combing through her hair, she crawled out of the tent.

Andorran, Tau, and Kodar were already breaking camp. The newlings were crouched around the fire ring, and Tiean stood stretching with a yawn.

Calla’s frown deepened as she scanned the clearing. “Where is Bal?” she asked, approaching the fire.

Tau looked up, surprised. “Bal? Isn’t he with you?”

“He’s not allowed, remember?” she said, voice dripping sarcasm.

Ignoring that, Tau turned to Andorran. “He was gone when I woke. I assumed he’d gone to Calla.”

Irritation flashed in her amber eyes. "I haven't seen him since last night."

"Maybe he's…you know…taking care of business." Niko gestured vaguely toward the trees.

Calla heaved a frustrated sigh and began circling the camp, calling Bal's name. No reply. No sign of the boy. Anxiety stirred in her gut. Widening her search, she looped further out, Caius joining her, but still they found nothing.

"This is your fault, Andorran!" she snapped when she stomped back into the campsite. "You should have left him with me!"

"No one made him go, Calla," Tiean said quietly.

Kodar and Tau finished stowing the last of their supplies, and Andorran gestured to extinguish the fire.

"We have to find him," Calla insisted.

"We don't have time," Kodar countered.

"We've lost enough already," Tau added. "Bal's a tough lad he can look after himself."

"He was doing it before we found him," Tiean reminded her.

Her fists clenched. "It's dangerous out there! He doesn't know these woods! We cannot just leave him!"

"Most likely he's just sulking and will follow from a distance," Kodar said.

Calla strode up to Andorran, glaring up into his unreadable eyes. "If anything happens to that boy, I will never forgive you."

His face was carved from stone, unreadable. "Tau," he said evenly, turning away and hefting his pack, "take them on. I'll catch up."

Tau's eyes widened. "Take them on? Where are you going?"

"To find the boy."

"We can all look," Niko offered quickly.

Andorran shook his head. "No. Keep moving. I'll catch up."

Without another word, he walked away from the camp, vanishing into the trees.

The rest of Una'savagi pressed onward in heavy silence. The sun had returned, but with the soaked earth and dripping branches, the air was thick and stifling. Cloaks were stowed away, and damp clothes clung uncomfortably to their skin.

By midday, their pace had slowed. None of them were hungry, but they stopped regardless, hoping Andorran would rejoin them. Though the Forest of Whispers had no clear path, Andorran was a skilled tracker. They made sure to leave a subtle trail for him to follow.

After more than an hour of waiting, they forced themselves to move on, worry tightening into fear. No one spoke. They avoided one another's eyes, unwilling to see their own unease reflected back.

By late afternoon, their pace had slowed to a crawl, progress all but stalling as another dense thicket forced them westward before they could resume south. Tau made careful marks along the trail for Andorran to follow.

Then a vast shadow passed overhead. All heads tilted skyward as the belly of a dragon momentarily blotted out the sun, its massive shape skimming the treetops on a course away from the mountains.

Calla froze, eyes wide. "Was that a golden?" she whispered.

"Impossible," Tau replied, gaze still locked on the skies. The dragon was already little more than a receding silhouette, but his tone was firm. "We are too far north."

"It looked like a golden," she insisted.

"Firebreathers never wander this far north," Tiean reasoned. "Even this time of year, it is too cold for them."

The newlings exchanged uneasy glances. They knew little about firebreathers, but they knew enough: the golden draxon was the most aggressive of all breeds. Dragonmasters had never subdued one successfully. Dozens had died trying.

Calla's amber eyes lingered on the sky. "I think we should make camp here."

Tau frowned. "A bit early to stop, is it not?"

"I don't care." Her voice was tight. "We need to stop here."

Kodar shrugged. "We may as well. We are not making much progress anyway."

The group set about clearing a site, raising tents, and coaxing a fire to life. Only once the camp was secure did Niko realize Calla was missing.

"Calla?" he called.

Caius looked alarmed. "Now what?"

"She was just here," Gan muttered, scanning the trees.

"Do you think she went looking for Andorran and Bal?" Caius asked.

Tau's jaw tightened. "Well, I don't think she went to pick wild-flowers for our dinner table," he snapped.

"I'll find her." Caius started for the treeline.

Kodar caught his arm. "We are not all wandering about and losing each other. Tau and I will find Calla. The rest of you stay put."

Tau cast Tiean a look. "Keep sharp watch."

"I will," Tiean assured him.

Together, Tau and Kodar retraced their steps. Tau pressed a hand to his collarbone, frowning. "She cannot have gone far...but I can barely sense her. She has learned how to shut us out."

Kodar scowled. "First Andorran blocks her, now she blocks us! I wish I knew how they were doing that."

"Calla's been casting spells no one has seen in centuries. Nothing she does surprises me anymore."

"Oh no?" Kodar arched a brow. "I think you are surprised by most of what she does."

Tau chuckled ruefully. "You may be right. She is unpredictable...and lately...distracted."

"Andorran," Kodar said flatly.

"You see it too," Tau murmured with a knowing laugh.

"What he said in Choran Sa...do you think he meant it?"

"I certainly hope not."

A sudden sound ahead made them both freeze. An instant later, a torrent of fire exploded from above. They dove for cover as the blaze scorched the trees and set the brush alight.

Calla crawled out of a nearby thicket, motioning for silence. With one hand she swept an arc. *"Eradicai,"* she whispered, and the flames snuffed out. Picking her way toward them, soot-streaked and irritated, she hissed, "Why did you follow me?"

Tau stared at the charred earth, then at the great beast circling above. His voice was hushed with disbelief. "A golden draxon."

"The bloody thing has been following us," Calla grumbled. "I asked you to watch the newlings while I tried to figure out what it was doing."

"No one heard you say that," Kodar shot back. "We thought you had gone after Andorran and Bal."

"Well, that would have been foolish."

"We thought so too," Kodar said dryly. "Much wiser to go dragon-hunting on your own."

She cast him a reproachful glare. "I was not hunting it."

The dragon swooped low, flames cascading across the treetops. The three of them scrambled on all fours to escape the inferno.

"I think it knows we are here," Tau muttered as Calla extinguished the blaze once more.

Wiping soot from her cheek, she grimaced. "What in Deius' name is it doing this far north? I have never heard of a draxon beyond the mountains."

Kodar tapped the bow strapped to her back. "Can you hit it with that?"

"Probably," she admitted. "But it would not matter. I cannot kill a dragon. I am a dragonmaster."

"But this dragon is trying to kill you," he pointed out grimly.

Pressing herself deeper into the shrubbery, Calla sighed. "Why do you think we called in dragonslayers?"

"We cannot kill a dragon," Tau confirmed, his tone grave.

"Well…that is an inconvenience," Kodar said, frowning. "I *am* a dragonslayer…but unless it lands, I cannot do much." His gaze slid back to the bow. "Unless I can manage that contraption."

Calla slipped the bow from her shoulder, drawing several arrows. "It is not terribly difficult. And you have a rather large target, which should help."

She quickly showed him how to grip the bow and nock an arrow her lesson cut short as another torrent of flame roared down. They tumbled for cover, Calla smothering the blaze with another spell. Coughing through smoke, she grimaced.

"He is determined," she muttered darkly. "I will give him that."

Kodar braced himself, Calla at his side giving quiet instructions. When the dragon swept overhead again, he released the arrow. It whistled through the branches, grazing the outer edge of the creature's wing.

The draxon loosed an outraged roar that shook the trees. All three of them clapped their hands over their ears.

"I suspect everyone within twenty miles heard that," Calla remarked dryly.

Tau rolled his eyes. "All you have done is make him angry! Now he will not just want to devour us he will want to make us suffer first!"

Kodar shot him a dark look. "I am a dragonslayer, not an archer!" he snapped. "And seeing that *you* can do nothing to stop this bloody dragon, I would thank you not to insult my efforts!"

Calla chuckled despite the tension. "Come now, boys play nicely," she teased. Turning to Kodar, her voice softened. "That was good. You have the right idea. Just remember…it's a moving target."

Kodar raised the bow again, nocking another arrow as the draxon wheeled above. Fire exploded around them, the blast knocking both him and Calla to the ground. His arrow went wide, vanishing into the smoke.

Calla scrambled up, smothering the flames with a sweep of her hand. She gave Kodar's singed hair a quick pat. "Close," she said lightly.

"A bit," he admitted soberly, climbing back to his feet. He took another arrow from her hand. "I'm not sure I can do this. I am no archer."

She met his gaze, smiling. "You once told me I would need you, remember?"

His brow furrowed, then he nodded. "The night of our bonding."

"Well, it seems you were correct." She gave him a saucy grin, patting his cheek. "I have confidence in you, dragonslayer."

A grin tugged at his mouth. He raised the bow once more, muscles taut as he drew back the string. The draxon circled low, preparing to strike. Kodar tracked its path, waited a heartbeat, and loosed the arrow.

This time it flew true, piercing the softer scales of the beast's belly.

The dragon shrieked, a deafening sound that made all three wince and cover their ears. It wheeled once more, keening in pain, then veered sharply toward the mountains, wings beating raggedly.

Calla let out a long, relieved breath. She turned to Kodar with approval in her eyes. "Not bad. He will be nursing that wound for days, but will should not be fatal. As a dragonmaster…I call that a victory."

Tau grinned, clapping Kodar's back with enthusiasm. "Very impressive. I take back my earlier cynicism."

Still smiling, Kodar handed Calla her bow. "Glad I could do my part."

They trudged back toward camp, brushing soot from their clothes and picking bark and leaves from their hair. Kodar frowned at the singed tips of his pale locks.

"Bloody dragon," he muttered.

Calla tugged gently at his hair. "Just be grateful it was not worse. Trim it off and you are as good as new." But her tone was heavier than her words.

"What is it, Calla?" Tau asked.

She hesitated, then said quietly, "That dragon came from behind us."

Tau nodded grimly, knowing her meaning. Andorran and Bal were somewhere behind.

"I did not mean it, you know," she added, her voice somber.

Tau and Kodar exchanged puzzled looks.

"I was angry…and worried…but I know it was not Andorran's fault that Bal ran off." Her voice cracked slightly. "I said I would never forgive him. What if…?" She shook her head, unable to finish.

"They're fine," Tau said firmly. "And Andorran has weathered your temper long enough to know words spoken in anger when he hears them. Would you not agree?"

She forced a smile and nodded. "I suppose."

"Of course he does," Kodar said, grasping her hand. Tau took the other. "We will return to camp and wait for them."

Calla hoped with all her heart they were right.

\>

That night, no one in Una'savagi slept. They huddled around the fire, discussing the golden draxon and speculating on its presence so far north. Perhaps it had lost its way during migration, a rare occurrence, but possible. At least the arrow wound would ground it for several days.

Their talk shifted uneasily to the Watch, to Tegoradaysol as a possible target, to the gray fairies serving the banedars. But none spoke of what weighed most heavily on all their minds: Where was Andorran?

Eighteen hours had passed since he set out after Bal. Normally, Calla would not worry. Andorran was the most capable man she knew. But the draxon's presence unsettled her. A dragonmaster could not kill a dragon and he had no dragonslayer with him. Only an eight-year-old boy, assuming he had found Bal at all.

Worse still, her own words echoed back, sharp and unforgiving. She did not want those to be the last he ever heard from her.

Frowning, she shook off the thought. Propping her chin in her palm, she kept her gaze on the forest shadows, resolved not to break camp until Andorran returned.

Gan touched her shoulder, snapping her from her reverie. "You should eat something."

"I am not hungry."

"Starving yourself will not bring them back faster," Tau reasoned.

"I know." She rubbed her face wearily, then froze. Movement flickered at the edge of the firelight. She stared into the trees. For a moment she convinced herself she had imagined it. Then came another shift of shadow. Slowly, she rose to her feet.

Even with her eyeshine, the timber was too dense to make out clearly. She narrowed her gaze, circling the fire with careful steps, watchful. The Forest of Whispers was full of dangerous creatures. Most would not dare face six dragonmasters but some might. Especially if hungry.

The others fell silent, eyes following Calla's gaze into the shadows. Slowly, they rose to their feet, hands on their weapons.

Then Calla let out a sudden whoop of joy, racing across the clearing and flinging her arms around Andorran's neck as he emerged from the tree line.

He hugged her back, chuckling. "Worried?"

Dropping to the ground, Calla beamed. "Why would I be worried?" She looked down at Bal. The boy stood sulkily at Andorran's side, tear stains streaking his dirty face, but otherwise unharmed.

Calla swept him into a hug. "You should not have taken off like that, Bal! You are lucky Andorran found you."

The boy stared at the ground, silent.

Calla sighed and ruffled his hair. "Go sit by the fire and get something to eat."

"He might be up to a meal," Andorran said, "but I expect it will be a day or two before he does much sitting."

Calla's eyes widened. "You did not?"

"I most certainly did," he assured her.

She cast Bal a sympathetic look. "Well, you can still eat even if you have to do it standing." She turned back to Andorran. "I said…" She stopped, drew in a deep breath, then pushed on. "I said things I did not mean."

He regarded her placidly, waiting.

"Well…Bal, that was not your fault, and I should not have…" She raked her fingers through her hair, flustered. "Deius help me, I am babbling like a fool." Shifting uneasily, she wrung her hands. "The fact is, I *was* worried. I said horrible things things I would not want to be the last words you ever heard from me." She pressed her burning cheeks with both palms. "I wish I were better at this."

"At what?" he asked in a low voice.

She let her hands fall to her sides and met his eyes. "At apologizing. At telling you how I feel." She shook her head. "But you are Kamborian, and I…I do not think I could ever be consort to any man. Even if…" Her voice faltered and she dropped her gaze.

"Even if what, Calla?" Andorran pressed.

Her eyes lifted back to his. "…Even if I loved him," she whispered.

He brushed a strand of hair from her face with gentle fingers. "A Kamborian who loves you would never ask such a thing. You are Soroni. I would never ask you to be my consort. A man cannot stake a claim on a Soroni woman without stripping her of her position. I would not do that to you."

"Are you saying…if I were not Soroni…?"

"I would have spoken for you long ago."

A soft laugh escaped her. Slipping her arms around his neck, she whispered, "Then let it be so. I ask you this night to be my mate, Andorran of Kambor Tine. Will you have me?"

Heat burned in his eyes, and the barrier he had always kept between them dissolved. A rush of emotions washed over her, filling her with warmth.

"There is nothing I want more," he murmured. His hands settled at her waist. "I have waited a long time for you, *mio'sync*." His lips brushed hers, soft and reverent.

"Then I stake my claim and offer you my body, heart, and soul."

"And I offer you my body, heart, and soul, and stake my claim," he vowed. His thumb caressed her cheek. "Kamborian tradition says I must ask for your family's blessing." He looked over her shoulder at the others. "You are Calla's family. I ask for your blessing on our claims."

Tiean smiled. "I cannot imagine a stronger bloodline for the next generation. You have my blessing."

Tau grinned broadly. "You have always had mine and about bloody time you got around to asking for it."

Kodar chuckled. "You have mine."

"And mine," Caius added quickly.

Gan nodded. "You have mine."

Niko, grinning from ear to ear, met Andorran's gaze. "Does this mean I am no longer in trouble?"

Andorran smiled faintly. "You have fortune on your side, newling."

"Then you have my blessing." Niko said proudly.

Calla arched a brow at him. "You were in trouble?"

"Your newling is sometimes too sensitive for his own good," Andorran said in a low voice. His gaze returned to Calla. "And he is not the only one who nearly landed in trouble. You took your time staking your claim. I thought I might have to do something drastic."

She rose on her toes to kiss him lightly. "Were you thinking to punish me as you did poor Bal?"

His voice dropped, rumbling. "Do not think it had not crossed my mind, Genesi Ney." His eyes held hers, unrelenting.

"Can you think of nothing better to do now that we have staked claims?" she teased.

His grip tightened, pulling her against him. "We have not yet petitioned the Triad," he reminded.

"We do not need the Triad's permission," she countered. "We have staked our claims, and our family has given us their blessing. You are my mate as of this moment. Nothing the Triad says can change that."

He nodded. "As you say." Then he kissed her again, this time with unrestrained passion.

Tau motioned quietly to the others, and they drifted back to the fire. Kodar found Bal some bread and cheese, ignoring the boy's sulky demeanor. "Go on, sit and eat," he instructed. Then, remembering Andorran's words, he smirked. "Well…eat anyway."

"I could heal him," Tiean offered.

Tau intervened. "No. A few days' discomfort is a small price to pay."

They crouched around the fire. Caius glanced at Tau curiously. "I still do not understand. If they both felt this way for so long, why did it take so long?"

Tau leaned back. "What do you know of Soroni customs?"

The newlings exchanged sheepish looks. "Nothing," they admitted.

"Not surprising," Tau said with a chuckle. "Few people do. Remember in Choran Sa, when Andorran said if she did not decide soon, he would do it for her?"

"Yes," Niko recalled. "And he said her pride be damned."

"Exactly." Tau grinned. "In Soronu, women stake the claim. It is a matriarchal society. If Andorran had spoken first, he would have put Calla in an impossible position."

"And in Kambor Tine," Tiean added, "men and women are not equals. A man goes to a woman's family, stakes his claim, and if the family consents, she becomes his consort. She is not even part of the decision."

"In fact," Kodar said grimly, "by Kamborian law, she is his property. Soroni women would never accept such a fate. They would never be property or consorts."

"So…Andorran could not speak first for Calla because she is Soroni," Caius said, working it through. "And she did not speak because she would not agree to be a consort."

"I suppose it never occurred to her that Andorran would ignore Kamborian tradition and take her as his mate rather than his consort." Tau decided.

"What about the Triad?" Niko asked.

Tau and Tiean exchanged brief looks. Tau explained, "No dragonmaster has ever claimed a mate without the Triad's consent before. But what is done…is done."

Bal finished his meal and began edging away from the fire, but Tau was ready. "I am shielding you, Bal. Do not get any ideas."

The boy scowled. "I need to be with Sera Calla."

Kodar barked a harsh laugh. "Go near her now, boy, and Andorran will do more than strap your backside, I can promise you that! You will sleep where we can keep an eye on you."

"I wonder if Tangor knew how Calla felt about Andorran," Tiean mused quietly.

"He did not miss much where Calla was concerned," Tau replied. "You were right about this union creating a powerful bloodline. I wonder why the Triad never considered it."

"Maybe they did," Caius said wisely. "Calla and Andorran are the two most powerful dragonmasters alive…maybe ever. I do not see how they could have overlooked the possibility."

"Maybe they thought they were too strong," Kodar suggested.

"And too much of a threat to the Triad," Tiean agreed.

Tau chuckled. "I think the Triad was right."

>

Andorran woke just before daylight, relishing the feel of Calla's body pressed against his, her head pillowed on his shoulder, her breath warm against his neck. He had always believed this day would come, despite all the obstacles set before him. He had known it from the first moment he saw her: a defiant sixteen-year-old standing in front of the Sovereign Master's quarters, back bared to the waist and crisscrossed with angry red welts, arms extended, sword pointed skyward as rain poured down from a dark, gray sky.

The long-awaited Genesi Ney was enduring a round of 'twenty-ones' less than a week after arriving in the village. Expelled from school for reasons unclear, and still reeling from finding her parents murdered in their bed, she should have been in mourning. Instead, she faced one of the harshest punishments a newling could receive.

Udaro, his counsel, had passed her by without so much as a glance, eager to escape the storm and report to the Triad. But Andorran had slowed, watching the newest dragonmaster with curiosity and no small amount of concern. He knew something of the prophecy, of her role, of his own. She was the Genesi Ney. If the reckoning depended on a spoiled, willful child, what chance did they have?

Then she raised her gaze to his, and her amber-bright eyes burned with such strength and determination that his heart skipped a beat. In that instant, he fell hopelessly in love.

Varzi called her a stubborn child with a malicious nature and an unrepentant spirit. Many in Tegoradaysol agreed, convinced the future was bleak if it rested in the hands of a dragonmaster so defiant, so unwilling to be tamed.

But Andorran, Tau, and Tiean saw what the Triad could not. Where the Triad saw defiance, they saw conviction. Where the Tribunal saw recklessness, they saw courage. What others took for insolence, they recognized as dignity.

Tangor, determined that no one should dictate Calla's path, fought to keep the Triad and Tribunal from molding her into their image of the Genesi Ney. Whenever possible, he took her away from the village, out of their reach.

Each time they returned, Andorran's certainty grew: Calla was meant for him.

Udaro, however, remained convinced she was better kept at a distance. He never pressed outright, but his opposition was constant.

First, he insisted Calla was too young to take a mate. Andorran was young as well; he could wait.

After her twenty-fifth birthday, Udaro argued she was too strong-willed for a Kamborian. Her temper was too volatile; she and Andorran clashed too often. Kamborian consorts were placid, obedient, everything Soroni women were not. But Andorran countered that he wanted no servile consort. He wanted a mate. A woman he could respect.

Udaro reminded him of Darmon's plan to unite Calla with the prince of Mim Tor. That had made Andorran laugh outright. He knew her well enough to know she would never bow to life in a royal court, no matter the Triad's persuasion.

His counsel even pointed to the letters Calla still received from an old classmate at Ackley's, rumored to be more than a friend. But Andorran knew she tossed those letters unread into the fire. Whatever feelings the classmate harbored, Calla did not share them.

Only once did doubt pierce him when Calla and Tau began spending more time together. Jealousy cut sharper than he expected, and, spurred by Udaro, he distanced himself from Tegoradaysol rather than watch them grow closer. The pain of it was more than he cared to admit.

On her twenty-eighth birthday, he resolved to act. She was of age, and nothing in her friendship with Tau suggested romance. All arguments had been countered; no obstacle remained. He sought Tangor. As her guardian, Tangor was the closest thing to family she had, and Andorran knew tradition demanded he ask.

Unlike Udaro, Tangor placed before him a stumbling block that stopped him cold.

"She is Soroni, Andorran," Tangor said gently. "If you stake a claim, she will lose her status as your equal. That is Soroni custom. She must stake the claim herself or forfeit her position and it could take years to reclaim it."

"I would never ask that of her," Andorran insisted.

Tangor, ever wise and patient where Calla was concerned, laid a consoling hand on his shoulder. "Wait. Calla is Soroni to her very heart. Even if you never asked her to surrender her standing, she would ask it of herself. Better she comes to you of her own will. Patience, Andorran. Calla will follow her heart when the time is right."

So he had waited. Not always patiently and more than once he had wondered if she was even listening to her heart. They had disagreed, argued, battled, and more than once he had been tempted to take matters into his own hands. But Tangor's words always stopped him. So he waited.

Now, looking down at her, he knew every moment of waiting had been worth it. He brushed a stray lock of hair from her face, his fingers lingering to trace the faint scar etched across her cheek. She had refused to let it be healed just as she had refused healing after every round of 'twenty-ones' she had endured. Scars, she believed, were reminders. Lessons to be carried, not erased.

Her eyes fluttered open and found his. She smiled, soft and unguarded, and leaned up to brush her lips against his.

"I like waking in your arms."

"I like waking with you in my arms," he answered warmly.

She sighed contentedly, then closed her eyes for a moment, drawing a slow breath as her mind reached out to sense the others of Una'savagi. When she opened them again, mischief sparkled in her amber gaze.

"The others are still asleep," she murmured, her hands wandering playfully across the hard planes of his chest. "…except for Kodar. He is on watch."

Andorran's brow arched, his expression deepening into something darker, hungrier. "Is that so?"

His mouth captured hers, and he knew with absolute certainty it had been worth the wait.

Chapter 19: Homecoming

The Mountains of the Condemned had sheltered the dragonmasters for over a thousand years, ever since the last reckoning and the fateful battle at Ackley's Castle. The range provided a perfect refuge for the wounded and the weary, most still reeling from the loss of so many of their kin.

The valley was accessible only by two passageways north and south both heavily guarded by spells and charms. Just beyond the northern passageway lay the small village of Tola Sol, a lively community of pixies and elves. Calla had always enjoyed visiting it. The villagers were spirited, warm, and welcoming, and like most enchanted beings, they held a good relationship with the dragonmasters.

It took Una'savagi four days to reach the hedges that ringed the village, and when Calla spotted them, twelve feet tall and impenetrable as always, a ripple of unease passed through her. Something was wrong.

The hedge served as Tola Sol's wall, with only two arched openings one east, one west leading in or out. From the outside, the tall greenery concealed everything within, and the surrounding forest kept even aerial eyes from seeing much. It had always been enough. The hedge, combined with a simple barrier spell, had made the villagers feel safe for centuries.

Calla tilted her head, peering through the dense canopy. She could just make out the jagged crest of Dragon's Peak, the tallest summit on the north ridge. The pixies and elves of Tola Sol had lived under its shadow long before the dragonmasters claimed the valley beyond. They considered themselves guardians of the northern passage, a duty they carried with pride.

"Someone should have come out by now," Calla murmured.

Tau nodded. "They usually send an ambassador. Maybe with the draxon flying about, they're staying behind the walls."

"Maybe." But her tone carried no conviction. She turned to Niko and motioned him forward. "What do you sense?"

He concentrated, his blue eyes narrowing as he stared at the hedge. Finally, he frowned. "Nothing."

"Nothing?" Calla pressed. "You mean no fear, no worry?"

"No," Niko said grimly. "I mean nothing at all. No emotions."

Her stomach tightened. That was impossible. A thousand lives at least dwelled within Tola Sol, pixies and elves alike. Enchanted or not, they should still give off emotions strong enough for Niko to feel.

"What is it, Calla?" Andorran asked.

She shook her head. "Something is wrong. I suppose a spell might be cloaking them, but I've never known pixies to work magic like that."

"Could it be a trap?" Tiean asked nervously.

"No…not a trap." Her voice was low, grim. "But we need to go in."

Taking a deep breath, Calla stepped through the east archway and froze.

The sight that met them was horrific.

The village of Tola Sol was gone. Where tidy homes and cheerful gardens had stood, there were only heaps of rubble, ash, and charred beams. Smoke drifted in thin ribbons from smoldering wreckage; flames still flickered weakly in places. The once-proud hedges were blackened husks, the west arch visible across a wasteland of ruin.

They stood in silence, their faces stricken. The air reeked of ash, smoke, and something fouler, burnt hair and flesh.

"What happened here?" Tiean whispered, his voice breaking.

"The draxon?" Tau offered, though without much belief.

Calla shook her head. "No. Dragons kill to eat, or to protect a nest. This…" she swept her gaze over the obliterated village. "…this is too much. Too deliberate."

"Slayers?" Kodar suggested, though doubt tinged his voice.

Something caught Calla's eye. She stepped forward, reaching down to lift a long, slender shaft of wood from the debris. The moment her fingers touched it, pain exploded in her skull. She cried out, stumbling backward and landing hard on the dusty ground.

"Calla!" Andorran was at her side in an instant, the others crowding close.

"What happened?" Gan demanded.

Her hand trembled as she pointed at the object. "That…that's a banedar's arrow." Her voice was hoarse. "I don't know if it's cursed, but when I touched it…" She broke off, her brow furrowing.

"What?" Andorran pressed, his tone urgent. "What happened when you touched it?"

She looked up at him, shaken. "I felt what the victim felt. The arrow, it holds the memory of their pain. Their death."

All eyes turned to the shaft lying in the dirt. Kodar reached out, brushing it with his fingertips. When nothing happened, he picked it up fully, examining it with a scowl.

"Maybe it only affects dragonmasters," he suggested.

"Or maybe the first person to touch it takes the burden." Gan countered. "Maybe Calla already absorbed the pain in that one."

Tau held out his hand. "Only one way to be sure."

Kodar passed him the arrow. Tau gripped it firmly, waited, then shook his head. "Nothing. Find another."

Another shaft was quickly found, and Andorran bent to pick it up. His jaw clenched, his eyes narrowing as the echo of agony swept through him.

"You felt it?" Calla asked, climbing shakily to her feet.

He gave a tight nod. "I felt it." Handing it to Tau, he waited.

Tau turned the arrow in his hands and shrugged. "Nothing."

"So…one time only," Tiean mused. "But why? What would be the point?"

"Maybe banedars just have a twisted sense of humor," Calla muttered, reaching for the shaft.

The moment she touched it, a fresh wave of torment surged through her. She dropped it with a gasp, clutching her head.

Tau's eyes widened in shock. "You can feel it again?!"

Calla pressed a hand against her side, half-expecting to feel blood. "Here this time."

Andorran nodded. "That must be where the arrow struck its victim. I felt it there as well."

"But why can she feel the pain if it already passed to you?" Caius asked thoughtfully. He stooped, lifting the first arrow shaft, bracing himself for some sensation but sighed with relief when none came. He held it out. "Where do you feel this one, Calla?"

She touched her temple lightly. "Here."

"I feel nothing," Caius admitted. He glanced at Andorran. "So perhaps it is not about being dragonmasters or the first to touch it. Care to test my theory?"

Andorran shrugged, reached for the shaft and grunted, dropping it almost immediately.

"You felt it in the same place?" Caius pressed.

Andorran rubbed his temple, frowning. "I did."

Kodar gave Caius an approving nod. "So it has nothing to do with being a dragonmaster or the first to touch it. Then why only them?" His pale eyes flicked between Calla and Andorran.

"Maybe not only them," Caius said quietly, scanning the others. "We have not all tried yet."

"Well, it had no effect on me." Kodar bent to retrieve the fallen shaft and held it out. "Who is next?"

Gan grimaced, but raised his hand. "I suppose me." He took it with a tense grip, then relaxed. "Nothing." He passed it to Tiean, who accepted it with determination.

"Nothing," Tiean confirmed.

Niko tried next, turning it over in his hand before shaking his head. "No…nothing."

Tau nodded slowly. "So it is only those two." He gestured at Calla and Andorran.

"What about Bal?" Caius asked softly.

All eyes turned. The boy already looked pale, fighting the urge to be sick.

Calla crouched beside him, resting a gentle hand on his shoulder. "Bal?"

He gave her a determined nod and held out his hand.

Niko placed the shaft into it.

Bal's expression shifted immediately. His dark eyes narrowed, his mouth twisted into a scowl. His small hand clenched tight around the wood as he retreated several steps, glaring at them all with contempt.

"He is not in pain," Tiean observed carefully. "But he is feeling something."

"Andorran and Calla felt the victims' pain," Caius said in a low voice. "What if…" He hesitated, then finished grimly. "What if he is feeling what the attacker felt?"

Calla's gaze fixed on the boy. She stepped forward, ignoring Andorran's hand when he tried to stop her. "I cannot cast it away I have already tried. But maybe I can take it from him."

"Let someone else," Andorran insisted. "It does not affect them."

But Calla shook her head. "He will not let them get close."

Bal's knuckles were white around the shaft, his dark eyes blazing with rage as she approached.

"Bal," she whispered soothingly. "You do not want to hurt anyone."

"Do not be so sure of that," Gan muttered, hand on his sword hilt.

Ignoring him, Calla reached for Bal's hand. "Just let me take it, Bal."

His gaze darted to her hand, only inches away and with a furious bellow he swung, aiming to drive the wood through her palm.

She jerked back just in time, seizing his wrist with her other hand in a firm grip. The boy screamed as she grabbed the shaft as well, both of them struggling.

Pain ripped through Calla's skull, nearly blinding her. Blisters flared on her palms from the heat radiating off the wood. Bal clung to it stubbornly, his thin frame trembling with rage. Calla matched his determination, refusing to let go.

The shaft shuddered violently in their hands, emitting a soft hiss. Then, with a sudden burst of heat and light, it vanished. Both Calla and Bal collapsed to the ground in a heap.

Bal stared wide-eyed at his empty hand, then at her. "I…I wanted to kill you," he whispered hoarsely.

"No," Calla said firmly, wrapping her arms around him. "You did not. The banedar wanted to kill me, not you."

He let out a ragged breath and then threw his arms around her, burying his face against her shoulder, sobbing brokenly.

The others watched in silence. Relief flickered through Caius, though unease lingered. Why had Bal absorbed the attacker's emotions, while Calla and Andorran had only felt the victims'? The question was etched on everyone's faces.

At length, Calla nudged Bal to his feet. "We should go," she said quietly. The boy rubbed his eyes with grubby fists, smearing more dirt across his cheeks.

"I am not sure Bal should come with us," Andorran said.

Calla sighed, flexing her blistered hands. "He comes with us."

"Why?"

Her shoulders stiffened. "He comes with us, Andorran."

He stepped forward, grasping her chin, forcing her to meet his eyes. "Why?"

Her amber gaze flashed, then softened. She closed her eyes, took a steadying breath, and looked back at him earnestly. "Do you trust me?"

"You know I do."

"Then trust me now. Bal stays."

"You will not tell me why?"

Her mouth curved into a sad smile. "If I knew, I would." She laid her hand over his wrist until his grip loosened. "Now let's go. I do not wish to linger here."

He searched her face for a moment, then nodded.

They filed out through the east arch, silent, Calla and Bal trailing behind. Several yards from the hedge, Calla stopped. She turned back, raising her blistered palms to the sky, then slowly rolling them down until they faced the ground.

"Mori interim," she whispered.

The hedges began to tremble, as if something were clawing from beneath. Then, to everyone's astonishment, they started to rise, the ground rupturing, black earth lifting in a swelling wall.

Calla stood at the center, trance-like, palms still pressed downward, eyes closed, her breathing shallow and quick.

The earth surged higher, cresting in a massive wave that came crashing down over the ruined village. Dust and ash swirled skyward as the others retreated several paces, watching in disbelief. In the middle of the chaos, a whirlpool of soil and stone spun open, widening as it devoured more of the wreckage.

Again, the ground heaved. Another wave of dirt collapsed into the vortex, swallowing the last fragments of Tola Sol. At last, a final crest rolled over the gaping wound, tumbling into the chasm like a great tidal wave. The earth gave a violent shudder and sealed itself.

Silence fell.

When the dust settled, only a wide patch of freshly turned soil remained, like a newly plowed field where a thriving village had once stood.

Andorran shook his head, his voice rough with awe. "How did you do that?"

Calla opened her eyes, lowering her hands. "They deserved to be buried."

He stepped forward, cupping her face in his hands. "I agree…but where did you learn such power?"

She hesitated, frowning. "I…I do not know."

"That was earth magic," Tau breathed, reverent. "Strong earth magic. No one has touched it in centuries."

"Sometimes…" Calla said softly, "…sometimes the spells just come to me."

Caius stared at the field of dirt where Tola Sol had once stood. "That is impossible. And yet…" He shook his head, still in shock.

Kodar's tone was steady but grim. "We should move. A spell that powerful will have drawn attention."

Calla gave him an apologetic look. "I should have thought of that."

"You did the right thing," Kodar reassured her. "They deserved burial."

"Yes," Tiean added. "Better that, than leaving them to scavengers."

Andorran caressed her cheek tenderly. "You did the right thing, *mio'sync.*"

With one last look at the field where Tola Sol had once stood, Una'savagi turned toward Dragon's Peak and the northern passage.

The journey back was hard. Exhaustion weighed on them, their spirits dampened by grief. Bal struggled to keep pace through the final stretch, his small body stumbling with fatigue. At last Andorran swung the boy onto his shoulders, and Bal, too weary to protest, rested his head against the Kamborian's neck.

By the time they reached the northern passage and sealed it behind them, the boy was bleary-eyed. When Andorran set him down, he immediately reached for Calla's hand.

"Everyone is likely asleep," Andorran said, glancing at the star-filled sky. "But I think we must speak with Camalaron at once."

Tau nodded. "You and Calla go. We will see that Bal is settled in our quarters."

"Put him in Calla's old room," Andorran added. "Somewhere we can keep watch."

Tiean frowned. "Are you sure it is wise, the two of you sharing quarters before the Triad has spoken?"

Calla managed a tired but certain smile. "There is no going back now, Tiean."

They descended the slope into the quiet village. At the door to their quarters, Calla gently released Bal's hand, giving him a nudge toward Tiean. Then she and Andorran continued on to the Sovereign Master's hall.

Vien was less than pleased to be dragged from his bed. He tried to insist they wait until morning, but their determination and his own unease around them was enough to win. Grumbling, he led them to the study and went to wake Camalaron.

Calla rolled her shoulders and stretched her stiff back. "I cannot wait to collapse into a real bed." She glanced at Andorran. "Do we tell him everything?"

Andorran smirked. "And what would you omit? The draxon? Tola Sol? Bal, perhaps?" He stepped behind her, kneading her shoulders until she sighed, eyes drifting shut. His chuckle was low. "Or were you thinking of keeping *us* to yourself?"

"I have nothing to hide," she said firmly. "But…I was thinking of the others. Tiean clearly has doubts not of us, perhaps, but of tradition."

"And you?" Andorran asked. "What do you think?"

She turned, eyes steady. "I think part of our destiny must be creating new traditions."

His hand slid down her neck, gripping her hips to pull her close. His voice dropped to a murmur, lips brushing her temple. "Tiean may be right…but I will not be parted from you just to appease the Triad."

Calla met his embrace with her own, fierce and unyielding. He was right. They had waited long enough, and she knew with every beat of her heart that they were meant to be together. She had known it, deep down, since the first time their eyes met.

It had been during her first round of *twenty-ones*. She had stood in the rain, arms trembling, sword raised to the sky, her back raw with welts. He had returned from Kambor Tine with his counsel, and when their eyes locked blue-green against amber her breath had faltered. She had wondered why this man unsettled her so.

It had taken years to name the truth. She was in love with Andorran. And that truth came with its own chains. A Kamborian man took consorts, not mates. Consorts were obedient, unequal, replaceable. Calla was Soroni, she would never bend to such a role, not even for love.

Pride forced her silence, the same pride that held her anger like a shield and turned her sorrow into fire. It was easier when Andorran traveled with Udaro and she with Tangor. Distance dulled the ache. But when they were together, the tension sharpened into clashes that left sparks in their wake.

Still what was meant to be could not be denied. The Triad would have to accept it.

Calla pressed a kiss to Andorran's jaw, then let her hands fall, stepping back to look up at him. "What do you suppose the Triad has been doing while we were gone?"

Chuckling, Andorran dropped into a chair. "What would *you* have been doing in their position, *mio'sync*?"

"Looking for a way to keep control," she replied flatly. "Exactly what they've been doing, I suspect."

He laughed, and Calla sank into the chair beside him. "And they say *I'm* stubborn."

"I'm curious…" Andorran leaned back, studying her. "What do you intend to say about Bal?"

"Bal?" Her brow arched with amusement. "What does one say about that boy? I don't understand him myself."

"Do you believe he can foretell?"

Calla looked surprised. "Foretell? I don't think that's what he does."

"Gan seems to think so," Andorran countered. "When the skeptic believes, I'm inclined to wonder."

She considered, then nodded slowly. "Bal does seem to know things things a boy his age shouldn't. Maybe that comes from foretelling…but I doubt it."

Andorran frowned. "What sort of things?"

"He knew Gan and I were dragonmasters. And he knew I am the Genesi Ney." Her tone was quiet but steady. "That was the main reason I paid that fool Yori to free him. I didn't want him talking."

Andorran's expression darkened. "Calla, why didn't you tell me this before?"

She sighed. "Honestly, I assumed Gan had. And it made no difference anyway he's just a boy."

"A dangerous one, it would seem."

Reluctantly, she nodded. "I know. Believe me, after what happened in Tola Sol, I'm very aware of the threat Bal might pose. But I can't get past the fact that he's only a child."

He studied her face. "Does this have anything to do with your parents' deaths?"

She tried to look away, but he caught her chin firmly. "Does it?"

"Perhaps…some." Her voice softened. "I know what it's like to be left behind and to feel responsible. Bal fears his parents were caught because of him. He blames himself for their deaths. That's a terrible burden to carry, Andorran. Most of his defiance is just an act."

"I know," Andorran said gently. "I asked Niko about him. He believes the boy is looking for you to replace his mother."

"I assumed as much."

His thumb traced along her jaw. "But you are not his mother, Calla."

"I know." She slipped her hand into his. "It's not my intention to try." A faint smile curved her lips. "But Andorran…he's supposed to be here."

"Because he *said* so?"

She placed his hand against her collarbone, her amber eyes unwavering. "Because I feel it here."

His fingers laced through hers. "Then he must have a purpose."

"Gan thinks I should bind him."

Andorran grew thoughtful. "And what did you say?"

She gave a short, humorless laugh and leaned back. "What could I say? He's just a boy. I don't know if he'd even understand what was being asked."

"I'd be more concerned about what might happen to *you* if he agreed."

Her brow furrowed. "Me? Why would anything happen to me?"

"You've forgotten what happened binding Kodar."

"That was different," she countered quickly. "It was the dragonslayer's oath, that has nothing to do with Bal."

"I wouldn't be so certain," Andorran warned. "Not after Tola Sol. Something about that boy attracted evil in that arrow shaft."

"So, you agree I shouldn't bind him?"

"I think Una'savagi needs to discuss it," he said firmly. "Gan may be right, binding might be the best way to test the boy's loyalty. And don't underestimate him, Calla. Bal knows more than he should for his years. I think he'll understand exactly what the binding demands of him."

Calla opened her mouth to answer, but the door swung open. She rose instantly to her feet, Andorran following suit, both turning to face the Sovereign Master as he entered with Vien on his heels.

Neither bowed nor touched their swords, and Vien's expression hardened in disapproval.

Camalaron, however, seemed not to notice. Dispensing with ceremony, he addressed them at once. "So you've made it back safely, thank Deius. We wondered what sort of trouble you'd found when the dragons returned alone."

"More than we bargained for," Andorran said grimly.

Calla dropped back into her chair, ignoring Vien's scandalized look. He clearly thought her insolent for sitting without being invited.

Camalaron turned to his aide. "Go back to bed, Vien. We won't be needing anything further tonight."

Vien looked as though he might argue, but with one last glare at Calla and Andorran, he bowed stiffly and withdrew.

Andorran reclaimed his seat while Camalaron settled into the chair opposite rather than taking his usual place behind the desk.

"Vien doesn't seem to understand that things have changed," Andorran observed.

"Perhaps he is simply slow to accept it," Camalaron replied calmly. "You may find that true of much of the village." His keen gaze flicked between them, noting the silent exchange that passed in an instant. "We waited for your return before making any plans for Tegoradaysol's governance. Nothing was decided in your absence...we left things as they were, for now. But that can wait. Tell me what you learned on this journey."

"Choran Sa, Kambor Tine, and Artiga are all held," Andorran reported. "But not by the slayers."

Camalaron frowned. "Then...who?"

"They call themselves the Watch," Andorran said. He gestured toward Calla. "She saw them. She believes they are banedars."

The Sovereign Master's gaze drifted to the bow strapped across Calla's back. "That explains your interest in such a weapon. Banedars are an unpleasant lot."

"They're aided by gray fairies," Andorran continued, "who point out the *sorcia* to them. The Watch prevents *sorcia* from leaving the cities. We don't yet know why."

"You were able to leave," Camalaron pressed.

"We had help." Andorran explained how Bal had led them through the smugglers' passages, then downriver. More than once Camalaron's eyes flicked toward Calla, but her expression betrayed nothing.

"So…this boy, Bal? He is *sorcia*?"

Andorran nodded. "His parents were chroniclers executed by the Watch as spies."

"You brought him with you?" Camalaron asked. "Another member of Una'savagi?"

"He is with us," Andorran replied vaguely.

"And you…" Camalaron was cut short by the sudden arrival of Varzi and Gira, both looking as though they had been roused straight from their beds.

Calla leveled a knowing glare at Vien, who stood in the doorway behind the two Triad members. "It seems Vien has taken the initiative and summoned the Triad," she said sharply, her gaze shifting to Camalaron. "Unless…it was at your request?"

Camalaron shook his head, frowning in his aide's direction. Vien's actions might have sprung from misplaced concern, but Camalaron was furious nonetheless. Dealing with Una'savagi was difficult enough without Triad interference.

"Vien did the right thing," Varzi said gruffly, his green eyes settling on Calla and Andorran. "What have you been discussing?"

Calla leaned forward in her chair, her mouth twitching. "A bit of this, a bit of that. But I'd be far more interested to hear what *you* were discussing while we were away."

Gira and Varzi exchanged troubled glances, then looked to Camalaron.

"Tegoradaysol and its citizens have always been our top priority," Varzi said at last, folding his arms.

"Good," Calla replied pleasantly. "…then we should have no problems."

"Problems?" Gira frowned.

Andorran nodded. "We made it clear before we left we intend to rule in Tegoradaysol."

Varzi's glare deepened, and Gira sank into the chair beside Camalaron. Clearly, the Triad had never truly believed Una'savagi would press this claim. They had not imagined they might one day take orders from the 'wild ones.'

"The slayers have united with banedars and gray fairies," Andorran continued. "They are holding all the cities surrounding the mountains."

"Hold them?" Gira echoed. "For what purpose?"

"That remains to be seen," Andorran replied evenly.

Concern shadowed Gira's face. "So you believe Tegoradaysol may be their true objective."

"The greatest threat they face is the dragonmasters," Andorran said. "Without us, they would have a clear path to the realm."

Calla nodded grimly. "Eliminating us is their logical first move."

"And the slayers know we will fight," Andorran added. "They know Una'savagi is a threat."

"Not yet, you are not!" Varzi snapped. "You are just seven overly confident dragonmasters!"

"I hope the slayers underestimate us as much as you do, Varzi," Calla shot back. "That would certainly be to our benefit."

"Calla, you know we are only interested in doing what is best for us all," Camalaron said quietly.

Her temper flared, her amber eyes flashing. "Your only interest has been making me into what *you* believe I am supposed to be! Shaping me to your interpretation of the prophecy!" She waved her hand impatiently. "I am not interested in what you think I am *supposed* to be!"

Outside, thunder rumbled. Remembering Tola Sol, Andorran glanced upward, wary.

"That is a very cynical view," Gira said solemnly.

"It is a realistic one," Calla countered.

"You must understand, Calla," Camalaron pressed, his tone measured. "The people here will not willingly accept you in leadership. Three of your number are newlings, bound less than a year. Three more have only recently been released from their counsels.

Even Andorran " the Sovereign Master nodded toward him, " has been free of Udaro's charge for only a short time, by our standards."

"Then you added a dragonslayer to your ranks," Gira pointed out. "That did not sit well with most of the residents."

Calla's brows shot up. "We brought Kodar to Tegoradaysol because we were *asked* to! Does anyone outside this room even know that?"

The shock on Gira and Varzi's faces made Calla laugh coldly. "Perhaps I should have asked if anyone outside of the Sovereign Master knew." She turned her gaze on Camalaron. "We brought him because you and Darmon asked it of us though we all knew it was more order than request."

Camalaron sighed softly. "That is true. They were asked to bring him back."

Gira looked at him incredulously. "But why were we not told? And what was the point?"

"Another matter of prophecy?" Calla pressed, rising to her feet and facing Camalaron. "It seems everything you do is tied to that bloody prophecy!"

The older dragonmaster took a steadying breath. "Many of my decisions have been guided by what I know of the prophecy that is true. But Kodar was not one of them. Darmon and I believed he was in danger in Mim Tor."

"And why would you concern yourself with the well-being of a dragonslayer?" Calla demanded.

"He refused to take the oath the others swore," Camalaron explained. "We thought that significant." He gave her a purposeful look. "Clearly, we were correct. You have bound him."

She shook her head. "You couldn't have known that would happen. I didn't even have the ability to forge a binding then."

"He refused the oath," Camalaron repeated. "We believed that important...that it spoke in the young man's favor."

Calla nodded slowly, though skepticism lingered in her eyes. "Does the prophecy say anything about assimilators?"

Camalaron shook his head. "Not that I know of."

Varzi frowned. "Now what is she talking about? What do assimilators have to do with this?"

Calla spun on him, fury in her voice. "*I* am an assimilator! Another secret the Sovereign Master has kept from you!"

Gira's face drained of color. He stared at Calla in horror. "An assimilator?" he whispered. "That is not possible. We have been watching you showed no signs…"

"I cannot control it," Calla cut in sharply. "But Camalaron knows, he has always known. That is why we were given quarters apart from the others."

Varzi's green eyes widened in shock, and he turned to Andorran as though seeking confirmation.

"She can assimilate," Andorran said. "…but not at will. She has been doing it since her binding. Tau, Tiean, and I have always known."

Varzi rounded on Camalaron, his expression thunderous. "How could you *not* have told us about this?!"

"I did not feel it was necessary for anyone else to know," Camalaron replied quietly. "As she told you, she cannot control it. It was not significant."

Gira shook his head slowly, disbelief etched across his features. "A dragonmaster with the ability to assimilate... Camalaron, how could you ever have thought that insignificant?"

"If she learned to control it learned to use it I would have told you."

"She is more dangerous *not* knowing!" Varzi snapped.

If Una'savagi had any hope of taking control without bloodshed, Calla knew the Triad had to be unseated. The cleanest way to accomplish that was to set them against each other. Revealing Camalaron's deception seemed to be doing exactly that, though she hated that her assimilator nature had to be laid bare to achieve it.

She crossed to the window, staring out into the night. "Una'savagi made it clear before we left we intend to be the ruling force in Tegoradaysol," she said bluntly. "It would have been prudent for you to spend our time away preparing for that transition."

Camalaron looked at her gravely. "We concede that you are in a unique position. You possess both the power and the strength to seize control. And I have no doubt you know how to use both to your advantage."

"But you still lack experience," Gira reminded them. His composure was strained, his confidence clearly shaken, but he pressed on. "Would it not be wiser to let us continue in our positions...allow you to rule through us? The people would cling to what is familiar, and we could offer counsel where you lack experience."

Calla turned to face them. "The Triad has ruled long enough. Some of the choices made under your watch were not sound...not in our best interest. We do not need the advice of the Triad."

Varzi's glare sharpened. "And you think it will be easy to overthrow us?"

"We do not intend to overthrow the Triad," Andorran said matter-of-factly. He glanced at Calla to see if she was reining in her temper; she gave him a faint, brittle smile. "We expect the Triad to step down of its own volition."

"Never!" Varzi shouted, his face flushed with fury.

Gira turned to Camalaron, who looked just as shaken. "This has never been done," he said quietly.

Camalaron nodded grimly. "I have a responsibility to Tegoradaysol."

"Which is *exactly* why you will do this," Calla pressed, stepping forward. "Overthrowing the Triad might spark riots, innocent people could die. There has been too much death already, with more yet to come. None of us wishes to spill more blood than necessary."

"Then consider what Gira suggested," Camalaron urged, rising to his feet. "You will be the true power, we all know it."

"The power behind a false front," Calla shot back. "Even if I *would* agree to such a deception, I would never hand that kind of control to someone I cannot trust."

Varzi planted his feet, his voice rising. "I will not step down and give Una'savagi free reign in Tegoradaysol! I will not be ruled by insolent young dragonmasters! I am a member of the Triad!"

Calla's fingers curled around the hilt of her sword. "And I am the Genesi Ney," she hissed, her tone dripping with venom. "A role I never asked for, in case you've forgotten. For years you have lectured me on my destiny, pushed me toward your interpretation of my responsibility." She whirled on Camalaron, her eyes blazing. "So be it! I accept what I am, and all that comes with it but on *my* conditions. On *my* terms. Una'savagi will rule Tegoradaysol!"

A thunderclap shook the chamber, and this time Andorran had no doubt of its source. He rose, laying a steadying hand against Calla's back.

She forced her anger down, her voice quieter but no less firm. "The Triad will step down tomorrow. You will make it known that you support Una'savagi, that this is what is best for Tegoradaysol. If you do not…we will be forced to take matters into our own hands."

Without giving them a chance to respond, she swept out of the room.

Andorran caught up with her in the corridor. "Well…that could have gone better."

She looked up at him in despair. "I do not wish to go to war with the dragonmasters. This has barely begun, and already I am weary of it."

"It will not come to war not here," he assured her. "They want what is best. I believe that. Do you not?"

Her shoulders sagged. "I am not sure anymore."

>

An arrow thudded into the target, dead center. Bal dashed forward, yanking the shaft free with a triumphant cry.

"You see, Sera Calla!" he exclaimed, racing back, his face alight with joy. "I told you you are camia'ol!"

She grinned, taking the arrow from him. After spending most of the morning in the blacksmith's shop discussing designs and advantages of different arrowheads, she was grateful for the cool breeze off the water. The smith had been eager for the challenge and promised her several dozen arrows in a few days.

Stepping behind Caius, Calla adjusted his grip, showing him how to hold the bow and nock the arrow. "It is really very simple."

Tau and Kodar, seated beneath Rait's Tree, looked up from their work as Caius loosed the arrow.

"Not bad," Kodar said appraisingly.

"You might just make an archer of him, Calla," Tau called out.

Calla patted Caius on the shoulder. "We may have found a weapon that suits you."

He chuckled. "I do like the idea of a little distance," he admitted.

Tau waved the shaft he was stripping. "Do you mean to make archers of all of us?"

"Not all of you," she assured him. She pointed at the half-finished arrow in his hands. "Now get back to work. Lodin says he'll have more arrows ready in a few days."

"Slave driver," he teased, turning back to his task.

Caius fired again, this shot striking even closer to the mark.

"Looks as though you've found another camia'ol," Andorran called as he, Tiean, and Gan entered the clearing.

Calla brightened. "Niko too. He is a natural."

Standing a few feet away, Niko executed a grand bow. "Thank you, m'lady," he drawled with a grin.

Caius rolled his eyes and laughed. "Compliments go straight to his head."

Looking amused, Andorran handed Calla one of the branches he had gathered. "These are flexible, but strong. I think they'll work."

Testing the branch, she nodded. "Perfect."

"That gives us five bows, plus the one you picked up in Choran Sa," Kodar tallied.

"Do not bother making one for me," Gan said with a grimace. "I would prefer to keep my eyes in my head, if you don't mind."

"And Tau is hopeless," Calla laughed.

He grinned good-naturedly. "She is absolutely right…though I prefer to blame her teaching."

"Niko, Caius, Bal, Kodar, and you," Andorran said, looking pleased. "Five archers then."

"Could be six, if you'd care to try?" Calla teased.

Chuckling, Andorran sat down at the water's edge. "Not me. I prefer to look my opponent in the eye."

Caius held the bow out to Tiean. "Care to give it a try?"

After several faltering attempts, Tiean finally struck the straw sack, and everyone cheered.

Calla sat beside Andorran, picking up a willow branch. They were using the bow and arrows she had acquired in Choran Sa as a model, crafting their own with willow for the bows, hemp fiber for the strings, and hickory shafts for the arrows.

"Any word from the Triad?" she asked quietly.

"Not yet."

She sighed. "I cannot decide if they mean to oppose us…or if they are simply stalling to annoy us."

Andorran patted her hand. "They still have a few hours of daylight. We'll wait and see."

"And Bal?"

"Tiean agrees with Gan and me." He gave her a questioning look. "And the others?"

Calla nodded, focusing on the willow branch in her hand. "They agree as well. Which means the only one left to ask is Bal."

"If he does not agree, he remains shielded."

Running her fingers through her hair, she set the half-finished bow aside. "I have no doubts about that…he will agree."

Andorran took her hands. "Are you worrying about what I said last night?"

"Partly," she admitted. She was not eager to risk another ordeal like the one she'd faced binding Kodar, but in the end, the result had been worth it. Kodar was now as much a part of Una'savagi as any of them.

"Calla, you know what Shiran Aku said, you will be betrayed by someone who does not share your dragonsheart."

"That could be anyone in Tegoradaysol."

He smiled faintly. "No, it could not. You are as much a skeptic as Gan. There are very few you truly trust." His gaze locked on hers. "We'll only feel safe with Bal among us if he is bound to you, Mio'sync."

She exhaled heavily. "Very well. We will do it tonight."

Niko, taking his turn with the bow, suddenly turned, alert. "Someone is coming," he announced.

All eyes shifted toward the path leading from the village. Several minutes passed before an older man came strolling into view, casual and deliberate. His white hair was neatly combed back and tied with a leather cord. His beard, trimmed to a perfect point, reached the middle of his chest, and his crisp clothes spoke of precision.

"Udaro," Calla muttered with clear resentment. She and Andorran's former counsel had never gotten along.

Tau glanced at Andorran, who nodded, giving him leave to lower the protection spell surrounding the clearing.

Udaro's dark eyes swept over the group, lingering last on Andorran. As a veteran dragonmaster and former counsel, custom dictated that the younger dragonmasters should rise and bow. None of them moved. They sat in silence, watching.

He stopped a few paces from Calla and Andorran, drawing in a deep breath before letting it out slowly. "The Sovereign Master asked me to speak with you," he said at last.

"About what?" Andorran asked flatly.

Udaro arched a brow. He was not accustomed to such insolence least of all from a former charge. He and Andorran had often clashed. Udaro was strict, Andorran obstinate. But never had the younger dragonmaster been disrespectful.

"I see he did not exaggerate," Udaro said coldly.

Tiean, Caius, and Niko moved to join Tau and Kodar beneath the tree. Bal and Gan drifted toward the bank near Calla and Andorran.

"This is not what you were taught."

Andorran felt Calla's hands tense in his grasp. He gave them a reassuring squeeze and leaned close, whispering against her ear. "Do not let him provoke you, Mio'sync." She nodded, offering him a small smile before he turned back to Udaro.

The older man studied Calla, then shifted his gaze to Andorran. "The Sovereign Master tells me you have some fool notion of ruling Tegoradaysol."

Andorran nodded. "We *do* rule Tegoradaysol," he corrected calmly. "We have for some time. The Triad has simply been reluctant to accept it."

"You do not have enough experience to rule," Udaro snapped.

Andorran rose to his feet. "If by experience you mean that we lack the skill in manipulation and deception that the Triad has mastered, then you are correct," he said sharply. "But no one is more qualified to rule here."

Udaro's scornful gaze swept over them. "Newlings, a dragon-slayer, a boy, and a handful of dragonmasters barely free of their counsel...this is your ruling force?!"

Calla rose as well, bristling at his condescension. Andorran set his hands on her shoulders, steadying her. She leaned back into him as the others moved closer.

"Do not underestimate us," Andorran cautioned. "We are more than we appear, and the Triad knows this. We know things the Triad has hidden, things you do not. Our purpose is not to divide dragonmasters, but to unite them."

"We *are* united!" Udaro snapped. "With the exception of Una'savagi!"

"Then stand against us," Andorran challenged, "and see how united you truly are."

Udaro turned abruptly, frustration etched deep in his face. These dragonmasters were far stronger than he had believed...he could feel it.

Without a backward glance, he walked away, his mind troubled. What did Andorran think he knew about the Triad? Udaro knew the young man well enough to see conviction and determination burning in his eyes. Well enough to know that Andorran believed, with every fiber of his being, that what he was doing was right.

Udaro headed for the Sovereign Master's quarters. He had spoken to Una'savagi at the Triad's request. Now, he meant to speak to the Triad for his own peace of mind.

>

Camalaron sat grim behind his desk while Varzi, Gira, and Udaro filled the chairs opposite, each trying to shout over the other until the Sovereign Master lifted a hand for silence.

"I think," Camalaron said, measured, "that if we give them what they ask, they will work with us be willing to compromise on certain issues."

"Compromise?!" Varzi's face flushed red. "I cannot see how you can even consider compromise!"

Udaro's dark eyes fixed on him. "How can you *not*? We have no control over any of them. The three still under counsel are Calla's charges. There is no room left to maneuver here!"

"So, you would yield to rebels?!" Varzi barked.

"They are not rebels," Udaro countered sharply. "Andorran says they want to unite the dragonmasters, and I believe he is sincere."

Gira sighed heavily, stroking his beard. "We have only two choices. If we step down and support Una'savagi, the rest of the community will follow in time. If we refuse…they *will* rise to the challenge. I do not doubt it. And I do not believe we are a match for even one of them let alone all."

Udaro nodded. "Gira is right. Defying them could bring consequences none of us want."

Varzi stalked restlessly across the room. "How can you even consider giving in to these…these *adolescents*?!"

Gira shot him a look of impatience. "Have you ever stopped to look past their youth, Varzi? Andorran, Tau, Tiean, Kodar they are young, yes, but not children! And Calla…" his expression softened sadly, "…I am not sure she was ever allowed to be a child."

"The four released from counsel were discharged in far less time than usual," Camalaron noted grimly. "That says something of their maturity."

"And they have not exactly been running to us for guidance," Gira added. "Calla has openly resisted our plans…sabotaged some of them."

Udaro leaned forward, curious. "In what way?"

"Her union with the prince, for one."

Udaro scowled. "Tangor told you long ago such a union was absurd. Prince Gadin was never a suitable match for her." He sighed, shaking his head. "I never liked the idea of Andorran and Calla either, she was always so defiant but I must admit, they seem well suited."

Camalaron furrowed his brow. Gira's eyes widened.

"Andorran and Calla?" Varzi repeated with disdain. "That match we already considered and dismissed."

Udaro frowned. "I do not understand."

"As Varzi said," Camalaron explained, "we considered it. They are the two most powerful sorcerers in the realm. But both are unpredictable."

Gira's gaze sharpened. "Are you saying Andorran truly entertains such a match?"

Udaro nodded. "Andorran has entertained it for years since he first met her, in fact. He even spoke to Tangor. Tangor told him that because Calla is Soroni, he would have to accept her as a mate, not a consort, and that she had to stake the claim. He urged Andorran to wait. I suppose he hoped the young man would abandon the notion. He certainly did not like it any more than I did. But it would seem our charges cared little for what we thought."

Varzi laughed bitterly. "A Kamborian and a Soroni? That alone was reason enough to dismiss it. How do you join them without bloodshed?!"

Udaro surged to his feet. "You are not listening. I am telling you it is *done*!" He strode to Camalaron's desk. "I assumed you already knew."

Varzi turned on Camalaron. "Did you consent to this?!"

"This comes as news to me," Camalaron said grimly. He looked at Udaro. "They told you this?"

Udaro shook his head. "They did not have to. I saw them together before I came here. The way he looks at her, the way he touches her it is more than familiar, it is intimate." He met the Sovereign Master's eyes. "I know Andorran. He has ignored Kamborian custom and taken Calla as his mate."

Varzi's face blanched. "But…they cannot! One does not simply stake a claim!"

Udaro's glare was sharp. "Do you hear nothing, Varzi? It is done! With or without the Triad, it is *done*."

Camalaron gave a weary nod. "I believe you, Udaro. Una'savagi follows their own code. They would not trouble themselves with the Triad's approval."

"Do you realize the bloodline those two will create?" Gira said quietly. "They are not only the most powerful dragonmasters in living memory, Calla can forge a binding. And she can assimilate."

"Assimilate?" Udaro breathed in shock.

Gira nodded grimly. "We only just discovered it ourselves," he said with a meaningful glance toward Camalaron.

Varzi's voice rose in fury. "How do we know this is truly the bloodline of prophecy?!"

Unexpectedly, Gira laughed. "I will relinquish my position in the Triad," he declared. "We have been trying to guide Calla down the path we *thought* she must walk, and we lost patience when she resisted. Perhaps she knows better than we do. Perhaps her instincts are leading her exactly where she needs to go. Look at the mate she has chosen...one of the most powerful dragonmasters ever born, and perhaps the only man strong enough to be her equal."

He crossed to the window, gazing out toward the clearing where Una'savagi waited for the Triad's decision. "Perhaps it is time we trust the Genesi Ney to do what she was born to do."

Chapter 20: Stirring Up Memories

The village was in turmoil for several days after the Triad resigned and publicly declared their support of Una'savagi. Varzi's words had been half-hearted at best, but Camalaron and Gira spoke with surprising conviction, declaring Una'savagi's rise to power as being, in their opinion, in line with prophecy.

The shift in power stirred suspicion among the people of Tegoradaysol. But when they saw that the young dragonmasters were not bent on dismantling their lives or making reckless changes, most citizens returned to their routines; watchful, curious, and waiting to see what might come next.

Una'savagi spent most of their time outdoors either by the river or high in the mountains with the dragons.

The bow had quickly become a spectacle for the villagers. People gathered daily to watch them practice archery. Calla's accuracy was near flawless, Kodar and Niko almost as precise, but it was Caius who drew the most admiration. Through clever adjustments to shaft design and arrow tips and no small amount of experimentation he managed to fire two or three arrows at once, striking separate targets. To him, the bow was less about strength or grace and more about calculation and logic.

Bal, proudly bearing the mystic dragonsheart, had at last found his place among them. He spent long hours at Caius's side, determined to learn the bow as well. The science of it baffled him, but his enthusiasm was undimmed.

Politics, however, remained a necessary evil. Several hours each week had to be given over to the tedious work of running a community. Calla, as the Genesi Ney, was expected at these meetings, though she detested them. She quickly learned that Tiean made an excellent second: diplomatic, logical, and able to resolve disputes with minimal confusion or frustration.

They were nearing the end of summer when grim news arrived: a rebellion had broken out in Choran Sa and Kambor Tine. The sorcia had attempted to overthrow the Watch with disastrous results. Po-lam-ti's report was bleak: all surviving agitators imprisoned, the remaining sorcia reduced to virtual prisoners in their own homes. Eight banedars lay dead, but more than sixty sorcerers had perished.

In the common room, Calla, Andorran, and Tiean listened with somber expressions as the dragon fairy relayed the events. They had warned against such an uprising when Po-lam-ti first told them it was being considered. The sorcia had ignored their counsel and paid dearly.

Calla rose to her feet, pacing, fingers combing through her tangled curls. "They should have waited!" she snapped. "We told them they were no match for banedars." She shot Po-lam-ti a sharp look. "You *did* tell them what we advised?"

The fairy, her pale gold hair cascading in spirals down to her tiny bare feet, fluttered uncertainly, twice vanishing behind Andorran's broad shoulders before daring to peek out again. "I told them, Genesi Ney. But they said…banedars have no magic."

"Gray fairies do!" Calla countered furiously. "And slayers! And banedars are not helpless!"

Po-lam-ti squeaked and darted out of sight once more. "They realize that now," she whispered from behind Andorran.

Calla's voice rose to a shriek. "Of course they bloody well realize it now! Sixty-three sorcerers are dead!"

The fairy's soft voice trembled. "They wish for you to come to Choran Sa."

Calla's head snapped up. "What?"

Po-lam-ti peeked timidly over Andorran's shoulder. "They say if the Genesi Ney comes, they can defeat the Watch."

Calla's laugh was bitter. "More likely I would walk straight into a trap!" She spun on Andorran, hands planted on her hips. "Tell the sorcia that if they want Una'savagi's help, they can *wait* until we have a fighting chance to get in and out alive! I am not marching against the Watch without the odds on my side."

Po-lam-ti gave another squeak and disappeared completely.

Calla glared at Andorran. "Will you *stop hiding her*!"

"I am just standing here," he said with a laugh. "Po-lam-ti, come out. Calla is not going to hurt you. She may yell, but she rarely bites."

Calla jabbed a finger into his chest, scowling. "*You* I would bite!"

He caught her hand, grin tugging at his mouth. "*You* I would allow."

She snatched her hand back, though a reluctant smile softened her face. "Perhaps later. As for you…" She turned her glare back to Po-lam-ti, who peeked nervously around Andorran's arm. "…remind the sorcia that we *warned* them. Before their revolt they were safe enough confined, yes, but not in mortal danger."

"You will not go to Choran Sa?" Po-lam-ti asked hesitantly.

"Not now."

The fairy sighed. "I will take them your message, Genesi Ney."

When she was gone, Calla sank onto the hearth, weary. "Why could they not wait?"

Andorran sat beside her, kneading the tension from her shoulders. "They were still prisoners," he said gently.

"No one wants to be held against their will," Tiean added. "Even if the walls are loose."

"They certainly have not improved their situation." Calla shook her head. "We could have smuggled them out one or two at a time. But the keep?" Her expression hardened. "I am not fool enough to break into the Watch's keep. I would end up in chains or worse before it was done. No need to make it easier for them."

Andorran chuckled, rising to his feet. "Your optimism is refreshing."

"You want optimism, talk to Tiean." Calla took his hand and stood. "I am a realist."

"I am a realist," Andorran corrected. "You…are a fatalist."

She shrugged. "Call it what you like. I prefer to expect the worst rather than be blindsided by it."

Tiean's expression was grim. "Do you truly think Choran Sa is a trap?"

"I think it is a strong possibility."

"You do not trust Po-lam-ti?" Andorran asked.

"I do not trust anyone who cannot look me in the eye."

"Is that why you bully her?"

Calla rolled her eyes. "Only a man would fall for that helpless act. Po-lam-ti plays the part of the pitiful victim very well. She hides behind you as if she is afraid of me."

"I think she *is* afraid of you."

Calla's smile was sharp and cold. "Not as afraid as she should be."

>

Since the failed uprising, the cities had settled into an uneasy kind of peace. The sorcia no longer dared risk provoking the Watch, while the Watch remained more vigilant than ever. Yet still the requests came relentless, insistent. Through Po-lam-ti, through pixies, sprites, and fairies, Calla was besieged with pleas from the sorcia for the Genesi Ney to come to them.

How many of them, she wondered, truly understood what it meant that the Genesi Ney existed at all? That her birth heralded a reckoning? Did they realize that in every reckoning before, blood had been spilled in rivers, lives lost in battles few survived?

"I heard you wanted to see me," a voice said behind her.

She glanced over her shoulder and nodded at Gira.

"Po-lam-ti has gone," he said mildly.

"After complaining about me, no doubt."

A faint smile tugged at his mouth. "She did mention that you shouted at her." He gestured to the ground beside her. "Would you mind?"

"Of course not."

He seated himself, and Calla leaned back on her elbows, letting the sun warm her face. Out on the water, Gan splashed Niko and Caius, their laughter carrying across the river. She smiled faintly at the scene.

"Gan seems to be improving," Gira observed, studying her profile. "Do they know why you do not join them?"

Her eyes stayed on the water. "They know I do not like it."

"But not the reason?"

"No."

He nodded, gaze drifting out over the river. "I was there that day…at the river. Do you remember?"

She drew a long breath, sat up, and wrapped her arms around her knees. "No…not exactly. My memories are…broken. Just fragments from my childhood."

"Tangor feared your childhood memories might harm you," Gira said quietly. "There weren't many happy ones in Soronu."

She bit her lip and nodded. That much she recalled.

"He was never certain whether it was better for you to have painful memories…or none at all."

Her brows drew together. She turned to him sharply. "He…he did something? To make me forget?"

"I think he did," Gira admitted. "At least once that I know of. Everything he did was to protect you."

Her voice softened. "I miss him."

"As do I. He was my closest friend before he took you on as his charge."

"He told me." She regarded him seriously. "That's why I wanted to speak with you."

He waited patiently.

"The people don't truly accept us," she said at last. "They pretend to because the Triad asked it of them, or because they are afraid not to. But acceptance? Trust? No."

"Do you blame them?"

She gave a crooked smile. "No. We know we're partly to blame."

"You have always kept people at a distance, even as a child. Una'savagi has followed your lead."

"Given what I am," she asked, "have I had much choice?"

"Perhaps not."

Her amber eyes narrowed. "Do you dislike me because of Tangor?"

He looked surprised. "I do not dislike you."

"Not as much as Varzi, perhaps…"

"That was never about you," Gira said quickly. "Tangor changed after he took you on. He argued with us constantly about your training. I knew he carried a great responsibility, but he refused any help. It was…frustrating."

"He told me to watch the Triad and the Tribunal. He said they wanted to use the Genesi Ney for their own ends. And he said I wasn't told the full prophecy." She studied him. "What do I not know?"

Gira looked puzzled. "I don't know. And I can't imagine how Tangor could, unless Camalaron kept more secrets from us. As far as I know, no one has heard the prophecy in full in centuries."

"Heard it?" she repeated, intrigued. "So someone must know."

"Someone spoke it once, though I don't know who or when. Since then, it's only been passed down piecemeal. Whether anyone alive knows the full prophecy now…I can't say."

"Well, someone must know how to *hear* it again," she reasoned. "How else am I supposed to fulfill it? I'd wager Camalaron knows...another secret he's keeping."

He frowned. "It's possible. He has not shared everything he knows."

"Did you ever just ask him?"

Gira chuckled softly. "Not all of us share your curiosity. We assumed we'd been told what mattered. At times…I think we were told too much."

She grinned wryly. "Then you may not appreciate why I asked to see you."

His brow arched. "Oh?"

"I meant what I said about not being the power behind a false rule. That is not how Una'savagi works. But we also know we need more than fear to govern. We need trust. You once suggested we keep an advisor. We agree. We want it to be you."

Gira looked stunned. "Me?"

"You are the natural choice."

"I'm…flattered. The others agree?"

"I wouldn't have asked if they didn't. We make our decisions together. You're free to refuse, but we'd like you to consider it."

He nodded slowly. "I will. But surely others will expect you to ask Camalaron."

Her expression hardened. "I do not trust Camalaron."

"I can see why," he admitted. "He has kept far too many secrets."

"My assimilating, for example?"

"A very good example," Gira agreed. "We knew it was possible and thought we were watching carefully. He should have told us." He tilted his head curiously. "How does it happen?"

Her frustration flared. "I wish I knew. Every time, it's in my sleep. I wake…different."

"Into what?"

"Different things," she told him. "A wolf, a deer, a snow leopard…even a mystic. But I never choose the form I take, nor when I change or change back."

"Andorran and the others they've known all along?"

She nodded. "They're the ones who kept me from going mad."

Gira shook his head slowly, astonishment etched across his face. "A mystic…I would never have believed it possible."

"According to Caius, it shouldn't be. He says *dali-daubs* cannot take the form of any creature considered pure of spirit. The Mistress of Mystics said the same."

"You actually saw her?!" Gira exclaimed.

"Shiran Aku," Calla replied. "She called herself the Mistress of Mystics, though I'm still not certain what she truly is. Not a fairy she has no wings." She gave a small shrug. "Whatever she is, she gave me this." She brushed her fingers across the silver marking on her collarbone.

Una'savagi had taken to wearing tunics that left their left shoulders bare, the mark clearly visible.

"She also gave me the ability to forge a binding."

The older dragonmaster tugged at his beard, regarding her with wonder. "You've become quite an extraordinary young woman."

"But still one in need of an advisor," she reminded him, her tone pointed.

Gira smiled faintly. "You realize that some of my ideas may differ from those of Una'savagi?"

"I should hope so." Calla's amber eyes gleamed with dry humor. "We admit we could use an advisor but that doesn't mean we'll always take your advice. I chose my mate without the Triad's guidance."

As if sensing her thoughts, Andorran glanced their way, a smile curving his lips.

"You and Andorran are an unlikely match," Gira observed. "I don't believe a Kamborian and a Soroni have ever vowed to be mated."

Calla chuckled softly. "I'm certain that's true."

Gira's gaze drifted to the newlings splashing in the water, Bal among them. "We accused Tangor of giving you too much freedom, of cutting you off from those who could help you…but perhaps he was right. Your bond with the newlings is strong even before the binding. And with Tiean, Tau, and Andorran as well. Tangor always insisted you would be ready. It seems he was right."

"Ready?" she echoed, brows knitting.

"To do what needed to be done when the time came."

She grimaced. "I wish I felt as certain."

Gira laughed softly. "How can you not? Look at what you've accomplished, and mostly by instinct. Tangor was right, you'll find your path…if others don't succeed in obstructing it."

"Perhaps," she conceded. "But there are things I must know first."

"What things?"

"The prophecy…all of it. If I could hear the whole rather than fragments, perhaps I'd finally understand what I'm meant to do."

"I see your point." Gira gave a slow shake of his head. "But I don't know how you expect to manage it. Perhaps Camalaron knows."

"Likely. Though he's shared nothing so far." Her amber eyes flashed, then softened as she waved the thought away. "I'll deal with him in my own time. For now, I want to know what Tangor did to my memories."

He sighed heavily. "I know of one time for certain at the river. He feared a memory spell might leave you afraid of water, but he was more concerned about what remembering that day might do to you."

"Was it so awful?" she asked ruefully.

"For a child yes. I think it was."

Her voice dropped. "How do I get those memories back?"

"Are you certain you want to?"

"No," she admitted, her gaze fixed on the rippling water. "…but I think I need to. I fear water, yet I don't know why. I know Lucan is my half-brother, but when did I learn that? Who told me?"

"Is it so important that you know?"

"It is to me."

"Even if what you remember is painful or frightening?"

She nodded firmly. "Even then."

His expression softened with compassion. "I can counter the spell Tangor used at the river. If he used the same spell at other times, it should bring those memories back as well." His voice grew grave. "But I must warn you, Calla if he used it often, you'll face many memories. This could be harder than you realize."

Calla drew in a deep breath and nodded.

Gira placed his fingertips against her temples. "*Memorare animatus.*" he whispered.

>

Soronu.

The city where she was born.

Crowded between the Garron Nir and the Dari San Rivers, it pulsed with life; traders, smugglers, gamblers, and merchants flooding its streets, bringing with them taverns, inns, and brothels. It was one of the fastest-paced cities in the realm, and for a child, even a Soroni child, it was not a safe place.

Lucan had been tasked with watching her, though everyone knew their father Harith cared more for reputation than for his daughter's safety.

Most who knew Harith thought him a heartless man, one who had broken his wife Bain and seemed determined to do the same with his children. But no one dared oppose him. Harith was Tribunal, powerful, untouchable. Bain, some whispered, had made her bed now she must lie in it.

But many pitied the children.

Lucan, eight years her elder, was tall and slender, with glossy blue-black hair framing his handsome face. His deep sapphire eyes gleamed with intelligence and mischief, his laugh was warm and contagious but his smile never seemed to touch those watchful eyes.

Calla was a petite child with bright amber eyes and a crown of golden-red curls. With her delicate features and wide eyes, she looked cherubic. But unlike her sociable brother, Calla was aloof and withdrawn. She watched everything warily, hanging back in the shadows. To most, she appeared merely bashful.

Lucan and his friends knew better. Since she was old enough to walk, Calla had been his responsibility, trailing faithfully after him wherever he went. And Lucan knew well enough there was nothing shy about his sister. She had a quick temper when provoked, a sharp tongue, and a deep dislike of being the center of attention. More than anything, she hated to be touched. Lucan had nicknamed her *little miss touch-me-not.*

Looking after her was rarely difficult. She asked for nothing, said little unless pressed, and usually followed at a safe distance. What irritated Lucan was not the task itself but the burden of her constant presence. His life had changed after her birth, and not for the better. His father had grown cold and perpetually angry, while Bain fell into a depression from which she never recovered. Lucan placed the blame for all of it squarely on his sister. Being saddled with her care only deepened his resentment.

Going away to Ackley's had been his first taste of freedom since Calla's birth. Returning home during term break, he was outraged to find nothing had changed, he was still expected to shepherd his six-year-old sister.

His friends Jarin and Olar sympathized, but they knew as well as he did that Harith's word was law. If Calla came to harm or worse, caused any scandal that embarrassed the family Lucan would bear the punishment. Their only consolation was reminding him it would last only until they returned to Ackley's.

Calla, though young, was not oblivious. She heard Lucan's constant accusations that she had ruined his life simply by existing and at first she even sympathized with him. But as the years passed and his bitterness grew, her sympathy soured into resentments of her own.

In previous summers, the children had spent their days along the Dari San, cooling off in its gentle waters. But after Lucan's first year at Ackley's, he and his friends grew bored of splashing children and anxious mothers. They sought instead the Garron Nir on the east side of the city a seedier bank where smugglers, traders, and rougher folk gathered. Families were discouraged from going there. The waters were swifter, dirtier, and hemmed in by steep, rocky banks. There was more water traffic and fewer safe places to swim.

But for Lucan, Jarin, and Olar, that was exactly the appeal.

Calla trailed several yards behind them along the cobblestone street, a curious sight in her clean cotton dress and starched pinafore. Her brassy curls were neatly pinned back with a satin ribbon, and her polished appearance stood out in the rough east side.

The path down to the river was steep and uneven, nothing like the grassy shores of the Dari San. The Garron Nir surged, fast and murky. Calla wrinkled her nose as she picked her way down after her brother and his friends.

By the time she reached the bank, the boys were already stripping to their under-breeches and racing into the water. Calla sat beneath a scraggly tree near the edge, tugging off her shoes. Sometimes she swam with them though always at a distance but one look at the treacherous river convinced her otherwise. If danger came, she could not trust Lucan even to notice. The bank was safer.

She pulled a book from the pocket of her pinafore and settled against the tree trunk. While the boys laughed and roughhoused in the river, she divided her attention between the pages and the constant traffic up and down the waterway. Barges and craft moved steadily along, their deckhands seldom sparing a glance for children at the bank, though now and then one called or waved.

Calla watched wistfully, wondering what it might feel like to board one of those watercrafts and sail away forever, never looking back.

Her daydream shattered when the book was suddenly snatched from her hands. She gasped and looked up, her amber eyes flashing angrily.

The boy looming over her was lanky and tall, perhaps a year or two older than Lucan. His chestnut hair was tied back with a wide leather band, and dark eyes gleamed with amusement as he held her book out of reach.

"Well, what have we here?" he drawled.

A second boy appeared beside him, shorter and broader, glancing toward the river. "Novices," he announced with a broad grin. "From the west side."

Lucan and his friends were already frowning as they waded out of the water, their expressions wary.

Calla jumped to her feet, reaching for her book, but the older boy lifted it higher, taunting her.

"Give it back, Gurin," Lucan snapped.

The pieces fell quickly into place for Calla. Lucan knew him from school.

Gurin's eyes swept over her. "She's cute, Lucan. Going to be quite the looker when she grows up." He cupped her chin, only to have her jerk indignantly away. His grin widened. "Friend of yours?"

"Sister," Lucan said gruffly. "Now give her the book."

Jarin and Olar exchanged uneasy glances. They had seen enough of Calla's temper to know trouble was brewing. She might be younger, but she was not helpless. Both boys had witnessed her cast before usually in anger, and usually with unpleasant results.

Gurin's companion snatched the book and squinted at the cover. "*Rules of Engagement in Sword Combat*," he read aloud, then laughed.

Calla lunged for it, but he yanked it out of reach again. Huffing in irritation, she planted her fists on her hips.

"Lir, give her the book," Lucan said tightly, his eyes fixed on Calla.

Jarin and Olar had climbed out of the water and now joined them on the bank. "Just give it back," Jarin urged. "She's only a little girl."

"What have you learned, little girl?" Gurin teased, twirling a stick like a sword.

Lir barked a laugh. "She's not reading this. It's far too difficult for someone her age." He flipped through the pages dismissively.

Calla's eyes narrowed, her jaw tightening as she tracked the stick in Gurin's hand.

"So?" Gurin taunted, tapping her lightly on the shoulder with it. "Can you actually read this, baby sister…or are you just pretending?"

In a blur of motion, Calla snatched the stick from him, swung it around, and cracked it sharply against his wrist.

Gurin grunted in surprise. Lir roared with laughter. "Maybe she *is* reading it!"

Lucan stepped in quickly, snatching the stick from Calla and tossing it aside. He shot her a dark look. "That's enough of your nonsense!" he snapped.

Calla jutted her chin out, glaring at him in defiance.

"Baby sister has a temper," Gurin muttered, rubbing his wrist. "You've got your hands full with this one."

Rolling his eyes, Lucan sighed. "You don't know how right you are. She's not worth the bother. Just give her the book."

Lir tilted his head, studying Calla with curiosity. "What's wrong with her? Can't she speak?"

Olar frowned, shaking his head at Lucan. The last thing they needed was trouble with upperclassmen from Ackley's.

"She can speak," Lucan said shortly. "She just chooses not to in front of strangers."

"Then we should become friends," Gurin drawled. He reached out, brushing his fingers through her curls.

Calla slapped his hand away instantly.

"She doesn't like to be touched," Jarin warned, clearly worried where this might lead.

Gurin smirked. "Well, she'd better get used to it. A looker like her, eh Lir?"

"Indeed," Lir agreed.

Calla pressed her lips into a tight line. One look at Lucan told her he wasn't going to force them to return the book. She lifted her hand, eyes fixed on the volume still clutched in Lir's grip.

"*Retrivus,*" she whispered.

The book vanished from Lir's hand and reappeared in hers. Without hesitation, she shoved it back into her pinafore pocket.

Lir stared at his empty hand in shock while Gurin grinned. "Smart little sister."

Turning on her heel, Calla began climbing the hill. She abandoned her shoes without hesitation, forcing herself forward despite the sharp rocks cutting into her bare feet.

A strong arm hooked around her waist and hauled her off the ground. She shrieked in protest.

"Shut her up!" Gurin snapped.

Even here, on the east side, a little girl's cries would draw attention. Lir clamped a hand across her mouth, muffling her screams as she thrashed in his grip.

"Just let her go," Lucan said quickly, panic edging into his voice. His father spent much of his time on this side of the city, and stories traveled fast. It wasn't hard to imagine this incident finding its way back to Harith and Lucan dreaded the consequences. Calla would never speak of it, she never did, but Harith always found out.

A sudden howl of pain from Lir silenced everyone. Blood ran down his wrist, dripping from Calla's chin. Her teeth were buried deep in the flesh of his palm, her amber eyes blazing with fury.

He dropped her with a curse, but Calla clung tenaciously, forcing him to yank his hand free. He whirled toward Lucan, anguish etched on his face. "Get her off me!"

Before Lucan could move, Gurin seized a fistful of Calla's hair and yanked hard. She released Lir with a yelp, twisting in fury to face this new attacker.

Gurin caught her small fist as she swung at him and pulled her head back, forcing her to meet his gaze. He expected fear, tears perhaps, but what he found was pure, unbridled rage.

He chuckled softly. "You're one tough little girl, baby sister."

Lir sat on the ground, cradling his bloody hand, while Gurin shook his head in disbelief. This pixie-like girl had bested Lir, one of the worst bullies at Ackley's and he couldn't help but be impressed.

Calla knew she was no physical match for Gurin. But she had learned something important in years of trailing her brother and his friends: boys always had one undeniable weakness.

She drove her foot upward with all the strength she had. Her aim was true.

Gurin released her with a howl of pain.

Calla bolted, but before she could escape, Lir managed to snag her bare ankle. She pitched forward, hands outstretched to break her fall.

Gurin caught her again, this time by the back of her dress, yanking her to her feet. His face twisted in fury. "You bloody, vicious wretch!" he spat, shoving her violently down the steep bank.

She tumbled into the Garron Nir with a splash. Spluttering, curls plastered across her face, Calla staggered upright in waist-deep water. She was still wiping the river from her eyes when she saw Gurin looming in front of her, his face dark with rage.

He lunged, his hand clamping around her throat. With brutal force, he shoved her backward, holding her just beneath the surface of the rushing water.

Her six-year-old mind screamed at her to fight back, to kick and claw, to break free and come up for air. Her lungs already burned, feeling as though they might explode in her chest. But another part of her refused to give in to panic. She resisted the urge to claw futilely at the hands gripping her throat and tried to ignore the strange buzzing in her head.

Gurin's image was beginning to blur, but she regarded him with eerie serenity and even managed the ghost of a smile. His grip tightened, but instead of fear, she felt an odd wave of satisfaction. She had won. She was not afraid to die.

"Repellius et ventias." The words echoed faintly in her head.

Intrigued, she whispered them aloud. Instantly, the pressure vanished, and she shot out of the water, crashing onto the rocky bank.

Lucan scrambled forward, turning her onto her side. He struck her sharply across the back once, twice, again. She tried to tell him to stop, but no sound came. Her head reeled, her chest heavy as if iron bands were strapped across it.

A final blow, and suddenly water gushed from her mouth. Her body heaved violently as she coughed and sputtered. Harsh, ragged breaths tore through her chest until, at last, her lungs remembered how to work.

Lucan leaned close, his sapphire eyes inches from hers, his expression hard with contempt. "Don't think I did this for you," he spat coldly. "He could've bloody well drowned you for all I care. But I'm not going to get into trouble because of you."

Shaking, still panting, Calla dragged her wet curls from her face and glared up at him. "I didn't ask for your help," she rasped.

He stared at her in disbelief. "You little ingrate!"

But Calla only tossed her head defiantly and started up the path. No one tried to stop her this time. Barefoot, dripping, streaked with grit and river-mud, she still carried herself with dignity head high, stride purposeful.

"You handled that very well."

Calla froze, eyes narrowing suspiciously at the pair of men waiting at the top of the bank. She recognized one of them faintly, though she had no name for him.

"Are you hurt?" one asked.

She glanced back at the river. Her brother and his friends were dressing, Lucan's furious gaze fixed on her. She shook her head.

"You knew the spell to use," the familiar-looking man said, a pleased note in his voice.

Both were older than her father, clad in long, dark robes, garb strange to her. Uneasy, Calla edged back a step.

"And it worked," the man went on. "Though it seems your brother intends to take the credit for saving your life."

Her fists clenched. "I don't know you."

"You will," he promised. With a casual flick of his hand, he murmured, "*Recessio.*"

"Calla!" Lucan barked, striding up the hill with his friends close behind. "Go!"

She looked down at her sodden clothes, confused.

"Now!" he ordered, marching past her.

Lucan moved fast, and Calla had to practically run to keep up. They rounded a corner straight into Harith.

"What are you doing here?" Harith demanded.

"We…we were just going home," Lucan replied quickly, eyes fixed on the ground. "We were at the river."

Harith considered that answer for a moment before grunting. "The Garron Nir is not safe for swimming."

"The Dari San was too crowded."

Harith's gaze shifted to Calla. His expression hardened. "What happened to her?"

Lucan frowned and looked at his sister. "She…um…fell in."

"Well, get her home! She's a mess!"

Calla stared at her dripping clothes, trying to recall what had happened. She didn't remember falling in.

The pretty brunette with Harith leaned toward her sympathetically. "Poor thing, she must be freezing. Bring her in we can get her cleaned up."

But Harith shot the woman a withering look. "No! Lucan, take her home."

"Yes, sir."

Lucan grabbed Calla's hand. When she tried to pull free, his grip only tightened, painful and unyielding. Once they were out of sight of Harith, he rounded on her furiously, jabbing her hard in the shoulder.

"If you get me into any more trouble, I swear…I'll drown you myself!"

Calla didn't understand what had prompted the threat, but she understood its meaning well enough. To be safe, she would keep her distance from water.

>

By her thirteenth birthday, Calla spent her days roaming Soronu alone. Lucan had finished school and was training under Inturo. Calla had briefly attended the local school, but it was quickly apparent neither she nor the teachers were prepared for each other.

When two classmates thought the smallest girl in class would be the easiest target, Calla retaliated with a spell that sealed their mouths shut. The administration had taken a dim view of her sense of justice. They insisted she didn't belong in a school with her peers given her advanced magic.

With Lucan away at Ackley's and Bian too weak-willed to control her only daughter, Harith had few options. A tutor or nanny was out of the question, he would never allow a stranger in his home.

So Calla was left to her own devices, under strict orders: no magic, no disgracing the family, and be home by dark.

Most of Soronu knew her on sight, Harith and Bian's only daughter, with brassy curls to her waist, wearing Lucan's cast-off tunics instead of dresses, and amber eyes flashing a silent warning: touch me not.

Unlike other children, Calla avoided the city's popular spots. She preferred musty bookshops and dim little stores crammed with trinkets and strange collectibles.

Tangor had become a regular part of Calla's life, appearing so often that she no longer believed it was coincidence. But she enjoyed his company. Other than Saya and Liab, he was the only person she truly liked spending time with.

On her thirteenth birthday, he took her to lunch at a café on the river, then browsing through several local bookstores. On the way home, he gave her a gold ring etched with strange symbols on the inside. Curious, Calla asked what they meant, but Tangor only smiled and told her she would discover the meaning when the time was right. Sensing a challenge, she grinned and slipped the ring onto her right index finger.

When they reached the end of her lane, Tangor stopped. He spotted Lucan, Olar, and Jarin practicing in the yard.

"I don't think I'll go any further," he said with a smile.

Calla nodded. Tangor was her secret, and she had no desire to share him with her family.

"Your brother wields well," Tangor observed, watching Lucan sparring with Olar.

Calla sighed. "I suppose." She carried the dagger Tangor had given her for her eleventh birthday and had grown proficient in its use, but what she really longed for was to learn the sword.

"Soon, Calla," Tangor said quietly, recognizing the wistful look in her eyes.

She smiled and nodded, waving goodbye before heading up the narrow cobblestone lane.

"Who was that?" Lucan demanded as she stepped through the gate.

Calla gave him a blank look. "Who?"

Lucan narrowed his eyes, lowering his practice sword. "The man you were just talking to."

Tossing her hair over her shoulders, Calla strolled past him, nearly reaching the front door before he spoke again.

"Maybe I should tell Father about him," Lucan said casually.

She turned slowly, her tone icy. "Why would he care? As long as I stay out of his way and yours what concern is it of yours who I speak with?"

Lucan's expression hardened. "Men that age only have one reason for latching onto young girls, Calla."

Her lips curved in a sly smile. "Not all men are like you and Father." She took five bold steps forward, meeting his gaze directly. "I have done nothing to be ashamed of."

Jarin sighed wearily. "Just leave her alone, Lucan."

Lucan laughed and shoved Calla toward Jarin. "It's no secret how you feel about my sister. Why not stake your claim, Calla, and let him take you off our hands?"

Jarin caught her reflexively, then jerked his hands away as she spun on him with her dagger clutched threateningly.

Lucan roared with laughter. "Perhaps not, Jarin. No man will ever get that close to little miss touch-me-not." With the tip of his practice sword, he flipped Calla's hair back. "Gurin was right you'll grow up to be a looker. Shame it'll go to waste. No man will get past that blade long enough to see you properly tamed."

Calla glared at him with contempt, then sheathed her dagger and murmured an apology to Jarin. She didn't blame him. In fact, she rather liked him though she questioned his choice of friends.

Lucan slung an arm around Jarin's shoulders. "Forget about her. The man Calla claims as a mate will spend more time in a brothel than at home if he wants affection. Just ask Father. If my mother were still alive, things would be very different."

Calla's face betrayed her confusion. Lucan smiled brilliantly.

"No one's told you yet, Calla?" he drawled, stepping toward her. "My mother died when I was six."

She recovered quickly, tilting her head with mock sweetness. "So...you're only my half-brother, then. You can't imagine how relieved I am to hear it. Don't worry I won't tell anyone I'm even half-sister to a dragonslayer."

Lucan arched a brow. "You object to protecting the sorcia?"

She shrugged. "From dragons?" she scoffed. "When was the last time you saw one?"

"You can thank the dragonslayers for that," Olar interjected gruffly.

Rolling her eyes, Calla tossed her curls again. "If we're finished here, I'll leave you to your game of playing at killing dragons."

Jarin grinned at Lucan's indignant look, and Calla flashed him a sassy smile as she sauntered into the house.

>

Calla drew in a shaky breath, resting her forehead against her knees as Gira studied her closely.

"Are you alright?"

"Fine," she murmured. "I just…had no idea." Slowly, she lifted her head. "It was Lucan who told me he was my half-brother, but I asked my mother later. She told me Lucan's mother died in child-birth. The baby too."

"Lucan blamed you for that?"

"No…not for that. For the way Harith changed after I was born." She hesitated, her eyes lowering. "I figured it out the night of my binding. It explained why my mother tolerated the way my father treated her. That was very uncommon for a Soroni."

Andorran climbed out of the water and sat beside her, concern etched on his face.

"Is everything alright?"

She nodded. "Just dealing with some childhood memories. And now…I understand my fear of water." She briefly recounted the incident at the Garron Nir. By the time she finished, Andorran's expression was dark with fury.

"If Tangor was there, why didn't he stop them?!" he demanded.

"Because he wanted Calla to do it," Gira replied. "And she did."

Calla met Andorran's eyes firmly. "Lucan knows what happened that day. He knows about my fear of water. I can't allow him to have that advantage. Will you teach me to swim?"

"If that's what you want."

"It is."

Andorran glanced back at Gira. "You were asked about being an advisor to Una'savagi?"

Gira nodded. "I hope I can live up to your expectations."

"So…you agree?" Calla asked hopefully.

"I do."

"Good." Looking relieved, Calla stood. "Now…time for swimming lessons."

Chapter 21: Traditions and Tantrums

On the ledge overlooking the valley, Tegoradaysol spread below her, picture-perfect along the riverbanks. Calla stood motionless, staring at nothing in particular. Behind her, Valor gave a snort and nudged her shoulder.

She glanced at him, shaking her head. "I haven't forgotten you," she said softly, patting his snout. "Forgetting isn't my problem."

Grasping the mounting ladder, she climbed into the saddle. At her murmured command, Valor eagerly extended his wings and stretched his neck forward. A heartbeat later, they were airborne.

Usually, flying soothed her mind, but not today. She and Valor circled high above the valley for more than an hour. Finesse joined them for a while, looping playfully around, but sensing Calla's mood, Valor refused to join in. Finally, Finesse veered off in search of more cheerful company.

Calla guided Valor down toward the river. The spiketail landed neatly on the bank, and she dismounted, whispering a spell to free him from the saddle. He stretched his wings and nudged her hard enough to make her stumble.

She turned on him with a faint smile. "I've enough people fussing over me without you joining in. Go find Finesse. He looked offended when he left."

Valor tossed his head, then took to the sky again. Calla watched him for a few moments before turning to stare into the water.

Outside their quarters, Una'savagi had been watching.

"She's up early," Tau commented, the last to rise.

Perched on an overturned water barrel, Niko frowned. "She and Valor were flying when I came out about an hour ago."

They looked toward Andorran. He shrugged. "Flying usually makes her feel better."

"Not today," Niko said grimly.

"I don't like this," Tiean murmured. "She's distancing herself from us."

"And angry all the time," Kodar agreed.

Andorran sighed heavily. "I know. She hasn't slept properly in days bloody nightmares wake her five or six times a night."

"Nightmares about what?" Tiean pressed.

He shook his head. "She won't say. But since she only had her memories restored a few days ago, I think it's safe to assume those memories are the cause."

Caius, leaning against the barrel, chewed thoughtfully on his thumbnail. "Having all those memories return at once…that would give anyone nightmares."

"Have you asked her about them?"

Andorran looked irritated. "Of course I asked! She just tells me she's working through them." His arms folded tight across his chest, his eyes never leaving Calla. "But I don't think she is."

Gira spoke quietly. "People in the village are talking. They're afraid of her."

"You shouldn't have given those memories back to her!" Andorran snapped, his tone sharp. "She was better off without them!"

"Calla didn't think so," Gira replied patiently. "And I had no idea there would be so many. I think Tangor was more overprotective than any of us realized."

Tau frowned. "How long was he doing this?"

"I don't know," Gira admitted. "But longer than I realized. It must have grown more difficult as time went on. Perhaps her later memories weren't repressed so much as dulled."

"Is that even possible?" Gan asked, concern etched on his face.

"Oh, it's a difficult spell," Gira said. "But Tangor was a master weaver, and she was young and vulnerable. I doubt he could cast such a spell on her now." His brows furrowed. He took a step forward. "What is she doing?"

Una'savagi exchanged uneasy looks. None of them knew.

Calla stood rigid at the water's edge, her hands clenched into fists at her sides, her breathing shallow and controlled.

Without taking his eyes off her, Andorran gestured to Niko. The younger dragonmaster hopped down from the barrel and moved closer, concentrating on Calla. She made no attempt to block him, and he could feel the anger and frustration pouring from her.

He touched the marking on his shoulder, strengthening their link. Caius gasped. Kodar swore under his breath.

Calla raised her left hand slightly, her index finger extended and turning slowly. In front of her, the water began to churn.

"Any chance she's not doing that?" Tau asked quietly.

"None," Caius replied.

Niko frowned, stepping closer, his voice low with amazement. "She's drawing on her anger."

Andorran's jaw tightened as the water began to swirl in the river's center. The wind picked up hot, heavy and mixed with the rising funnel. Slowly at first, then faster, a towering waterspout formed, spinning violently.

Gira glanced at Andorran. "How long has she been able to touch earth magic?"

"A while," Andorran admitted. "We first saw it in Tola Sol."

The storm grew into a ferocious sight, towering above Calla, its outer fringes whipping at her hair and clothes, drenching her with spray. She stood unmoving, oblivious to the chaos she'd unleashed.

"Can you reverse this?" Gira shouted over the roar of wind and water.

Tau shrugged helplessly. "We've never tried to reverse her spells."

"How can you counter a spell you don't even know?" Tiean asked.

"You can't," Gira replied. "But nature spells can be reversed if the sorcerer is powerful enough." He turned to Andorran. "Do you think you can do it?"

Caius frowned. "She's not going to like having her spell reversed."

Gan nodded grimly. "Do we risk angering her further?"

Andorran looked back at Calla. The storm's reach was spreading, its fringes pushing toward the village's outer structures. He knew Gira was right. He'd have to try. She might be furious afterward, but better her anger than innocent lives lost.

Niko laid a hand on Andorran's arm. Expecting an argument, Andorran turned, but Niko's tone was calm.

"Don't focus on the storm," he advised. "That feels like the right thing to do…but it isn't. Focus on Calla. On her anger. That's what's feeding it."

Caius nodded in agreement. "That makes sense. To reverse the spell, you should try to soothe her anger."

Taking a steadying breath, Andorran pressed his hand over his mystic dragonsheart, eyes fixed on Calla. He could feel her rage and pain not as Niko could, fully immersed in it, but as a heavy, oppressive force pressing against him. He had known the return of her memories would stir strong emotions, but he hadn't realized just how powerful they had become.

Reversing her effects on the water and wind was no small feat, but Andorran drew strength from the thought of Tegoradaysol's people. Little by little, the winds began to die, the towering funnel sank back into the river, and the waters settled into violent ripples that slapped against the banks.

Calla turned, amber eyes locking onto his. Even from a distance he saw the flicker of realization, she knew he was the one who had undone her storm.

Kodar dropped heavily onto the upturned water barrel. "Tell her it was our idea," he suggested dryly.

Andorran smirked. "I doubt it will matter whose idea it was." He glanced toward the river. "I should go speak with her."

"Maybe wait," Tiean advised.

Niko shook his head. "No. It'll be fine. Go."

Gan eyed him warily. "You haven't just sent him to his doom, have you?"

Niko laughed. "Of course not. She vented most of her anger just now. She's better."

If Calla's greeting was any indication, Niko was right. When Andorran reached her side, she slipped her arms around his waist, resting her head against his chest. Relief surged through him as he held her close, not caring that she was drenched.

"I didn't expect a warm welcome," he admitted.

She tipped her head back, managing a weary smile. "You did quench a rather lovely storm."

"It was getting dangerous." He tugged gently at her wet hair. "Truthfully, I wasn't sure I could stop it."

She studied him. "How did you manage?"

"I didn't counter it," he said. "I reversed it."

Her brows lifted. "Impressive."

Andorran shrugged. "I had help."

She slid her arms back around him, sighing. "You say that as if you couldn't have done it on your own."

"Caius is the logical one, not me."

She shook her head. "That's not true. You can be just as logical as Caius when the situation calls for it. Camalaron says we all have dominant traits, but that doesn't mean we don't possess the others. We simply draw on what we need at the time. You can be as skeptical as Gan, and he can be as stubborn as I am." Her eyes danced impishly. "And so can you."

He chuckled. "Fair enough."

"And not just the so-called last generation," she added. "Kodar and Bal have just as much strength, courage, and loyalty." She frowned up at him. "But how are we the last generation? That can't be right."

Perplexed, Andorran asked, "Aren't we?"

Her agitation rising, Calla quickened her pace toward their quarters, Andorran falling into step beside her.

"I don't see how he could've gotten this wrong," she muttered. "If we're meant to begin a new bloodline, that makes us the first generation, not the last. Those born before us should've been the last...unless..." she winced. "...unless we're the end of the dragonmaster line."

The others caught the tail end of her mutterings and shot Andorran questioning looks. He only shrugged.

Calla stopped abruptly in front of Gira. "I need to know the entire prophecy."

He looked startled. "But I already told you...I don't know any more than I've shared. I suspect Camalaron might, but I doubt he'll be forthcoming."

"I suppose not," she conceded. "If he'd wanted us to know, he'd have told us already."

"You think he's hiding something?" Gan asked.

"Possibly. Though I can't imagine why." She looked over her shoulder at Andorran. "I'll send a request for him to come speak with us. Maybe we can sort this out."

"A request?" Tiean asked, brows raised.

"I expect he'll respond more willingly to a request than a summons." She turned her gaze on Niko and Caius. "You two should come with me."

Niko's eyes widened. "Us?" He exchanged a dubious glance with Caius. Neither had ever been included in a formal meeting with the Genesi Ney.

"Calla, are you sure?" Tau asked carefully. Noting the indignation on their faces, he added quickly, "…I only mean they're newlings. This could get complicated."

Caius felt the sting but held his tongue, waiting for Calla's answer.

"Caius stays calm and sensible in precarious situations, and Niko can read the mood of the room," Calla reasoned. "But it does present a problem." She chewed her thumbnail thoughtfully.

Tiean nodded. "A charge isn't usually included in a summons…certainly not as part of the party itself."

"And let's be honest," Tau added. "You call this a request, but we all know what it really is."

Andorran agreed. "Camalaron may not feel inclined to speak freely in front of your charges."

"Then there's only one solution." Calla's eyes lit with sudden resolve. "Caius, Niko, Gan..."

"Wait just a moment." Andorran cut her off with a frown. "Calla, I know what you're planning, and I'm not convinced it's a good idea."

"Why not?" Tau asked, curious.

"What is she thinking?" Kodar muttered.

Tiean glanced at Gan, Niko, and Caius, his expression contemplative. "It's never been done so soon after the binding. Andorran was under counsel for the shortest time, and even that lasted over a decade."

Andorran nodded. "Your charges have been under your counsel for just short of a year."

Calla saw her charges watching her with questioning eyes and gave them a reassuring smile. "If I release you as my charges…"

"Release us?" Gan and Niko blurted together, stunned.

"Release them?" Tau echoed in disbelief.

Calla laughed. "Tau, when Madoral released you, did you stop seeking his advice?"

"Well…no, but…"

"They're not ready," Gira said flatly.

Calla turned to face him. "Ready? Are any of us truly ready for what's coming?"

Tau eyed her with apprehension. "But…less than a year?"

"You sound like Varzi," Calla shot back, planting her fists on her hips. "Time and age are irrelevant. Yes, they're young, but we are Una'Savagi. We work as equals, learning from one another. We don't need those old labels and rules."

Gira tugged fretfully at his gray beard. "I'm not certain the others will accept this."

Calla's brows lifted sharply. "I don't see that they have a choice. It's the counsel who decides when a charge is ready for release."

"But Calla..." Andorran began.

"No," she interrupted firmly. "They are my charges. My decision." Her gaze returned to the three boys. "I will no longer be your counsel, but that changes nothing. Not really."

Gan's bright eyes flicked toward Niko and Caius, then back to Calla. To the citizens of Tegoradaysol, the three of them had never been considered equal to the other dragonmasters. They were newlings, still beneath the guidance of a seasoned dragonmaster. And perhaps, he thought, Gira and Andorran were right the others might never see them differently, no matter what Calla said.

Her fingers brushed his cheek lightly, pulling his attention back to her. "Do you doubt that you're ready?"

He met her gaze steadily. "No…not about that."

"Then it makes no difference what others think."

Niko grinned wide, and Caius bounced cheerfully on the balls of his feet, their excitement making Gan smile and relax. "I just hope you know what you're doing."

Laughing, Calla draped an arm around his shoulders. "That makes two of us."

Andorran stepped in, exasperated. "As much as you enjoy defying tradition, could you at least hold the ceremony properly when you do this?"

Calla stuck her tongue out at him but nodded.

>

Calla sent a message to Camalaron requesting an audience, her wording polite and leaving it to the former Sovereign Master to choose the time and place.

Vien had accepted the parchment warily, as though unsure whether he wanted to deliver it even with Calla's assurance that there was nothing offensive written within.

The rest of the day passed in a blur for Niko, Caius, and Gan as they prepared for the evening's ceremony. Calla had agreed to hold the traditional rites, but she insisted on several changes.

First, it would be held outdoors, no one argued.

Second, it would not be publicly announced until after the fact, rather than beforehand as tradition dictated, again, no one objected.

But the third alteration sparked resistance. Traditionally, a released charge was expected to give a final oath, pledging themselves to Tegoradaysol. Calla herself had nearly refused her own binding because of this requirement. Tangor had crafted a compromise for her allowing her to pledge not to the city itself, but to what the city represented.

"Let them make the oath you made," Gira suggested when the debate began.

Calla shook her head stubbornly. "No oath."

"Why not?" Tau asked, perplexed.

"Why shouldn't they pledge allegiance to the city?" Tiean pressed. "It is their home, after all."

Calla frowned. "No, it isn't. This isn't home for any of us." Her tone sharpened. "You are Baldarian, Tau you've never renounced your citizenship to Baldar'tine, any more than I've renounced mine to Soronu. I think it matters that we come from every corner of the realm."

Kodar's brows knit. "In what way?"

Calla turned to him. "Do you really think it's coincidence that I'm Soroni? The only female dragonmaster born of the only matriarchal society in the realm?" She gave a quick, sharp laugh. "Imagine if I'd been raised a Kamborian." She shot Andorran a grin. "No offense."

"None taken," he assured her with a grin of his own.

"But seriously," she continued, "Tegoradaysol has been our refuge, yes but it isn't our home. Even if I never return to Soronu, I am always Soroni."

Tau nodded slowly. "I can see your point. But how does it hurt for them to pledge to the city that's given them sanctuary?"

Calla sighed wearily. "Given what's expected of us, do you honestly believe we'll remain in Tegoradaysol? You are bound to me by the dragonsheart and to your virtue stones by birth and binding. I won't ask you for another pledge." Her voice softened, almost sorrowful. "You've given enough of yourselves already."

Andorran laid a hand on her shoulder. "Very well, Calla. I vote no pledge."

Around the circle, the others echoed the vote.

>

Under a canopy of stars, Una'Savagi minus Andorran and Calla gathered in the clearing by Rait's tree, settling into their familiar circle. Gira, citing old bones and stiff muscles, perched on a low stool between Kodar and Tau.

"What's keeping Calla and Andorran?" their advisor asked.

Gan snickered. "They were having a row over traditions."

"An argument Andorran actually won for a change," Tau added with a huge grin.

"Oh?" Gira's brows arched curiously, and the others burst out laughing.

"Over hair, if you can imagine it," Tiean explained. "Calla's never minded plaiting Andorran's hair in fact, I think she rather enjoys it."

"But she wasn't keen on letting Andorran do the same for her," Kodar added.

Gira smiled knowingly. The plaiting was a Kamborian ritual, and for a Soroni woman to relinquish control, even over something as trivial as her hair, was unheard of. Still, he had to admit, Calla was learning to compromise for her Kamborian mate.

That became even clearer when the pair arrived a few moments later, freshly scrubbed, their wet hair neatly plaited. Andorran's dark tresses were in their usual single braid, but Calla's wild curls had been subdued into two tightly woven plaits, twined together and fastened at the nape of her neck. A few soft tendrils curled along her neckline, giving her a more elegant appearance.

Gan stared in amazement while Niko grinned, marveling at how Andorran had managed to tame Calla's unruly hair.

"Sorry we're late," Calla said cheerfully, settling between Niko and Andorran. "There isn't much to this ceremony, but I don't want you to take it lightly. Being released from counsel means you're no longer considered newlings. But you're still only fifteen, all of you not adults yet. So don't get the idea you're grown and ready to step out on your own."

Niko grinned sheepishly, Caius looked shocked as if such a thought had never occurred to him and Gan simply nodded in understanding.

Holding out her hand, Calla met Gan's gaze. "As you were bound first and are the oldest, we'll begin with you." With a muffled pop, his stone appeared in her palm. "Your virtue stone, Gan. If you accept that you're ready to be released, summon it into your own hand."

His eyes dropped to the stone, then back to hers. A sudden doubt struck him; was he ready? Being Calla's charge had given him a sense of safety, of always being watched over.

A warm tingling in his left shoulder startled him. He glanced down and saw her free hand resting over her dragonsheart. He felt the reassurance through their bond, took a deep breath, and nodded. She might no longer be his counsel after tonight, but he was part of Una'Savagi. He would never be alone. Closing his eyes, he concentrated. A moment later, the stone appeared, warm and weighty in his hand.

Calla repeated the process with Niko, then Caius, sending each of them the same reminder through the dragonsheart: their bond was stronger than counsel and charge.

Gira was the only one outside that link, and when Caius tucked his stone back into the pouch under his tunic, Bal leaned in, giving him a one-armed, brotherly hug.

"Any word from Camalaron yet?" Kodar asked as the group rose and began drifting out of the clearing.

Calla shook her head. "No but I didn't expect to hear before morning. I assume he'll want time to decide how he wants to respond…and what he thinks we want."

"You're a thorn in that man's side, you know that?" Tau teased.

Calla shot him a mischievous smile. "Do you think so?"

"Just remember," Tiean cautioned in a sternly paternal tone, "Caius and Niko are going with you to keep you from losing your temper. Listen to them."

"Yes," Tau agreed, "you'll get nowhere with him if you start shouting."

"He hates that," Tiean added. "And being interrupted."

"Or being told what he has to do," Tau chimed in.

"And it wouldn't hurt to address him as *Master* Camalaron," Tiean suggested seriously.

"That's a good point," Tau nodded.

Calla smiled, hands clasped behind her back, clearly entertained.

"You could bow your head slightly, too," Tiean continued. "Nothing drastic, just enough to show respect."

"Yes, he'd appreciate that," Tau agreed, glancing at Tiean. "She wouldn't need to put her hand to the hilt, but the nod would be a nice touch."

"Yes," Calla finally piped up, her tone playful. "Eyes down, hands like this…" She clasped her fingers demurely and hung her head, staring at the ground. "What do you think?"

Before they could respond, she snapped her head up, eyes bright with enthusiasm. "I know!" she exclaimed. "I could bring tea and cookies and offer to fluff his pillows!"

Gira chuckled in amusement while the others roared with laughter.

Tau and Tiean exchanged insulted looks.

"We're only trying to help," Tau said indignantly.

Laughing, Calla patted his cheek. "I know and I promise, I'll be on my best behavior."

Andorran caught her hand. "Just remember your goal. To learn the prophecy, you may very well need Camalaron."

She nodded. "I know."

>

Calla and Andorran were roused early the next morning by Bal, who bounded excitedly into the room, waving a roll of parchment.

"A reply!" he exclaimed, landing with a bounce at the foot of the bed.

Groaning, Andorran pulled the blanket over his head. "We must put a locking spell on that door," he grumbled.

Grinning, Calla propped herself on one elbow, resting her head in her hand. "We have spoken of this before, Bal. You should knock and wait to be invited."

Oblivious to the gentle scolding, Bal crawled up beside her and pushed the parchment into her hands. "Read it, Calla."

"Read it *to me*," she teased, flopping back onto her pillow.

Bal furrowed his brow, lips pursed tightly as he broke the seal and unrolled the page. He leaned against her hip, holding it up.

"What does it say, Bal?" Calla inquired sleepily, feeling Andorran drape an arm over her stomach.

Bal squinted at the text. "What language is this?"

Calla's eyes opened, surprised. "It is the Language of the Old Age."

Intrigued, Andorran poked his head out from under the blanket, studying the parchment. "Why would he reply in the Old Language?"

"I cannot imagine," Calla admitted.

Andorran sat up, taking the paper from Bal nearly sending both him and Calla tumbling. Once they had hastily repositioned, he scanned the page.

"He refuses to meet," Andorran said irritably.

"Refuses?" Calla echoed, rising to her knees to peer over his shoulder. "*It would be unwise to meet at this time,*" she read aloud. Her amber eyes flashed. "Unwise? What does he mean?"

Andorran shook his head, reading on. "*I know what you wish to discuss, and I have no further information.*"

Calla leapt out of bed, Bal scrambling after her. "He cannot do this!"

Sensing trouble, Andorran threw on his clothes and sword belt, catching up as Calla stormed for the door, Bal at her heels.

"Wait a minute," he protested, grabbing her arm. "Where are you going?"

"You know where!" she snapped.

"That is not a good idea."

"I am not interested in whether or not it is a good idea!"

"You're supposed to bring Niko and Caius," he reminded firmly, tightening his grip as she tried to pull free. "To prevent you from losing your temper."

"I do not *want* to be kept from losing my temper!"

"Obviously." Andorran marched down the corridor, Calla still in tow. Raising his voice, he called: "Una'Savagi!"

Her glare was scorching. "What are you doing?"

"Calling the others. Majority rules."

"We do not need a vote!" she spat.

He released her at last, folding his arms across his chest with calm finality. "We vote on all matters concerning Una'Savagi."

Her frown deepened. "Do you expect me to just give up on learning the entire prophecy?"

"Of course not," he said evenly, forcing his tone to remain steady.

Kodar was first to appear, rubbing his eyes. "What is it?"

"We have heard from Camalaron," Andorran explained, holding up the parchment.

"So early?" Tau asked, entering with Gan, who looked half-asleep on his feet. "Does he object to waiting until the sun comes up?"

"I suspect the intention was to catch us off guard," Andorran replied.

"Vien brought it," Bal chimed in as Tiean, Niko, and Caius stumbled in. Caius yawned and dropped onto the hearth.

"Brought what?" Niko asked.

"A reply from Camalaron," Bal said, nodding. "He was tossing rocks at the door."

The others looked amused. Vien never dared approach their quarters without assurance the shielding spell was down, so he had resorted to throwing rocks. Bal, a light sleeper and nearest the front door, always heard him. Though not strong enough to drop the shield entirely, Bal could create a small safe opening.

"What did he say?" Niko pressed.

"Nothing," Bal replied. "He just handed me the roll and left." A crooked grin crossed his face. "I think he's afraid of me."

"Yes… you are *terrifying*," Gan said dryly.

Tau took the paper from Andorran, his eyes widening. "The Old Language?"

Kodar frowned at the symbols. "You can read this?"

Tau nodded. "One of the first things we learn in Tegoradaysol is how to read and speak the Language of the Old Age."

Kodar passed it to Gan, who glanced at it and shrugged. "We've not learned enough to read it."

"It says he *refuses* to meet," Calla said sharply, her eyes blazing.

They all turned to her in surprise.

"Refuses?" Tau repeated in disbelief.

"Does he say why?" Tiean asked, taking the parchment. "*Unwise at this time,*" he read aloud, brows furrowing. "What does that mean?"

"He adds that he knows what she wants, but has nothing else to tell her," Andorran clarified.

"Do you believe he truly knows what she wants?"

"I believe he is making an educated guess," Andorran said. "A good one, most likely."

"Then why refuse to at least meet?" Caius asked, perplexed.

"That is what Calla would like to know," Andorran said, gesturing toward her. "But I thought we should vote on the wisdom of pressing the matter."

"Go anyway?" Tau's dark eyes filled with apprehension.

Tiean shook his head. "If he already rejected a written request, he'll be even less receptive if you storm in and demand answers."

Calla scowled. "Who said I was planning to storm in?"

He gestured at her. "Look at yourself, Calla. You're ready to explode."

Niko turned quickly to hide a smile. Tiean rarely risked provoking Calla, but today he was standing squarely in her path. To his credit, he held her glare without flinching.

"Calla," Tiean went on logically, "you said yourself it was best to meet with him along with Caius and Niko."

"That was before," Calla snapped. She was in no mood for logic.

"Exactly," Tiean pressed, taking a step closer. "But we all know that if you go in this mood, he is not going to tell you anything." He shook his head firmly. "I vote against it."

Calla drew in a sharp breath. She did not want debate. She did not want logic. She wanted to lash out at Camalaron for continuing to control them.

"I vote against," Tau said quietly.

One by one, Una'Savagi cast their votes each opposed to Calla going to see Camalaron.

When the last voice fell silent, Calla nodded stiffly. "Very well...if that is the vote." Turning sharply, she strode from the common room, the outer door swinging open at her nod and slamming shut behind her.

Groaning, Tau shook his head. "She is not going to forget this."

At the window, Niko watched her march toward the clearing, his expression grim. "We have to do something," he murmured, more to himself than to the others.

Kodar joined him. "She would not go anyway." But his tone lacked conviction.

"No," Niko agreed. "She does not like the vote, but she will abide by it." He turned to Andorran. "But the anger is getting worse."

"I know." Andorran sighed. "I can see she tries to fight it, but it gets the better of her."

"It is all those bloody memories," Tau burst out. "Gira should never have reversed that spell no matter what Calla said!"

Tiean dropped onto the hearth beside Bal, his brow furrowed. "We knew her childhood was difficult Camalaron told us as much before she ever came to Tegoradaysol. But to stir up this kind of rage… it must have been far worse than we realized."

"I wonder if Gira knew," Kodar said gravely, "that the emotions bound to those memories were suppressed along with them. Or that they would come flooding back too."

"All of that anger unleashed at once," Tau muttered. "Overwhelming."

Andorran nodded. "And it is becoming more than she can handle."

Caius exhaled heavily. "We all agree she's overwhelmed. The question is what can we do for her?"

"I will go talk to her," Andorran decided.

Tau's brows shot up. "Now? While she's in a mood?"

Andorran looked to Niko, who shrugged uncertainly. "She is furious…but there's…" He shook his head. "…there's something else."

"Something else?" Caius repeated.

"What else?" Andorran pressed.

Niko's brow furrowed in concentration as he turned back to the window. Calla's emotions were a stormy anger foremost, but beneath it… fragments of something smaller, rawer.

"It's complicated," he said slowly. "The feelings tied to the memories are those of a child, the child she was when they happened. That's the problem. She doesn't know how to deal with a child's emotions, because she's no longer a child."

Andorran nodded grimly. "Whatever her mood, she should not be alone right now."

The sun had only begun its climb over the mountains, painting the clearing in a soft glow. Calla stood on the riverbank, her right hand resting on her sword hilt as if for comfort. The brisk wind made the water choppy, waves slapping hard against the bank and spraying the air with mist.

Andorran approached carefully, watchful. At times her anger spilled into spells without her even realizing it. Being caught in the backlash would be… unpleasant.

He stopped a short distance away, laying his right hand against his dragonsheart.

At once Calla turned, amber eyes brimming with tears but still blazing. Her jaw was tight, her fingers flexing against the hilt of her sword.

"You know we were right, Calla," Andorran said, his voice low. "Logically it makes no sense to storm in demanding to see an elder dragonmaster."

Calla's eyes narrowed. "He is no longer Sovereign Master."

"That has nothing to do with it." Andorran kept his tone calm. "He is still an elder. A senior dragonmaster. That gives him a certain status, even without the title."

Calla shook her head sharply. "Not anymore! That's just an old tradition we follow because we're told to! Do you even realize how many things we do just because they're tradition? We don't even know the reason half the time!"

"I agree completely," he assured her, his voice serene. "But you want to resist all our traditions cast aside everything we've held to. You are the Genesi Ney, Calla." His blue-green eyes caught and held hers. "You have a responsibility to our past as well as our future. Would you have everyone forget all that has brought us here?"

"Yes!" she hissed. "Yes, I would!"

"Just because *your* past was painful does not mean everyone's was," he reminded gently. "Some traditions should be held sacred."

With an indignant huff, Calla turned away.

"Some traditions," Andorran continued, stepping up beside her but resisting the urge to reach for her hand, "are a very real part of who we are. We staked our claims according to tradition."

Calla's body went rigid, but she said nothing.

"Some traditions," he pressed softly, "bind us to our past."

"There is nothing in my past I want to hold on to!" Calla's voice was hard as steel.

"Nothing?" Andorran pressed, turning her to face him. "I find that difficult to believe."

She glared, her amber eyes sharp. "What do you know of my past!?"

"Very little," he conceded, "but only because you refuse to share it with me. I do know it was not all bad, though. Tangor, for instance."

Her teeth caught her lower lip. She said nothing, gaze shifting to the whitecaps forming on the river.

"The two of you were close," he continued softly. "Closer than any counsel and charge I've ever seen until you took the boys. There must be pleasant memories there."

Still, Calla did not speak, but he saw her throat work as she swallowed hard.

"And your mother," he pressed gently. "In your sleep, you sometimes call out for her. Did you know that?"

She gave the barest shake of her head, her grip tightening on her sword until her hand trembled.

"And no matter how it ends, everyone has good memories of their first love."

This time Calla's head snapped toward him, her frown puzzled. "First love?"

He reached out, tucking a stray lock of hair into her plait, letting his thumb graze her cheek. "You know. The first boy who made you self-conscious. The one who made your heart skip. The one who gave you your first kiss."

She recoiled from his touch as if burned, scrubbing at her cheek with her fist. "I have no idea what you're talking about."

Andorran grinned. "Are you telling me Dak never kissed you?"

Her scowl deepened. "How is that relevant? And how did we even get on this bloody subject?"

"My point," he said evenly, "is that not all your memories are bad. You *have* had good days."

"Well, I am not having a good day today!" she shot back.

"You can do something about that."

She gave him a reproachful glare. "Perhaps I have no wish to."

"The rest of us might like to vote on that."

Calla folded her arms. "Andorran, did you come out here just to antagonize me?"

"As a matter of fact, I did," he confessed, hand resting lightly on his sword hilt. "Wield with me, Calla."

Her frown deepened. "I do not feel like wielding."

"Come now, Calla," he coaxed. "It will be good for you. A chance to work off some of that hostility."

Her eyes widened indignantly. "Hostility?"

Laughing, Andorran drew his blade with a casual slash through the air. "Wield, Calla. Excise your demons."

"You are talking nonsense." She waved him off impatiently.

"Then tell me about your memories," he countered, spinning his blade in a smooth arc. "Tell me what Tangor was suppressing."

"I am handling it!" she snapped.

"You are not."

"I do not wish to talk about it."

"I realize that." His sword whistled through the air, grazing just past her shoulder. "But sometimes we must do what we would rather not."

He raised his weapon into position. "Draw and wield."

When she stood stubbornly in place, he chuckled. "Afraid?"

The word hit its mark. Calla's hand dropped to her hilt, eyes flashing furiously. "I am not afraid to wield with you!" she bit out.

"Prove it," he said softly, falling into combat stance.

Her sword cleared its sheath in one fluid motion, both hands gripping the hilt. Andorran nodded once, lowering his blade to meet hers, their tips raised to the sky. For a moment, they stood in silence blades locked, eyes locked. Then Calla struck. Steel clashed with a ringing clang.

"So tell me what the nightmares are about," Andorran urged, deflecting her swing with ease.

"They are of no importance."

"Then why not tell me?"

She swung again, harder, their blades locking. "Why is it important to you?"

"You are my mate, Calla. Anything that affects you is important to me."

The valley echoed with the crash of their blades.

"Does that include Dak?" she demanded bitterly.

"Is he part of the nightmares?"

"Why would he be?"

"The man wrote to you for years after you left school, though you never wrote back. He was clearly smitten."

Calla rolled her eyes, swinging furiously. "Like most men, Dak did not know when to back off! A problem you seem to be having right now!"

Andorran grinned as their swords rang again. "Forget Dak then. What about your parents? Do you blame your father for your mother's death?"

"Should I?"

He shrugged, countering easily. "I do not know. But you seem angrier with him than with her."

Calla slashed again with a grunt. "My mother was hardly innocent. She lied about her bloodline just to secure her place by bonding with a tribunal member. That deception, that risk of birthing a dragonmaster meant nothing to her!"

"She paid for that error in judgment," Andorran reminded quietly.

"She deserved to pay!" Calla raged, her fury lending strength to every blow. "But *I* was the one who really paid!"

"She was still your mother."

"Saya was more of a mother to me!" Calla snarled. "Bian was afraid to be in the same room with me! I was nothing but a reminder of her deception!"

"And Harith?" Andorran pressed.

"He was a fool! His bloody pride cost him and my mother their lives! If he had not been so ashamed of what I was…" She broke off, blocking his blade with a sharp clang. "I wonder what he would not have sacrificed to keep the truth hidden, to protect Lucan! He could have saved himself so much grief!" Her laugh was bitter, harsh. "If he had just told Lucan the truth, his problems could have ended long ago!"

Though the morning air was cool, Calla was drenched in sweat, her muscles aching under the strain of her wrath-driven wielding.

At the edge of the clearing, the rest of Una'Savagi had gathered, watching anxiously.

Andorran was clearly forcing Calla to confront her anger giving her an outlet to vent it. Yet they could not help but wonder if it was wise. If anything, she seemed angrier than ever.

"And now Lucan thinks he will hunt me like prey!" Calla spat, her tone venomous. "That bloody fool taught me half of what I know about survival. I know his tricks. And he seriously believes he can tether me?!"

"He may try."

"He will fail," she said coldly.

Her sword cut through the air in another vicious arc. Andorran barely dodged the tip, sweat stinging his eyes as he dragged the back of his hand across his brow.

"He will regret every injustice he ever inflicted on me! Every strapping I took for *his* actions! Every cruel word he ever spoke!"

"He was a child," Andorran reminded gently.

"So was I!" she snapped.

"Yes," he admitted, their swords clashing again, ringing loud in the valley air. "But you are not a child now, Calla. This is not about getting even." Their blades locked, eyes burning into each other's. "This is not about revenge, Genesi Ney."

Calla froze, staring into his face. Slowly, her sword lowered, her head tipping back, eyes closing as ragged breaths tore from her chest. Her skin glistened with sweat, the fury that had fueled her wielding leaving her trembling.

Andorran sheathed his blade, his own shoulders aching from the strain. He had never seen her wield with such ferocity. Her wrath had given her strength, but it robbed her of precision. She had been pure attack relentless, reckless and he had allowed it, forcing himself only to deflect, never strike.

"Tangor should never have blocked my memories," Calla whispered bitterly, sheathing her weapon.

"It is easy to say that now," Andorran conceded. "At the time, he thought it was protecting you. He likely never considered the cost."

Calla's fists clenched. "The consequences aren't even the worst of it. He lectured Camaleron about trying to control me. How is this any different?"

Andorran brushed damp tendrils from her face, his gaze steady. "You have every right to be angry with your parents, with Lucan. But Tangor? He always acted in your best interest…did he not?"

She let out a long sigh. "I wish I knew." Her eyes lifted to his. "Would you ever do something to protect me, even if you knew it was something I would not want?"

A small smile tugged at his lips. "I would like to say no. But truthfully…until the moment came, I cannot be certain." Her brow arched, and he clarified, "I do not believe what Tangor did was right. I would never block your memories. But I would do everything in my power to keep you safe. You are the most important part of my life. How could I not?"

Her hands came up over his, pressing them against her face. "It is so frustrating all these memories and feelings, jumbled up inside me."

"Who are you most angry with, Calla?"

Her eyes shut. "What does it matter?"

"Who?" he pressed. He felt her jaw clench, her fingers digging into his hands. "Your parents? Lucan? Tangor? Who else?"

Her eyes flew open, blazing. "My whole life feels like a deception! And all of them were part of it not just my parents! Tangor, Camaleron, Fane! All of them, manipulating me!" She slipped free of his grasp, temper surging again. "Hang me for a fool, but that bloody Arrio was the most honest one of the lot!" A harsh laugh broke from her throat. "Imagine that! Perhaps I owe him an apology."

Andorran darted a glance toward the others, gathered uneasily at the edge of the clearing. He turned back as Calla's voice dripped with sardonic bite.

"That would shock him, would it not? My friends all rallied to 'protect me' when he started his ridiculous campaign to fence with me. For nearly two years he persisted, and Dak and his friends ribbed him endlessly for it."

"Tangor told us you were making friends at school," Andorran said quietly.

"Is that so?" she snapped, her tone sharp as broken glass. "Then he clearly had no measure of the truth." Her hand flexed on her hilt. "When I started school, Tangor and Fane warned me to keep hidden. No one could know what I was. And I believed them. After the way my parents behaved at my binding, I had no wish to repeat it." She rolled her eyes bitterly. "For nearly three years, I was allowed to be like other girls. I should have known it was too good to be true. My fault I cast for the rapier, after all."

Her voice dropped, quiet and heavy. "I saw it in Arrio's eyes first. He was shocked, but he knew. And then just like that he said it. 'You are a dragonmaster.' And the truth was out."

Her arms crossed tight over her chest, hands digging into her shoulders. The words kept tumbling, though she seemed powerless to stop them.

"After three years of late-night study sessions, of competing over scores, of quarreling for the best tables…I thought I could count on those I called friends. But in seconds, I saw the truth. Fear. Anger. Contempt. That was what looked back at me." Her voice went flat, emotion drained. "Not one of them stepped forward. Not one. Not even… "

She broke off, closing her eyes, her body rigid. When she spoke again, her voice was quiet. "…Not even Dak. The one person I thought would surely stand by me. He did not move. He did not speak. Nothing."

Andorran caught Niko's signal out of the corner of his eye. The young dragonmaster's face was drawn, his blue gaze darting from Calla to Andorran. He signed caution, and Andorran gave a subtle nod of understanding.

Niko's warning proved true. Calla's fury flared again, her face flushed, eyes blazing.

"That is why I never read his bloody letters!" she burst out. "Tangor took those memories from me! I had forgotten how Dak betrayed me that day how they all had, those fools who pretended to be my friends! And I had forgotten how Fane offered to go before the Tribunal to plead my case, but Tangor told him not to. He said I was too angry to remain at Ackley's, that it would be too dangerous!"

Her words came sharp and fast, a flood of rage. "And he was right! Arrio was the first one to cross my path, and he paid for it. But I wanted to cast against the whole lot of them! That is why there was no hearing, no mention of the incident! Tangor got me out before I could do more damage, and the Tribunal had enough to deal with. Better to let Tangor handle me than risk more blood."

Her chest rose and fell with quick, furious breaths. "I learned that day first at school, then at my parents' house it did not matter who I was. Not to anyone. Not even to those who knew me best. It was always what I was. Dak. Liab..." Her voice cracked. "That was the worst day of my life. I wanted to make them pay, to hurt them as much as they hurt me. And Tangor stopped me."

Her rage ebbed again, shoulders slumping, head bowing low. When she lifted her gaze to Andorran, her eyes shone with tears. "Maybe Tangor did not suppress my memories to protect me...but to protect others from me. What is wrong with me? Even now, I am so angry."

Andorran reached out, and she placed her trembling hand in his. He drew her into his arms.

"There is nothing wrong with you," he told her firmly. "All of us feel rage when we are hurt or betrayed. The difference is that you are powerful, Calla. When you lose control, your anger has consequences others can only imagine. Tangor likely feared that, so he chose to intervene until you were strong enough to face both your emotions and your gifts."

He stroked her damp hair, holding her steady against him. "These memories came back all at once. Along with them, all the anger you buried. No one could be expected to master that overnight."

Calla leaned into him, weary. "I suppose."

"Did wielding help?" he asked gently.

Her lips curved in the faintest smile. "As a matter of fact…it did. You are clever."

His grin was quick and warm. "I try."

She placed her hand over his dragonsheart, amber eyes steady now. "Gira was right. I chose well when I chose my mate."

Andorran covered her hand with his own, his voice low with conviction. "So did I."

About The Author

Hi, my name is Anne Renee Schellen, but I go by Renee. I'm married and proud to be a mom to three wonderful daughters and a stepson. Life has blessed me even further with three beautiful grandchildren who bring so much joy and laughter into our family.

I live just outside of Houston, Texas, where things are always a little warmer—both in weather and in spirit. Our home is a lively one, shared with three rescue dogs and two cats who keep us on our toes and fill our days with unconditional love and a bit of chaos.

Every day is an adventure in our busy, blended household, and I wouldn't have it any other way.